FINDING HER CHANCE

A STEALTH OPS NOVEL

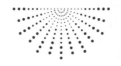

BRITTNEY SAHIN

EMKO MEDIA LLC

Finding Her Chance

By: Brittney Sahin

Published by: EmKo Media, LLC

Copyright © 2019 EmKo Media, LLC

This book is an original publication of Brittney Sahin.

Editor: Deb Markanton

Editor: Anja, HourGlass Editing

Proofreader: Judy Zweifel, Judy's Proofreading

Cover Design: LJ, Mayhem Cover Creations

Photography: Eric Battershell

Paperback ISBN: 9781097895274

❀ Created with Vellum

To our military spouses.

PROLOGUE: RECRUITMENT

CORONADO, CALIFORNIA

"You know, you're a walking stereotype."

Liam's gaze slid sideways to match a face to the voice. A pretty redhead with pale green eyes studied him.

"You should try a little harder if you want to hide the fact you're a SEAL." A smug smile skirted her glossy lips. Clearly, she was proud of herself for identifying him as a Teamguy.

Liam planted his palms on the bar top counter and straightened his back. He scanned the wall of liquor bottles before his eyes landed on Brent Flannigan, the owner of the pub.

Brent gave him a light shake of the head, a signal the woman was trouble.

Yeah, Liam knew her type. Since joining the teams, a decade ago at nineteen, he'd encountered plenty of women who loved to hook up with Teamguys. And it was a major turn-off.

"Oh, really?" Liam wrapped a hand around his glass of Coke and feigned interest in the napkin beneath.

"You've got an American flag on your shirt. Probably made by Forged." She paused. "The G-shock watch on your wrist and Gatorz sunglasses on your head are also dead giveaways."

He glimpsed at her out of the corner of his eye before casually gulping down half of his drink.

"Probably have a frogman or trident tatt somewhere beneath that T-shirt of yours, too. But . . . I'll let you buy me a drink, anyway."

Brent shot him another look, a smile tugging at the corners of his mouth. The guy was enjoying every minute of this. He'd been on the teams until an IED stole part of his leg.

Brent was a survivor, though. He'd gone on to train the Naval Special Warfare Developmental Group—DEVGRU—recruits for Green Team after that. And now, he ran an Irish pub, often frequented by women hoping to score with SEALs.

"You're right. You caught me." Liam lifted his palms in surrender and faced her with a smile.

And in three, two, one.

She scoffed and stood, then backed away like he was some disease carrier. "No way are you a SEAL. Obviously, you're a fake." She rolled her eyes. "No real SEAL would admit to being one."

Her sandals smacked against the concrete floor as she sashayed to the door, then slammed it so hard it rattled some of the nearby framed photos of war heroes on the wall.

"Well played, brother." Brent stood before him and pressed his hands to the counter. "But really, she was right. You look like a fucking Teamguy," he said in a low voice.

"Why do you think I dress like this?" Liam laughed.

"Hell, it doesn't matter what I do. When I'm in Coronado, I get accused of being a SEAL, so—"

"Act like someone pretending to be a SEAL?" Brent smiled. "Brilliant."

Liam finished his Coke. "But this is why I rarely come down here. No offense." He loved getting laid, but Coronado was swimming with frog hogs—women who wanted to screw as many SEALs as possible—and sex because of his job title? Nah, he was good.

Brent wiped down the counter, tossed the rag over his shoulder, and then crossed his arms. "You have that look, like your skin is all itchy. You must be on standby."

"It's the worst, man. No drinking. No partying. Nothing." He spent most of his time prepping for missions that Washington inevitably turned down. But on the off chance he got the call for an op, he had to remain sober at all times.

"I remember those days," Brent said, even though it hadn't been that long ago since he'd been active duty. "How's your grandfather doing? He still living in Virginia?"

"Yeah, I owe him a visit when I get some time off. My mum flew in from Sydney a few months ago and stayed with him for a couple of weeks, but I was overseas." Liam stood.

"Well, next time you see him tell him I said 'hello.' He's a good man. Served our country for a long time."

"Yeah, and he left some pretty big shoes to fill," Liam said with a smile.

"You're not doing so bad yourself." Brent nodded. "When was the last time you went Down Under to see the rest of your family, mate?" His imitation of Liam's Australian accent was comical.

"A few years."

Brent's gaze locked on something over Liam's shoulder, and Liam pivoted to follow his stare.

Luke Scott strode through the pub with another Teamguy, Wyatt Pierson, at his side.

He didn't recognize the blonde to Luke's left, though.

"Flannigan. Been a long time, man," Luke said once he closed in on the bar.

"You here for this guy or me?" Brent jerked a thumb Liam's way. "Or is this a chance run-in?" He came around from behind the bar to embrace Luke in a quick one-arm hug.

"I'm here for Liam." Luke reached to shake Liam's hand. "But seeing you is a bonus." He pointed to the woman at his side. "This is my sister, Jessica."

Liam adjusted the band of his watch while Brent shook her hand, then he followed suit. "Pleasure to meet you."

"You, too." A damn firm grip.

Tall. Blonde. Ice-blue eyes. A walking cover model.

Not his usual type, though—especially since she was Luke's sister.

Liam greeted Wyatt next. "What brings you all here?"

Luke looked at Brent. "You mind if we steal him for a few minutes?"

"Of course. Drinks on me when you come back."

Luke nodded, and Liam followed the three of them out of the pub. "How's it going, man? I assume you're on standby?" Luke patted him on the shoulder as they headed toward the beach on the other side of the street.

"Yeah, unfortunately." The sun beat down on the water, and the golden sand sparkled. He slipped on his sunglasses and tucked his hands into the pockets of his board shorts as they walked. "So." He dragged in a deep breath, suddenly feeling like a recruit again. The nerves in his stomach trekked up into his throat.

Luke Scott didn't make social calls. The man was a legend. And here he was, walking on the beach with Liam.

And Wyatt, well, he'd all but reinvented what it meant to be a sniper for the SEALs.

Liam had mad respect for both of them.

The presence of Luke's sister . . . that was throwing him off, though.

"Wyatt and I left our teams."

Luke's words stopped him in his tracks. He slowly removed his hands from his pockets.

Liam's job as a sniper was to recall details about every setting at any given time. Snipers were intelligence gatherers first and foremost, which most civilians didn't realize.

But at the moment, he barely noticed the two women in matching red string bikinis in his peripheral vision.

"What? Why?" He scratched his beard, which he'd finally had trimmed upon his return from Kandahar four weeks ago.

"Technically, we're still SEALs," Luke said once the two hotties in bikinis were out of earshot. "Just on a different team."

He took a beat to absorb the words before focusing on Luke's sister, hoping for some clarity. "What's going on?"

She removed her black aviator sunglasses. "We're forming a team of covert operatives to run missions for the president, CIA director, and a few other higher-ups. Only a handful of people will know what we're doing; our ops will be off the radar."

Liam tilted his head skyward, attempting to corral his thoughts. If they were telling him about a newly formed, secret group that meant only one thing: they wanted *him* on the team.

"You're one of the best bloody snipers in the world." Wyatt's British accent still clung to his speech despite his time in the U.S.

"We'd like you to join our team," Jessica said.

Liam still wasn't sure how she fit into the equation.

"I was CIA," she said softly, reading his thoughts. "And, in part, forming this team was my idea. I want to conduct missions that won't get caught up by red tape. We'll use an alias, Scott and Scott Securities, as our cover."

That explained her role, but he still had a lot of questions.

Although, the idea of sidestepping the bureaucratic bullshit was damn appealing.

Hell, how many target packages in the last few weeks had his people presented only to be blocked by the suits sitting comfortably in Washington?

Of course, would working directly for POTUS or the CIA director be any different?

"We're creating two five-man teams. Bravo and Echo," Luke explained. "I'll be Bravo One. And I've asked Wyatt to be Echo One."

"And between ops, what will we do?" He hated idle time.

"We'll take on legit security jobs for Scott and Scott Securities," Jessica answered.

"I understand this is a lot to take in, but—" Luke started.

"I'm in," Liam cut him off.

"Told you he'd be down." Wyatt grinned and slapped Luke on the back.

"Welcome to the team, Bravo Four," Luke said. "The president will be speaking to your CO this afternoon to explain your departure."

"I assume my CO will get an alternate version of the truth?" He'd prefer to be the one to tell his platoon why he was leaving, though.

Jessica nodded.

"Why don't you enjoy the surf today," Luke suggested. "We're gearing up for our first op. We head out tomorrow."

"Oh, yeah?" A burst of excitement traveled up his spine, and he arched his shoulders back. "Where to?"

"Argentina," Jessica said. "Short notice, I know. Not much time for goodbyes, but—"

"No, I'm game." He'd miss his platoon, but damn, he couldn't pass up this opportunity. "Let's do this."

CHAPTER ONE

CÓRDOBA, ARGENTINA
Six and a Half Years Later

LIAM SPREAD HIS ARMS WIDE, SLOWING HIS VELOCITY TO catch the wind. He was traveling three hundred and five meters every six point five seconds. The dark sky quickly released its embrace of him as he neared his destination.

His team was performing a high-altitude-low-opening, or HALO, jump over enemy territory. It'd been a while since he'd jumped. And ironically, his first op as Bravo Four had been twenty kilometers away from today's drop zone.

Joining the team was a decision he didn't regret, and he knew he never would.

All the ops. The lives saved. Every single moment. It'd all been worth it.

He took a few seconds to enjoy the silence, having forgotten how much he loved the feeling of flying, of sailing through the air like man was meant to be there.

Liam spied the green numbers on his altimeter, checked his compass, then pulled the release to his chute.

The parachute filled with air, slowing him down, and he gently tugged on the steering lines to bank into a turn and head toward the landing area. "This is Bravo Four. I'm in position," Liam announced over his radio to the lead jumper, Asher Hayes.

Asher was Bravo Three, but he often took over for Luke Scott as Bravo One whenever Luke was unable to join operations. At the moment, Luke was on his honeymoon in Hawaii.

Only a few days ago, Luke and Eva tied the knot in Vegas. And at the same time, Bravo Two, Owen, also married the love of his life. And unbeknownst to everyone, Liam—

"This is Bravo Five," Knox's voice came over the line, interrupting Liam's thoughts. "I had a cutaway."

"You good, Bravo Five?" Asher asked.

"Yeah, I'm good. The reserve saved my ass," Knox answered.

Liam lined himself up with the target and the rest of the jumpers as they closed in on their position.

The Argentinian government probably refused to green light an American-backed op, so the president had to call in Liam's people. Of course, if anything happened to them they'd be screwed, but that was the risk they took with every mission, even the ones on their own soil.

Once Liam grounded his chute, removed his oxygen mask, and gathered up his gear, he approached Knox to make sure he was okay. "What the hell happened up there?"

Liam's mind had been off ever since he'd left the hotel in Vegas after the double-wedding on Sunday. Even now, it was as if the frequencies in his brain were jammed, and static cut through every fifth thought. So, if anyone should have had a bad jump, he thought it would have been him.

"It's been a long-ass time since we've done this." Knox knelt to check his gear. "I jumped stiff, pulled too early . . . let's just say when we get home I'll be jumping from a plane every weekend to ensure that shit doesn't happen again."

Knox always owned his mistakes. He didn't sugarcoat anything, and Liam appreciated that about him.

"Yeah, I should probably go with you," he replied, even though his mind kept whipping back to what had happened in Vegas. And no matter how many times he'd hit the kill switch, his thoughts had begun to convert from a slow trickle to an end-of-days type of flood.

"I'm thinking we all should get our asses up in the sky after we're home," Asher joined the conversation. "Been too long for everyone."

They weren't exactly jumping from C-130s with jumpmasters, either. Since their teams didn't technically exist, they had less to work with.

Liam surveyed the rest of the crew as they gathered to prep for part two: the extraction.

Jessica and their latest CIA recruit, Harper Brooks, waited in position five kilometers away at the exfil site.

He positioned his night-vision goggles until the green hue filled his line of sight. "How certain are we our target is at this compound?"

"Eighty percent," Asher answered. "Trust me, I'm not a fan of relying on intel from the CIA, but they said she'd be inside. So, let's hope the CIA's asset got this right."

"And we're not walking into a trap," Wyatt pointed out.

It wouldn't be the first time.

Asher held his palms in the air while tilting his head to

the side, his way of saying, *Shit happens, and if it does, roll with it.*

"How many guards are there supposed to be again?" Liam asked.

"Eight to ten." Asher shifted his NVGs atop his helmet to find Liam's eyes, which prompted Liam to do the same. "Yo, you sure you're good?"

Maybe he wasn't. *Shit.* He never forgot the details of an op.

"Yeah. I'm fine." More like six tequila shots past screwed, but he wasn't about to unleash his feelings on the boys as they geared up.

"Why'd this damn drug lord have to crawl out of retirement?" Knox brought his gloved hands beneath his chin in prayer position. "He get bored sitting by his pool?"

"This fucker would make El Chapo quake in his boots, so heads on a swivel tonight, boys," Asher said, repeating Luke's typical line before shit could go sideways and fast.

"No chance Ricco Carballo will actually be at this compound tonight," Wyatt said. "But wouldn't it be nice to take the bastard down once and for all? A quick double-tap right in the forehead?"

Carballo wasn't their target, but yeah, it'd be a nice bonus to bring his head back with or without the body.

"Anyone want to wager on whether CIA intel is actually accurate?" A.J., Echo Two, asked. "Loser buys next rounds for a month," he added, his Southern drawl winging through his words more heavily than normal.

Harper's voice popped over the radios, "Aren't I already on beer duty for a month as the newbie?" She laughed. "I mean, I'll happily take the bet and relinquish my—"

"A month's round of beers says CIA intel is wrong," A.J. interrupted.

"Deal," she answered far too confidently.

"Brother, you're gonna lose this bet." Knox stood and patted A.J. on the shoulder. "All right, we ready to roll out, or do you boys need a group hug first?"

Liam rolled his eyes before placing his NVGs back on. "Let's do this." He took a moment to collect his thoughts and then followed the team.

After a ten-minute walk through the woods, which was more comfortable to Liam than a stroll through Times Square during holiday rush hour, he and Wyatt arrived at their destination and set up.

They'd be on overwatch, banging on their long guns so the rest of the team could infiltrate the compound for the rescue.

"Bravo Four, radio check," Asher said over the line.

"That's a good copy," Liam answered and examined the scene. "I have two tangos outside the entrance."

"Looks like we showed up to the right party after all. You lost the bet, Echo Two," Wyatt added over the line with a light chuckle. "I have five heat signatures inside the main building at the center of the compound. Two on the post-exterior of that building. One on each side."

Liam put his crosshairs on his first target and calculated the distance. He was about one milliradian tall in his scope, which meant he was roughly a thousand meters away. Liam adjusted for the range, and then noted the wind was currently moving right to left, so he shifted one mil dot to the right and upward by two mils.

With one eye closed, he stared through the scope, but his mind blazed straight back to Emily and their night together in Vegas, even though he had no business thinking about her at a time like this.

When Jessica and Asher had been running through the

operational details yesterday and again today—it'd been like a flashbang grenade had gone off in front of him, and all he'd been able to see was red, orange, and purple smoke.

All thoughts centered around Emily—the friend he'd been given strict orders to stay away from by Sam, Owen's wife.

He'd been drawn to Emily since the day they met last fall when he had to hold her back from knocking the shit out of a guy she'd been dating.

And frankly, the fact that his feelings went beyond physical attraction had scared him enough to behave—well, up until he'd overdone it with the shots the night of the wedding.

Relationships were a fuck-no with flashing red warning signs for him.

And Emily, she was the kind of woman who deserved more than a few orgasms and a thank-you-for-the-lay breakfast in bed.

The morning after Luke and Eva's, and Owen and Sam's weddings, Emily had lifted the sheet, taken a look, and with a gasp had quickly clutched it to her body. Her cheeks had ignited into the brightest red Liam had ever seen, and her eyes said it all.

"Did we have sex?"

"Yeah, I, uh . . ." He hadn't been sure what the hell to say to her as he stood next to the bed.

Her hand had darted to cover her eyes, and he'd lowered his gaze to find himself buck naked. And for some reason, her shyness about that fact had him smiling instead of reaching for something to cover himself with.

"I'm an asshole," he mumbled to himself *off* comms. He didn't need to hear rapid-fire agreement from his teammates over the line. They wouldn't need a frame of reference to understand his words—they knew his MO.

"Bravo Four. Echo One," Asher interrupted his thoughts. "We're in position. Take your shots."

Liam stiffened and held his breath, which was never good for sniping.

An unusual tremble traveled down his spine, and Liam squeezed the trigger. The tail end of the round caught the wind and—*shit, I missed.*

Before Liam could figure out how the shot went sideways, Wyatt pinged Liam's target.

"Both targets down," Wyatt said.

Liam felt his gaze. Wyatt was probably wondering how the hell he could have butchered the shot.

"Breacher up," Asher ordered next.

Liam examined the dead guard on the ground through his crosshairs, trying to analyze his error to ensure he didn't repeat the same mistake on his next shot.

He heaved out a deep breath at the realization he hadn't accounted for the disparity in elevation, which had impacted his depth perception. The guard had appeared closer than he actually was, and it was a mistake Liam didn't make.

A hard knot fisted in his stomach as he considered how he'd allowed himself to lose focus. He thought back to the time in sniper school he'd nearly been booted for missing a shot.

"You miss again, you're done," his instructor had said during their morning session. Morning shots were the worst; you had to shoot through the bore of a cold barrel—one of the hardest shots to take.

He'd missed the day before because he'd been thinking about what he'd given up to be in the Navy . . . and if he missed again, he was done.

"Good," his instructor had said after Liam nailed the target.

Of course, he had no intention of telling him he'd slept with the bullet under his pillow to warm it up. Every guy did it, though. Well, the guys who wanted to pass.

After sniper school, Liam had made a vow to himself to never lose focus.

And he hadn't come close to missing a shot until three years ago. In his defense, it'd been right after visiting his family in Australia and discovering something that hit a twelve out of ten on his shit meter—but even then, he'd still managed to take down the hostile on the first try.

But now . . .

"Bravo Four, you good?" Wyatt asked.

"Yeah." He had to get his head back in the game. He couldn't let his team down.

Once the compound had been breached, both Liam and Wyatt took their next shots.

All successful.

And thank God.

Liam caught sight of Asher and Knox exiting a building at the center of the compound with the hostage a few minutes later.

"Uh, TOC?" Liam pulled away from the rifle for a second then looked back through the scope. "I thought we were rescuing a woman."

"Yeah, Elaina. What's wrong?" Jessica answered.

"She's a she," Asher came on over the line, "but she's also a kid."

"And she doesn't seem to want to go with us," Knox added.

The girl couldn't have been more than seven or eight, and she was flailing her arms, protesting the abrupt departure.

"I wasn't aware of her age." Jessica's normally calm tone conveyed surprise.

"You sure this is a rescue?" Liam asked when the girl continued to struggle with Asher as he pulled her toward the exit. "We didn't, uh, just kidnap Carballo's daughter or something, did we?"

* * *

"Someone else want to try talking to her?" Jessica surveyed everyone in the back of their current ride, an eighteen-wheeler grocery truck. They were heading to Chile to hand over the girl to two agents.

"We showed up with painted faces and annihilated everyone at the compound," Liam pointed out. "Of course, she's going to be hesitant to talk."

Elaina's long, black hair framed her face, hiding her eyes as she stared down at her worn-out Nikes. Her arms shook beneath her white fleece jacket.

He spied a gray blanket, the kind used to wrap furniture or whatnot, beneath a bench. He dusted it off and draped it around Elaina's shoulders.

"Good call." Jessica's lips pressed into a hard line as if she were kicking herself for not thinking to offer a blanket first. It was wintertime in South America, and although it wasn't too cold, the girl was freezing.

Elaina's chin lifted, causing her hair to swing away from her face, revealing her brown eyes.

The tiniest nod of thanks from her had his pulse picking up.

"We're not going to hurt you," Liam said. "We're here to help."

"We already told her that back at the compound." Asher sat next to Jessica with a tablet in hand, a map of their destination on the screen.

"You also look like you," Knox said. "You know, muscles on muscles." He placed a hand on his chest and smiled as he stood before Asher. "Hell, brother, I was intimidated by you when we met."

"Fu—" Asher's curse faded into the air when his eyes landed on Elaina. "Yeah, well, it's called working out. You ever try it?"

"Anyway." Liam's eyes connected with A.J. He had a niece the same age. Maybe he could get through to her?

"I can try." A.J. tugged at the bill of his American flag ball cap and sat next to Elaina on the bench. "*Mi nombre es A.J.*"

Liam grabbed a hand towel and began wiping the green and black paint from his face as A.J. continued to talk to her. When Elaina didn't respond, A.J. tried Portuguese, and then French. All a one-way conversation. She never even looked at him.

"Sorry." A.J. shot him an apologetic look and returned to his original seat.

"She's been through a lot," Liam said, unable to hold back his concern for the kid.

He'd seen a lot of shit in the world, but whenever a kid was involved, it made his stomach tighten to the point of pain, and a hollow ache would always gather in his chest.

Elaina's shoulders began to relax, but when the blanket started to slip, she pulled it tighter around her body.

"Liam, can we talk?" Asher pointed to the back end of the truck.

"Yeah, sure." He followed him, but he could feel someone else trailing behind him.

Jessica. Of course.

"What's up?" He crossed his arms, feeling the need to

build a wall between them since they stood two to one. Not a fair fight.

"You good? We're worried about you." Asher spoke first.

"I, uh, missed, I know." He bowed his head, disappointment in himself cutting a sharp line down his spine. "I'm sorry."

"You missed?" Asher's question barreled out low and deep.

"Wyatt didn't tell you?" That was surprising. "Then why are we talking?" He let his arms fall to his sides, but the tension didn't melt away. Hell, he felt worse.

Emily. He couldn't get the woman out of his head. Even now, of all times. Her beautiful face, pouty lips, and an innocence that could bring a man to his knees . . .

He'd inventoried every detail about her, even though his heart had warned him against it.

"What's going on?" There was a soft plea to her tone. The new Jessica—no longer so icy—was front and center. A woman who now stole kisses from Asher when she thought no one was looking.

And if she could change, maybe there was hope for him.

Liam had worried Asher and Jessica's first mission working together as a couple might interfere with the op, and yet, it was Liam who'd been off-balance and had screwed up.

"Let's focus on the girl." Deflection wouldn't work, but he'd try damn hard. "We either unknowingly kidnapped someone, or she's been in captivity hell." Anger at either idea roared to life in the pit of his stomach.

He chanced a look at Jessica, hoping she'd returned her focus to the mission. Where his should've been all night.

A slow exhale left her barely parted lips.

"I have a lot on my mind, but I'm fine," he answered as honestly as he could.

"Liam." Jessica reached out for his forearm and squeezed.

"I missed the shot." The inconvenient truth hung on the tip of his tongue.

"Yeah, man, I got that. But why?" Asher wasn't looking for an explanation about his technique, but damned if that wouldn't be easier.

"I, uh, had my mind somewhere else," he admitted, feeling the need to unburden what he'd done. But he knew there'd be hell to pay when he did.

"Like where?" Jessica released her hold of him. "Liam, I'm worried about you."

She'd expressed her concern about him on their flight from Vegas to Argentina, too. Somehow this new Jessica had the uncanny ability to pick up on his problems.

Just great.

"I did something in Vegas. Something really damn stupid."

"What?" Jessica's gaze slid to Asher's briefly before her eyes moved back to Liam's.

"I got married."

CHAPTER TWO

LIAM PUSHED AWAY FROM WHERE HE'D BEEN LEANING against the eighteen-wheeler truck and eyed the dark Chevy Tahoe kicking up dirt off in the distance as it closed in on their location in Chile.

"I don't like this," Knox said. "Are you sure we can trust them?"

"We don't have a choice." Jessica didn't seem too excited about handing her over either.

"How does Elaina fit into the Feds' plans?" Liam asked. "*Was* this a rescue or something else?"

"I honestly don't know." Her arms anchored to her sides. "But she's important enough for the president to send us down here to extract her and risk ruining relations with the Argentinian government if we got caught."

"Like we would've gotten caught," Asher grumbled, standing next to her.

"Why didn't POTUS mention she was a kid?" Knox's eyes caught Liam's briefly. They appeared to be on the same page.

"Gotta admit, that part's strange." Asher glanced at

Jessica. Her eyes shot daggers back at him. "What?" He lifted his shoulders and held his palms open to the night sky. "You know something is off about all of this, too."

"This is a win," she insisted. And yet, her voice faltered. "Let's trust our orders, and leave it at that."

"And what about Elaina's family? Does she have any back in the States? Is she American?" Liam asked.

"I would think so." Jessica's words didn't carry the confidence Liam was used to hearing from her, though.

"Well, I, for one, don't like the idea that we're about to meet up with Feds." Asher's breath visibly sailed in the cooler air.

"You never do, man." Knox lightly laughed.

"These guys may think we're pulling this gig as private contractors," Asher began, scratching at his full beard, "but they're bound to wonder why POTUS chose us in particular."

"We can trust Jared Morgan," Harper chimed in. This was her first official operation since Jessica had brought her over from the CIA.

Harper Brooks had first helped the guys on an operation in Monte Carlo over a year ago—the same op where Luke fell in love with Eva—and Harper ended up badly shot and left for dead.

Liam had found her body and gotten her to the hospital in time. Honestly, he'd been surprised when Harper agreed to join the team in a permanent capacity.

"You two worked together back at the agency?" Knox asked Harper as the SUV came to a rolling stop twenty meters away from where they all stood.

The headlights were left on, illuminating the two men who'd climbed out of the vehicle and now approached the group. "Yeah, we did."

"Brooks," one of the two guys called out as they closed in

on their position. "I didn't know you worked in the private sector now." Must've been Jared Morgan.

Harper stepped forward. "Yeah, I just started with Scott and Scott Securities a week ago, actually."

"And this is your first gig?" Jared asked in surprise. "Well, damn."

Liam rocked back in his boots at the stretch of tension that filled the night air beneath the canopy of stars.

"Yeah." Harper pivoted toward where the team stood, practically in a line, as if blocking the path to Elaina.

"I heard about what happened to you in Monte Carlo," Jared said instead of greeting the team. He dropped his eyes to the ground for a beat. "Sorry I didn't reach out. I was deep under in . . ." His voice faded into the air when his gaze finally cut over to Liam and the crew as if remembering their presence. "Which one of you is Scott?"

"Which Scott?" Jessica offered her hand. "I'm the better sibling," she said with a smile. "My brother is on his honeymoon."

"From where I stand, you're certainly the better looking of the two."

Jared's compliment had the boys locking their focus on Asher, waiting to see how he'd react to the situation.

"I'm Asher." He was doing his best not to go all caveman and mark Jessica as his—she'd never let that fly, anyway.

"Yeah, uh, well, did everything go as planned?" Jared stepped back, picking up on Asher's vibe and added space between them.

Good idea.

"All the guards were taken out as requested, and Elaina's inside. She's also scared shitless." Jessica tipped her head toward the truck behind them.

Jared fingered the collar of his button-down shirt and

tipped his head toward the other man at his side, but the guy didn't offer a name. Typical. "We should get the girl and head out."

"What are your plans for her?" Liam asked. He hated the idea of Elaina leaving with these two.

"It's classified." Jared's reply came quick, a common turn of phrase used in his line of work. "You're civilians," Jared noted as if he didn't actually want to be a dick. "Sorry."

Liam still didn't like the idea of passing her off, though. He looked Jessica's way. "A minute?" He motioned for her to step off to the side, and both Knox and Asher joined them as well. "I don't want to do this."

"Liam." She pulled at her earlobe, and whenever she did that it usually meant it was a shit time to engage with her. But he didn't have a choice.

"What if we bring her Stateside, and—" Liam started.

"We're flying as civilians. We can't bring her with us," she replied. "I'm not a fan of handing her over either, but we don't have a choice. We completed our mission."

"She's safer with Jared than she was with Carballo's armed guards. That's something we can all agree on." Asher's eyes drifted over Liam's shoulder, and Liam followed his gaze to see Wyatt escorting Elaina toward Jared and the other agent.

"How about one of us go with them?" Liam's stomach squeezed. A growing discomfort there.

"I'll ask, but—"

"Protocol will dictate their answer to be a hard *no*," Knox finished for Jessica, and Liam hated that he was right.

"I'm sorry." She looked toward the sky, maybe wrestling for the right words.

"Fine." Liam moved to where Elaina now stood.

"I don't want to go," Elaina spoke up for the first time.

Jared placed a hand on her shoulder. "It'll be okay, honey. We're the good guys."

The distinction between good and evil had become more and more muddled these days.

"I'll come with you." Liam stepped forward, and her attention snapped to his face.

"I'm sorry. We can't bring any of you." Jared pointed toward the Tahoe with his free hand. "We've got this covered. I'm afraid this is where we part ways."

"We have to let them go," Asher said from behind, and Liam sort of hated his friend right now. "She's in good hands."

Tears started to fill Elaina's eyes, and Liam crouched to eye level with her. "You'll be okay. Whatever happened back there . . ." He couldn't bring himself to finish his words because he had no idea what had actually happened to her. He added a nod, hoping to reassure her—maybe himself, too. "I'll check on you."

He'd keep his promise no matter what.

When she didn't speak, he unsnapped one of the pockets on his right pant leg and reached inside. "This is my lucky charm." He uncurled her fingers and placed the old coin in her palm. "It's been with my family for a long time. It's kept me safe. I want you to have it."

His throat thickened at the realization of what he was giving up, but something told him she needed it more than he did.

Liam forced himself back upright after they exchanged goodbyes. "You promise to keep her safe?" he asked Jared when the other man placed her in the back seat.

"She's away from Carballo and his people. You're going to have to trust us." Jared's gaze winged toward where Harper stood. "See you around, Brooks." He added a salute.

The night sky and tinted windows made it too hard for Liam to see Elaina, but he waved in case she was looking.

"She'll be okay," Jessica said once the SUV had taken off. "That was sweet of you to give her your coin. I had no idea you carried it."

"There's a lot you don't know about me."

Jessica's fingers brushed down the column of her throat before her palm rested on her collarbone. "This was a successful operation, and you—"

"Missed a shot and handed a kid over to strangers."

"We should get going," Asher called out, interrupting a conversation Liam was in no mood to have, anyway.

He lifted his head to find Asher flicking his wrist, motioning for the team to get back inside the truck.

Liam released a deep breath, hoping to let some of his worries go with it.

"I have a feeling Elaina will always remember you," Jessica said as they walked to the truck. When he didn't respond, she asked, "Where are you headed when we're back Stateside?"

"D.C." He stopped when they reached the truck. "I have some things to make right."

CHAPTER THREE

"I CAN'T BELIEVE YOU CUT YOUR TRIP SHORT." EMILY PUSHED her fettuccini around in the bowl. She'd opted for the skinny version instead of the 1172-calorie dish.

The whole calories on the menu thing was starting to lose its appeal, especially when she wanted to stress eat, and right now, she was regretting the lighter option.

"It's only Thursday, which means you had probably less than three full days in Hawaii." Emily scoffed.

"I was needed in D.C. tomorrow for an emergency meeting." Emily's best friend, Sam, worked for the Intelligence Committee. They'd been friends since college, and they'd both gotten each other through some tough times.

And right now, she wanted to cry on Sam's shoulder and confess her Vegas mistake, but at the same time she didn't want to share the news.

"You could've said *no*," she reminded Sam. "It was your honeymoon." She set her fork down and leaned back in the chair at Mariano's, her favorite Italian eatery. "And you," Emily shifted her gaze to Owen, "could've tied her down and kept her in Hawaii."

Owen flashed a smile and glimpsed Sam out of the corner of his eye. "As much as I wanted to, you know I can't stand in the way of a woman trying to save the world."

"You deserved those ten days of sheer bliss. Sunbathing. Drinking. Swimming with sharks. You know, whatever makes you happy."

Sam tucked her short, dark hair behind her ears. "A couple of days is better than nothing." She reached for Owen's hand atop the table, and he clasped her palm.

"Well, it's not like you two do anything at half-speed." She thought about their last-minute decision to get married at the same time as another couple: Luke Scott and his wife, Eva Reed.

And great, Vegas was back on her mind. What if Sam spotted the afterglow she couldn't seem to shake every time thoughts of Liam buzzed around.

Emily's eyelids sealed tight as memories from Vegas obliterated every other thought in her head.

Liam on one knee.

The pinging slot machines filling her ears.

His kill-me-now-greenish-blue eyes focused on her.

"How about we make it three weddings?" he'd asked.

Only fragments of that night were filed in her memory bank; the rest of the evening was one messy blur.

It hadn't been a full-on *Hangover* movie kind of evening, but still, she'd woken up naked in bed with Liam. And, oh yeah, married to the guy.

Emily's tongue pinned to the roof of her mouth, resisting the impulse to blurt out what else had happened the night of the double-wedding ceremony—no—*triple* wedding.

"We're going to head to Charleston after my meeting tomorrow. You want to come?" Sam asked, ripping Emily's focus back to the present.

She opened her eyes. "Did your wife just invite me on a romantic getaway with you two?"

Owen smirked and lifted his free hand in the air as if to say, she does what she wants.

"I think I'll pass." Emily's lips stretched into a smile. "Besides, I'm working a pretty intense case right now."

Plus, there was the other issue. She needed to get Liam to sign annulment papers. One minor problem: she didn't have his phone number or address. And he wasn't exactly listed online.

Despite all of her resources working cases for the FBI, ATF, DEA, and so forth, she couldn't find much of anything about Liam. She managed to find only one next of kin Stateside, which was his grandfather.

"When are your friends getting back from their trip?" Emily casually asked Owen. It'd been the trip that stole Liam away from her before they could really make sense of their wild night.

"Luke and Eva?" Owen wrapped a hand around his beer bottle.

"No, your, uh, other friends. Like Liam." *Way to be discreet.*

A smile teased his lips, but when she chanced a look at Sam, there was only concern in her eyes. Her best friend was way too protective of her. But in all fairness, Emily was the same with Sam.

"The boys got back this morning. It was a quick trip." He straightened in his seat and brought the rim of the bottle to his lips. It hovered there as he studied her as if trying to read her thoughts.

"You ever going to tell me the truth about what you all really do?" Emily crossed her arms, trying to maintain control of her nerves.

He took a long swig before lowering his beer. "You know what we do."

Yeah, she knew what he'd told her they did, but she'd bet her life savings on the fact there was way more to it than that.

"Did they fly into New York?" She was pushing the envelope, and probably about to trigger some major red flags, but stealth-mode had never been her signature go-to.

Some said she was honest to a fault, especially when it came to prosecuting cases. But it'd take a hell of a reason for her to deviate from her norm.

"You okay?" Sam let go of Owen's hand.

"Uh, yeah."

Owen rested his elbows on the table on each side of his empty plate. He hadn't ordered the skinny option, and considering how much he and the guys worked out—they probably had the annoying ability to eat eight full meals a day.

"They went to our home office in Manhattan."

"Scott and Scott Securities?"

"Yeah."

"Would I be able to get Liam's number?" *There. I said it.*

"Why?" Sam leaned forward.

"After this case, I was thinking about heading to Australia for vacation. If anyone would have advice on how to avoid getting bitten by a snake, or uh, a crocodile, it'd be him, right?" *Bull. Bull. Shit.* And . . . she was lying. Moral compass out the window—heading for Australia, apparently.

"You planning on kicking it in the outback?" Owen reached for his beer again, and she used the moment to buy herself some time to think.

"Sydney." She swallowed, attempting to dislodge the bullshit from her throat. "Have you been there?" She grabbed her wine glass and sucked it bone-dry.

"Once for work." Owen tilted his head, amusement in his eyes. She didn't want to know what he was thinking.

"Since when do you have time for a vacation, especially one so far away?" Sam grabbed her martini and took a sip.

Wine gave Sam headaches, but since Emily loved it, Sam always kept her place stocked with Riesling and Cabernet Sauvignon. Talk about a real friend. A friend she needed to come clean to about Liam, and soon.

"You barely made it to Vegas for our wedding," Sam added.

"In my defense, you gave me a three-hour heads-up."

"Well, why don't you wait until I can join you? Maybe we can make a girls' trip out of it?"

"Sure, and let you get attacked by a shark or something?" Owen rolled his eyes, and Sam swatted his bicep.

"Anyway, would you mind if I call Liam and ask him about Sydney?" She lifted her shoulders. "You know, for whenever I get a chance for some R and R?"

"How about you give me your number, and I'll have him call you?"

"What? You don't trust Emily with Liam's number?" Sam twisted to the side, her lips pinched in a hard line.

"No, babe, it's not that." He shook his head. "Liam won't answer a call from a number he doesn't recognize. Trust me, I know him."

"I can leave a voicemail, and he can call me back," Emily blurted, because the idea of Owen talking to Liam about her . . . *just no.*

Then again, wouldn't Liam seek her out, too? Wouldn't he want the wedding to cease from existence?

Since he was back from wherever he ran off to for work —he'd find her, right?

"You know, never mind. I'll just Google Australia."

"No, you most certainly will not." Sam's hand disappeared under the table.

"Not in public," Owen said with a laugh.

"Funny," Sam grumbled. "I'm trying to get your phone out of your pocket."

Owen rattled off Liam's digits a moment later. "I'll let him know to expect a call from you."

Why didn't I just keep my mouth shut? "Thanks." She programmed Liam's number before she forgot it, then stowed her phone back in her purse. "I should get home. Thanks for dinner."

"What's the rush?" Sam asked.

"I kind of have a curfew." And now she knew Sam would take worrying about her to an all-new level.

Sam's palm landed on the table by her plate. "Say what?"

"The man we're trying to prosecute is dangerous, and my boss and the FBI think it's best if I stick to daylight hours."

"Emily!"

"You know my job has some risks." She jerked her thumb toward the window which overlooked the street. "I have a bodyguard. He's driving me around, and he and another guy rotate the night shift."

Sam gathered in a deep breath and slowly let it go. "I don't like this."

"Comes with the territory."

"Owen, do something." Sam elbowed him in the side.

"We can pull some guys from Scott and Scott to keep an eye on you, too," he suggested after eying Sam's pout. "We have a few people in the area. Former Teamguys who take gigs like these."

"No, that won't be necessary," Emily was quick to reply. "The extra protection I'm already getting is overkill." She reached across the small table and placed her palm over

Sam's hand. "I'll be fine. I've been doing this job for forever. Besides, I don't even know if we have a case, yet."

Sam's forehead creased. The familiar guilt crossed her face. "And last year you could've gotten shot because of me, and—"

"But I didn't." Emily retracted her arm and settled her hand in her lap.

"Because of Owen and his team," Sam replied. "So, let his people help you this time."

"If I feel like things are getting dangerous I'll ask for help. But like I said, we're still in the preliminary stages of the case."

"Yet, you have a bodyguard." Sam folded her arms. "How about you stay with us?"

"No," she shot back right away. "You just got married." *And you have way too much sex.*

Sex. She stiffened at the thought, wishing she could remember what sex with Liam had been like. Of course, *that* part of the night had to be foggiest of all.

She shifted off the seat and stood, but her jaw clenched at the sight of a tall and super well-built man at the bar, his narrowed gaze on her. He gave her the creeps.

She closed her eyes, trying to chase away her paranoia. But her thoughts immediately landed on Liam.

"We pulled a Ross and Rachel. This isn't supposed to happen in real life." She'd clutched the bedsheet to her body as if it were the only thing protecting her from the truth of what had happened.

"A what?" Liam had smiled.

"The Friends episode where they get married. You've never watched that show?" She'd gawked at him. Mouth unhinged. Floor, meet jaw. Jaw, meet floor.

33

"Ah, no." His hands had gone to his hips, and his gaze had journeyed to the carpet beneath his bare feet.

"Emily?" She opened her eyes to find Sam standing in front of her next to the table. "You okay?"

"Too much wine, and I drank it too fast." More lies. She owed her friend a really nice purse after all of this. "Good thing I have a driver, huh?"

"I don't like this," Sam said as they left the restaurant a few minutes later, the sun starting to trade places with the moon in the sky.

"You promise I won't wake up with ten bodyguards outside my door tomorrow?" Emily pressed an index finger against Owen's chest.

He held a palm in the air. "Promise, but if anything happens to you Sam will kill me. So, if you care about me, you'll—"

"Call you if I feel I'm in danger," she finished and released an Oscar-worthy sigh.

"Fine." Sam hugged her. "I love you, but maybe find a new job?"

Emily chuckled. "Um, you're one to talk, missy."

"She has a point," Owen said with a laugh.

After they parted ways, Emily climbed into the back of the black town car. She stared at Liam's saved number on the screen of her phone.

Maybe he was already on his way to end their marriage.

CHAPTER FOUR

"WE LOST A LOT OF GOOD PEOPLE." HIS GRANDFATHER'S fingers skimmed over the names of the fallen from the Vietnam War as they walked alongside the memorial in D.C. "We lost a lot of frogmen, too."

Liam eyed the black band on his wrist, a reminder of a frogman he'd lost from Bravo. He inhaled a breath of the night air, forcing the memory away, and tucked his hands into his pockets as they walked.

He still had to figure out how to tell his grandfather he'd given away the coin, a coin his pops had carried with him throughout the Vietnam War.

"It was 1967 when I was deployed as a SEAL to Vietnam." His grandfather stopped walking and pointed toward a bench, and Liam followed him over and sat next to him. "Your mom was barely four at the time. Fighters would hide in those thick mangrove swamps and attack our squad." He placed his cane across his lap and leaned back, eyes still on the memorial.

Liam had heard his grandfather's stories dozens of times since he'd first started spending his summers as a kid in the

U.S.—and he'd never grow tired of listening to him talk. He couldn't be prouder of the fact his grandfather had been one of the first SEALs.

He waved a hand through the air, his eyes closing in the process. "Our boys wore Levi's, not the Navy-issued fatigues." He grinned. "We had our own set of rules." He swallowed as if a painful memory had snagged in his mind. "But it wasn't easy."

"You're an inspiration, Pops." Liam thought back to the summer of '94 when his grandfather had first taught him to shoot a rifle. "I always knew what I wanted to do—follow in your footsteps and make you proud."

His grandfather shifted on the bench to face Liam, pale blue eyes locking on to his face. "You make me proud." He patted his shoulder.

Liam looked up at the cloudless night sky. "There's something I have to tell you." He found his grandfather's eyes again. "I was on an op in Argentina this week, and we rescued a little girl." He tensed at the memory of when he'd had to say goodbye to Elaina.

His grandfather was the only one in his family who knew the truth about Liam's job. He'd never lied to him, and he didn't want to start. More than that, he trusted him, and he knew his grandfather would never tell anyone the truth, not even Liam's mother.

His grandfather had been a Teamguy, after all. There was a code they lived by. A trust they shared with each other.

"What happened?"

"Well, she was scared, and I didn't know what to do, so I gave her my coin to make her feel better. *Your* lucky coin."

"You always do the right thing, Liam," his grandfather answered without even taking a pause. "I'm sure she needed it."

"I'm sorry, though." He'd had that coin with him since before his first deployment. It'd become like a piece of his body—and somehow, he'd handed it off so easily to Elaina.

"Don't be sorry." He started to stand, and Liam helped him up all the way.

They began walking again, heading for Liam's truck, which he always kept in his grandfather's garage for whenever he visited.

"How's work otherwise?"

He wanted to tell him about Emily because, well, he didn't keep secrets from him. But for some reason he couldn't get the words out.

Liam reached for the keys in his pocket. "Work's busy. Back when we started, we carried out an op for POTUS once every few months at most, so the majority of our jobs were for Scott and Scott." He unlocked the truck and helped his grandfather inside. "But," he began once he was in the driver seat, "now I feel like we're constantly spinning up for the president."

"Sounds like you've got your hands full." His grandfather fiddled with the radio as they pulled away from the curb. "Still hiring vets for your security company?"

"Of course." Liam smiled. "Who better to run protection?" Plus, he'd never been a fan of the way veterans were often treated after they'd returned home—and so, it felt good to be able to do something about it. Even if in a small way. "Someday I'll retire from Bravo and test out the civilian life. Not any time soon, though, I hope."

"Nah, son. Once military you're never really a civilian again. Military's in your blood."

"True." Liam nodded.

"But, I'd like to see you settle down and have kids someday. I'm pushing eighty," he said with a laugh. "I'm lucky your mom had you when she was young, or I might not be alive to see some great-grandkids."

"Well, I don't know how long it'll be until one of us has kids." He was one of four boys, and he certainly wasn't going to be the first to have children.

"When's the last time you talked to your mom?"

"I checked in with her earlier today to let her know I was safe." He'd called her on the plane from Vegas to Argentina before his op. He never told her where he was going, but since there was always the chance he wouldn't make it back, he liked to chat before heading out.

He'd stayed at JFK when they'd arrived today and caught the next flight to Dulles instead of heading back to HQ with the team. Thinking about facing Emily later had his heart doing some sort of awkward and unfamiliar dance, though.

His grandfather reached for the controls on the radio and turned up the volume. "You think this Bennett guy will run for president?"

"Knox's dad?"

"Yeah, won't that be strange if he wins and you all report to him?"

"I'm guessing it'll change the dynamics quite a bit." He clutched the wheel tightly as he considered a future with Knox's dad as Command.

"Well, Bennett's got my vote if he runs." He coughed into his fist. "Unless you don't want him to win, and then I'll vote for the other guy, even if he's—"

"A different party." Liam chuckled. "You'd do that for me?"

His grandfather placed a hand over his heart and glanced at him. "Anything for you." He winked.

"Thanks, Pops." They fell silent and listened to the news as the radio guest discussed a potential presidential run for Bennett. "We're here," Liam announced when they pulled into the long, curvy driveway. His grandfather had dozed off, lulled to sleep by the monotone voice on the radio.

"That was fast."

"Er, Pops . . . who's here?" Liam parked behind a black Audi, but before he looked at his grandfather, he caught sight of two people exiting the house.

He grasped the steering wheel and gathered a deep breath as his stomach did a full-on freefall.

"Did you know he was coming? And bringing *her*?"

"I wanted to tell you, but . . ."

Liam chanced another look at his older brother.

"When Brandon found out you were in town and going to visit me, he asked if he could come over." He reached for Liam's forearm. "I thought maybe it was fate you were both in D.C. at the same time."

"Not fate," he said, almost under his breath. "Mum."

"You haven't spoken to him in years." There was a note of sadness in his tone.

Liam's gaze locked on to his brother's wife. "They're having a baby?"

"Yes," his grandfather answered after a stretch of silence filled the car.

"Looks like you're gonna get a great-grandkid sooner than you thought." Liam exited the truck and walked around to help him out. "I'm sorry, Pops. I love ya, but I just can't do this."

He had his limits, and this was one of them.

"Liam!" The sound of Brandon's voice was like a stab to Liam's heart.

"I have to go. I'm, uh . . ." His mind blanked out for a moment. "I'm gonna take the truck into the city." He'd taken an Uber to his grandfather's house earlier, and he didn't have time to wait for a ride. He had to get out of there.

"Liam, please." Brandon strode toward him, but Liam quickly circled the truck.

His eyes connected with Melissa's as he opened the driver's side door and climbed in; she remained on the porch, her hand beneath the curve of her belly.

He rolled down the window and let go of a heavy breath. "Congratulations," he said to his brother, then shifted in reverse and left before anyone could try to stop him.

CHAPTER FIVE

"WHAT ARE YOU . . ." EMILY'S WORDS FADED AS SHE dropped her gaze to the white tee she was wearing, and her eyes widened. "Shit!" She slammed the door shut and staggered back.

She'd answered the door in only her T-shirt and underwear knowing full well it was Liam since she'd checked the peephole first. *What was I thinking?*

"I have seen you naked before," he said loud enough for her to hear. Probably loud enough for Miss Peterson next door to hear even over her seven constantly yapping Chihuahuas. Another reason Emily was anxious to move into her new place next month.

"One second!"

After putting on a bra and pulling on a pair of jeans, she checked herself in the hall mirror and frowned. No time for makeup, damn it.

She swung the door open to see Liam in the same spot, his palm pressed to the frame of the door.

His lips briefly rolled inward before a lazy grin exposed the devastating dimple in his right cheek.

41

"You're not in the townhouse anymore."

"Would you have stayed there if someone you dated, even if it'd been super casual, was killed right in front of you?" She waved a dismissive hand. "Never mind. Don't answer that."

She shrugged, trying to act casual even though the entire event had been insane—but it'd also been how she met Liam and his buddies, and so . . .

"I'm renting this place until my new home is ready." Her brows stitched together when a thought occurred to her. "But um, how'd you get up here?"

Her building had top-notch security—plus, she had a bodyguard outside.

"Does it matter how?" He dropped his hand, and her gaze followed one of the veins in his forearm up to his bicep. The sleeve of his shirt battled against the muscle there. Every time she looked at his arms the word *damn* popped into her brain. No exception now.

"Did Owen call you?" She forced herself to tear her eyes away from his muscles as she considered whether or not Owen may have dialed Liam after dinner tonight.

"Why would Owen call me?" He once again braced the doorframe as if he needed the support.

Was he drunk? It was hard for her to believe a guy like him couldn't handle a few drinks, but then again, alcohol had been the culprit in their whole saying *I do* debacle.

She leaned forward as if she might be able to smell booze like she was one of the old hunting hounds her grandfather had kept back on the ranch in Montana.

She blinked a few times at the realization that the only thing she could smell was the intense odor of garlic coming from her neighbor in 3-B. The guy loved to bathe his food in garlic to the point she could feel the natural benefits just from a few daily whiffs on her way in and out of her place.

"When did you get to D.C.?" she asked, ignoring his question about Owen once he was inside, and she'd closed the door.

"This afternoon. I stopped over to see my grandfather in Virginia first." He pointed at her living room, which was five feet away from the area serving as her foyer. "This doesn't look like you. Not a place you'd live in."

How many times have we hung out? She did a quick count in her head—six.

Was it really only six times they'd been around each other?

First time—he'd shown up at her door with Owen and Asher and warned her the guy she was dating was dangerous and also an asshole of the highest order.

The next time she'd hung out with Liam was at Luke and Eva's baby gender reveal party, and although several of the guys had stolen her away to chat, she'd had her eye on Liam the entire time. How could someone not? The guy could've been Chris Hemsworth's twin. Accent and all. The God of Thunder from Down Under.

She breezed through the other times they'd spent together, trying to get a handle on how he seemed to know her well enough to determine her current rental wasn't "her."

There was the Christmas party. Liam had been devilishly charming that night, but she'd had too many eyes on her to even think naughty thoughts, let alone act on them.

Then a quick trip to Owen's pub in Charleston in January with Sam—but Liam had been on his way out, and so, they'd only shared a few hours together over breakfast.

Dancing with Liam at a club on Valentine's Day in New York had only left her with a case of female blue balls.

And then there was Vegas.

"How would you know what kind of place I would live in?" she asked since she couldn't come up with an answer during her brief walking tour of their past.

"I was at your townhouse last year when that D.C. wanker—"

"Right, but surely you don't remember what it looked like, or the kind of person I am to assume this place isn't my style." Her hands went to her hips as she eyed him.

"The main hall had artwork on the walls—watercolor, right? Scenery, not graphics," he said without taking pause. "Two brown suede couches and an armchair in your back living room. Lots of family pictures on the far-side wall in there. A fireplace. And your bedroom . . ."

"Okay, I get it. Your memory is off the charts."

He swirled a finger in the air as he did a three-sixty, examining her apartment. "This place is cold. Barely lived in. Like it's almost—"

"So sterile a surgeon could operate here?" She smiled. "Well, the place came furnished. Super minimalistic, and my guess is it belonged to a doctor before, given the smell of antibiotic soap the walls sort of absorbed." She motioned for him to have a seat on the black leather sofa. "Of course, that smell does act as a barrier to my neighbor's love of garlic, so I can't complain."

"Ah, that's what I smelled in the hall." He jerked a thumb toward the door then dropped down onto the leather.

There weren't any other seats aside from the sofa, but she wasn't quite sure if she could bring herself to sit so close to him. Not yet, at least.

She had to first reduce the hammering of her heart to a near-normal level.

"The bed is mine, though," she noted, feeling the need for

him to know she wasn't sleeping in some other guy's bed. The idea had creeped her out, and so it'd been written into her rental agreement to swap the beds. "The rest of my stuff is in storage until moving day."

"Good call." He swiped a hand over his blond head. His hair was shorter on the sides and a bit longer on the top with a touch of gel to style it.

"So, um, did you get shitfaced with your grandfather before you came here?"

His green eyes, rimmed in blue, locked on her face. A palpable tension that no way could only she be feeling moved through the air and hit her.

"No." He cleared his throat. "I stopped at the bar around the corner until I got the nerve to come see you."

She wondered if this was alcohol-induced honesty.

But she was also currently suffering from the warm and fuzzy effects that had kicked in after she'd moved on to her second bottle of red.

A fluttery sensation traveled from her stomach up to her chest. "Owen told me you were back. I was hoping to see you soon. I just didn't realize it'd be tonight." She would've dressed for the occasion at the very least. Then again, how does one dress to sign annulment papers?

"Does he know what happened? Does Sam?" He could've been asking about the weather—he didn't sound nervous or concerned.

"No, but um, how was your trip?"

He crossed his ankle over his knee and held it. "It was good, but . . . I wasn't focused, and then there was this kid that I was worried about. *Still* worried about."

"Oh." Her mouth rounded in surprise. More honesty and she almost felt guilty about listening to him talk. She had to assume Liam was like Owen, who was super tight-lipped about his work. Liam probably wouldn't normally share so much if he hadn't hit the corner bar first.

So, she decided not to prod. She didn't want Liam having any more regrets when he woke up tomorrow. Surely, they had enough already.

"Well, I have the papers to sign. I assume that's why you're here." She'd been drinking wine and staring in a daze at them when he'd startled the hell out of her by ringing the bell.

"You work fast."

She found his eyes again. There was a sadness there. She hadn't noticed it before, maybe because she'd been too focused on his panty-melting smile.

"We used to have a no-marriage rule at work," he blurted.

"What?" She inched closer to the couch, which she instantly regretted because, when he rose, they were inches apart.

His chin dipped so their eyes could meet—he had at least half a foot on her height of five-eight. Her legs were beginning to feel unsteady, and she had the urge to grab hold of his arms to stay upright.

"You're so damn beautiful." He lightly gripped her biceps, doing what she'd wanted to do to his arms moments before.

My husband. Husband!

"I, um, I doubt I'm your type," she said, trying to deflect. To protect her heart from the look in his eyes that could surely ruin every other man for her.

"You're right, you're not my type." His words were rough, like the touch of an uncut diamond drawing blood as it scraped over her skin.

She tried not to flinch, to let him know how crushing his comment had been.

He released his hold of her and shut one eye. "That didn't come out the way I wanted." He looked heavenward, and she took the chance to create space between them and stepped back.

"I'll grab the papers."

A couple of signatures away from being Emily Summers again.

She thought about her few memories from their wedding night as she went to her bedroom.

"Mrs. Evans. It sounds good," Liam had said.

"Well, husband, what do you want to do with me now?" She'd hooked her arms around his neck.

"Make love." The words had brushed across her lips before he'd kissed her, taking command of her mouth, and she'd surrendered and let him. Gave him complete control, too.

"You're not my type because you *are* my type."

Startled, she turned to find him standing in her bedroom doorway, his shoulder leaning into the interior frame as he observed her.

"Yeah, that doesn't make much sense either," she mumbled.

"Your brother would probably kill me if he found out about this," he said once her back was to him as she reached for the papers.

Yeah, her brother, Jake, wouldn't exactly roll out the red carpet for Liam, but she had no intention of telling anyone in her family what she'd done. "Jake's harmless."

"Sure." He barked out a laugh. "He does what I do, so . . ."

The on-the-books stuff or the other top-secret work? She almost spoke her thoughts, but she was worried Liam would assume Sam had betrayed Owen's trust and told her the truth, even though she hadn't. Emily wasn't an idiot, she'd pretty much figured it out.

"Do you remember more of our, uh, wedding night now that some time has passed?" he asked, his voice low and sexy, and his question derailed her thoughts.

"I, uh. Yeah, a little."

He was behind her now. She could feel him. Smell his cologne. A touch of mint with smooth notes of vanilla as the base.

Desire unfurled inside her belly when his hand matched the curve of her hip. "Liam."

Her pulse broke out into a full-on Mt. Everest type of climb with him so close, and she tried to hide the chill sweeping down her body as if it were his hand running smoothly over her skin.

He leaned in and brought his mouth near her ear. "You've been drinking, too?"

She spied the glass of wine on her nightstand. She'd left it there when she went to answer the door. "Mmhm. A lot on my mind. Work." She paused. "You."

He released his hold of her, and she turned to face him. "I should go then."

She extended the papers, a slight tremble in her hand. He didn't even look down. No, he kept his eyes on hers, his chest lifting ever so slightly as he studied her. She'd give anything to have the power to read his thoughts.

"Maybe since we got married while we were drunk, we should get divorced when we're sober." A sort of sad resignation moved through his words.

"It, uh, won't be a divorce. It'll be like it never happened." Her stomach turned at her last statement, and she wasn't sure why.

"'Never happened,' huh?" His eyes dipped to the papers.

Even beneath his beard, she witnessed the strain of his jaw as if he were attempting to pulverize stone with his back teeth.

When he peered at her again, with his lips set into a hard line and his brows drawn inward, she couldn't tell if he was angry or confused.

She wished it'd been more than six times they'd hung out so she'd know him better, so she'd know how to handle this moment.

"I'll come back tomorrow," he said. "What time will you be out of work?"

"Six-ish."

"I'll bring food. Thai okay?"

"That's not necessary."

"Please. We should at least eat a meal together before you stop being my wife."

Wife. Why did that word sound so amazing coming from his mouth?

"Okay," she finally caved.

He continued to stare at her, words seeming to fail him.

"Well, thank you," she added, feeling like she needed to fill the space of the silence since he hadn't talked in a solid minute. She'd been slowly ticking off the seconds in her head waiting.

"I'll be back tomorrow, then." His focus wandered to her bed as if a memory from their night together had hit him. "I, uh, should go." A touch more of his Australian accent flowed through his speech this time. Or maybe she'd imagined it, she couldn't be sure of anything at the moment.

A dizziness grabbed hold of her as she stood before a man who, according to the state of Nevada, was her husband.

"You've been in the U.S. for a while, right?" She tossed the papers back on the bed and strode toward him.

"Since I was nineteen."

"So, you've lived here for almost half your life?"

He folded his arms and angled his head. "Why do you ask?"

"Just wondering how you're still so very Aussie."

His lips quirked into a slight smile. "Do you not want me to be?"

"No, I love your accent," she admitted, probably too quickly.

"I happen to love yours, too."

She poked her chest with her index finger and arched a brow. "Mine?"

"Your Southern accent is very . . ."

He looked at the ceiling instead of finishing his thoughts. Maybe that was for the better.

He gritted out, "You're making this hard for me."

"I don't understand."

His eyes seized hold of hers again. "You're making it hard for me to walk away right now, Emily."

Ohhh.

He scratched his trimmed blond beard. What was it about a man with facial hair, and why did she find herself wondering if his beard would tickle her inner thighs if he kissed her there?

"Are you always this candid, or is it the alcohol?"

"Probably the whiskey."

She set her hand against his chest and maintained eye contact. "Maybe you could try it when you're not drinking?"

He wrapped a hand around her slender wrist, then bowed his head closer to hers.

She wasn't sure if he was going to kiss her. And was it wrong she wanted him to?

He was still her husband until they signed the papers. And

right now, this ruggedly sexy man seemed to be looking at her like he wanted her.

His forehead touched hers, and he cursed under his breath.

Yeah, the struggle was real.

"I really should go." His words were heavy. Gritty. Like he had to force them out.

"Yeah," she whispered but didn't pull away. "You have a place to stay, right?"

She was dangerously close to offering her sofa, which she knew would be a stupid idea given this very moment.

No way would she be able to sleep under the same roof with him, not after they'd had sex last weekend, and not with her wishing he'd rip off her clothes.

Damn her brain for not remembering everything about that night in Vegas, especially the between-the-sheets parts. Or on top of the sheets. She wasn't sure if they'd made it to a bed until the moment they actually decided to sleep.

He stepped back, and she lowered her hand to her side.

"There's a hotel within walking distance. I got a room there when I first arrived this afternoon."

"Oh. Good. Well, then I'll see you tomorrow night."

His hand moved up to cup her cheek, and his thumb swept in circular motions as he stared at her lips. "Goodnight, Emily."

Her cheek grew cold at the loss of his warm palm.

She followed him to the door, and once he was outside of her apartment, he glimpsed one last look at her before disappearing into the stairwell. Alcohol or not, the man still took the stairs instead of the elevator.

After he was out of sight, she closed the door and rested her forehead against it.

At the sound of a text alert coming from her phone a beat

later, she locked up, then went to the living room to retrieve it.

Liam: *This is your husband. ;) I thought you should have my number.*

Emily: *How'd you get mine?*

Clearly, he hadn't known Owen had given her his digits.

Liam: *This is me we're talking about. ;)*

God, he even winked in his texts. Why did he have to be so frustratingly sexy and charming?

Emily: *Good point.*

She clutched the phone, considering what to say next.

So they got drunk and married and became a TV cliché—why not own it, at least?

Emily: *I'd expect nothing less from my husband.*

Liam: *And now I kind of want to come back up there and kiss you like I wanted to before.*

She almost dropped the phone. *Holy shit.*

Emily: *You never told me—what do you remember from Vegas?*

Liam: *Probably more than you. Because I remember how you kiss. How you taste.*

A blazing trail of heat traveled from her stomach down to between her legs.

Liam: *I should probably turn off my phone before I get myself into more trouble.*

Liam: *Goodnight, Emily.*

She was going to need her emergency stash of Oreos tonight.

And more wine.

Hell, a lot more wine.

CHAPTER SIX

ATTORNEY GENERAL JERRY DRYDEN RUBBED HIS FOREHEAD, which had a few faint lines from years of stress on the job. When he lowered his hand so she could find his eyes, she knew the news he was going to hit her with wasn't going to brighten her day, that was for sure.

He sat taller in his chair, and his palms went to the maple desk in front of him. The man intimidated a lot of people with his Dwayne "The Rock" Johnson body type, but then he had the handsome face of Idris Elba, which always had both sexes fanning themselves whenever he walked through a building or stood in a courtroom.

Dryden didn't look anywhere near his age of sixty, either. Well, not normally. Today he sure as hell did, which spelled more bad news.

"She's not talking," he said, explaining his forlorn look. He pushed away from his desk and stood. "This case will end before it even starts if she can't tell us anything."

No. Shit! She didn't even understand how the FBI managed to get this witness, but they couldn't back down now. "This might be our last chance to finally nail this son of a—" Emily let go of her words since she was speaking to Dryden. Of course, he'd dropped quite a few F-bombs while she worked for him as a trial lawyer for the criminal division, but still, he was her boss.

Dryden scratched his dark beard, untouched from white or gray, and he fixed his light brown eyes on hers, but before he could say anything there was a knock at the door.

"Sir?" It was his admin.

"Come in."

"FBI Director Mendez is on the line," his admin announced. "He says it's urgent."

"Why didn't you just patch him through?" Dryden dropped back into his seat.

"You were with Miss Summers, and I didn't want to disturb you."

Mrs. Evans now. "You think it's about the case?"

"Maybe." He thanked his admin and answered the phone once she closed the door. "Any news?" He paused to let the director talk. "Yeah, okay, I'll call you back on a secure line."

"Everything okay?" Emily sat in front of the desk while he switched to a burner cell.

"I don't know."

She glanced off to her left at the wall of law books as she waited for Dryden to begin speaking.

Six more hours until she'd be out of the office and having dinner with Liam. And then after, she'd be single again. It was all so strange. Like she'd fallen asleep but was having someone else's dream.

"Really?" He waited for the director to continue. "Well, has she indicated she does, in fact, know something?"

Dryden's words had her refocusing on him.

"He's a civilian now, we can't—"

She could hear the director talking over the line, but not loud enough to understand what he was saying.

"Fine. I'll talk to the president, but for the record, I don't like this." He ended the call and grabbed his blazer from the back of his chair before standing. "I gotta go."

"Are you going to tell me what that was all about?" Once on her feet, she smoothed her hands down the sides of her black pencil skirt, resisting the urge to unzip the back a little so she could breathe. She was regretting all the wine and Oreos she'd consumed last night.

Her emergency wardrobe for such occasions—Thanksgiving, post-breakups, losing a case, and oh yeah, nearly getting shot last year . . . well, those flowy dresses were in a box in storage until her new home was ready.

She needed to buy some post-marriage outfits now. Maybe an entire month's worth of more comfortable clothes.

"There's been a development." He moved past his desk, flicking his wrist for her to come along. "The witness knows something, but there's only one man she'll speak to, and I need approval from the president to make it happen."

"Who?"

He stopped in front of the door. "The less you know, the better," he said and left before she could protest.

And maybe he was right because Dryden would probably force a bodyguard to move in with her next. Or worse, pull her from the case.

Emily started for her office, but at the vibration of a text on her cell she stopped in the hall, nearly bumping into an intern.

Jake: *Can you talk? I'm outside your building.*

What? She blinked a few times and re-read the message.

She hadn't seen her brother since last fall, especially since he mostly worked in London as of late. So, she couldn't imagine what he was doing in her neck of the woods.

Emily: *Be right out.*

Once outside, she shielded her eyes with her hand, having forgotten her sunglasses, and searched for Jake.

He was leaning against a black Escalade with Alexa at his side. When he spotted Emily, he started for her and then lifted her into the air in a hug as if she were light as a feather—and you know, not weighed down by the double-stuffed cookies from last night.

"What are you doing here?" she asked once her heels touched the ground.

"We're flying to Australia, and we chose D.C. as our first stop," he answered while she hugged Alexa. "We wanted to see you, then Mom and Dad next, before we head to Melbourne."

"Australia?" She tried to hide her surprise as they approached the Escalade and out of the way of foot traffic. "Why Australia? And why do you need to see me? Or Mom and Dad?"

Jake looked at Alexa briefly before his gaze wandered back to hers.

Something was definitely going on.

"Don't kill us. But um . . ." She lifted her left hand, and her engagement ring, which Emily had helped Jake pick out, sparkled in the sunlight. But it was the accompanying eternity band that had her grabbing hold of Alexa's hand and gasping.

"You're married?" Her eyes grew wide at the sight.

"It was a last-minute thing. We literally grabbed a buddy we work with as a witness and went to the courthouse," Jake announced. "We were working a case for a friend, and well . . ."

"We decided life is too short, and why the bloody hell don't we just say *I do*?" Alexa finished for Jake.

"You look shocked. You gonna say something?" Jake braced a hand over her shoulder, and she forced her gaze to his.

"Australia. A wedding. Am I on *Punk'd*?" She looked around for a camera. "What's going on?"

"'*Punk'd*'?" Alexa smiled. "No, it's true."

How was it possible? And if there were ever a time to tell her brother about Liam—well, yeah, nope—now wouldn't be it.

But seriously. Maybe she was still passed-out drunk in the hotel room in Vegas.

"I, uh . . . congratulations!" She looped her arms around Alexa's neck. "I just wish I had been there, you know?"

"I'm sorry." Jake hugged her next.

"Mom and Dad are going to kill you. Maybe you should wait until after the honeymoon Down Under to tell them." She lightly laughed because hell, if she ever switched careers from lawyer to stand-up comedian, she'd have a lot of content to work with.

"I'd rather rip off the Band-Aid and get it over with," Jake said. "You have time for dinner when you're off work before we head to see them?"

She was supposed to have dinner with Liam before she became single once again. But she couldn't exactly tell Jake and Alexa no. "I can change my plans."

"Were you hanging out with a friend tonight? You can bring her along." Jake reached into his pocket for his keys.

"Oh, um."

Alexa studied her for a beat. "Oh, you have a date, don't you?" She stepped closer and smiled.

"It's not like that." *I have an annulment date.*

"Bring him," Jake said with a nod, and Emily knew that look.

No guy would ever be good enough for Emily in his eyes, especially after her two-year relationship with Mr. British, as Sam liked to call him, ended so badly. Then there was the D.C. douche last year. Her track record with men was shit.

"I'll call you when I get out of work," she said instead, not sure what to do.

But maybe dinner with Liam *and* her brother would be safer than dinner alone with Liam.

She waited for Alexa and Jake to leave, then whirled around like a crazy person on the sidewalk one last time in search of the cameras for a show she hadn't watched since the days when getting your hair permed was still a thing.

She tapped out a quick message to Liam as she headed up the steps and back to her office.

Emily: *My brother and his wife just popped into town for today only. They want to have dinner.*

Liam: *Since when is your brother married?*

He'd responded almost right away which surprised her.

Emily: *He just got married. News to me. And . . . they're going to Australia for their honeymoon.*

Emily: *And yeah, I know—it's weird.*

Liam: *Are we on Punk'd? ;)*

She stopped walking and grinned.

Emily: *You've watched that show, but you've never seen an episode of Friends?*

Liam: *Mm. I might have watched a few episodes of Friends this morning while I recovered from last night.*

She almost laughed out loud.

Emily: *I don't believe you.*

Liam: *I swear. I watched the Ross and Rachel wedding,*

too. I mean, at least we didn't write on each other's faces like they did.

Oh my God. She was going to fall in love with this man, which would not be a good idea.

Liam: *Anyway, am I invited? Or am I your dessert?*

Liam: *Shit, I meant to delete that last part before I hit send. Fingers were trigger happy.*

Liam: *P.S. I can't blame alcohol right now.*

And now she couldn't stop smiling.

Emily: *I'll text you when I'm out of work. You're invited to dinner.*

Emily: *But maybe don't mention the "you're my husband" thing.*

Liam: *I don't have a death wish.*

Liam: *It's a date. ;)*

CHAPTER SEVEN

EMILY OBSERVED HER BROTHER FROM ACROSS THE DINNER table, amazed by how well he seemed to be getting along with Liam. She'd honestly never seen Jake react so positively to a guy she'd hung out with before.

Apparently, Liam's charm extended to everyone, even her tough-as-nails brother. It was mind-boggling.

Liam had come bearing wedding gifts. A thick travel guide to Australia, along with a copy of the DVD *Crocodile Dundee*. She was pretty sure the other present was a gag gift.

"Are there really snakes, spiders, and crocodiles everywhere in Australia?" Alexa asked.

"Oh, we get a bad rap for that kind of stuff. You're going to Melbourne, not the outback." Liam waved a dismissive hand.

"Well, any advice?" Alexa leaned forward a touch.

"Thongs are flip-flops, not G-strings," he answered while glimpsing Emily out of the corner of his eye.

She'd been wearing a pink thong the night of the wedding last Saturday, and she was sure her cheeks now matched the color as he continued to list off a few other signature Aussie terms.

"And just don't go around asking for shrimp on the barbie," he added, "or you'll look like a bloody tourist."

"No?" Alexa asked with a smile and reached for her wine.

They were sitting on the outdoor patio of an Irish pub not far from Emily's rental. The weather was far too amazing to be pent up inside.

"We don't call 'em shrimp. They're prawns. And we usually boil the suckers not barbecue them."

"Well," Alexa began, "I still think you're being modest about the snakes and spiders."

"I've got your back when we're there," Jake said. "Although, I might be jumping into her arms if I see a friggen snake."

"Or a spider." She nudged Jake in the side. "I swear, I'm not sure if I've ever heard a man scream so loud at the sight of one."

Jake held both palms up. "She's leaving out the part where it was actually a tarantula and in my sock drawer at our hotel."

Alexa chuckled.

"He made you check out right after, didn't he?" Emily asked.

"Oh yeah." Alexa reached for the bottle of wine on the table and offered her some.

"I think one glass is enough for me tonight." They had to sign the papers later, and so, she'd behave herself.

Of course, part of her almost wanted an excuse not to sign.

But why put off the inevitable?

Besides, Liam was drinking soda, so apparently, his mind

was set on officially ending things between them tonight. His playful texting banter threw her for a loop, though.

Too bad they couldn't have sex one more time before they broke things off so she'd have a few memories to save away.

"You're vibrating," she announced a moment later and pointed toward Liam's jeans.

When his gaze met hers as he retrieved it, he smiled—the kind of smile that read: *Yeah, I know you're thinking dirty thoughts about me.*

He tucked the phone back into his pocket after studying the ID.

"Not going to answer?" she asked.

"I never answer a number I don't know."

Guess Owen was right.

He leaned back in his chair and focused on her brother. "How's work in the private sector?"

"You know how it is, right? It has its benefits but makes things tricky when you don't have the entire government behind you for ops."

"Not having a helo or QRF on standby is a pain in the ass."

Jake smiled at Liam's words and took a drink of beer. "I heard rumors Scott and Scott may rebrand. Is that true?"

Really? She was surprised Sam hadn't mentioned the news. Well, unless she didn't know it yet herself.

"You remember Luke Scott?" Liam asked, and Jake nodded. "His wife's family is famous, and Luke thinks it might be better for the agency. You know, draw some attention away from him by changing the company name."

"You guys have been expanding like wildfire," Alexa commented.

"Heard the same about your business," Liam responded. "Maybe we'll work together someday."

Yeah, that'd be weird.

"You also work with Wyatt Pierson, don't you?" Jake asked.

She caught sight of Liam sitting taller in his seat.

"Isn't he from London originally?" Alexa looked to Liam for an answer.

"Yeah," Liam replied. "He got his citizenship through marriage when he was eighteen."

"Well, I was just gonna say he single-handedly saved my ass and a bunch of other Marines back in Iraq ten years ago. He was on overwatch while my guys cleared houses in Baghdad." Jake finished his drink, and Alexa reached for his hand. "A guy nearly took me out, but Pierson double-tapped him just in time."

"He's one of the best snipers on the damn planet," Liam said in a low voice.

"Yeah, and word is so are you," Jake pointed out.

She couldn't take her eyes off Liam, and he casually shrugged away the compliment.

"I think I need to powder my nose," Alexa said, and when Emily managed to tear her eyes away from a very stoic Liam, Alexa was cocking her head, a silent request for Emily to come with her.

"Aw, babe, didn't they teach you to be a bit more subtle in spy school?" Jake's lips spread into a grin.

"Smart arse." Alexa stood. "You coming?"

"Yeah." Emily quickly rose. "Be back."

Alexa hooked her arm with Emily's, and they went inside the pub. "So, he's gorgeous. How long have you two been shagging?"

Emily nearly stumbled in her heels. "What?"

"Oh, come on, the way you've been looking at him all

night, and the hot looks he's been shooting your way . . . you must be having sex."

"We're friends," she said once in the bathroom. "That's all it is."

Alexa met her eyes in the mirror over the counter. "If you truly aren't shagging you will be soon. I promise."

"I don't want to—"

"Emily, you're a horrible liar!" Alexa turned and leaned her hip against the counter. She placed both hands on Emily's shoulders and looked her in the eyes. "You've been through a lot, I know, but I have a good feeling about this one."

"His nickname is Ladies-Man-Liam." Something that had apparently suited her fine after doing shots of tequila in Vegas. "He's probably really good in bed, and maybe I'd love to know just how good, but—"

"But what? At least have some fun with the guy. You know, some hot, sweaty sex."

"Alexa," she said with a chuckle.

"But seriously, Jake's practically ready to ask Liam to marry you, just so they can be brothers."

Yeah, about that. "He's charming, that's all."

Alexa released her hold of her shoulders. "And he's Australian, Em."

"Okay, well, your accent sounds almost the same to me," she said with a smile. "Very sexy."

"And your brother's Southern accent is hot to me, so I'm betting Liam feels the same about you."

"What's gotten into you? Marriage making you crazy? You going to start singing Disney songs to the birds?"

Alexa waved a hand in the air. "Maybe I'm still feeling a bit high on life right now, and I'm so looking forward to this vacation. I don't know. I just want you to be as happy as I am."

"And I appreciate that."

Liam was hot, but his humor was going to be her undoing. A guy that could make her laugh—how long had it been since someone had been able to do that, even with a text?

"Give him a chance is all I'm saying. He might surprise you." She was quiet for a moment. "Not all guys are like your ex-fiancé. They won't—"

"I know," Emily whispered. "We, uh, better get back out there." She hugged her. "I'm glad to have you as a sister," she added, leaving before her mascara started running.

She caught sight of Liam and Jake at the bar inside the pub when she exited the bathroom.

"Are they doing shots?" Alexa asked as they closed in on them at the bar.

"It's a celebratory thing." Jake gave Alexa a shot, and Liam's eyes connected with Emily as he handed her the clear liquid.

"Just one." Shots got them into the Vegas mess in the first place.

"Cheers," Jake said as they all clinked their glasses together.

After downing the shots, they made their way to the outside table, but Alexa remained standing.

"We have an early drive." She reached for the gifts. "We should get going."

"Oh, so soon?" Emily widened her eyes Alexa's way, knowing exactly what she was up to.

"I trust you'll get Emily home okay?" Jake reached for Liam's hand.

"Of course. And congratulations again. Be careful when you head Down Under."

"Thanks, brother."

Oh, God. Technically you are kind of brothers now, right? Maybe he meant brothers-in-arms. Of course, he did. Damn it.

Jake kissed her on the cheek. "Love you, Sis. I'll call you when we're back in London."

"Have an amazing time. Good luck with Mom and Dad." She hugged Alexa goodbye next, and then seconds stretched to minutes once she was alone with Liam. "So."

They remained standing alongside their table, Liam with his hands tucked into his back pockets. "Ready to roll?"

No. She looked skyward, willing herself to find the right answer, and then sputtered, "Yes."

* * *

"WHAT'S WRONG?" EMILY ASKED WHEN LIAM STUCK HIS ARM out in front of her, bringing her to a halt on the sidewalk. She pivoted to find Liam's focus dead set on a black town car on the road off to their right.

"You have a tail. Same car was parked outside your place last night now that I think about it. He was parked near the pub earlier, too."

"It's not a tail. But how do you remember that? You were pretty drunk last night."

"It's my job to remember details. Preferable to be sober, though." He jerked his thumb toward the car. "If it's not a tail, care to explain why this guy's following you?"

She didn't need him going all overprotective on her, but she owed him the truth, she supposed. "He's my bodyguard."

"And why do you have a bodyguard?"

"Just a precaution because of a case I'm working on. Well, possibly working." She started walking again, expecting him to follow suit.

"Oh . . . kay." He dragged out the word, unconvinced. "Is this normal in your line of work?"

"No, but I really can't say more about it." Her gaze slid to the side to observe him as they walked. "If anyone should know about needing to keep secrets it's you."

"You know I'm not going to just let this go."

"Well, you don't need to worry about me." They stopped at the crosswalk, waiting for their turn. "So, um, why is remembering details part of your job?"

"Being a sniper isn't just about shooting."

She quirked a brow and eyed him, waiting for him to explain further.

He lifted his chin, signaling the walk sign had popped up. "When I was back in sniper school the part of the program most recruits struggled with was called stalking."

"'Stalking'? Yeah, you're going to have to unwrap that lingo and expand it for me."

"Capturing locations and scenes perfectly in your mind. Intelligence gathering. You know, relaying intel back to headquarters to help take down the bad guys. But the memorizing stuff can be brutal."

"But not for you?" She was intrigued. Another new piece of the puzzle that was Liam. And for some reason, this had her jonesing to learn even more about him.

He stopped walking and faced her. "Not sure if there's truly such a thing as a photographic memory, but since I was a kid, I could pretty much look at something and remember it. Not permanently, but long enough so I could pass my exams in primary," he said with a smile.

"Yeah, teachers must've had a love-hate relationship with you." She matched his smile with one of her own, and then looked over at the building to their left. "Oh, is this your hotel?"

He nodded.

"Well, you don't need to walk me the rest of the way. I've got the bodyguard. Remember?"

His smile dissolved. "Well, the papers are back at your place."

"Papers?"

She wasn't sure if there'd ever been a time in her life when she felt like her mind was empty. Just a bunch of negative space.

But there was always a first time. And that time was now.

"The it-never-really-happened papers."

Shit. "Right." She wet her lips, ready to start walking again, but Liam had shifted toward the street, and his body went completely still.

"What are you doing here?" Liam started toward a blond man who looked eerily similar to him. "I don't know how you found me, but you need to go."

"Liam, please." There was a desperation to the man's voice. A gritty plea.

Emily stood awkwardly off to the side of the hotel entrance, watching the scene unfold, even though she felt like it should've been a private moment.

"Mum told you where I was staying?"

Emily clutched her purse strap, hugging her bag close to her body to try and kill some of the nerves.

"Please, I came all the way here to try and make things right. With the baby coming, we want—"

"Go back home." Liam turned away from him, catching Emily's eyes in the process. A dark look crossed his face.

Regret. Sadness. She wasn't sure. Maybe both.

"Yeah, run," the guy snapped. "That's what you're good at."

"Don't you dare," Liam rasped in a hard voice as he spun

back around. "You're my brother. You're supposed to be on my side." His voice elevated as obvious anger radiated to the surface. "You may have won over Jesse and Greyson. And Mum and Dad. But I can't forgive you for what you did."

His brother was quiet for a moment. "Liam, we need to make this right."

She wanted to do something, to help him somehow, but she stood frozen in place, simply watching. It was a family issue, what could she possibly do or say?

"You married her, Brandon." Liam's hand curled into a fist at his side. "There's nothing to talk about."

She replayed Liam's words in her head, barely noticing her bodyguard now closing in on her location, probably worried a fight was about to break out.

"You chose the Navy over her. And I—" He paused. "It was years later. We never . . ." His brother's voice trailed off as he stepped back. "I thought you'd want to know you're gonna have a nephew. But I guess I was wrong." He turned and went around to the driver's side of a nearby parked Audi.

"You should leave, Miss Summers." Her bodyguard, Hugh, reached for her arm. Liam spun around at that moment, his eyes landing on Hugh.

"What are you doing?" Liam crossed the space between them to get to her.

"He's my bodyguard," she quickly replied, worried Liam would misdirect his anger onto Hugh.

"You okay, ma'am?" Hugh kept his focus on Liam, his hand still protectively wrapped around her bicep.

"Yeah, I'm okay," she said, never losing hold of Liam's eyes.

"Can you see that she gets home okay?" he asked, defeat in his voice.

"Of course," Hugh answered, and her heart stuttered.

"What about—"

Liam massaged his right temple as if a headache stirred. "I can't do this right now. I'm so sorry."

CHAPTER EIGHT

L IAM FINISHED HIS M AKER'S M ARK AND ORDERED ANOTHER round. The familiar and intoxicating scent of a sexy perfume drifting from his right side caught his attention. He pivoted on the bar stool to find Emily sliding onto the seat next to him.

"I thought you might be here." She'd changed out of her skirt and blouse and into a pair of jeans and a black tee. She forced a smile, which wasn't quite broad enough to showcase her dimples. "I convinced my bodyguard to let me break curfew, so I hope you don't mind me showing up."

He wished she hadn't witnessed the confrontation with his brother, and he'd give anything to take it back.

He wasn't sure if he'd ever forgive his brother for marrying his ex, even if his family may have been right about why Melissa left him—it didn't matter. His brothers on the teams would never betray him like his own flesh and blood had.

The bartender slid a fresh whiskey to Liam and directed his attention on Emily. "Would you like something?"

"You know we don't make the best decisions when we get drunk together," Liam reminded her.

"Good point," Emily said. "A glass of your most watered-down wine, please."

The bartender laughed. "Coming right up, ma'am."

She remained quiet until he delivered the drink, and Liam guessed that was for his benefit. He wasn't sure what the hell to say, or how to explain what had happened. He was waiting for her to ask, though, and so, he'd need to come up with some sort of answer.

He shifted on the stool and her eyes lifted from the drink, and he'd swear his heart stopped. There was such a sweetness about her.

Her white teeth flashed his way. Her lipstick had faded after having eaten dinner earlier. And either her cheeks always had a natural pink glow, or she had the tendency to blush whenever he was around because he didn't think she had any other makeup on. Mascara maybe, but she already had long, dark lashes, which showcased the depth of her espresso brown eyes.

"So, how'd you find me?"

"The beer on tap at your hotel is shit so you wouldn't drink there," she answered; those lashes of hers rising and falling a few times, drawing his attention. "And since you were here last night, I took a chance." She combed her fingers through her brown hair, which had streaks of blonde framing her face. Her palm went to her collarbone, drawing his eye straight to the neckline of her shirt like a target in his crosshairs, and he forced his gaze to the bar top to refrain from looking like some creep ogling her breasts.

Shit. How could it feel like both an eternity and yet only five minutes since they'd gotten married?

"Thank you for the flowers, by the way. Lilies are a favorite of mine. I don't know how you knew that or how you got them into my place while I was at work today . . . but thank you."

He'd been walking by a flower shop earlier when looking for a wedding gift, and the impulse to buy her the flowers had struck him. Roses hadn't felt right, so he'd gone with the lilies. "You really need to upgrade your security. I got in way too easy." He held up one palm. "I was in and out quick. I didn't snoop around. No worries."

"The thought never crossed my mind." She shot him his own signature wink right back at him, and damn, did he love it.

"But seriously," he said with a nod, "I'll be calling a few guys I know in D.C. to beef up your security system."

"I move in a month."

"I don't give a damn if it's three days or thirty, you need to be better protected." He scratched the side of his neck. "Please," he added, hoping to soften what he realized had come out more like an order than a friendly request.

"I'll consider it." She shifted on her seat and looked at the color-coordinated bottles lining the shelves.

"Listen, I know we're supposed to sign the papers tonight," he began, thinking about his brother screwing the night up, "but—"

"We have time," she said, saving him from having to muster up some sort of explanation.

They could leave now and get it over with, but for some reason, the idea of signing the papers created a dull ache in his chest.

"You shoot darts?" he asked when his eyes fell upon the board at the back corner of the room.

She tracked his gaze before returning her focus to his face. "What, go up against someone who graduated top of his class from sniper school?"

"What makes you think I didn't almost wash out?" He squinted at her.

"Based on what I already know about you, you don't seem to be the kind of man who'd do anything half-assed. You'd whole-ass it for sure." Liam laughed, and she gave an innocent lift of her shoulders. "And as for me and darts—well, do you know the expression, 'you can't hit the broad side of a barn'?"

"Is that a Southern thing?" He grinned, and the smile actually made him feel a little better.

Her dimples popped.

God help him.

"The point is," she started, talking with her hands, which he couldn't help but find sexy, "I'll probably hit the wall instead of the dartboard, even though my career military father and grandfather taught me how to shoot a gun like it's my job."

He smiled. "What branch were they in?"

"Army." She sipped her wine then winced. Guess it really was the cheap stuff.

"Betting they wished your brother hadn't gone the Marine route."

"Only every Sunday and Friday. And you know, all those other days in between." She chuckled. "But, um, you never told me, how'd you end up living in the U.S.? You said Wyatt moved here for marriage, what about you?"

"I, uh." He smoothed a hand over his jawline. "My mum's American. My father had been traveling in the U.S. on business, and she was working as a waitress while an undergrad—they met and fell in love. They got married and moved to Sydney six weeks later."

"Wow. Sounds like a fairy tale."

"Guess so." He didn't want to think about Australia right now, though. Not after the run-in with his brother.

"So, you decided to move to the U.S. when you were nineteen, right?"

"Yeah. I'd been coming to the States every summer since I was a kid. My grandfather was one of the first frogmen, and it'd been my dream to become like him someday."

"He must be so proud of you." She beamed, her lips stretching into a gorgeous smile.

He looked to the beat-up wood floors beneath his boots, not sure what to say.

He wasn't an A-plus student, not even a C-minus one, when it came to conversations revolving around his personal life.

Give him a question on adjusting a shot to account for wind, and he could talk for days. But his past—nah, he was good.

When Emily remained quiet, he figured she'd sensed the wall he'd erected between them at lightning speed. She didn't deserve a guy with walls, though. She was a good person. He could feel it in his bones.

"Okay." She said the word on a sigh, dragging his attention to her lips. "I'll challenge you to a game of darts, I suppose."

"Why do I feel like a bet is about to follow, and that you're actually hustling me?"

She laughed, and damn, did he love the smooth sound. "Yeah, I'm no shark, I promise." She held a finger between them. "And I'm also a horrible liar, so you can believe me when I say that."

"Okay, then." He grabbed his drink and stood, then watched the sway of her hips as she moved away. He didn't think she was intentionally trying to direct his focus to her heart-shaped ass, but hell, he'd take that distraction over thinking about his brother.

You're my wife. For maybe only hours. Or another day. But still—wife.

He nearly stopped walking at the thought as he maneuvered around the pool tables to get to her.

She beat him to the dartboard and began gathering the red- and black-tipped darts. "You okay?" she asked, facing him as if she could sense the bone-crushing pain that had found a way to wreak havoc on his insides—pain he'd thought he'd squashed years ago was now suckering him into a rematch.

He forced the lump down his throat, but it wasn't hard to do with her beautiful eyes beholding his.

He didn't think she was even going to press about what happened with his brother. "You're . . ." he whispered without thinking.

"What about me?" Her lower lip caught between her teeth, and it brought him back to Vegas, to the sweet sound of his name coming from her mouth when she'd surrendered to her first orgasm that night.

He wanted to hear his name from her again. He wanted to listen to it a thousand more times. Even if he wasn't good for her, he couldn't seem to stop himself from flirting, from wanting more of her.

"Here," she said when his lips remained glued shut.

He blinked and looked down to see three darts in her palm.

He set down his drink, took the darts, then positioned himself at the line and threw the first one.

"What? No bull's-eye?" Her hands went to her hips, and she flashed him a smile.

He sucked in a sharp breath, glanced back at the

dartboard, then closed his eyes and tossed the second dart. Then the third.

"Wow." She clapped her hands when he reopened his eyes. She edged closer to the dartboard to view the two darts that had landed dead center next to each other. "That's kind of hot, not gonna lie." She pulled them free and strode back toward him. "Twenty bucks you can't do it again."

He laughed. "I thought we weren't betting."

"On my skills, no." She pursed her lips, her eyes moving to the ink on his arm.

She wanted him. And in his drunk-ass state last night, he'd felt it then, too.

He didn't want to hurt her, though. Maybe it was better she didn't remember much of Vegas. Maybe she'd be able to move on easier than he could.

At the feel of someone's eyes on him, he turned to catch Emily's bodyguard observing them from across the room. "Why do you really have the bodyguard?"

She set aside the darts and whipped her hair into a ponytail. "It's classified."

"I don't feel good about it." He stepped closer to her.

"You probably shouldn't feel anything about it." Her brows drew inward. "I'm not someone you need to worry about. I get the feeling you have enough on your plate without adding me to it."

"You're not just . . ." He didn't even know what to say, or how to finish his line of thought.

Emily was the newbie to his group—an off-limits friend. A woman he'd hung out with only five times before Vegas.

"I'm sorry." The apology left his lips quickly, and it had him bracing a hand on the empty bar top table off to his left.

"For what? For caring?"

"For what happened between us."

"Oh."

One syllable. One quick word. And yet, he could feel the impact of it like the perfect shot fired center mass. He almost gripped his chest as if a slug had hit him.

He needed to explain, but at the moment, he didn't really know how to. "I feel like an asshole."

She looked back at him, the glow to her skin gone, and it burned him to know he was the cause. "It's been a long day."

He'd give anything to bring the smile back to her face, to make her happy again.

"I think I could use some Oreos."

"Are you, uh, offering?" He waggled his brows a few times, and her smile nearly reappeared.

"You have a thing for milk and cookies, too?"

He lifted his shoulders. "Who doesn't?"

She raised a finger between them. "On one condition. Do you dunk then twist?"

A warmth flowed up and into his chest. "Is there any other way?"

CHAPTER NINE

"Mm. So good," she mumbled around a mouthful of cookie and grabbed another. "Better than sex."

He dunked his Oreo into his full glass of milk and looked over at her on the sofa. "I wouldn't go that far."

Her bottomless browns widened a fraction, and she rolled her tongue over the drop of milk on her lip. "It's been forever. I can't even remember what sex is like." Her eyes closed and that adorable pinkish hue bloomed on her face, overlapping the slight dusting of freckles that crossed over the top of her nose and beneath her eyes.

"And I can't believe I'm so forgettable."

She set the Oreo on the napkin atop the glass coffee table in front of them, then pressed her hands to her jeaned thighs. Her attention averted to the lilies he bought her positioned at the center of the table in a plain cream-colored vase.

"There's something you should know." She paused to take a breath. "I distinctly remember jumping into your arms and attempting to climb you like a tree once we were in the hotel room." Her blush deepened, her eyes now on the hardwood beneath her bare feet. "After that, I don't remember anything, but I don't want you to feel like you took advantage of me. We were both super drunk. It's also fairly possible I took advantage of you."

He coughed into a closed fist, taking a moment to gather his thoughts. "Regardless of who did what, I should've taken responsibility and not let it go that far. Alcohol or not. I'm really damn sorry." He set down the uneaten Oreo and dusted the crumbs from his hands.

She reached out and gently pressed her palm atop the back of his hand, and the gesture had his heartbeat dialing up as if he were back in BUD/S about to enter Hell Week.

"We're two responsible adults." She looked him in the eyes. "We're both to blame for the wild sex."

"What makes you think it was wild?" He couldn't help but smile.

He'd had her up against the wall naked.

On the hotel couch naked.

Then in the shower—obviously naked.

Yeah, it'd been . . . *damn*, his dick stirred in his pants as he thought about that night.

She retracted her hand. "I'm sure it was, and I wish I remembered it."

"You do?"

"Yeah, I mean"—she made a circle in the air with her hand—"have you seen your body?" She chuckled. "Sorry, I'm honest to a fault."

And he loved that about her. It was refreshing. "You didn't tell Sam, though?"

"No, and I'm guessing for the same reason you didn't tell anyone."

"I told Jessica and Asher," he said before thinking his words through, but the admission was almost freeing. "I mean, I didn't go into detail, but I mentioned we got married."

"And were they pissed?" Her voice slightly wavered.

"I think they were too busy removing their jaws from the floor to say much," he said as she stood and walked across the room to stand before the floor-to-ceiling window. "You ought to keep your blinds closed, especially at night."

"Normally I remember to close them, especially because of the apartment across the street."

"What about it?" The idea of some creep spying on her had him quickly at her side, his trigger finger itchy.

She pointed toward a softly lit-up room on the other side of the two-lane road. A guy had a woman pinned to the wall, and by the looks of it—maybe cuffed.

"Pretty sure that's his red room of pain, and he's clearly not shy about it." She shot him a look and scrunched her nose with disgust.

"A red what?"

"I know you're busy saving the world and all," she said with a smile, "but how could you not have heard of—" Her mouth opened into a cute O-shape before she playfully swatted his chest. "You just wanted to hear me explain, didn't you?"

He pressed a palm to the glass at his side. "Just a little bit."

That laugh of hers he loved so much—the infectious one —well, right now, it had his pulse elevating, and had him officially forgetting the confrontation with his brother.

"So, yeah, I usually have these blinds closed at night."

"I don't blame you." He reached for the string to close them, but then his gaze veered toward the street below.

"Something wrong?"

He fully faced the window, trying to get a better view of

her bodyguard's car. "Your driver looks like he's asleep. He's face forward over the wheel."

"We're on the third floor, how can you tell?" She paused. "Right. You and details."

"You still have a gun?" He kept his voice as steady as possible.

"Yeah, but—"

"We need to get you out of here." He dropped the blinds closed then reached for her arm, his heart pounding as a sense of urgency grabbed hold of him. "You have a fire escape?"

"It's an old drop-down ladder, and it's broken. I placed a work order to get it fixed, but it won't—"

"Okay. Change of plans." His hand slid down her forearm before he held on to her wrist. "Where's the gun?"

"In my safe," she said as they moved. "Why don't we go out the front door? And why do you think there's danger?"

"Because someone may have just killed your bodyguard, which means they're probably on their way up here now."

"My-my closet," she said, almost breathlessly. Panic clearly setting in. "The, uh, gun."

Once inside her bedroom, he closed and locked the door, and she went into her closet. He flicked off the bedroom light, then turned on the adjoining bathroom light as well as the shower.

They returned to the room at the same time, and he grabbed hold of her shoulders instead of taking the 9mm from her outstretched hand and looked into her eyes. "Listen to me very carefully. I want you to go into your bathroom and lock the door. Then call your boss and let him know what's happening. This could be a coordinated attack against everyone working your case—have him phone the cops." He let go of her and grabbed his cell from his pocket, entered the passcode, and placed it in her free hand. "If anyone other than me tries to get into the bathroom, you don't hesitate. You shoot. Remember how?"

She blinked rapidly as if trying to summon a response. "Ye-yes."

He pointed toward the bathroom. "You're going to be okay. I promise."

"And what about you?" Her lips tucked inward, as if biting back a *Please, don't do this*. "Don't you need the gun?"

"I'm fine." He shifted his head to the side and listened to the familiar sound of a door being breached. "Someone's here." Her mouth parted, and for some crazy reason, he brushed his lips over hers then whispered, "Shoot if it's not me."

"I, uh . . . be careful."

He motioned for her to get into the bathroom, and then he quietly unlocked the bedroom door.

He grabbed the knife strapped near his ankle beneath his pant leg—his emergency go-to if shit ever got hairy when he was in civvies—and then he pressed his back flat to the wall alongside the door and waited.

The knob twisted, and the door slowly moved inward, light from the hall spilling into the room.

Liam raised his free arm like an axe and dropped it onto the man's wrist, knocking the intruder's gun to the floor.

The guy was a freaking goliath. Taller than pro-basketball tall. And as big as an MMA heavyweight.

The man jerked to the side to face him and shot Liam a who-the-fuck-are-you look. The good news—Liam had the advantage of surprise. The bad—the guy was still a damn beast, and within seconds, he deflected Liam's attempt to stab him.

He sucker punched Liam in the side, then got in an upper

punch beneath his chin, before using his body weight to push Liam back a few steps.

Liam bobbed and missed the next swing and brought the knife back to the guy's right side this time, but the son of a bitch not only dodged and missed, he whacked the blade free from his grip.

What the fuck?

Maybe he'd gotten too comfortable on the long gun and needed to up his game in hand-to-hand, but first, he had to drop the bastard.

Another left hook to Liam's jaw sent his head over his shoulder, but he shook it off, cracked his neck, and lifted his guard in front of his face.

"Where's the girl?" Goliath's gaze veered to the bathroom door, and Liam took the split-second distraction to grab hold of him and yank him forward while forcing a knee to the groin. Yeah, he'd play dirty if he had to.

The guy groaned, then Liam swept the intruder's leg with his own and dropped him to the floor.

The gun had been kicked around when they'd fought, and now Goliath made a play for it.

Liam lowered his weight atop the man, both legs on each side of him, but Goliath had already secured the weapon.

Liam locked his hands around the man's forearms and tried to force the muzzle toward the ceiling, using all of his muscle and energy to try and wrangle the gun away.

"Drop it!"

Liam blinked at the sound of Emily's voice—at the fact she was in the room and now putting herself in danger to try and help him.

The guy squirmed but didn't drop the firearm.

"Take the shot," he yelled, knowing he might get hit in the process. "Just take it!"

"I don't want to hit you."

He couldn't look back to see where she was standing, but he knew what he had to do. She'd never shoot with him in harm's way, and he'd have to trust her training.

"Now!" He slid off the guy and to the left, losing hold of his forearms so she could take the shot, and hopefully peg him before Goliath could squeeze off a round.

A familiar ping hit his ears, and the guy's arm fell, letting go of the gun.

"Oh, God. Are you okay?" She crouched to Liam's side.

"Yeah. Nice shooting." He secured the other firearm and checked the man's weak pulse. He'd been shot center mass. A perfect fucking shot.

"No one else came with him, right?"

"Doesn't look that way." He pressed his hands to the wound. "Can you get me something to help stop the bleeding? I doubt we can keep him alive, but I'm going to try. We need answers."

"Shit. I'm sorry. I didn't mean to—"

"You were brave," he rasped as she stood and turned on the light. "You should've stayed in the bathroom, but you may also have saved both of us."

"I heard you guys. I got worried, and I didn't want anything happening to you."

She handed him a shirt, and he folded it three times and pressed it down onto the wound, soaking up some of the blood.

"You brought a knife to a gunfight. You should've taken my gun."

"And risk him getting both weapons and leaving you defenseless?"

Her fingers wrapped over the top of his bicep after a moment of silence passed. "I think he's dead."

He checked for a pulse again, but Emily was right. "Do you recognize him?"

Eyes wide, she nodded, her color a ghostly pale now. The woman had just killed a man in her bedroom. Thank God for rentals, but still.

"He was sitting at the bar the other night when I was having dinner with Sam and Owen. I thought he was just checking me out."

"And you never saw him before that?"

"No."

He motioned for her to sit on the bed then checked the guy's pockets. "Nothing. No phone. No ID. Not even emergency cash." He removed the guy's boots and checked beneath his blood-stained clothes.

There were no visible tattoos. Nothing to connect him to a gang or organized crime.

"Police should be here soon," she said in a near whisper.

"You got ahold of your boss?" He stared at his blood-stained palms.

"Yeah, I didn't have much time, so I rattled off the info and asked him to call the cops."

"Good." He went into the bathroom and quickly scrubbed the blood from his hands, then turned off the shower that'd been running now for . . . hell, he had no idea. He grabbed his cell phone from the counter where Emily had left it and returned to the bedroom. "I want to get a copy of his prints and a blood sample for my people to check." He snapped a few photos of the man with his phone.

"The Feds will do that," she said, her voice hollow as if in shock, and who could blame her?

"Yeah, well, I want to know who he is, and I don't want to have to cut through red tape to get answers."

She stood, her eyes trained on the blood oozing like a spilled can of paint beneath the body. "I, uh, killed someone."

"It was him or us." He squeezed her arm, hoping to knock her out of her trance-like state. "Try and remember that."

She dragged her attention to his face. "Was he here to kill me, or to get information out of me?"

"Probably both," he admitted, but he also knew someone else would be coming after her to finish the job. "But I'm not going to let anything happen to you."

"The government will keep me safe."

He jerked his head back. "Like they did tonight?" He let go of her arm and tipped his head skyward.

Before he could say more, she whispered, "My bodyguard, Hugh, is he dead? Should we go out there?"

"Let the police and medics handle it. I'd say we already took too many risks with your life tonight." He motioned for her to sit, but she remained before him in a daze. "I'm going to grab a glass from the kitchen to put his prints on." He gently gripped her arm, ensuring she heard him. "Okay?"

"Yeah, okay." She staggered out of his reach and dropped back into a seated position on the bed, her gaze landing on the corpse. "So much blood from one bullet."

"Yeah, that happens." He cleared his throat and rushed from the room. With the police closing in he didn't have much time to work.

He lifted the man's prints by wrapping his hand around a glass tumbler, then used his knife to rip a piece of Goliath's bloody shirt for a DNA sample. He put the cup and cloth into a freezer-size Ziploc bag and set it on her bed.

"You good?"

"I, uh," she began, her eyes on the bag, "this is the only piece of furniture that's actually mine in the place, and now I kind of want to burn the bed."

He patted her shoulder like she was one of the guys, nearly forgetting he was with an attorney and his *wife*. And just because she was capable of such a phenomenal shot didn't make her someone who should be putting her life on the line like she did. No, he'd never want that for her.

"Can we put that bag in your safe until after the police do a sweep of this place? They're not going to let me walk out of here with it."

"Better than on my bed." A tiny curl of her lips had his heartbeat steadying a touch.

She gave him the code, and once the items were locked away, he escorted her back into the living room, worried her legs may give out at some point.

"I'm missing the garlic smell from my neighbor right about now. It beats the stench of death." Humor to hide from the shit reality of what happened—maybe she was more like his teammates than he realized.

"Emily, I need you to tell me what case you're working on so I can better protect you."

"I'm not your responsibility just because—"

"Because you're my wife?" he asked. "Well, you're also a friend. You became one of us when Sam married Owen. You and Sam are best friends, so you're sort of a package deal."

She crossed the short bit of space to get to him and rested her hands on his biceps. "I almost got you killed."

"You kidding? You saved my ass."

"But you shouldn't have been in danger in the first place." Her fingertips buried a little deeper into the muscles of his arms.

"Everything happens for a reason." She let go of him, and so, he brought his palm to her cheek. "Emily," he started, but he didn't have a chance to say more because the sirens outside cut him off.

"They're here," she whispered.

He lowered his hand and separated the blinds to look out the window. "Medics are checking the bodyguard."

She stepped up next to him. "They're putting him on a stretcher with an oxygen mask."

"That means he's still alive."

"Thank God. I couldn't handle anyone dying because of me."

A black Mercedes pulled up behind a squad car. "That's your boss, right? The AG?" He'd seen the guy on the news before. The AG had been an Army Ranger back in the day before switching from a battlefield to a courtroom.

"He's not going to let you be my protection because he'll never let me tell you about the case we're working on."

"I can handle him."

Accidental marriage or not, Emily was his wife, and if anyone was going to keep her safe it'd be him.

CHAPTER TEN

Attorney General Dryden came through the door a few minutes later. He looked over at her with bloodshot eyes. He was in a crimson Harvard sweatshirt and jeans instead of the suit she was used to seeing him in.

He swiped a hand over his bald head as if forgetting he'd shaved it last week. He surveyed her apartment and let go of a massive breath when his eyes connected with Emily.

"Are your wife and daughter okay?" she asked straight away.

"After you called, I caught someone on camera trying to get into my home. I set off every damn alarm in my house, and he took off. Thank you for the heads-up."

She slung her arms around his neck, allowing the boss-employee lines to blur. "I'm so glad you and your family are okay." She let go of him after a moment. "I killed the guy," she forced out the admission.

"I heard, but how'd you know . . .?" He must've set eyes on Liam.

"He saved me." She jerked a thumb Liam's way once he stood alongside her.

"More like Emily saved me," Liam said. "The guy who came after her was well-trained." There was a hint of frustration in his tone, and she was certain he was upset about not having personally taken the guy down.

But the guy had been big. Like—really big. Plus, he'd had a gun and Liam had a knife.

Dryden took a small step away from them. "Liam Evans?"

"You know me, sir?"

"Yeah, I know who you are, and I've been calling you all afternoon." He looked around the room, eying the men and women in uniforms going through her place. She supposed Liam was right to hide the evidence in her safe.

"I never answer numbers I don't recognize." Liam added a shrug. "Should've left a message."

"Well, we can't talk here." His attention wandered back to Emily. "After you give your statements, I'll arrange for a police escort to take you both to the White House."

"The White House?" She opened her mouth to ask for an explanation, but he held his palms in the air and shook his head.

"Not here." And then he went to talk to the FBI agent in charge of the crime scene.

Shit. Crime scene.

"What was that all about?" she whispered to Liam out of earshot of her boss. "And why would he be calling you?"

"No idea."

She smoothed a palm over her cheek, not sure if she could break the seal of confidentiality she'd been sworn to in her line of work. Maybe if she was sparse on details it'd be okay?

"The case we're working," she began in a whisper, "we have a witness, and she'll only talk to one person, but it's not like that'd be you." She pivoted to face him, finding his eyes closed. She reached for his chest and rested her palm over his heart, noticing the fast beats. "What are you thinking?"

"Maybe I do know something." He opened his eyes and motioned for her to go out into the hall, but before they could make it a federal agent blocked their path.

"We're ready for your statements."

"Yeah, of course," she answered, catching sight of Liam's jaw tightening beneath his beard, anger rising to the surface.

Whatever he knew—well, he looked pissed.

* * *

"Who are you texting?" she mouthed in the back seat of the squad car as they were driven to the White House.

"My team," he returned in a low voice. After he tucked his phone into his pocket, he reached for her hand and threaded their fingers together, allowing their clasped palms to rest in the small space between them on the back seat.

His gesture had been unexpected. But somehow, it felt right. Like her hand belonged with his. Like she was already his in every possible way.

But a paper that declared they were married was merely a piece of paper, and so it was crazy she'd feel such an intense connection with him.

"I don't want my brother hearing about this. And I'd rather Sam not know as well. She and Owen are in Charleston this weekend." The last thing she wanted was to endanger her best friend. Sam had been through so much already, and Emily would fight like hell to keep her safe. "Please."

"What happened to being honest?" His grip tightened, but his thumb shifted side to side in a calming manner atop her hand.

"It's an omission, not a lie," she said, not meaning to snap out the words in the way she did. "It's for her protection," she added softly.

He dragged his focus to their hands. "I'll do my best to keep her out of the line of fire."

"Thank you," she said when his eyes met hers again, and this time she was the one squeezing his hand.

"You two okay back there?" the officer behind the wheel asked, interrupting whatever moment they'd been sharing.

"Yeah, thanks for the lift." Although she regretted the ride because she hadn't had two seconds alone with Liam to learn what he might know about the case she was working on with Dryden.

And the fact he even knew *anything* was insane.

"We're going to get you through this," Liam said to her once they'd arrived. "Together."

Secret Service took over for the officers and escorted Liam and Emily to the Oval Office after going through security measures.

No one was in there yet aside from the president's Secret Service.

"You ever been here before?" She took a seat on one of the two couches in the center of the room. It wasn't her first time in the Oval Office, and normally she'd survey the scene, take in every little detail, and try to feel the presidents of the past as if they were in there with her, but today wasn't the norm. Today was a nightmare.

"Yeah," he answered.

She picked at the lint on her T-shirt, not sure what to do with her hands. The memory of shooting the man popped back to the forefront of her mind, and she stared down at her palm and curled her right hand into a ball.

Am I a murderer? When she'd heard Liam struggling she'd reacted on instinct. She couldn't let him die for her.

"You're not a killer." His words were rough, like a command she needed to hear—to understand. Her focus drifted up to find his light eyes pinned to her face.

She wasn't sure how he knew what she'd been thinking, but then again, he'd said he was an expert at noticing details. The man could probably read her like a book. Extra-large font. Bold letters. Maybe he'd been reading her long before this moment.

"I barely know you," she whispered. "But I feel . . ."

He sat next to her and pressed a hand to her knee, catching her gaze, and she realized she didn't need to offer more. He got her. Somehow, he just knew.

"I owe your grandfather or your dad—whoever taught you to shoot—a proper thank you someday." His lips curved but stopped short of a full smile. He was trying to distract her, to remind her of the good that had come from the bad.

"My grandfather first taught me to shoot." She smiled as she thought about him. The memory of such a strong man who'd help shape her into a strong woman.

"Mine, too." He reached for her hand again, locking their palms, and a warmth flowed from the tips of her fingers all the way up to her shoulders.

The band of discomfort in her chest dissolved, replaced by a strange sense of ease. Of home. Forgiveness for the death she'd caused. Acceptance of her actions.

"I've had to kill a lot of people," he said, his tone somber. "I mean, as a sniper, you have to point your weapon at a stranger and snuff the life out of them." He glanced at the two men standing guard on each side of the door before meeting her eyes. "But in the SEALs, the way we looked at it—the way we got through it—was to focus on the lives we were saving back home rather than the lives we were taking."

She absorbed his admission, but before she could

respond, the doors opened and her boss and the president entered the room side by side.

Liam released his hold of her hand, and they both stood. She glimpsed at him out of the corner of her eye, noting his hands positioned behind his back as if at attention, as if he were still in the Navy and standing before his commander in chief.

The president moved toward them and reached for her hand first. "Good to see you made it out alive, Miss Summers. Glad you happened to have a friend like Liam with you at the time." His gaze snapped to Liam. "Interesting timing, though." He reached for Liam's hand.

"Mr. President," he greeted him.

"I guess next time we need to get ahold of you, I ought to call you myself. Maybe send my people to locate you?" He went over to a rolling bar cart alongside the couch. Made of rich dark wood with a high-gloss shine, it had two crystal decanters and four matching tumblers.

"You could've called Jessica," Liam said. "Why didn't you?"

"I had hoped the fewer who knew what was going on the better." He swished the brownish-gold liquid around in his glass. Probably Scotch. "But after tonight's turn of events, well, I'll have to rethink things." He took a drink. "Tell me, how'd you happen to be with Miss Summers tonight?"

"Sir, if I may?" Emily smoothed her palms over her shirt then let her arms hang tensely at her sides. "We're friends, and he was in town—"

"I don't buy it." He polished off his drink and set the glass down, then loosened his tie. "This can't be a coincidence," he said. "One of you must've told the other what's going on, and before we continue, I need to know who else you told."

"About my case, sir?" What was she missing?

"Emily didn't tell me anything, Mr. President," Liam said. "After the operation, I headed to D.C. to visit my grandfather, and then I had dinner with Emily and her brother earlier this evening."

Operation? So, he had, in fact, obtained their witness. But . . .?

"Jake Summers is in town?"

"I didn't tell him anything, either," she rushed to clarify, feeling the walls of the room closing in on her.

The president tossed his tie, popped the top button of his shirt, then leaned back against his desk, arms crossed. "Who knew about the witness? About our retrieval team?"

"FBI Director Mendez and CIA Director Rutherford. Plus myself, of course. Then the two men who were sent to meet up with the rescue team in Chile—Jared Morgan and Don Hopkins," Dryden answered.

"And the girl's safe house?" President Rydell asked. "Who knows about her present location?" The president's eyes lifted to the ceiling as if trying to piece together what might have happened.

"Only Morgan and Hopkins. The rest of the task force was aware we had a team going after the girl," Dryden began, "but they didn't know the details about the operation."

"Does this mean a member of the task force may have sent someone after me? After Dryden?"

She chanced a look at Liam. He remained rigid, his arms pinned to his sides, his biceps tight and flexed—or was he just *that* chiseled?

"Possibly. And if so, they probably hoped you knew the safe house location," the president answered.

"I didn't recognize the guy who came after me tonight

aside from seeing him at a bar," she said, thinking back to the dead man from her apartment.

"Hired help," Liam said in a low voice. "A hitman."

"Are we assuming someone on the task force is in Carballo's pocket?" Dryden asked.

"No," Liam responded. "If they knew about the mission they would've tipped off Carballo before we ever got there."

"This is why you left Vegas," she said almost under her breath. "And now—"

"We hired Liam and his associates as civilian contractors to handle the job since we couldn't," the president explained.

Liam kept his eyes on Emily for a moment before directing his focus to President Rydell. "Our orders were for a rescue op. This is the first I'm hearing Elaina's a witness."

"And who is the witness?" Emily asked.

Liam brought a closed fist to his lips and tapped it there. "Elaina's an eight-year-old kid we rescued from one of Carballo's compounds in Argentina." He drew in a sharp breath and glimpsed the president. "But please tell me we didn't kidnap the daughter of Ricco Carballo opposed to rescuing her."

The floor became quicksand beneath Emily's feet. She needed to sit, but she also couldn't get herself to walk.

"It *was* a rescue," the president said in a firm voice. "We don't make it a habit to kidnap people. Not on my watch."

The slight spinning sensation refused to relent, so she forced her feet to carry her to the couch.

"But Elaina may know something that can help us, and she's only willing to talk to you, Liam," the president added and pushed away from the desk. "You must've made quite an impression on her."

"Sir, why'd we need to send Liam and his team into Argentina? Why couldn't we send our own agents?" It was hard for her to believe By-The-Book-Dryden would back the president on something like this, but clearly, he had, or they wouldn't be in the White House right now.

"Carballo has high-powered men in the Argentinian government, just like he did in Mexico when we went after him there and failed five years ago," the president explained. "We couldn't risk someone tipping him off we were coming."

"And you really supported this?" Emily asked her boss.

He dipped a finger into the collar of his sweatshirt and pulled the material away from his body. "I wasn't made aware of the methods of retrieval, only that Liam's team, in some capacity, was involved."

She called bullshit, but she wasn't about to voice her thoughts so blatantly. Not in the Oval Office, at least. "Room for legal deniability?" she asked in a sharp voice, the lawyer in her rising to the surface.

If word got out about the president's or Dryden's involvement in a secret mission to Argentina . . . it could go one of two ways, depending on the media's mood.

"I still don't understand what an eight-year-old abductee might know to help take down Carballo," Liam interrupted her semi-derailed thoughts. "You couldn't get at him before with the help of the Mexican government when he lived there, so what makes you believe you can get to him now that he's hiding out in Argentina?"

Was this really what Liam did for a day job? Went up against people like Carballo?

Worry climbed up her spine, leaving little marks, like the kind her mom placed on her bedroom doorframe to measure her growth as a kid.

"Carballo's old school. He doesn't have digital files. He records his transactions in notebooks. Scribbles plans on whiteboards. You think the girl saw something that can help us?" she asked before the president could answer Liam, but she still had doubts. What could a kid have possibly seen to help take down a ruthless cartel leader?

Instead of responding, the president's attention pivoted to Dryden. "I need to speak with Liam alone. I'll need you and Emily to leave. My apologies."

Dryden pointed to his chest. "Mr. President?"

"As AG of the United States, it's better if you don't hear what I'm about to say," he said. "You already know too much which could compromise your position. Or your future—"

"Someone came after my family and Emily tonight," he cut him off, not seeming to care about his political career.

"Which is why you need to officially close the case against Carballo for now, and be under twenty-four-hour surveillance and protection."

It was an order. The set-in-stone kind based on the president's tone. But she couldn't resist a rebuttal. "Close the case, sir? But we're so close."

"This is an instance where the justice system won't be able to help us out," he answered. "Close the case."

"Yes, Mr. President." Dryden nodded.

"I don't want to go." Emily stood and crossed her arms. "I killed a man tonight." She wet her lips, trying to find the words. The backbone to stand up to the Commander in Chief of the United States. "I'm in this now. And I want to help."

"Emily." Liam turned to face her, his eyes meeting hers. A plea in his intense gaze, but she couldn't back down.

"I'm not going to be locked away with guards. I can't live like that." She shook her head. "You've already admitted to me you sent a team of civilians to a sovereign nation without permission to rescue a girl who you also want as a witness. And what about her family? Where are they? Don't they want her back?" Hands to hips now, she eyed the president. "You need someone on your side from legal to ensure you don't get yourself impeached, sir."

"Mr. President, I don't think we should put Emily in any further danger," Dryden began, "but she does know the Carballo case inside and out, and maybe it wouldn't be a bad idea to have someone from legal in your corner."

The president let go of a long sigh. "Fine." He maneuvered around his desk. "You'll need to sign some documents if you stay in this room."

"Of course."

Dryden wrapped a hand over her shoulder. "Stay safe."

"You, too, sir." She hugged him goodbye, and once he was gone, her attention returned to Liam, to the line darting through his forehead. The unease evident in the slight bow of his normally straight spine.

"You sure this is what you want? There's no going back once you know the truth." Liam studied her, worry in his eyes.

"Yes." She kept her shoulders rounded back, her posture straight. No weakness allowed.

The president came between them and extended a folder in her direction. "Here."

As a lawyer, she'd never been one to speed read and sign —but honestly, she just wanted answers, and so, she scribbled her name on every paper and handed them back to the president. "What about him?" She gestured toward Liam. "He doesn't need to sign anything?"

"I've already signed away my life," Liam said, and she wasn't sure if he was joking or not.

The president motioned for them to sit after he placed her signed documents back on his desk.

"Given the probable leak in the CIA-FBI task force, I don't know who we can trust, so I'll need your people working this case." He sat on the couch across from them. "I'm also pretty sure this extends beyond Ricco Carballo."

"Because of the girl, sir?" Liam asked.

He nodded. "What you both already know is that Carballo gave up selling drugs for a new hobby." He crossed his ankle over his knee. "After he evaded capture and took off to South America, he became an international tradesman of sorts."

"Smuggling weapons, artifacts, people . . . mostly to Europe." This much Emily knew.

"Weapons which often go to the Middle East and are used on our soldiers." He caught Liam's eyes now. "We've never been able to locate Carballo because he doesn't leave a digital trail, and he's always on the move. It also doesn't help that he buys off so many officials we don't know who we can trust." The president paused briefly. "But Jared Morgan did manage to acquire a high-ranking official as a CIA asset, and he's become our eyes and ears down there."

"That's how you knew about the girl and the compound?" Liam spoke up.

"Yes. So far, all of Morgan's asset's intel has been spot on, so the CIA has trusted him. The asset wants Carballo gone as much as we do, but he's playing both sides. He has to, to keep up appearances. But he still hasn't gotten close enough for us to pinpoint Carballo's exact location. Carballo never gets his hands dirty himself."

"But who is Elaina?" Liam asked, his tone gritty. "Why is someone on the joint task force willing to throw their career away to find her location?"

"Because Carballo isn't the one who wants her, is he?" Emily asked before the president answered Liam. "Someone else does, right? Carballo's just a middle man."

"The asset informed us that Carballo had learned

someone—the asset had no idea who—had negotiated to pay Carballo ten million dollars for Elaina."

A slight tremble moved down her spine at the news. "Does Elaina's family know we have her?"

"We can't risk letting anyone know about our involvement, yet," he answered. "To make matters more complicated, Elaina's mom died in a car accident three months ago. Elaina moved in with one of her mother's colleagues from the university."

"No father? Grandparents?" Liam asked.

"No records of any living family. Elaina was American by birth, but her mother was originally from Chile. The birth certificate from Texas had no listed father." He took a breath. "Elaina's mom moved to Santiago right after Elaina was born to conduct research for a university there. Talia, the mother, was one of the most brilliant minds on the planet. We're talking ranked in the top ten to have ever lived in the modern era."

"What was her research?" Emily asked.

"She was working on finding a cure for memory loss."

"I still don't understand who'd be after Elaina," she murmured.

"You don't actually think Elaina knows enough that can bring down Carballo." Liam was on his feet now, standing in front of the president. "She's worth ten million dollars to someone, and you want to know why." The president rose to meet him eye to eye. "Would you have sent us to rescue her otherwise?" The muscles in his back snapped together, drawing a line down his tee.

"Honestly," the president said, "no, I probably wouldn't have risked sending a team, not without a green light from the Argentinian government."

"But you want to take down Carballo, too, right?"

Distress cut through Emily's voice, panic at the idea Carballo could get away again. "He's killed a lot of Americans, and now he's supplying weapons to terrorists—"

"It's a top priority, yes. But first, I'd like to know why Elaina is so important," he cut her off.

"Money," Liam sputtered. "Someone from the task force is after the ten-million-dollar payout Carballo had been offered. If we identify that person, we might be able to discover who is after Elaina and why."

"Carballo might try and get Elaina back," she pointed out. "He'll be pissed she was taken from under his nose."

She reached for the small charm dangling from the white gold chain around her neck. Her mother had given it to her as a law school graduation present: Lady Liberty blindfolded with the scales of justice in her hand.

She rarely took off the necklace, a reminder she'd always be a champion for justice and what was right.

Smoothing the charm between her fingers, she couldn't help but wonder if maybe there was a time and a place when justice had to travel outside the courtroom walls.

In Carballo's case, there'd never been boundaries to begin with. He slaughtered an entire team of DEA agents five years ago.

"We go after everyone," the president said after a beat. "But are you sure you want to put your life on the line for this?"

He had to have been asking Emily since Liam probably put his life on the line almost every day for the nation.

"Yes," she said without hesitation.

"She's my wife, sir." Liam bowed his head. "I'd never let anything happen to her."

Shit. Shit. Shit.

"You want to run that by me again?"

"Um." The words were stuck in her throat, so she'd have to leave it up to Liam to explain.

"Luke married Eva last weekend. Owen married Sam. And well, Emily and I got married, too."

"Yeah, I didn't see that coming." He leaned against his desk and observed them. "Is Luke still on his honeymoon?"

"Yes, sir."

"Then call Jessica. Assemble Bravo and Echo Teams."

Bravo and Echo?

"I'll have you coordinate with Jared Morgan and Don Hopkins, the men you met up with in Chile. We'll keep it to just the two of them."

"I want my team taking point on this. I don't want to take orders from Morgan, and my team will feel the same."

"That's fine. I'll let them know." He nodded. "I'll get CIA Director Rutherford and FBI Director Mendez in here next to discuss what's going on."

"If you can find out who requested to be part of the original ten-person task force that might help narrow down our leak," Liam said. "My guess is someone heard chatter about the ten mill before the task force was even assembled."

Good thinking. The kind of hollow ache from a two-day fast hit her core, and she resisted the urge to press her hands to her abdomen as nerves tangled inside of her. *I can do this, damn it.*

"And, sir?" Liam said. "The next time an American kid is being held hostage in a foreign country, you send our team regardless of whether you deem him or her valuable to a case."

Wow.

"Noted, but talk to me like that again, and I'll make your life a living hell, understood?" There was a casualness to his tone like it wasn't his first time threatening someone.

"Anything else, sir?" Liam asked.

"Yeah, do I owe you two congratulations, or was this a drunken Vegas mistake?" He crossed his arms and eyed them both.

"I, um . . ." She didn't know what to say.

"We should get going," Liam said, coming in for the save. "Given what happened tonight, I suggest we relocate Elaina to a new safe house."

"Agreed." The president looked at Emily. "You do realize if anyone finds out we're playing outside the legal system it could mean your job, right?"

And that was why he'd sent her boss out of the room.

"Yes, but I'll do everything in my power to ensure we have the evidence we need for a *legal* takedown." She started to turn but then glanced back at him. "And if not, then I'll make sure no one ever sees the evidence of what was done to take him down."

Did I just say that? She tried to keep her cool, to act like she belonged.

"You're planning on saving all of our asses, legally, huh?" There was an amused twist of the president's lips.

She cleared her throat as subtly as possible. "Without a doubt, sir."

CHAPTER ELEVEN

"WE HAVE EVERYTHING, RIGHT?"

Liam slid behind the wheel of his truck. They'd picked it up after grabbing his belongings from his hotel before heading to her apartment. Thank God the body was gone from the room, but it sure as hell couldn't be rented out as "surgery sterile clean" to the next tenant.

"The evidence. Your clothes. And—"

"The annulment papers?" She hadn't noticed him grab them from her desk when they were up there.

"I didn't want anyone discovering we were married. If someone knew you were my wife . . . well, it could be dangerous for you." He handed her the folder, and she didn't know what to do with it, so she set it on her lap.

"Does that mean Sam's in danger? Eva?"

"They knew what they were signing up for when they married my friends." He pulled the truck away from the curb. "You didn't."

"How far away are we from the location?" she asked after letting his words sit with her for a few minutes.

"About four hundred kilometers. My team will meet us there at thirteen hundred hours tomorrow."

"Are you up for driving that far tonight?"

It was now technically Saturday since it was one in the morning, and she wasn't sure about Liam, but she'd been running on adrenaline up until this point. And she was beginning to fade.

"I can handle it," he said, glancing over at her, "but we'll stop in a few hours or so since we have time." He turned his focus back to the road. "I also need to make a pit stop at my safe house in Alexandria. We should swap vehicles, plus I need a weapon and ammo."

Safe house? Wow, she was in the big leagues now, and there was no turning back. "That's smart," she said as his phone began ringing.

He checked the ID and brought the phone to his ear. Clearly it was someone he knew since he answered.

"We're on our way," he said straight away. "Yeah, I understand the consequences of—" The person on the other end cut him off, and he let them talk before adding, "Yeah. We'll meet you there. You get the pictures of our vic I texted you?" Another pause. "Okay. Good. And yeah, let's not pull Luke or Owen into this until we know more." He ended the call a moment later.

"Was that Jessica?"

"Yeah."

"She really is kind of badass, huh? A wizard with computers?"

"You could say that," he said, a smile to his tone. Or pride, maybe.

"And now Harper works with you, too, right?"

She thought back to the wedding in Vegas. The place had been swarming with Teamguys—the same group she'd met at the Christmas party when Owen had made his epic proposal to Sam.

But for the most part, Emily and Sam hung out with the same five or six guys, Liam being one of them.

"Harper will eventually take point on operations with Echo Team to free up some of Jessica's time."

She did a mental count of hot guys in her head. "You, Luke, Owen, Asher, and Knox—you're one team, right? It's mostly you guys when we've hung out, and sometimes Wyatt, so I assume—"

"Wyatt's Echo One. And I'm on Bravo."

"Do you have a number?"

He swung his gaze to the right to capture her eyes for a quick second. "Bravo Four."

"And those other Navy SEALs at the wedding? They're not on your team, just friends?" Maybe she could finally fill in the blank spaces that had been in her head since the day Liam and his team had come into her life last year.

"Most of the vets you met at the wedding work for Scott and Scott, but they're not privy to missions like these."

"They don't do the president's bidding, you mean?"

He checked the rearview and side mirrors, then focused on the road again. "It's not like that. It's not like in the movies where you see some black ops group wiping out villages of people or taking out world leaders in foreign nations in a staged coup."

"I would never think you—"

"But people would. They'd think the worst if they knew about us."

She splayed both palms atop the folder and stared down. "If you were to get hurt or caught on an operation, what would happen to you?"

He was quiet for a minute. Well, it felt like a minute, at least. The silence stretched and stretched.

He pressed the heel of his palm to the wheel to steer and rechecked his mirrors. "As far as anyone is concerned, we're not connected to the government, and we'll never betray our oath to save our asses if that's the case."

Patriotic through and through.

She worked for the justice system, and so every bone in her body should've been against what he was doing. But for some reason, she wasn't, because she knew Liam and his team had rescued a kid who would've been sold to God-knew-who all because the government wouldn't have given operational authority for the mission.

"I admire you."

He kept his eyes locked on the road, the traffic thinning as they moved farther and farther from the city.

"Emily, the more you know about me, the more danger it puts you in."

"But some part of you wants to talk to me about this, right? You want to share?" The man probably had to keep everything bottled inside of him, and it had to be tough. Owen and Luke had someone to share their lives with, but who'd Liam have? He had his team, but that was different, wasn't it?

"I don't want you to get hurt because of me."

She touched her chest, an achiness developing. "I'm already deep in this, so you don't have to worry about further endangering me."

"I probably shouldn't even have you with me." He stopped at a light. "I should have you locked away somewhere with twenty guards."

"But you care about this girl and what's right, and you know I can help."

"I care about you, too, Emily."

More knots in her stomach. Twisting. Twisting. Twisting. A never-ending entangled mess.

"Selfishly, I want to keep you with me for as long as possible."

A flutter of nerves worked into her chest and up to her throat. "Well, I'm in no hurry to go."

* * *

SHE STARED AT THE TWO QUEEN BEDS SEPARATED BY A nightstand, not sure which one to pick. They were at a motel in Harrisonburg, Virginia, about ninety miles from her place in D.C., and she was beginning to wonder if it'd been pointless to stop. No way would Liam sleep, even though he'd said they hadn't been followed.

They'd made a million turns and took empty stretches of country road that had nothing on each side as they drove. He wanted to ensure they weren't leading someone straight to Elaina.

"Get some rest. We leave in four hours." He tossed a duffel bag of weapons he'd picked up at the safe house on one bed, which now narrowed down her choice.

"Yeah, okay." She opened her overnight bag and grabbed a clean pair of underwear and pajamas to change into.

She'd expected to toss and turn once her head hit the pillow, but instead sleep had grabbed hold of her and sucked her in deep, so when she'd woken up startled and in someone's arms, she'd gasped.

"It's okay. Shhh." Strong arms held her tight and rocked her body. "It's a nightmare. I've got you." Liam's deep voice soothed the remnants of her nightmare.

She forced her eyes open and pulled her head back,

struggling to see in the dark. "When did it start raining?" she asked as the heavy patter-patter against the hoods of cars outside seemed to intensify.

"An hour ago."

She shifted a little, realizing she was cradled in his lap. He must've scooped her into his arms and held her to try and calm her down. She sort of didn't want to move yet, though.

"You haven't slept, have you?" she whispered, his face beginning to come to focus.

He brushed the back of his hand over her cheek, keeping his hold on her. "No rest for the wicked."

She didn't need to see his face to know he'd probably winked. "When do we leave?"

"Two hours."

She lifted her arms to drape them over his shoulders with her eyes now adjusted to the dark.

The truth of what happened last night became a distant memory. Someone else's bad dream.

Her right hand slipped down his chest, a light sheen of sweat on his bare skin causing her to expand her awareness.

The room was hot. Like Devil's playground kind of hot. "Air-conditioning not working?"

She skimmed her fingertips back up the center of his chest and flattened her palm over his heart. It was slow and steady. Calming.

"No. It's been hissing and making some rattling sound, so I finally turned it off." His thumb pulled down her bottom lip, and she leaned her cheek into his touch, her eyes falling shut.

"Liam." His name came out as a desperate cry, even though she hadn't meant it to.

She shifted on his lap, and a light groan left his lips.

His length bulged, hardening beneath her. "Sorry," he

rasped, his tone gravelly. "Your ass is sort of, well—right there, and my dick doesn't know it's not appropriate."

She couldn't help but smile at his apology, as well as lose hold of whatever hell from last night had been trying to wrestle her away like those freakish dark shadows from the movie *Ghost*—a longtime favorite of hers.

She opened her eyes and pulled her right knee up between them, then stretched her leg out on the other side to straddle him.

"What are you doing?" His hands slid around to her back, holding her firmly in place. "That won't help my, uh, situation."

"I'm getting more comfortable." She swallowed away reason and bit back rational thought.

She was alive because they hadn't signed the papers last night. Because she hadn't left him at the bar alone after the fight with his brother. And because Oreos were a weak spot for both of them.

Alive because they'd been together.

And now, well, that's what she wanted. To just be with him.

"You've been through a lot," he said, the words a whisper over her mouth.

Her teeth skirted her bottom lip as she caressed the hard edges of his triceps. She rocked forward, relishing the feel of his cock pressing against her center, the cotton pajama shorts and panties barely a barrier between them.

"I know what happened." She inhaled a sharp breath and let it go. "And I don't want to think about it right now." She leaned back and reached for the hem of her camisole and peeled it over her head and tossed it.

His eyes dropped to her breasts before she leaned against

him, allowing her nipples to press to his chest, needing to feel the warmth of his body.

He swept her hair over one shoulder and brought his mouth to the sensitive part of her neck and kissed it.

Her eyes fell closed, and her lips parted, her panties growing wet. She rubbed against him again, desperate for him to fill her.

She wanted to remember their one night together, to know how he felt inside of her.

Liam worked his lips up the column of her throat as she buried her fingertips into the corded muscles of his back.

A gasp of surprise escaped her when he grabbed her hair and gave a sharp tug. He kissed her hard then sucked at her bottom lip. Met her tongue with his.

He nearly bruised her mouth, his need as pressing as hers. And she wanted more. More of him. More of anything he would give her.

She rotated her hips in a circular motion, on the verge of coming from the friction between them. That hollow ache she'd had earlier was gone, replaced by desire.

He kissed away her soft curses as she rode him until she climaxed.

"Damn, Emily." He shifted her off his lap and onto her back, then braced himself on top of her.

She was still reeling from the orgasm, struggling to find a steady rhythm of breath.

She reached for his belt buckle, needing to free him of his pants, to hold his shaft and give him the same pleasure he'd given her.

She'd just dry-humped him, hadn't she? *Gah.*

His forehead met hers, their bodies now too close for her to try and unbutton his jeans. "What's wrong?"

He dropped to the side and covered his face with both

hands. "I can't do this." He hissed a sigh of frustration, which she assumed was directed at himself, then got off the bed.

She snatched the comforter and pulled it up to cover her breasts, even though it was still hot in the room. At least in the dark, he wouldn't see the flash of crimson that no doubt colored every inch of her.

"You don't have to hide your body."

"I kind of do. Rejection and all." Her eyes went to the ceiling as her mind flew through a million different possible replies he might offer her in the next moment.

"I'm not rejecting you, but you know who I am. What I'm capable of."

She sat upright. "You mean what you're *not* capable of?"

He cupped his mouth.

"Listen," she began, her shoulders relaxing, "I'm not interested in forever right now. Not with anyone."

"Well, we are married." Humor touched his tone, and he dropped his hand from his mouth.

"You know what I mean." She grabbed her top and pulled it over her head and stood. "The point is, you won't hurt me because we want the same thing."

"Sex?"

She tried to harness the impulse to step closer, to run her hands over his bare chest.

"You just woke up from a nightmare."

She took a hesitant step his way. "Yeah, but I woke up to you." She lifted her hand and pressed her index finger to his pec.

God, she wanted him.

Wanted this.

"I can have casual sex." She turned but was brought up short when his firm grip captured her wrist.

"I'm trying to do the right thing." His voice was rough,

and if she could see better—she'd probably witness the familiar strain of his jaw she'd grown accustomed to observing when he was around her. "You deserve it."

"I want to remember," she said under her breath. "I want to remember how you feel inside of me."

His chest lifted, and he let go of a hard breath.

Barely a moment passed, and before she knew it he lifted her up, guiding her legs around his waist.

He walked backward as he claimed her with his mouth. When his back hit the wall, he spun around and pushed her up against the wall instead.

When her feet touched the ground, he slipped a hand beneath the hem of her shorts and glided a finger over her slick center.

"Fuck, you're so wet." He secured one hand around her hip, holding her in place as she bucked, while his other hand stroked her harder and faster.

Her toes curled into the carpet, and she clung to his body, her short nails biting into his back.

His mouth traveled up her neck, kissing and sucking before wandering to her earlobe and biting.

"I want you." Guttural. Raw. His tone sounded almost defeated. "But not here. Not this place."

She pressed her hands to his chest and peered up at him. "So, you're not just charming, you're a romantic, too?"

A smile pulled at the corners of his mouth, but instead of responding, he placed two fingers inside of her. In less than a minute she was shattering and collapsing into his arms.

He carried her back to the bed and placed her beneath the comforter. "Now, get another hour or two of sleep."

CHAPTER TWELVE

"At least the rain let up," she said as Liam drove, and he only nodded.

He'd remained quiet since they'd been in the car. A beat-up faded ball cap backward on his head and a pair of Gatorz sunglasses shielding his eyes were preventing her from getting a better read on him.

Every so often he'd fidget with the material of his plain gray tee as if it were hot in the car, even though she was pretty sure he was trying to freeze her to death with the blasting AC.

Right now, he was rocking the look of a surfer playboy with his laid-back clothes and golden skin. Yet, despite his board shorts, tee, and flip-flops—he couldn't shake the badass SEAL vibe he gave off.

But every time she thought about what had happened between them only a few hours ago, her cheeks would burn, and she was grateful for the ice-cold temperature of the Suburban.

She couldn't help but wonder if maybe Sam was right about Liam.

"Honey, I love you, but this guy is not like the guys you date in D.C. He's great. But he'll break your heart," Sam had warned her on Valentine's Day when they'd all been together at a nightclub in Manhattan.

Sam had brought Emily to New York City for a girls' night back in February, but the boys had come home from work earlier than expected. When they walked through the club doors, her heart had catapulted into her throat at the sight of Liam.

Knox had pulled her to the dance floor, but then Liam had stolen her away from him not even a few minutes later.

"Happy Valentine's Day," he'd whispered into her ear when the DJ had switched the music to a slower song.

"You want to be my Valentine?" she'd half-joked, her brain knocking down Sam's warnings swimming in her head with Liam's body so close to hers.

"I'm not allowed to," he'd said near her ear, his breath tickling her. *"But I'll be damned if I let some wanker at this club try and bother you."*

"So, you're going to be like a big brother to me, huh?"

He'd pulled back and grinned. *"I'd prefer you never think of me like a brother,"* he'd said, the huskiness of his tone hard to miss despite the music.

And now they were married.

"You okay?" It was the first time actual words had escaped his lips since they'd gotten into the SUV.

"Trying to be." But she also wanted to clear the air, just pull off the Band-Aid and talk about what happened at the motel.

She clutched the coffee he'd grabbed her at the drive-through but didn't take a sip. He hadn't asked her how she took her coffee because of course he'd remember the one time she'd ordered a vanilla latte at breakfast with him in Charleston.

"What'd you do after I fell back asleep?" She only hoped her question didn't sound as awkward as it did in her head.

His gaze winged her way, a hard look in his eyes. "What do you think I did?" His brows rose. "Prepped for the trip."

"Before or after you jerked off?" *And . . . I just said that.*

He looked back at the road and remained quiet, but he clenched his teeth, that familiar tightening of his jawline evident. He slightly shifted on his seat as if uncomfortable and his free hand settled atop his lap.

"Well, are we going to talk about what happened or not?"

He made some sort of grunt noise, like it was the last thing he wanted to do. But she needed to talk about it, so she wasn't ready to give up.

"I get why you refrained. I probably even owe you one for it because wrong time wrong place, but—"

"Yeah, I knew a 'but' was coming." A lighter tone touched his words.

"*But* I don't like that you think you're bad for me, or that I can't handle you." She positioned her coffee back in the cup holder between them. "I'm well aware of your reputation. And sex can be cathartic."

He chuckled. "'Cathartic,' huh?"

"After what we've been through, it's okay to let loose and let go." *As long as I don't fall in the process.*

"You don't really want to let go. Not with me."

"Why do you say that?"

"You're conflicted." He removed his sunglasses and looked over at her. "You know how I know? Because I'm confused, too."

Confused? "You wanted me back at that motel as much as I wanted you. You admitted it, and—"

"I wanted to rip off your panties and use your shirt as a blindfold while I robbed you of every last breath—fucking you so hard you wouldn't be able to walk today. And then I wanted to do it again. With you on top. Your tits bouncing while you rode me."

A string of *holy shits* flew through her mind, and her knees bumped as she squeezed her thighs together.

"Basically, I wanted to do what we did back in Vegas. But for longer. A bit harder. And with you remembering this time."

Her palms went to her cheeks, and she knew she wouldn't be able to hide her reaction to his comment.

He slipped his sunglasses back in place and returned his focus to the road as if he hadn't just dropped her jaw.

"But we're about to meet up with my team to go after one of the sickest bastards in cartel history, in addition to some unknown asshole wanting to buy an eight-year-old girl for ten million dollars. A girl who, as it happens, will only talk to me." He clenched the wheel so hard his knuckles whitened. "So, I'm going to do my best not to pull this car over and have you hop on top of me and grind on me like you did last night."

Her entire body flushed with warmth, buzzing from the heat of his words.

When he slowed the car and actually did pull off to the side of the road a moment later, she grabbed the oh-shit handle as he spun in his seat.

He was breathing hard like he was fighting his desire to grab hold of her.

"But this is why you're my not-type type."

She almost laughed at his choice of words, especially when a small grin swept to his lips.

"Because I can't resist you, and that makes you

119

dangerous." His palms went to his legs, and he dropped his head. "When I was going after Elaina in Argentina, I missed a shot. I never miss. But I was thinking about you and Vegas, and I missed."

She closed her eyes at his admission, at the meaning of his words.

"I'm telling you because you said you're honest to a fault, and maybe I want to be more like you."

"I don't want to be the reason why you or your teammates get hurt." She forced her eyes back open.

He reached across the console, steam still drifting in the air from their drinks, and grabbed hold of her hand. "I'm not blaming you or telling you to make you feel guilty."

"You just want me to understand I can make you lose your focus." She took a deep breath, hoping to sidestep the mounting emotions rising to the surface. "But if I'm so dangerous why'd you bring me along? Why not tell the president I'm a distraction?"

"Like I said before, I'm also really selfish and not ready to let go of you. Plus, I don't trust anyone else to keep you safe." The back of his skull met the headrest, and he released her hand. "See . . . I told you—I'm fucking confused."

She reached for his glasses and removed them, needing to see his eyes. "What do you want me to do? What do you need from me to make it all okay?"

A smile skirted his lips. "Stop being so funny. So amazing. And sexy." His throat moved with a hard swallow. "You know, stop being so you."

CHAPTER THIRTEEN

HE'D LOST HIS MIND. THE BOYS WERE GOING TO HAVE A FIELD day the second they saw him and Emily together. If Jessica and Asher hadn't yet spilled the news to the team, they'd figure shit out and fast just by how he acted around Emily.

The woman was like no one else he'd ever met.

Smart. Beautiful. So damn funny.

And honest. The kind of honesty you don't find in many people anymore.

They were friends. *Only* supposed to be friends.

"Sam practically threatened to cut off my balls if I ever made a move on you," he admitted. "I get she's protective, and you went through hell with that asshole last year"—a man he wished he could bring back from the dead right now just to kill again since he'd slept with Emily to get to her best friend, resulting in a bullet through Emily's window—"but is there more to it than that?"

She pulled her silky hair into a ponytail, and he'd give anything to tug on it while devouring her mouth.

"We both have our pasts, right? Mine has shaped me the way I'm sure yours has. Plus, Sam's protective like a sister."

And now, he was trying to protect Emily, too.

You're not mine. She couldn't be. He'd only screw with her head and rip her heart to pieces. Or maybe she'd even destroy him, too. He wasn't so sure. Love wasn't in the cards for him, not now, at least, and that was the only truth he knew.

He glimpsed his cell when it began ringing, but he couldn't bring himself to answer.

"It says *Pops* on the ID, so you obviously know the number this time. Not going to answer?"

He switched the call to voicemail and clutched the wheel with both hands, irritation springing to the surface as he remembered the reason why his grandfather would most likely be calling. "He's trying to apologize. I'll call him back."

"For?"

"Ambushing me with a visit from my brother back at his home the other day," he quickly rushed out.

She was quiet for a minute, probably absorbing his words. "You don't have to talk about it. You've probably maxed out on your honesty for today." He could hear a tiny smile in her tone. "At least you took my advice. You know, testing out telling the truth without the use of alcohol for courage."

He almost laughed. *Shit.* This woman.

"My brother married the woman who left me standing at the altar when I was younger." The words flowed from his mouth before he could catch them.

"I, uh, don't understand."

"Yeah, sort of the problem." He gripped the wheel even tighter. "Neither do I." And that's all he'd be saying for now.

They were two klicks from their destination.

Jessica, Asher, and Knox were going to be meeting up

with them at the safe house, and he had no choice but to reset his focus to the mission. Somehow. Someway.

He wasn't sure what to say to Elaina, to the girl who'd lost her mother only to be kidnapped and sold by Ricco freaking Carballo.

"What will happen when we get to the safehouse?" she asked as they took a left onto the last road leading to their destination.

"We'll bring Elaina to a new location, one that's off the map and no one in the CIA or FBI knows about."

"I've worked with Jared Morgan and Don Hopkins," she said. "They're honest guys. They've wanted to bring Carballo down for some time now."

"That's good to know." Harper had vouched for Jared in Chile. Emily vouching for both men gave him a sense of relief he hadn't realized he needed.

"And what does Jessica have to say about me being with you, especially since she knows we're married?"

"She's not exactly excited about bringing you in, but she also knows Sam would kill her if we let anything happen to you, so it's best you're under our protection."

"Does she know we haven't had a chance to sign the it-never-happened papers yet?"

"I didn't bring it up," he said as he parked the Suburban, then removed his sunglasses.

She reached for his hat and took it off, then mussed up his hair. "You look less intimidating this way." She gave a small shrug. "Is that why you decided to dress like you're at a beach instead of going into a war zone? For Elaina?"

He hadn't thought about it like that, but maybe he had. "Guess so."

"Aside from Jessica, who else from your team is inside?"

"Asher and Knox. The rest of my people will meet us at the next site."

He killed the engine, and she reached for the door handle. "What happened in Argentina that made Elaina only want to talk to you?"

He shrugged. "I don't know. When we handed her over in Chile I gave her a coin."

"What kind of coin?"

"It was my great-grandfather's. He carried it through World War Two, then passed it on to my pops, then it came to me."

Her lips lifted at the edges. "That was nice of you."

"She was scared. I was trying to make her feel better."

"Well, clearly that's why she asked for you." She pushed the door open but looked back at him. "For the record, you make me feel better, too."

He gripped the wheel, giving himself a second to collect his thoughts, then headed outside. "We'll leave the rest of our stuff in the car since we won't be here long."

"Okay." She slung her purse strap over her shoulder and tucked her hands in her pockets as they walked alongside two other vehicles to get to the house.

It was a yellow two-story colonial. White picket fence. Tire swing hanging from the oak tree off to the side. Honeysuckle plants and pops of wildflowers. A normal-looking place and not the front for a CIA safe house in Charleston, West Virginia.

Jared was the first to greet them once inside. "I didn't expect to be seeing you so soon after Chile."

"And I was kind of hoping never to see you again," Liam said, only half-kidding.

"Hey, Emily." Jared's eyes rolled like a wave over

Emily's body as if assessing her for damage—or checking her out. "Damn. You okay? I heard about what happened to you."

"It's hard to believe someone from your team would hire people to come after us." She folded her arms, an unease crossing her face as she stood before Jared. "Any ideas who'd sell us out?"

Jared closed and locked the door then faced them, still hanging back in the foyer. "Must be FBI. I personally handpicked my people from Langley for the op. They wouldn't roll on us for ten mill."

"Yeah, well, what about for thirteen?" Jessica spoke as she came down the hall.

"What are you talking about?" Jared asked.

"Looks like the price tag on Elaina's head got bumped to thirteen million since Carballo didn't come through." Jessica started to reach for Emily's hand, but then blinked a few times and pulled her in for a hug instead.

Damn, the woman was changing.

The Ice Queen had melted.

"Glad to see you're okay. Thank God Liam happened to be with you." Jessica released her hold of Emily and looked over at Liam. He saw the question in her eyes—*were they still married?*

"Can you track the source of the bounty?" Liam asked.

"Unfortunately, no. Whoever wants Elaina went old school like Carballo. Zero communications online. All by word of mouth." She motioned for them to follow her.

They walked down a hallway, and she pointed to the last door on the right. "Elaina's in there watching TV."

"Alone?" Emily asked.

"Don's with her," she answered as they entered a different room where Asher and Knox were working on laptops.

"Emily." Asher rose and pulled her in for a giant bear hug, then Knox gave her a quick one-armed hug next.

"Glad to see you don't have any bullet holes in you." Knox sat back on the couch and pulled the computer onto his lap.

Liam was pretty sure Asher and Jessica hadn't spilled the news about their accidental marriage. That was a relief.

"So, if the bounty is all word of mouth, how do we know it's true?" Liam motioned for Emily to have a seat on the chair off to the side of the couch by Knox.

"Because I'm good at my job." Jessica glimpsed him out of her peripheral view and remained standing at his side. "Hired mercenaries and assassins began gearing up all over the world today. Our mystery buyer might not use the internet, but everyone else does, and word spread online fast."

"So, we're going to have a ton of people gunning to get to Elaina first?" Emily placed a hand over her chest as if trying to process the news.

"Yeah, which is why I'd like to get out of here and to the next location as soon as possible," Jessica said. "Echo Team's already there setting up for us."

Asher tipped his chin. "Maybe now's a good time to say *hi* to Elaina, so we can get on the move."

"Right." He wiped his hands on the sides of his shorts, his palms suddenly sweaty. Why was he nervous to talk to a kid?

He left the team, and when he opened the door to Elaina's room, he found Don sitting on the couch opposite of Elaina with a phone in hand.

"Hey." Don tucked his phone into his pocket and stood. "You're here."

Elaina looked away from the TV and hopped to her feet at the sight of Liam. She was in jeans, a tee, and a pair of bright-orange Chucks. Jared or Don must've gone shopping for her. At least they were taking good care of her, that was something.

"I'll go meet up with the team." Don left, and Liam approached Elaina.

"You came." She reached for his hand, and the gesture had his heart fracturing into a million pieces for some reason.

"Of course, I came." He resisted the impulse to rub at the growing ache in his chest.

He gently wrapped his hand around hers, afraid he'd hurt her. Her hand was so damn small compared to his.

"I want you to have this back." She unfurled her free hand and showed him his coin. "Having you here is better than this, and I feel like you might need it for luck."

He smiled but didn't take it from her. "You can have both. The coin. Me. Whatever makes you feel better. Safer."

"I want you safe, too." She lifted her palm, encouraging him to take it.

"Are you sure?"

Her big brown eyes widened with a plea. "Please."

He took a steadying breath and reached for it, the memory of his grandfather giving it to him before his first deployment skirted the front of his mind.

"I'm sorry to make you come here," she said while pulling her other hand free of his, "but I—"

"No apologies." He tucked the coin in his pocket.

"You're like me." Her little hands became fists at her sides. "I can tell."

"I am?" He smiled at her words, even though he didn't understand.

"Smart." She looked up to find his eyes. "You see things how I do, don't you?"

"And how do you see things?"

"I . . . I can take pictures with my mind—like a camera."

His heart stammered. "I take pictures with my mind, too. You're right."

She grinned and reached out to hug him, and his body went still. "I knew it!"

He tried to remember what he was supposed to do in situations like these. He hadn't been around kids all that much.

Hug her back! He lifted his arms to hold her.

"I took some pictures with my mind of anything and everything I could while those bad men had me." She let go of him, and he stood tall. "When you and your friends saved me, at first, I thought maybe you were bad men and there to hurt me, too—but you're a good man."

"And I promise we'll keep you safe." He considered his next words. "It's better if we move to another place first before we talk, though. I—"

"My mom died," she said, cutting him off. "She was smart, too."

"I, uh, know." He crouched to eye level again. "I'm so sorry."

"I don't think you should tell Miss Maria where I am right now. She wasn't home when the bad men took me, but I'm afraid they would've hurt her if she had been . . . and they might try and hurt her if they think she knows where I am."

"Maria's who's been taking care of you?"

"Yeah. I was supposed to be at school, but I snuck away and went back to the house, and that's when those bad men got me." She scratched her nose, her long lashes lifting and falling with a few quick blinks. "I don't like school." She swallowed. "I get bored."

"I used to feel the same." He could never pay attention in

class. He was always five steps ahead of the teacher, especially in math.

"See, I knew you were like me."

His heart was going to split into two. *Shit.*

She nodded. "Okay. Let's go to the next place."

For being only eight, she was handling everything like she was one of the guys on his team. She was a little champ.

She'd been scared out of her mind when his people rescued her, but like she said—she trusted them now, and so, damned if he wouldn't stop until he knew the kid was safe.

She reached for his hand, and he held on to her little palm as they left the room.

"Hey." Jessica's eyes went to their clasped palms once they joined the team. "Everything okay?"

"Yeah." He didn't know what else to say because this was outside his comfort zone.

"We can roll out, then?" Asher closed his laptop and stood.

"Should we find out what Elaina knows before we go?" Don leaned against the far side window with crossed arms and one booted foot propped to the wall beneath the window pane.

"I think it's best if we wait until we're at the next location," Liam said, knowing his team would agree. Elaina's safety was the priority.

"We can take Elaina in our car," Don said, but Elaina's shoulders slumped at his words, and she scuttled closer to Liam's side. "Why don't you ride with us, Emily? She might prefer—"

"I, uh, think Elaina wants to stay with us. And Emily rides with me," Liam was quick to reply.

Don kept his hand on his *unsnapped* holster—something no agent would do unless they were on the verge of grabbing their weapon. "Well"—he cleared his throat—"let's do this then."

Liam angled his head and reached around to secure a grip on the gun tucked at his back, hidden beneath his shirt. "Did someone get to you?" His gaze darted from Don's holster to his face.

Beads of sweat dotted Don's scalp despite the blowing A.C., and a touch of red moved up the column of his throat.

Jessica drew her weapon at the same time as Asher and Knox.

"Hold up." Jared patted the air, trying to diffuse the situation.

Liam kept the girl close to his side and backed a few steps away, not wanting her near the drawn weapons.

"He's on our side, guys." Emily moved to stand in front of Don, offering herself as a shield, and Liam cursed under his breath.

Wrong man to defend. Wrong fucking time.

The son of a bitch wrapped a hand around Emily's abdomen and pulled her tight against him, training his pistol at her temple while keeping his back to the window. "I'm sorry," he said, and Liam wasn't sure who the hell Don was apologizing to, and it didn't matter.

The bastard had a gun on his wife, and there was an eight-year-old kid in the room.

"What the hell, Don! Put the gun down." Jared focused his Glock on Don now, too. "Don't you dare tell me this thirteen mill has you—"

"I'm sorry," Don said again, his hand shaking. The sweat on his brow dripping down the sides of his face.

Liam shifted Elaina around to stand behind him, then retrieved his gun with his free hand. "Let her go." He removed the safety on his firearm. "It's five to one. You know you can't win this."

"You won't take the shot. You can't risk I'll shoot Emily." Don's words nearly rattled.

Liam tightened his grip on Elaina's wrist as she stood behind him, and Emily closed her eyes but remained still, her palms in the air as if in surrender.

"Why are you doing this, man?" Knox spoke up. "Put the gun down and let's talk."

"I-I don't have a choice." Desperation flowed through Don's tone. "Please."

"Who were you texting back there?" Liam asked, remembering Don's phone when he'd arrived in Elaina's room. "Who got to you?"

"Just tell us what's going on," Jared demanded. "You don't have to die today."

The president had trusted Don; something didn't add up.

"Tell us so we can help you." Jared kept his voice level. "You could've taken Elaina when you were on watch last night, or even shot me and taken her earlier before these guys arrived. Why wait until now? What happened?"

Don blinked a few times. "I don't want to do this, but . . . they have my wife." His voice caved in, and the arm pinning Emily to his body loosened a little.

"They have Becky?" Jared lowered his gun to his side.

"I got a text this morning. They said if I don't give them Elaina and Emily, they'd kill Becky." Tears welled in the man's eyes.

"Emily, too?" Liam's heartbeat rose even higher, and Emily opened her eyes at the sound of her name.

Jared holstered his weapon and raised both palms in the air and sidestepped Liam's teammates. "You don't have to do this. I can't imagine what you're going through, but you can't trade one life for another."

"I can't lose Becky. The baby. She's four months pregnant. We didn't want to tell anyone and jinx it, but . . ." He finally released Emily and lowered his gun. Asher quickly pulled Emily away from Don and secured his weapon. "I'm sorry. I panicked." He sank to his knees. "I'm so sorry, Emily. Elaina."

Liam tucked his gun away as Emily hurried across the room to get to him. He wrapped his arms around her, thankful she was out of danger and okay.

When he released his hold of her, Elaina approached Don. "I forgive you." Her words had Don's silent tears turning into the sob of a man who'd lost the love of his life.

But they wouldn't let that happen. They couldn't.

Too many people were in danger, though, and it didn't make any damn sense.

When Elaina turned back toward Liam, she smiled and pointed at Emily. "Is she yours?"

"My what?" he asked, bending forward to meet her eyes.

She lifted her shoulders. "You know . . . *yours*."

"I, uh." He blinked and stood back up.

The kid was unflappable.

"We'll get Becky back," Jared said, pulling Liam's attention to the situation at hand. "I promise."

Don extended his phone out to Jared. "They sent me this video of Becky. She's strapped to a chair. It's not at our house."

Jared dragged his free hand through his jet-black hair and cursed as he watched the video.

"Can you trace it?" Don looked at Jessica.

"Maybe." She sounded grim as she took the phone from Jared. "What were your next instructions?"

"To text that number back once I got away with Emily and Elaina."

Jessica bowed her head for a moment. She was thinking. Strategizing. And she was the damn best person to have in their corner in a situation like this.

"Here's what you do," Jessica began, "tell them you have Emily, but Elaina ran off during the fight. And now you need some time to hunt her down in the woods."

"What?" Jared stood before Jessica, his brows snapping together with concern.

"We need to buy ourselves some time," she explained. "Send them a picture of Emily as proof, then tell them you'll text as soon as you have Elaina."

"You want to strap Emily to a chair and tie her down for—"

"If it keeps Don's wife safe, it's fine," Emily interrupted Liam, sitting down in the chair she'd been in before as if preparing herself to get tied up.

"They want Emily for a reason." Jessica glanced at her. "Two people were sent out last night. One went after Emily, and the other after the AG. I'm betting the guy who got away, the one the AG scared off—he's who has Becky now."

"And you think he's pissed his partner was killed, and he wants Emily for payback?" Liam pressed two fingers to his left temple, processing the news.

"Which might help me narrow down a suspect list," Jessica said. "I've already got Harper working on the identity of our dead guy, and once we get to the next safe house, you can give me the fingerprints and blood you pulled off the vic to speed up the process."

"Find out who died last night, and we might be able to link him to whoever he's working with," Liam said, following along Jessica's line of thought. "This could work."

"Let's send Echo Team back to D.C." Jessica handed Don's phone to Jared. "We need them there and ready for when we locate Becky."

"I'm going, too. I have to be there for her." Don surveyed the team, a look of panic a permanent feature in the set of his brows.

"I can't let you go and risk—" Jessica started.

"I'll keep an eye on him," Jared said. "I'll make sure he doesn't get hurt or in the way of your team."

Jessica peered Asher's way.

"Your call," Asher said even though she hadn't asked him anything.

"Fine." She pointed to Don's phone. "Buy us as much time as possible so we can get our people to D.C."

"I hate to say this, but we should probably film a video of Elaina, too," Jared said. "I'm sure whoever has Becky will want evidence Don managed to capture her."

"We need to wait until Echo Team is in D.C. to send it. When our abductor uploads the video, that'll be my best chance to track his location. Are you okay with doing that?" Jessica looked to Elaina, who then tilted her chin up to view Liam as if asking his opinion on the matter.

"It's up to you." He didn't want to pressure her into doing anything.

"Okay," she said as casually as if she were saying yes to going to a movie or out for ice cream—something she should've been doing. Not this.

"We're going to get Becky back." Jessica's tone remained steady. "The baby will be okay."

"While you're en route to D.C., we can try and identify who on the task force hired these men to get Elaina in the first place," Knox said to Jared. "If we find that person we can get them to point us in the right direction to find Becky as a backup plan."

"Doubtful they'll talk. Not fast enough, anyway. But we need to find the traitor regardless," Jared answered.

Jessica's eyes darted back to Elaina who was observing them and taking inventory of every detail. Liam knew what that was like, a habit he couldn't shake.

"You okay?" Liam gripped her shoulder.

"Who wants me this badly to do all this?" she softly asked.

"I don't know," he said. "But we're going to find out."

CHAPTER FOURTEEN

"How'd Elaina know about Don?" Emily spoke quietly as she sat on a twin bed, the only piece of furniture in the ten-by-ten room. The space may not have had much, but at least it lacked a typical musty basement smell given they were underground.

They'd arrived at the property thirty kilometers east of the last location in West Virginia—a place his company had purchased under a fake name. The massive estate had been built by a millionaire during the Cold War era, worried the Russians were going to attack someday. So, the guy had created an extensive underground bunker to withstand a nuke. It was where they were currently located, a perfect site for the team.

"She's super smart, that's all I know," he said, leaning with crossed arms against the closed bedroom door. "A photographic memory, too. Maybe she also has a sixth sense about people."

"She did about you." She clasped her hands, hanging them loose between her knees. "I still can't believe they got to Don."

"They moved fast. Since they failed to get you or your boss, they had to go after the weakest link."

"Don having a wife makes him weak?" Emily sat upright.

"I didn't mean for it to sound like that, but loving someone can make a person vulnerable."

"And what would you have done today if you were Don?" Her palm flattened against her breastbone. "What would Luke do? Owen?"

"I wouldn't exchange one life for another. Neither would the guys," he answered as honestly as possible, even though he knew it'd be painfully more complicated if the situation were to ever, God forbid, present itself.

"Owen would let Sam die?" Her voice pitched higher in surprise, and she stood.

He shook his head.

"Then what?"

"My team would get her back like we'll get Don's wife back."

"You're that confident everyone will be okay?"

"I have to be. And if I ever stop believing we can pull off miracles, then I need to switch professions." And that was the truth.

Her mouth rounded in surprise, but no words came out.

"I, uh, meant to tell you—your bodyguard's surgery was successful. The bullet should've killed him, but somehow, he survived."

"Thank God."

He reached for the ball cap he'd put on after they left the last safe house, slid it backward, and crossed the short space to get to her. "You've been so brave. You act like one of us and not a lawyer hell-bent on following all of the rules."

"Well, I've had to deal with my fair share of lions in and out of the courtroom, so I gotta adapt or die, right?"

He cupped her chin, but before he could speak, Knox opened the door.

"You guys ready?" Knox asked.

"Uh, yeah," Liam said, even though he wanted to finish his conversation with Emily.

"Where's Elaina right now?" she asked once they were in the hall.

"She's in the room with us, drawing on the whiteboard. Doodling. I don't know. We didn't want to let her out of our sight, though." Knox reached for the door handle to their temporary command center.

"And Don and Jared are on their way to D.C.?" she asked.

"Yeah," Knox answered. "Hopefully we bought ourselves enough time to get our people in place." He opened the door and stepped back to let Liam and Emily through.

The place was much larger than the bedroom. Well, it was big enough to accommodate his team so they could work. One long brown table down the center of the room with eight chairs, and a projector screen on one wall, and a whiteboard on the other.

Asher, Jessica, and Harper sat around the table working on their laptops. And Elaina was doing exactly what Knox said, drawing on the whiteboard with headphones covering her ears.

She was too young and innocent to be caught up in the kind of depravity that no one—especially not a child—should ever face.

Liam pulled out a chair for Emily at the table, but she pointed to the whiteboard, letting him know she was going to hang out with Elaina.

Good call. He tipped his head in thanks, then rounded the table to join his team.

"What do we have?" He gripped the back of a rolling chair for support and eyed his teammates.

Wyatt and the rest of Echo were on their way to D.C. so they could be in position to rescue Becky as soon as Jessica and Harper worked their magic and located her.

Harper looked up from the screen. Her faded navy Yankees ball cap was on backward, her long, dark hair in two braids that draped over the words *Kiss Me, Buttercup* on her red T-shirt. "We're running the dead guy's prints, bloodwork, and picture through every database in the world."

"And I'm doing my best to track down the source of this thirteen-million-dollar bounty." Asher used his fingers as combs, pushing them through his short dark hair. He'd lost a bet in Mexico a few months back, forcing him to chop his long locks. A few more months and it'd be back to the length he usually kept it.

"I thought you said there wasn't a digital footprint," Liam said.

"Yeah," Asher began, "but the buyer will have to give a drop-off location at some point. If someone were to capture her, they'd need to know where to bring her. It's not like he's going to have a carrier pigeon deliver an address."

"You're not going to suggest we pretend to have found her to get the money, right?" When Asher didn't say anything, Liam knew the answer. "That's how you're going to try and find the location, isn't it?" He let go of the seat and crossed his arms. "We're not using her as bait," he said in a low voice in case Elaina could hear them over the volume of her headphones.

Liam glimpsed a look at Emily and Elaina from over his shoulder. Emily was drawing funny faces on the dry-erase board, and Elaina was chuckling.

Damn. He didn't remember ever feeling such an intensity of emotions crammed inside his chest.

"Of course, we won't." Jessica caught his eyes when he veered his focus back to the team. "But Asher's working on locating a hitman we can use as a cover."

"What do you mean?" Emily must've been listening in because she left the board and joined Liam at his side.

Jessica leaned back in her chair and studied Emily. "We don't want our buyer to sniff out a fake. It takes time to build up an assassin profile. We need confirmed kills and abductions that can be verified—"

"The buyer might do a hitman background check?" Emily's brows darted together in surprise. "Is that a thing?"

The team glanced at each other, and then lifted their shoulders to say *yes.*

"Okay, let me get this straight." Her hands went to her hips. "You're going to abduct a hitman." She paused as if letting her words sink in. "Then pretend to be him and put the word out you have Elaina."

"It's one possibility," Asher was quick to respond. "But we'd never actually put Elaina in the line of fire, we just need a drop location to make some headway."

"I know where those men were taking me." Elaina's little voice had everyone swiveling in their chairs to face her. "The bad men wrote it on a board before they erased it."

Liam slowly looked at the girl who was somehow stealing his heart. She lowered her headphones and pointed to the whiteboard. He'd recognize those kinds of numbers anywhere —longitude and latitude coordinates.

Jessica was on her feet, crossing the room in a matter of seconds.

How could Elaina possibly know what the numbers meant?

"I thought you were just doodling." Jessica wedged her thumb between her teeth and studied the whiteboard.

"Are you inputting the numbers into the system?" Jessica faced Harper, her cheeks flushed.

"Yeah, give me a minute." Harper squirmed in her chair a bit as if excited about the new information.

Jessica motioned for Liam to meet her in the hall. "Did you know she's a genius?" she asked once they were alone.

"She told me back at the last safe house she takes pictures with her mind. Her mom was a genius, so I guess it makes sense her daughter's smart, too."

Jessica pointed to the room. "That's more than smart. You don't think her mom was experimenting on her or something, do you? Her mom was studying memory loss at Universidad de Chile. What if—"

"She discovered a cure within her own daughter, a kid with an off-the-charts memory?" He highly doubted it.

"If it's true, or if someone thinks it's true and believes she holds the answers to a cure . . . wouldn't she be worth a lot of money?"

"Like to a big pharma company or something?" He gripped the back of his neck, the tension spiking. "That's a stretch, but I guess we can't rule anything out."

"I think it's time we talk to Maria, the woman who was taking care of Elaina." Jessica reached for the door handle. "She might know something. Plus, maybe Maria can tell us more about Elaina's mom since she worked with her at the university."

"I'll head there tomorrow. If too many of us go it could tip someone off." He lowered his hand to his side. "Let me do it."

"You sure you want to leave Elaina and Emily?" She let go of the handle. "They'll be safe with us. Although, Maria might be more apt to talk with a woman present, and I need Harper working here with me."

"I don't want to put Emily in danger," he snapped, knowing what she was thinking.

She waved her hand in the air. "Of course." She went back into the room and over to where Harper sat.

Elaina and Emily were now playing Hangman on the other half of the whiteboard.

Both of them were so damn strong. And both were somehow penetrating his walls, which scared the hell out of him.

"Thank you," he mouthed to Emily when she caught his eyes.

She tucked a strand of loose hair from her ponytail behind her ear and gave a quick nod before laughing at something Elaina had said.

"The Port of San Lorenzo." Harper looked up from her screen. "They must've planned on putting Elaina on a ship out of Argentina."

"You get the final destination?" Jessica braced the back of Harper's chair and eyed her screen.

"Port of Adra. Spain," she answered. "Arrives late Tuesday night."

"Whoever made the deal with Carballo won't show now," Knox pointed out. "Surely they've heard he lost Elaina."

"But maybe the government can use this information about the ports for a lead on Carballo," Asher noted. "Carballo might have weapons or other cargo on that ship. We can at least use this information to stop some guns from going to terrorists. I'll take any wins we can get."

"Get the information to the president," Jessica instructed Harper. "Send everything we have." She walked over to Elaina and knelt before her. "Thank you."

"I hope you can stop them." Elaina smiled at Jessica then focused back on the game they were playing. "Are there any P's?" She tipped her chin, a knowing smile on her face.

"Two." Emily playfully rolled her eyes and filled in the letters.

"Who do you think chose the port, Carballo or the buyer?" Knox asked.

"My guess is Carballo," Liam said. "Do we have any contacts over there who'd have picked up on chatter about this?"

"I know a guy." Harper found his eyes. "I'll reach out to him."

"The first priority is saving Becky, but yeah, see if he can get us eyes on the port when the ship arrives." His gut churned. "What can I do to help?" He sat at the table across from Knox.

Asher glanced his way. "Find out who the hell on the FBI and CIA joint task force needs the money bad enough to throw away their career for it."

CHAPTER FIFTEEN

"YOU ALWAYS SHOOT TO LET OFF STEAM?"

Emily lowered her earmuffs and removed the clip of ammo from the 9mm. "How do you think I got to be such a good shot?" She took the last bullet from the chamber and set the weapon down, then pressed a button to bring the paper target closer to view the damage.

"I'm getting the feeling you were going to hustle me at darts the other night." He smiled as he examined the target. "No way are you that precise of a shot but can't hit a round board with a dart."

"I guess you'll have to rechallenge me someday and find out." She removed her protective eyewear. "I'm not sure why I was surprised you had a shooting range here." She turned toward him. "Then again, I also assumed you no longer needed the practice."

"Yeah, well, we can't afford to get rusty now, can we?" He slipped his hands into his pockets. He'd changed into faded jeans, and by the looks of it, they were nearly as old as Elaina.

His hair was slightly mussy and a little wet. He must've

hopped into the shower before finding her. She could probably use another one herself to try and calm her nerves.

She was doing her best to wear a brave face and act like she belonged with a team of covert operatives.

"You get Elaina to sleep?"

"She asked me to sing to her."

"So, you sing, too?" She cracked a smile.

"Not well, apparently," he said with a laugh. "She told me as much, at least."

She was the one chuckling now, which was surprising given they were in some sort of underground bunker trying to find so many targets her head felt like it was on a swivel. "Did she really?"

"She's honest like someone else I know." The rich tenor of his voice dropped lower, and it was as if he'd reached out and touched her using only his words.

"I like her even more." She looked back at the target, contemplating whether she wanted to reload and take a few more shots to relieve some of the tension that didn't want to relent from thumping up her spine, scattering into her back, her chest—hell, everywhere. The tension was even in her mouth, which had her biting down on her teeth.

But given the situation, and her lack of emergency wine and cookies, what could she expect?

"She almost looks like a mini-you." He lifted his hands from his pockets and began kneading the flesh at the back of his neck with both hands.

Her knot of tension doubled at his words, but she realized he was possibly suffering from the same problem. "You hold all of your stress back there?"

"Yeah." He closed his eyes and kept rubbing, and so, she circled him and pushed his hands out of the way.

"Let me."

"No, that's . . ." His head rolled forward, and he softly groaned as she began massaging.

"You're tall. Mind sitting?"

"You don't need to do this." He reached back and grabbed hold of her hand. "Echo is closing in on D.C., and hopefully we'll know Becky's location soon."

She pulled her hand free of his. "Then we can spare a few minutes to relieve some of your stress. You're hard as a rock."

"Normally around you I am, but—"

"Liam!" she rasped as he faced her.

His mouth tightened, and his shoulders trembled as if fighting a laugh.

"Just sit. Take your shirt off, too."

"Yes, ma'am." He peeled off his tee, then sat in the only chair in the room, draping the fabric over his thighs. The seat was only a little bigger than the kind you might find in a high school, definitely not big enough for his frame, but it'd have to work.

She eyed his golden skin—his back as hard and firm as his chest. She tried to ditch her desire so she could focus, but the second her fingertips touched his muscles, she was a goner. She bit the inside of her cheek, resisting the urge to close her eyes and relish in how he felt beneath her palms.

Her hands slid over the blades of muscles and to the sides of his arms, and she squeezed his biceps. "You're so tense."

"Having your hands on me doesn't help if I'm being honest."

Her eyes widened. "Want me to stop?" she asked, her voice soft.

"Fuck no," he said without pause.

She sucked in a deep breath and worked the knots beneath

his flesh. The lilac-scented soap floated off his skin and met her nose. "No cologne tonight?"

"I was worried you might jump me."

She playfully smacked the back of his head. "So, your cologne is why women are so drawn to you?"

"Yup. My secret weapon. Don't tell, though, okay?" He twisted around to look at her, but she pointed toward the wall. He grinned but did as he was told.

"When Owen and Sam get back from Charleston, are you going to tell them what's going on? Well, Owen, I mean." Emily clenched her hand into a fist and used her knuckles to grind at his muscles. He really was hard. Her hands were going to give out fast, but she was enjoying this far too much to stop.

"It's going to be difficult keeping this from him. Luke's gonna kick our asses as well for not bringing him back from his honeymoon."

"Would someone go after Sam to try and get to me?" Her hands came to an abrupt halt. "Or my family?"

"I considered that." He stood and circled the chair. "We put the word out there you don't know anything." He reached for her shoulder. "And we'll nail this son of a bitch who has Becky tonight so he won't be a threat to anyone else." He gently squeezed. "But maybe we'll have Owen keep Sam out of D.C. until this blows over."

"And my parents?" Her brother was in Australia, but if she let him know what was going on, he'd come back immediately. The last thing she wanted was to ruin his honeymoon.

"I'll assign some guys from the company to establish a perimeter around your parents' home and keep an eye on them just in case."

"Could you do it without them knowing so they don't get worried?"

He nodded. "What about your brother?"

"I think he's safe in Melbourne, but if he comes back before this ends, we can fill him in."

He let go of her shoulder. "You should know I might be going to Chile tomorrow."

"Just you? Why?"

"I want to talk to the woman who has been taking care of Elaina and see if she knows anything."

"Will you tell her Elaina's okay?" She crossed her arms, a chill moving through her.

"As much as I'd like for Maria to know Elaina's safe, we can't take the risk."

She took a moment to process his words, and the fact he could be leaving her tomorrow.

"If we can't get anything out of the person on the task force—whoever it is—or out of the guy who has Becky . . . I'll visit Maria."

"How big of an 'if' are we talking? You think your people can find both the leak and Becky tonight?" *Is it even possible?*

Of course, she was used to dealing with the slow-turning wheels of politics and procedure. Liam and his team had the luxury of bypassing rules and red tape.

"If we don't get to Becky soon, she won't survive. We don't have a choice but to move fast." His words were so matter-of-fact. Like he'd done this a million times before and knew all the potential outcomes. And she supposed he probably had.

"Was this your job in the Navy? I thought you followed orders from the Department of Defense, or whoever . . . and prepped for ops. But it seems like you're also an FBI or CIA agent now."

"We weren't just picked because of our muscles," he said with a smile.

"Your brains, too, huh? Smart and sexy. A dangerous combination." She uncrossed her arms, her shoulders wilting in the process. "Do you have to go alone tomorrow? If you go, I mean."

"It's the best idea. I'd prefer not to draw attention." He pressed a palm to her cheek. "My team won't let anything happen to you or Elaina."

She turned away from his touch, her gaze dropping to the floor. "Did you come here to ask me to sign the annulment papers before you leave?"

Was he worried there was a chance he'd make her a widow?

"Er, no, but do you want to?" His hand went right back to his neck, and she wished she could relieve more of his stress. The man put his life on the line daily, and he was carrying too much weight.

"No," she rasped, almost too quickly. "And nothing will happen to you."

He reached into his pocket and produced a coin. "I got this back, so yeah, I'll be good. No worries, love." He tucked it back into his pocket.

He was trying to act casual, and maybe it was a regular day for him—but not for her, not even close.

"Crazy how our worlds suddenly overlapped in so many ways in the last week, huh?"

"Emily." His voice was gruff. And yet, that one word coming from his mouth was as if she'd been wrapped in a soft, silky embrace.

She turned away, worried he'd witness the effect he had on her. Of course, he already knew. Surely her feelings were written into every line on her face, in every movement of her body.

His hand curved around to her abdomen, and he pinned her back against his chest. It was a place she wished she could stay forever.

Safe and protected. And if she closed her eyes and pretended for a minute . . . maybe even loved.

CHAPTER SIXTEEN

"WE GOT A HIT ON OUR ASSASSIN. ANTHONY LAMOND," Jessica announced when Liam and Emily rejoined the team twenty minutes later. "He arrived at the Dulles airport the same day our team rescued Elaina."

"Who is he?" Liam asked as Jessica broadcasted her screen onto the opposite wall, showcasing two men. She also had Jared and Don on Skype so they could see her screen.

Emily zeroed in on the man on the right, the same man whose blood had soaked her floor.

"He's the guy I killed." She pointed to the screen as she sat, and Liam joined her and reached beneath the table, locking their hands together.

"Anthony was Italian Special Forces before he went AWOL seven years ago. He has a brother. Mickey Lamond. They're both on Interpol's wanted list for the abduction and ransom of three high-ranking officials, as well as four assassinations." Jessica zoomed in on Mickey. "I think they took the job together."

"Any CCTV footage get a hit on Anthony's brother, Mickey, being in town?" Liam asked.

"No, but that doesn't mean he's not in D.C.," she answered.

"The brothers always work together. They probably travel separately under aliases to avoid detection," Harper noted. "Mickey would be pissed his brother died, which is why he wanted Emily delivered along with Elaina."

"So, it's gotta be him, right? Mickey has Becky," Don said over the line, anger piercing his tone.

Don looked horrible. The stress lines on his forehead had tripled. Bags beneath his green eyes. She couldn't begin to imagine what he was going through. She even forgave him for holding a gun to her head and trying to take her. Love could make a person do crazy things, she supposed.

"Mickey's our best bet right now," Jessica said. "If it's him who has Becky, when we text him at the agreed upon time I'll try and ping his phone to get a location."

"You can't do that now?" Emily asked.

"He must've removed the battery from his phone to remain off the networks," she answered. "But when Don sends him the video of Elaina as evidence he has her, it should give us enough time to pinpoint his position."

"And if that doesn't work?" Don asked.

"We have a few ideas," Jessica said.

"We've been scouring through all the CCTV footage around Emily's apartment to trace Anthony's prior steps, plus examining the cameras near Dryden's place," Harper explained. "I located three suspicious vehicles, and I'm in the process of tracking their whereabouts."

"Wow. You guys are incredible." Emily peered at Don on the screen. The man needed good news and soon. They all did. "What about the agent on the task force? Any luck finding him?"

Liam let go of her hand and began working at the tension in his neck again.

"Not a *him*," Asher said.

"Patty?" Emily asked in surprise.

FBI Director Mendez had introduced Emily to everyone on the CIA and FBI joint task force when Dryden brought her onto the case, and Patty was the only woman on the team, and she was from the CIA.

"Patty invited me out for drinks last Monday after we met," she explained, "but I said *no*, I'd been too . . ." Too hungover from Vegas. Too married. Too out of it.

Had it really been only a week since she and Liam had tied the knot?

"You didn't tell her about Vegas, did you?" Liam asked as if forgetting not everyone in earshot knew what he'd be talking about.

"No, of course not." Her voice was a near whisper, and she was fairly certain red streaks now advanced up her neck and to her cheeks. She glanced at the computer screen where Jared appeared now instead of Don. "I thought you said you hand-picked everyone for your team?"

"I did," Jared said a little defensively. "Patty's been working on catching Carballo for years. She must've picked up chatter about the abduction before my asset told me about it, and maybe she thought if we grabbed Elaina, the buyer might offer her the same deal."

"She probably didn't expect it'd become open season for assassins to come after Elaina with Carballo out of the picture," Harper proposed. "But our traitor has to be Patty. She used an alias to fly to Belize, and we have her on camera checking into the same hotel Anthony Lamond happened to be staying at."

"And then shortly after that trip, Anthony Lamond

showed up in D.C. on the day we rescued Elaina," Knox pointed out. "No way is that a coincidence, especially with Anthony trying to kill Emily."

"Why would Patty do it?" Emily pushed back from the table, the sting of such betrayal sickening.

"Money's a strong motivator. It makes people do stupid things." Jared briefly bowed his head. "She made me think it was my idea to assign her to the case, but she must've manipulated me somehow."

"Isn't that a special skill you guys learn at your spook's academy?" Knox asked.

"This isn't Hogwarts, man," Jared responded flippantly.

A tiny smile met the edges of Knox's lips. "Hog-what?"

"Anyway." Jessica dragged out the word as if trying to clear a sudden bout of tension rising in the room. It was obvious Liam and his people had some sort of beef with the CIA.

"CIA Director Rutherford dispatched a team to pick up Patty," Harper said. "If she knows something about our buyer we'll find out."

"Can't she tell us where Mickey Lamond is?" Emily asked.

"Patty's been trained to defeat lie detectors and withstand interrogation. It'll take some time to break her," Jared answered.

"And time is something we don't have." Don's face filled the display screen again. "She's going to pay for this, but first we need Becky back."

"Hopefully the plan works so we can catch Mickey," Jared said in a steady tone. "And preferably alive."

* * *

"MICKEY HAS BECKY TIED TO A CHAIR IN AN ABANDONED warehouse three klicks from the Potomac," Wyatt said over the line. "We're looking for the best angle to get a clean shot."

"That's a good copy," Jessica answered, her eyes focused on a computer screen in front of her.

Emily was grateful Liam's team had let her stay in the room during Echo Team's operation; she wouldn't have been able to wait alone in that small bedroom, which was more like a prison cell.

Liam squeezed her hand beneath the table, offering his support.

His free hand was curled into a fist atop the table, and he took slow and measured breaths.

He wanted to be with Echo Team, didn't he? To be part of the action.

Knox. Asher. Jessica. Harper. They all had the same looks on their faces. The same clench of their jaws. Barely blinking.

Liam and Emily sat across the table from the rest of his team, and as much as Liam probably wanted to be on their side, he chose to sit with her. To comfort her.

"This is Echo Three. I have eyes on the target, TOC, but I don't have a shot. What about you, Five?"

TOC? She forgot the meaning of that acronym. She'd watched the show *SEAL Security*, which Luke's wife was the lead writer for, and she remembered hearing that term. *The command center or something?*

She was used to reading reports by the FBI, CIA, and other three-letter agencies while working for the criminal division at the AG's office, but she never crossed paths with the Navy.

"This is Five. I don't have a clear view either."

"Echo One? What about you?" Asher asked.

155

"Mickey keeps circling Becky's chair," Echo One, Wyatt, answered. "I don't want to—"

"I've got the shot!" Jared said, and a loud snap followed before anyone could respond.

Jessica and Asher exchanged a concerned look, and she was on her feet in a split second. "Echo One, come in. What's your status?"

"This is One. Mickey Lamond is down. Repeat. Mickey Lamond is down."

Emily's hand swept to her chest, and she sucked in a deep breath. Was it really over? That fast?

"And Becky?" Jessica's eyes pinned to the ceiling as she waited for an answer.

"She's fine," Wyatt said, and a chorus of *thank fucks* left the lips of the teammates across from her in the room.

"I had no choice but to take a kill shot," Jared said. "Sorry."

"You were supposed to stay in the van with Don." Jessica's shoulders shrank a touch. "But thank you."

Asher was on his feet next to Jessica, his palms on the table. The guy didn't look like someone you wanted to mess with. Well, no one on the team did, but Asher was . . . a bit intimidating. "Now we can't question the son of a bitch," he mumbled.

"We already know Patty hired him. He probably wouldn't have known anything beyond that," Jared responded.

Jessica shifted her dark-rimmed glasses up to pinch the bridge of her nose. "Yeah, okay. Call it in, Jared. I want my people gone before the Feds roll up."

Emily pulled her hand free from Liam's and left the table.

She hurried out of the room, on the verge of puking.

After arriving in the connecting bathroom to her bedroom,

she turned on the faucet and leaned forward. Her stomach shook, but nothing came out.

"Just breathe." Liam pulled her hair away from her face.

She met his eyes in the mirror then cupped the running water and splashed it onto her face.

He kept hold of her hair and rubbed the center of her back in an up-and-down motion with his other.

"How do you do this all the time?" She turned off the sink and braced the counter with both palms. "That one minute aged me five years."

He let go of her hair and went around to her side, perching his hip against the vanity. "It's easier when you're with the team. Even I get heart palpitations when I'm on the other end like this. I don't like being helpless."

"But you're not. You helped save her. You and your people worked so fast, and you somehow found her. She's alive because of you all."

She turned into him, and he brought his forehead to hers and rested it there. She held on to his arms so she didn't wobble. "You should get some rest," he whispered.

"What about you?" she asked once they were back in the bedroom. "How long has it been since you've slept?" She kicked off her Nikes and toed them under the twin bed.

"I'm used to this." He shut the bedroom door and turned to face her.

"No one should be used to going without sleep." She sat on the bed, wondering if he'd sit with her. She didn't want to be alone, but would it be selfish of her to keep him from his team any longer?

He casually shrugged. "I can stay with you until you're asleep?"

Her lip went between her teeth as she considered his

words. She couldn't get her voice to work, so she nodded and shifted to her back before rolling to her side atop the covers.

The weight of the twin bed shifted when he joined her.

He draped his arm over her side, pulling her close against his chest, and she relaxed into his warmth and closed her eyes.

She could get used to falling asleep and waking up in this man's arms.

Then again, maybe being close to him was actually dangerous because this moment wasn't about lust or desire . . . which had been her safe go-to rationalization for her feelings up until now. What she was feeling right now was so much more.

"Liam?"

"Yes?" he whispered near her ear, his breath tickling her there.

"Thank you."

"For what?"

"For marrying me."

He stiffened against her.

"I mean—if you hadn't . . . I'd probably be dead."

CHAPTER SEVENTEEN

AFTER SHOWERING THAT SUNDAY MORNING AND PUTTING ON clean clothes, plus a touch of mascara and some ChapStick, she left her room to find out if the team had learned anything new.

She hadn't expected to find the main room crowded with five other men. She recognized the guys, but she didn't really know them. Not even by name. Well, she knew Wyatt—but he'd made a point to get to know her by shamelessly flirting a couple of times—right in front of Liam, too.

"Hi." She lifted her hand in greeting when she entered the room and everyone turned to look at her.

Computers, wires, all kinds of tactical gear, as well as other stuff she didn't recognize cluttered the table now.

Were they prepping for war? Did they have news?

The feeling when you're walking down a hall wearing squeaky sneakers or noisy heels, drawing eyes—that's how she felt right now. Like all eyes were on her, and they weren't enthused about having an outsider present.

"Hey, beautiful," Wyatt spoke up.

Unlike the rest of his buddies who were in plain tees, he

had on a black shirt with a skull holding a SEAL trident in one hand and flames spiraling around it which read: "Brotherhood Forged by Fire."

"How are you?" Wyatt motioned for her to get out of the doorway and come into the room.

"Okay. Uh, where's Liam?"

"He's checking on Elaina," Wyatt replied.

"Oh. Maybe I'll do the same." She quickly turned and left the room before anyone could object, then pressed her back to the hallway wall once the door had shut.

"Hi, Emily."

She turned to see Liam and Elaina walking hand in hand her way. She tucked her hair behind her ears and pushed away from the wall.

"How'd you sleep?" Liam shot her an innocent smile once they stopped in front of her.

"Better than I expected." No bad dreams, which was surprising. Given the fact she'd killed a man thirty-six hours ago and an FBI agent pointed a gun at her head.

She pressed her hands to her thighs and leaned forward to connect with Elaina's eyes. "And how about you?"

"I'm good," she said, her tone almost upbeat. "I like being here. I'd like to stay in America."

"You don't want to live with Maria?" She wrapped her hand over Elaina's shoulder but switched her focus to Liam, wondering if the same rush of concern moved through him at her words.

"She doesn't want me." Her words were flat. Just so matter-of-fact. Like she'd come to terms with the truth and had moved into the acceptance phase.

"I'm sure that's not true." Emily's heart shattered, the shreds like broken glass puncturing her lungs, making it hard to pull in a deep breath.

"Can I ask you something?" Liam voiced the question slowly. Elaina's gaze wandered up to his face, and she nodded her permission. "Did anyone ever run tests on you, did they—"

"You mean my mommy, right?"

"Yes," he said, but it was as if the word pained him to say it.

"She said my brain might be able to help people get their brains back. Memories, I mean."

"Did she teach you how to memorize stuff? Is that how you remembered those numbers?" Elaina had been spot on about the two ports, which had blown Emily's mind.

"She didn't teach me how to remember stuff. I just can. She did teach me how to tell what people are thinking by the faces they make." She looked to Emily. "Like, I know that every time you scrunch your eyes, it's like you're trying really hard to be okay when you're not. And whenever Liam squeezes the back of his neck, he's worried about something. Maybe you, Emily. Maybe me."

Emily forced herself to stand all the way upright and released Elaina's shoulder.

"You like him a lot, don't you?" A smile touched Elaina's lips. "I don't blame you. He's very handsome."

Emily fought a nervous laugh bubbling in her throat. "We should probably—"

"See what the team has to say," Liam finished for her, never losing his hold of Elaina's little hand. "You sure you want to come in there with us?"

"I can wear the headphones." She started to walk to the door, forcing Liam to move, too.

He looked back at Emily from over his shoulder and mouthed, "Wow."

Yeah, she felt the same.

Her mind switched gears once they were back in the room, though. How could it not with what they were facing?

"I just got off the phone with POTUS," Jessica said straightaway. "Someone tipped off the Argentinian government that Americans took Elaina. They're calling it a kidnapping."

"Shit." Liam let go of Elaina's hand, and with a tilt of his head sent a silent request to Emily to distract her at the whiteboard like yesterday.

"President Rydell denied everything, of course. But we don't need the extra heat, or any added tension between our nations," Asher said. "It's probably Carballo pushing the government to get her back."

Emily helped Elaina put on her headphones, then she handed her a marker. They were both out of place in there, weren't they?

Elaina deserved to have the life of an eight-year-old. A chance to have fun and be carefree.

"Looks like more people are coming out of the bloody woodwork," Wyatt said, his British accent thickening. "Mercenaries and other freelance blokes are flooding the States since the Argentinian president went on TV to announce Uncle Sam has Elaina." He paused for a moment. "Speaking of which . . . heard of Brittany and Henry Simpson?"

"A married couple in their thirties or forties, right? Canadian? Work together as a hit team?" Liam asked, and the idea of such a team had her stomach turning.

Of course, Anthony and Mickey Lamond were brothers, and also a killing duo. Thank God they couldn't hurt anyone else now.

"The border patrol picked them up when they crossed the

Canadian border into New York near Niagara Falls an hour ago," Wyatt said.

Emily kept drawing on the board, but she pivoted to the side to observe the group, her curiosity piqued.

"Who knows they've been detained?" Liam's hands went to his hips.

"It's not been made public yet." Wyatt flipped his screen toward Liam, and Emily craned her neck a touch to try and get a view of the man and woman.

"I'll go to Chile as Henry," Liam said a beat later. "I'll use one of his aliases to travel, and maybe I can—"

"Get the drop location from the buyer," Jessica finished.

"Can't we just ask this couple for the location?" Emily set the marker down and looked at the group.

"We'll see what they know," Jessica said. "But there's no way the buyer provided a location without evidence Elaina's in their custody."

"But now we might have a way to reach out to the buyer to let them know we have her," Asher explained.

"I want access to everyone the couple has been in contact with," Jessica instructed to Harper. "Pull everything from their phones and any other records you can find."

"Won't it be weird if Liam travels alone considering they, uh, work as a husband-and-wife team?" The focus whipped Emily's way once again, and she could feel it . . . the wheels of their minds turning. Ideas spinning. "You all need to stay here, right? To track down leads."

"You're not suggesting you go as Liam's wife, are you?" Asher's arms went across his chest in a defensive position.

You could hear a freaking pin drop in the room.

"I, uh." She wet her lips and blinked, summoning the words.

Elaina pulled on her hand, and so she looked down at her.

"You should go with him. I think he needs you. I think he needs you more than I need him."

When Emily looked up, Liam stood mere inches away, his eyes steady on her. "Can we talk in private, please?"

She dragged in a breath, not so deep she'd become lightheaded, then followed him out into the hall.

"Are you out of your mind?" Throwing his hands up, he did a three-sixty as if he didn't know which direction to face, before settling on a stance dead-center in front of her. "You're not an operative. You can't just run off to Chile disguised as a fucking hit woman and—"

"And what?" she challenged.

"You're a lawyer, Emily. A lawyer."

"I know that. You don't need to remind me. This is just an intel op, right? You're going to see if Maria knows anything that could shed some light as to why someone's after Elaina. But Maria may be skittish around you. She may not even speak English. I can help."

"So, you speak Spanish?"

He let go of a heavy breath and placed his hand on the wall above her shoulder, caging her in without actually touching her.

"Yes."

He was quiet for a few seconds as if contemplating the idea of her coming along. But then he said, "No. I can't let you do this. If I pick up a tail, or someone is watching Maria, you could get hurt."

"It's Chile, not Argentina."

"That doesn't mean Carballo won't have his people there waiting for someone to show up. Or whoever this buyer is might have someone waiting as well."

"Then why are you going alone if it has the potential to be so dangerous?"

"Because this is what I do," he said, his voice almost hollow.

The man put himself in danger all of the time. Something could happen to him.

She knew that. Understood it. But the normalcy of it didn't soften the blow. How could it ever ease the pain of what could possibly happen to him or someone on his team?

A loss. It'd be an unbearable loss.

"And you really think there's something in Chile that might help?" she asked, needing to redirect her thoughts to what was at stake right now. "Why not wait and see if we can get a drop location from the buyer first by—"

"While the team is working on that, I can make use of my time by gathering whatever intel I can in Chile."

She placed her hand over his fast-beating heart, but kept her gaze on her hand instead of looking into his eyes. "I don't want to be here without you."

"Elaina needs you."

"*You* need me," she said without thinking her words through. But she was right, wasn't she? "Please. Let me go as your wife on this trip."

"You are my wife," he said in a near whisper.

Her eyes journeyed to his face as a hot beat of tension burned her lungs. "Let me come." She'd attempted to use her authoritative courtroom tone, but the break in her voice failed her.

"I'd never forgive myself if something happened to you." He cupped her cheek with his free hand, and as she leaned into his touch, her mouth brushed over his thumb.

She wrapped her hand over his wrist, keeping his hand in place. "So, you know how I'd feel if you leave and don't come back," she said, her tone soft. The touch of weakness, of worry, still there, even though she didn't want it to be.

165

"This is who I am. And this is why—"

"You don't settle down," she finished so he wouldn't have to.

He was quiet for a moment. Studying her as if contemplating the idea.

"Even if I can get the team to agree, I highly doubt we'll get the OK from the president." He lowered his arms to his sides and stepped back.

"So don't tell the president."

"Aren't you supposed to make sure we stay on the right side of the law and out of legal trouble?" A flicker of a smile caught the edges of his lips.

"All the more reason I should go with you." She might not have a job when this was all said and done, but as long as everyone made it out alive and safe, that was more than enough for her.

* * *

EMILY STARED AT LIAM, ANTICIPATION RACING THROUGH HER, as he talked to Jessica and Asher off to the side of the room ten minutes later. Judging by how they all kept swinging their gazes Emily's way, she sensed the decision about her going to Chile hadn't yet been made.

She kind of liked the fact a woman was in charge of a bunch of Navy SEALs. The guys not only didn't seem to mind, they had an obvious respect and admiration for her. She knew Luke and Jessica co-led both teams, but based on what Emily had witnessed so far, Jessica was the glue.

And now they'd added another badass woman to the team.

Emily had met Harper in Vegas. And wow, that seemed so

long ago, even though it'd only been last Sunday when Emily had woken up naked and married to Liam.

"You really have to leave so soon?" she'd asked Liam as he'd hurriedly dressed in her hotel room. Asher had blown up his phone a dozen times, and he'd finally given in and answered it. *"Shouldn't we talk about what happened first?"*

"You said you don't remember much of what happened." He draped the blazer from his tux over his arm and approached her, needing to leave her room in the clothes he'd worn the night before. *"So, what should we talk about?"*

"I remember a little." She'd tossed a hand in the air. *"Like the getting-married part."*

"Shit. Okay. I was going to bring that up when I got back from—"

"Wherever you're running off to? Which is where exactly?"

"Emily, are you sure you want to do this?" Both Jessica and Liam stood before her now, abruptly roping her back to the present.

"Yeah," she answered, no doubt in her mind. "So, who can I be? What alias?"

Jessica and Liam exchanged a quick look. "Heidi and Decker Hoffman are the least used aliases," she answered.

"Me? A Heidi?" She pulled on the strands of her dark hair. "I guess I'm going as a blonde, but, uh"—she glanced at her jeans—"I don't exactly have legs for days."

"You're not going as Heidi Klum," Jessica said with a laugh.

"And your legs are damn perfect to me." Liam's eyes trailed a path along the curves of her body.

Jessica cleared her throat. "But yeah, Heidi's blonde, so I'll get you a wig. We have everything you'll need here. No worries." She squeezed her shoulder.

"Are we flying commercial or private?" Maybe Liam could get some sleep on the flight to Chile.

"Since the Hoffmans always fly first-class commercial, we'll stick to their usual routine," Jessica answered. "Jared's heading to New York to the CIA black site where the couple's being kept. Since Patty still denies involvement, hopefully, he can get something out of them. And Harper's going to see what she can pull from their records. Maybe we can find out how they learned about the bounty in the first place."

"Will Elaina be okay with us gone?" Emily asked.

"I'm not great with kids, but Harper has a few nieces— and she's got a better singing voice than this guy." Jessica jerked a thumb Liam's way.

"So, Elaina told you how bad I am at *Twinkle Twinkle*?" He flashed his white teeth.

"She may have mentioned it." Jessica returned his smile.

"Would I be able to talk to Sam before I go?" Since Liam had told Owen what was going on to protect Sam that morning, there was no point in keeping secrets from her best friend anymore.

"Yeah. I'll get you a secure line." Jessica left her alone with Liam.

"What are you going to tell her?" Liam asked.

"I don't know. Maybe everything." She leaned in closer to him, tipped up her chin and whispered, "What about the rest of your team? You planning on telling them the truth about us? That we're already married?"

Liam's eyes were a bit bloodshot, and his lids were heavy, no doubt from exhaustion. The man was a machine, but he also needed to rest at some point. "Do you want me to tell them?"

Her mouth was dry and cottony like she hadn't eaten in days. And if it weren't for Liam reminding her to eat since they'd been underground, she probably would've forgotten to.

"Here you go." Jessica came back with a phone in hand, saving Emily from stumbling through an answer to his question.

"Thanks." She tapped it against her palm.

"I'd keep it short. You two need to gear up and leave soon." Jessica looked to Liam. "I couldn't scrounge up anyone in Santiago to provide you with weapons, especially since you're going undercover, so you'll need to get something on the black market when you're there."

"Shouldn't be too hard to do."

"I'll be right back." Emily went to her temporary bedroom.

She dialed Sam's number and bit her thumb as she waited for the line to connect. She'd lied to her best friend about Liam, and now . . . how would she drop the truth bomb to her over a cell phone in an underground nuclear fallout bunker?

"This better be you," Sam said upon answering.

"Hey," she nearly whispered and sat on the bed. A tingling sensation moved through her limbs. The nerves and guilt strangling her words.

"Emily? Can you hear me?" Her voice pitched higher. "Hello?"

It was now or never. "I know what you're going to say, but I promise, I know what I'm doing."

"Was there ever going to be a trip to Australia?" Sam asked, and Emily could picture her brows snapping together, her lips pinching tight as she worked at putting the pieces together.

She closed her eyes. "There's something I have to tell you, but I'm afraid you'll be angry." Hell, she knew Sam would be pissed. But probably at Liam and not her.

"You're scaring me, Em. What's going on?"

I'm married. I'm married. She chanted the phrase in her head for what felt like a solid minute, hoping eventually the words would slip out.

Silence.

Crickets.

Nada.

"Emily, please."

"I'm sorry," she forced out. "It was supposed to be *your* day, Sam." Guilt at what she'd done had her stomach tucking in, hollowing her out.

"What are you trying to say?" Sam's voice had lowered to a soft, nervous tone.

"The, um, reason Liam happened to be at my apartment when that guy busted in to, uh, kill me . . . well, he was there to sign annulment papers."

Silence and then, "I don't understand."

Oh, God. She was going to make her spell it out for her. "We got drunk and married the night of your wedding," she blurted.

"I'm going to kill him," Sam gritted out, using the tone she reserved for only the people who pissed her off on a nuclear level—often politicians.

"It's not his fault," Emily quickly came to his defense.

She was back on her feet and began pacing the small space in front of the bed as she waited for Sam to say something. Hell, anything. She'd even take anger over the death-trap of silence.

"Did you sign the papers already?" Sam finally spoke. "Are you no longer married?"

"We got sidetracked by the—"

"Assassin. Shit. I'm so sorry." A hard sigh crackled through the line causing static. "Are you okay?"

"You don't need to worry about me. I'm just sorry about what I did and for keeping what happened a secret from you."

"Don't be. I'm not mad at you," she said, almost a hushed tone. "I'm just glad you're alive."

"I'm so sorry if my work has put you in danger."

"Well, I did get you mixed up in the craziness of my life last year."

"That wasn't your fault."

Sam grew quiet for a moment. "Just stay safe. I know you're with the team, so I'm confident you'll be okay . . . but . . ."

"What is it?" she asked, her voice rising a touch. "What are you afraid to say?"

"Liam." His name snapped through the line like she hadn't wanted to say it. "He'll hurt you. You've stuck to casual dating since Mr. British broke off the engagement two years ago, but Liam—well, I don't think you should—"

"I know you care about me, but I just can't talk about this right now. And I promise, everything *will* be okay." She hoped she knew what she was doing, at least. "Try not to worry about me."

"Not possible," she said, and Emily could hear the cut of emotion—the brink of tears about to hit Sam's cheeks. And damn if it had her eyes watering now, too. "Call me with updates when you can. I love you, Em."

She cleared her throat. "I love you, too."

She ended the call and took a few minutes to gather herself—to put her head back on straight before she faced the team. Before she set eyes on the man who did have the power to cut a sharp line through her heart, splitting it into two.

CHAPTER EIGHTEEN

THERE WAS A PURPLISH-PINK HUE TO THE SKY, THE SUN having now disappeared, as Liam and Emily walked to their hotel in downtown Santiago. Palm trees lined the streets, and colonial architecture was sprinkled in between the colorful homes in the city.

If they weren't on a mission, it'd feel almost like they were on a date, just walking along like a normal couple, not undercover as a murdering duo.

"Sorry I slept the entire flight here." How had he passed out that hard? That wasn't like him, but when he'd woken up as the plane began its descent to the airport, he'd found his fingers laced with Emily's. He didn't remember reaching for her, but maybe he did it in his sleep.

"You needed it." She played with the blonde bangs of her wig as if annoyed with them cutting across her forehead. "Besides, I need my protector full of energy."

"Good point." He surveyed the scene as they walked, checking to see if they had a tail.

"This place is beautiful." Her eyes were trained on the

snow-capped Andes Mountains off in the distance. "I could get used to a view like this."

He kept his grip on their one bag of luggage and used it to point to the hotel off to their right.

They checked in with no trouble, and when they arrived in their room, she did a three-sixty in the living area and smiled. "The presidential suite?"

He dropped the bag at his side and locked up. "Trying to keep up with appearances." He turned to find her standing before him—looking like sin. The kind of sin he craved.

Her long blonde hair fell in lustrous waves over her shoulders, and although he liked her natural color—well, the woman looked hot as hell staring at him with her thick lashes framing her big brown eyes.

Hell, she looked like a sexy spy in her leather jacket and brown boots. Someone who could go to bat with bad guys and drop them down with a flick of her wrist.

She was strong. Tougher than he'd realized upon first meeting her.

But he couldn't shake the feeling she was hiding some sort of pain deep inside, and he knew what that was like, and how it could eat at you.

"We'll go back out soon to secure a sidearm. I don't like being without one down here." He tipped his chin toward the window—to the view of the Andes he made sure they had when he checked in.

"You'll take me with you, right?" She whirled away from the window after observing the scenery and removed her jacket.

"I don't like risking bringing you along to buy a gun from an illegal dealer, but I don't want to leave you alone, either."

Having her there made him uneasy. Hell, in more ways than one.

The white jersey fabric of her long-sleeved shirt molded to her body, accentuating her breasts. He remembered how her tits had felt cupped in his hands.

He could see the outline of her bra beneath the material, and there wasn't much padding based on the fact he could see her nipples poking through.

But if she kept staring at him like he was the sun and the fucking moon he'd probably lose his bloody mind.

She strode closer to him, and he wanted to back the hell up. To take a second to remind himself they weren't in this suite for fun, but because they were trying to track down the sons of bitches who were after Elaina. "You good?" she asked, a hint of humor in her tone as if she'd picked up on his obvious desire.

"Still just a little tired," he lied, hating himself for it. But what could he say? *I want to screw you all day. All night. Every day after that.* And he was more than confident in the fact he'd never grow tired of it. Of her. And when he made her breakfast in bed, he wouldn't slip out afterward like the dick he normally was.

She sat on the couch and unzipped her boots, freeing her legs. "Do you think someone might be after Elaina's mom's research?"

Her question was the reset to his focus he needed. *Thank God.*

He grabbed two bottles of water from the fridge in the kitchenette off to his left and handed her one before sucking his dry.

"If that were the case, why not grab Elaina immediately after her mother was in the accident?" He sat next to her but kept enough distance to prevent him from reaching out and touching her.

She removed her wig and held it in her hands. Her brown

hair was pulled back in a tight bun. "What if someone caused the car accident to get the research, but they didn't know Elaina was important until later?"

He considered the idea. "But why put a bounty on her head instead of just grabbing her themselves?"

"Maybe they couldn't come after her yet, or they wanted to keep some distance to prevent exposure." She set the wig on the glass-top coffee table in front of her. "I'm just thinking aloud. I don't know."

He scooted closer, but if he touched her—if he reached for her—he'd be done. "I still think the timing is a factor. It's been too long since her mother's death, and if there was anything in her mom's notes about Elaina somehow having some sort of genetic marker in her DNA for memory loss, they wouldn't have waited to get her."

"So, coming after her must be for another reason."

He stood again, but when he roped a hand around the back of his neck, he remembered Elaina's words about him. The girl was perceptive. And since she was only eight, maybe she'd grow up to be even smarter than her genius mother. "The question is . . . what?"

"I guess we'll have to wait until tomorrow to find out." She joined him on her feet. "And speaking of which, what's the game plan?"

"Maria's first class on Monday is at ten. We'll stop by the lecture hall close to eleven and try and get her to talk." He looked to the one bedroom that branched off the living space. "You want to wash up before we head out? I could use a shower, too."

"At the same time?" she said, a playful sweep of her tongue over her bottom lip.

Damn it. As much as he'd love to watch water rolling

down her naked body . . . "Funny." He cupped his mouth, willing his dick to calm the hell down.

"I'll just clean up, and the bathroom is all yours."

He grabbed the luggage and carried it to the bedroom and set it atop the bed.

"Were we followed?" she asked, the touch of teasing gone from her tone, replaced with concern.

He unzipped the bag and began removing the clothes Jessica had packed for Emily's role as Heidi. "No."

"How can you tell?"

He faced her. "My job is to notice things, remember?"

"Well, um, do you think anyone is watching Maria?"

"It's possible," he said, his voice falling flat.

"But we should be safe until we visit her tomorrow?"

He nodded.

"And are we endangering Maria by visiting?"

"If someone wanted her, they would've gotten to her already. But that's also why it's best if we don't tell her the truth about Elaina. The less she knows about us and where Elaina is—the better."

"Makes sense." She reached around him and grabbed a red bra and matching underwear from the suitcase.

Holy hell. Emily must have slipped a few of her own items inside.

He really didn't need to know she'd be wearing red lace beneath her clothes. Maybe he should've let her unpack.

Once she was in the en suite with the water running, he dropped onto the bed and clutched his cell in his hand. Closing his eyes, he let his mind slide back to the memories he'd stored away from their wedding night in Vegas.

"I can't think when I'm around you. You make me crazy." His tongue had roamed her mouth right after, and he had her positioned before him against the wall of the coat closet

outside the wedding reception area. *"I don't remember ever wanting someone so much."*

"I want you, too." She'd moaned against his mouth while tearing her fingers through his hair.

"Then let's get out of here."

"Liam?"

He rolled to his side and was greeted by the view of Emily standing in the doorway of the bathroom clutching a towel to her chest. He couldn't help but look at her legs—legs she didn't seem to realize were absolute perfection.

"Forget something?" He dropped his feet to the floor and sat up, hands braced on the bed at his sides.

"Yeah. You."

She let go of the towel and stood naked.

"Liam?"

He jerked upright at the sound of his name. *Shit.* He'd fallen asleep.

What's wrong with me?

Emily stood *fully* clothed at the side of the bed. "Your turn."

He then followed her eyes to the bulge in his pants. He grabbed one of the pillows and set it on his lap. "So, uh, how cold does that shower get?"

CHAPTER NINETEEN

EMILY'S FOREARMS RESTED ATOP THE RAILING OF THE HOTEL rooftop bar, her gaze on the indigo and amethyst sky. So much more colorful than what he was used to back home.

"The empanadas we had at dinner were crazy good, but now I feel like I'm stuffed with cheese."

He lightly laughed and switched his focus to her. She was far more interesting to look at than the sky.

"Worth every calorie, though." A close-lipped smile deepened the dimple in her right cheek. Kryptonite for him. "This is not how I anticipated the trip going, though."

"Yeah, this is definitely not how these sorts of trips normally go." He'd never spent the evening buying weapons illegally with a gorgeous attorney at his side, that was for sure.

"It's like someone took a paintbrush to the sky. Never seen such beautiful colors before." Her graceful hand raced through the air as if she were throwing shades of purple onto a canvas.

"I've been to Chile quite a few times, but I never really noticed how nice it is."

"I thought you noticed everything." She faced him, fidgeting with the zipper of her leather jacket and pulled it all the way up.

"I don't always notice beauty, I guess." *Not until it's right in front of me, staring me in the eyes, stealing my focus. My thoughts. My breath like a dying man.* "You must be cold." He pointed to the sofa in front of a fire off to their side.

He grabbed one of the rolled blankets, which were set out for guests, and draped it over her shoulders once she'd taken a seat.

"Thank you. Much better." She leaned back on the sofa but kept her eyes trained on the fire that burned bright from the bed of what looked like hundreds of three-carat diamonds.

A light breeze had the flames flickering his way as if reaching out for him like a demon trying to rope him back to the hells of Afghanistan, to the day he watched a Humvee of Marines get hit by an IED right in front of him nine years ago.

He coughed into a closed fist, trying to force away the thoughts. "Would you like something to drink?"

"Do you normally drink on assignment?"

"No." But there was nothing normal about this night or the company. "One's fine."

"Wine, then. Something red. Thank you."

He went to the bar tucked beneath an overhang not too far from their couch and ordered their drinks. He scanned the area, checking for anyone or anything abnormal as he waited.

"I thought you needed my help with Spanish," she said with a smile when he returned with their drinks. "I heard you order," she added when taking the glass he offered.

"I never said that, you did."

"So, you do speak the language?" She tightened her grip on the blanket with her free hand. "How come you didn't

179

when you were, uh, making the purchase from that man tonight?" The flames threw shadows on her face when a slight gust of wind hit them again.

"Because Heidi and Decker don't speak Spanish." And his Spanish was only decent; his Arabic, Mandarin, and Urdu were much better.

He thought back to an hour ago when he'd clutched Emily tight to his side as they navigated the bustling streets to buy a 45 and 9mm from an illegal vendor. Yeah, not the most thrilling moment of his life.

"You want to come back here and take that arms dealer down, don't you?" She sipped her wine. "I saw the way you basically inventoried every detail about him and his operation in your mind."

"He sells weapons to criminals. Of course, I want to come back here and take him off the streets. Wouldn't be my first time either."

No flutter of her lashes or downturn of her lips at his words. Maybe she didn't view him as a killer? "A double-tap to the chest. A bullet to the head, perhaps."

She angled her head, thinning her eyes as she studied him. "That's what you'd like to do to him?"

"Yes," he answered through barely parted lips. "And if that son of a bitch had even looked at you sideways I would've snapped his neck."

No flinch. Zero reaction. How was that possible?

He was attempting to press on a nerve. To see if the softness of her eyes would harden with every beat of the truth he dropped.

His job was to kill. To sit on the long gun and wipe scum from the face of the earth. And he was okay with that. He meant what he'd said back at the White House, those deaths were about keeping people safe. Keeping his brothers in arms safe. So, no regrets.

"Do most snipers keep count of their kills? I saw the movie about that well-known SEAL and—"

"It's a force of habit, I guess."

She took another sip of wine and stared into her glass. "Well, this part of the night is much more my speed. I'm hoping that was my first and also last weapons buy."

A touch of silence ate up the space between them, allowing his mind to quiet, a nice change from the constant parade of details rolling through like an early morning fog.

"I love the smell of a fire. Reminds me of when my brother and I used to go camping with our parents." She set her glass on the wide ledge surrounding the firepit and lowered the blanket from her shoulders. "My brother has always been protective of me. He'd bring my dad's gun when just the two of us went hiking, worried a bear would try and maul me."

"And what about with guys? Did he have a gun on our dinner date the other night?"

She cracked a broader smile. "Probably. But he really liked you. I've never seen him like that. You have an effect on people."

She scooted over a hair and rested a hand on his knee. Ideas of her hand in other places on his body popped to mind.

"It has to get exhausting, though. I mean, the woman at the front desk downstairs when we checked in earlier couldn't take her eyes off you."

He wasn't sure about that, but then, he didn't notice other women with Emily at his side.

"I wasn't much to look at growing up. I had to work my ass off to get in shape," he admitted. "I was kind of a geek. My brothers loved to play American football—they were obsessed with the Cowboys—and they always made me play, even before I learned how to make use of a gym." His throat thickened at the memory. "Brandon, my oldest brother, he'd always be the quarterback, but he could never remember the plays."

"So, he had you memorize them and tell him, huh?"

He shifted his beer bottle around, the liquid sloshing up. "They said I couldn't ever be a SEAL because I was too weak. Mum said my brain was my greatest asset. My biggest muscle."

"And now you have both." Her teeth skirted her bottom lip, and he forced his focus away from her mouth before his dick tented his jeans.

"I still have to work out a lot. Six-packs are irritatingly annoying to keep up with."

"Yeah, I prefer food to a perfect body myself, but—"

"Whose definition of perfect are you using?" He leaned a little closer, covering her hand with his free one. "You're not insecure. You're confident and strong." He was sure of it. He saw how she handled herself at the apartment with the hitman. And he could picture her slaying it in court as well. "But someone got to you. Someone somehow made you feel like you're less than, at some point. Sometimes I see the vulnerability. I see what he or she did to you."

"I was engaged," the admission came quick. A deep, almost painful sounding breath followed as if she were reliving a memory or letting one go. "He's a lawyer, and I met him at a conference. We tried the long-distance thing since he lived in London." She pulled her hand from his knee and gripped the blanket, pulling it back around her body. "But I couldn't give him what he wanted, and so he broke things off almost two years ago."

There had to be more to her story, but he wouldn't press.

"Sounds like an asshole to me." He brought the rim of the bottle to his lips and swallowed, trying to cool off the flame of anger burning up the center of his body. There was a fizzy after-kick he wasn't used to in his beers, but he drank it anyway. "He's why you're not looking to settle down?"

She deserved way more than her wanker ex could ever give her, that was for sure.

"With my track record, can you blame me?" She reached for her wine and finished it in one long swallow.

"At least the guy from last year got what he—"

"A bullet might be a bit extreme."

"More like too generous. Anyone who hurts you should have a fate worse than death." And he meant every damn word.

She grew quiet, her lashes lowering as if considering his words. "I, uh, remembered something from our night in Vegas." She set the empty glass down.

He arched a brow. "Oh, yeah?"

"You were kissing me in the hall near the hotel room door, and then you pulled back and said, 'You're nothing like her, are you?'" She paused for a moment. "Your ex, right?"

A stone dropped in his stomach. Skipping a million times. He leaned back and rested his beer bottle on his thigh, his eyes on the fire. "Melissa and I had been dating since high school. She knew all I'd ever wanted was to join the Navy. She didn't like the idea, but she said she supported me and would move to the States."

He touched the beer bottle to his forehead, needing to cool off even though it wasn't warm out.

"But she didn't?"

"She kept putting the move off while I was in BUD/S. She started acting distant."

Emily took his hand and squeezed.

Hell Week. It was hell in more ways than one. It was the first time he truly felt her pulling away. Or maybe it was him who'd drifted? He couldn't be sure. But memories of Melissa had begun to fade while he focused on the drive to complete his training and become a SEAL.

"She asked me if I had to make a choice between the SEALs and her which would I choose. I said her, of course. She never actually asked me to choose, though." He cleared his throat. "I ignored the warning signs on my first deployment, and after I rotated back home—I thought maybe she'd finally move to the base once we were married. I thought things would go back to normal between us." He set his beer on the table and stared at their clasped hands atop his left thigh. "I never thought she'd stand me up at the altar."

He faked a laugh because what else could he do?

"For a guy who pays attention to details I really dropped the ball, huh?"

"I'm so sorry." She pulled her hand free of his and placed her palm on his cheek, and he turned into her touch to look at her eyes.

"Don't be. Everything happens for a reason. And it probably really is my fault because I'm pretty sure I lied to her. I don't think I would've chosen her if she'd actually given me the ultimatum to choose between the teams and her. So, I guess she was right to leave me."

"You don't ask someone you love to make that choice. It's not fair."

"My family blamed me for the split. Blamed me for losing her. But being a SEAL was all I'd ever wanted. More than anything. More than her." It was the first time he'd said the words aloud. Spoken the truth.

"Then maybe she wasn't the love of your life." She let go

of his face, and he missed her touch. "Maybe being a SEAL is."

His job, the missions, his teammates—it was everything to him. And in the last ten or so years he hadn't thought he needed more. Better for his focus anyway.

"What happened next?"

"After we broke up, I went to sniper school, and when I nearly got booted for missing a shot—I realized I had no choice but to move on." An image of Brandon rose in his mind, but the anger he'd experienced whenever he thought of him and Melissa together over the last several years didn't feel quite as heavy right now. "My brother didn't have the balls to tell me he'd started dating my ex. I found out myself when I went home to visit. I decided to go tactical on his ass and breach his place to surprise him."

"Oh, no."

He nodded. "They were on his couch in the dark having sex when I dropped in."

Her lips twisted into a scowl, the first he'd ever really seen her wear.

"Brandon says nothing happened between them while we were together, and even if that's true, he's my brother . . . But he says I chose the Navy over her, and so, I never deserved her."

"How is that right? How can your family side with him?" She shook her head. "Shit, I'm sorry. It's not my business, but it just pisses me off."

He thought back to Melissa standing on his grandfather's porch, which seemed like an eternity ago. "I'm going to be an uncle. Brandon flew to Virginia to let me know."

"That's why you showed up to my place drunk that night?"

"Yeah, sorry about that."

She reached for his face again, her cold palm heaven against his warm skin. "And now you and I are married, and—"

"And you'll be leaving, too." He shifted out of her reach, stood, and moved back to the railing. He linked his hands together behind his neck and tried to focus on the beauty of the sky Emily had been so enthralled with before.

"Liam." Her hand splayed on his back over the fleece fabric of his jacket. "Look at me."

He lowered his arms to his sides but didn't turn. "I don't think I should."

"Why not?"

His chest tightened. Hell, it burned.

"Please."

"I'm too scared to look at you."

"Scared? What could you be scared of? You're a hero. A warrior."

He slowly maneuvered around to face her, his chest rising and falling as he struggled to pace his breathing. Wanting nothing more than to take her into his arms and be with her.

"You make me feel shit I haven't felt in a long time." His nostrils flared. "You make me wonder if . . ." He let go of his words because voicing what he wanted wouldn't be fair to her. He knew how it'd end with them. How it had to end.

She placed her hands atop his forearms over his coat and held on to him. "Your brother showed up. Melissa's pregnant. And now there's this eight-year-old kid who has entrusted her life to you, and so, you're confused." Her lips pressed into a hard line before she added, "It's not me."

He stroked her cheek with the pad of his thumb. "There it is again."

"What?"

"That brush of insecurity courtesy of your ex-fiancé."

God, he wanted to kill him for ever thinking it was okay to hurt her. Emotional pain often left far more damage than the physical. Guess he knew that firsthand. "But, uh, what makes you think *you're* not the reason why I'm so fucked up right now?"

A tiny smile skirted her lips. "When you put it like that . . ."

He brought his hands to his face and slowly dragged them down. "I didn't mean for it to sound like that."

She shrugged. "I'm not your type, remember?"

"Because I can't let myself feel this way, because I've done my best not to feel this way since—"

"She broke your heart?"

"No. Since I chose the Navy over her." He turned back toward the Andes Mountains. "I don't want to hurt someone because of the choices I make."

"Or get hurt, you mean. Casual sex is much safer. I get it."

He cursed under his breath and forced himself to face her again. "What happened in Vegas, there was nothing casual about that night." And that was the problem.

"Yeah, well, I'll have to take your word for it."

He rested a fist beneath her chin, and she wrapped her hand around his wrist. They remained quiet for minutes. Eyes simply locked.

It was almost as if someone hit the fast-forward button on his life, and he was trying to catch up to the speed. To figure out what he was feeling right now.

"This song is screwing with my head," she said, breaking the silence. Her entire body gently swayed back and forth to the music, and her eyes dropped closed. "Music like this makes me feel everything. Makes me want things."

"Define 'things,'" he said as his gaze zeroed in on her

mouth. He wanted to suck her bottom lip and pull it between his teeth. When she didn't answer, he couldn't help but blurt, "I take back what I said in the car the other day."

"About what?" She opened her eyes.

"Blindfolding you with your T-shirt," he said, recognizing the deep timbre of his own voice, the desire flowing through. "I'd want to look you in the eyes while we make love." *Make love?* What was he saying?

She pushed up on her toes, bringing her face closer to his like an invitation to kiss. And hell, he took it. His mouth slanted over hers.

He matched her almost light, feathery kisses, then he demanded her lips to part, to make way for his tongue.

Kissing her was better than taking the perfect shot. Sweeter than riding the perfect wave back home with the sun hitting his back.

Her kiss. Her touch. It was everything. Innocence masking some of the X-rated things he wanted to do with her.

"Is anyone watching us?" she murmured against his lips.

"Probably everyone."

"I meant bad people."

He reluctantly stepped back. "No, we're good, but let's get the hell out of here, anyway."

CHAPTER TWENTY

"YOU WANT SOMETHING TO DRINK?"

That organ in her chest—it was beating harder and faster than the moment she took a life back at her apartment on Friday. Being alone with Liam and the anticipation of what was to come was like the tantalizing promise of rain on a hot and sticky summer day. The cool taste of a better tomorrow after a shit day in court.

She wanted him. Needed him more than that rain or a win on a case.

"You know how we get when we drink together." A tiny smile met her lips as she unzipped her boots and tossed them.

He removed his black fleece jacket and knelt in front of the mini-bar and opened the fridge. She had a weakness for a man in well-worn jeans, and damn did he wear them well.

She resisted the urge to angle her head and study his backside. Well, not too much, at least.

"Yeah, but I'm thinking we might need something to—"

"Keep our hearts from leaping out of our chests?" She got rid of her leather jacket and the wig next. "Maybe I like the fast-paced beats." She freed the bobby pins and shook out her mass of hair so it dropped over her shoulders and to her chest.

He stood but didn't face her. His hands went to his hips, and he dropped his head. "You should know something."

Oh, God. "What?"

"I want you," he said in a husky voice. A voice that said he was hanging on the edge of his need the same as her.

But?

"I'm worried tonight won't be enough for me." He slowly turned, his chest expanding as he filled his lungs with air.

Her lips parted but her voice was gone. It was trapped inside the little jar she saved her father's air kisses in when she was a kid—the kisses he used to send to her over the phone whenever he'd been deployed.

She'd saved them all. Placed those air kisses in that glass jar, a jar she still had tucked into the drawer in her nightstand by her bed.

"I've never been nervous about sex." Both palms went together and his fingers steepled beneath his chin as he studied her. The blue rim of his eyes absorbed some of the green, taking over.

"Why are you nervous?" she asked, thankful she found her voice again.

He let his arms fall to his sides. "Because it's not just about sex." He paused, his voice deeper this time when he spoke. "It won't be just sex with you."

She stepped closer and placed a palm to his chest, discovering his heartbeat matched her own. Roller-coaster intense. "What will it be?" Her words were whisper light.

"I'm not sure, but I don't know if we can . . ." He hissed, his warm breath touching her. "All I know is that I want to kiss you right now, but I'm afraid I'm never going to want to stop." He wet his lips, his eyes falling to her mouth. "You don't want anything serious, and I don't . . . *didn't*—shit, I don't know."

"I want you," she admitted, even though a cruel pain gathered, pressing against her breastbone, "but there are things you don't know about me. We both have bag—"

He cut her off with his mouth, and she gave in to him. Surrendered to her desire. To her need. To the rain. The wins in court. The air kisses. He was everything to her at that moment. He was what was right and good in the world.

She kissed him back, allowing him to seal his lips to hers, to suck her into the vortex of his universe where she could stay forever.

He guided her legs around his hips, and he walked them backward and to the bedroom. He shouldered open the door without losing hold of her.

"No baggage, then. Not tonight, at least," he said against her mouth before releasing his hold of her, and her feet found the carpet.

"Okay."

His fingers threaded through her hair.

"Make love to me like this is our first time."

"So . . . all the sweet spots of yours I remember," he said while his free hand worked at the button of her jeans, "I should forget?" His hand slid beneath the waistband of her panties and skimmed down to the V between her legs.

Her nipples hardened almost to the point of pain as desire eclipsed her thoughts. "Maybe you can—"

He stole her words again with his mouth, and he yanked at her jeans and shoved them down to her thighs along with her panties.

Her body collided with his, needing to be closer to him. He palmed her wet center, teasing her with feather-light touches.

She fought the urge to tilt her head back and stare at the ceiling as if the stars were visible instead. Because the way he touched her made her see light—see so far beyond it was as if she could see their future. And he was in it.

"Do you have protection?" Her voice was throaty, the achy throb of desire squeezing her vocal cords. She lifted his shirt and helped him get rid of it, so she could brush her palms over the hard planes of his muscles that he said he had to work hard to achieve.

"Yes, I have something," he said once he relieved himself of all of his clothes and helped her finish getting undressed as well. "I want the lights on." He was at the door and flicking on the switch before she had a chance to protest.

His legs were as muscularly perfect as the rest of him. A tattoo of a trident on the back of his right calf. Another tattoo of a frogman on the back of his left shoulder blade. And then several others colored his right arm. He was a work of art. She'd never been drawn to ink before, but then there'd never been a man like Liam standing naked in front of her either.

"I feel a little exposed right now." She hugged her arms when he faced her.

"You're so beautiful." His gaze roamed from her pink-painted toenails and slowly swept north before meeting her eyes.

She did about three double takes of his impressive length and tried not to clear her throat at the shock of the size. "You're, um, big."

He flashed her a smile. "You really don't remember Vegas, do you?" He ate up the space between them, and she rested her fingers on his abdomen, tracing a line with her index finger down his happy trail before wrapping her hand around his shaft and lightly squeezing.

He groaned at the touch, and she dropped to her knees without a second thought. She had to taste him.

He braced her shoulders as if he might fall as she swallowed as much of him as she could. "Emily," he barked out gruffly. "Fuck."

She cupped his balls with one hand and circled her tongue around his tip. When she deep-throated him; his groan of pleasure was so loud it had her doing it again.

"Stop," he rasped a minute later, gently pushing at her shoulders for her to back away. "I don't want to come yet." He urged her to her feet, took her in his arms, and kissed the hell out of her. Kissed her like it was their first and maybe their last time.

His hand went to her center, and he slid his finger over her slit, rubbing her swollen pussy. He shoved his fingers inside of her. Two. "You're tight."

She clamped down on her back teeth.

"I don't want to hurt you," he said, a throaty touch to his tone. "Last weekend the alcohol probably helped ease—"

"Stole the memories from me." She nipped at his lip. He removed his fingers and palmed her hip. "I can handle you." She brushed her mouth over his. "I can handle everything you give me, I promise."

His hand dipped to the curve of her ass, and he squeezed her flesh so hard it drew a ragged breath from her. "This ass," he growled.

"Hard-earned with my love of Italian food and Oreos," she said with a laugh. "You enjoy the extra padding?"

"It's fucking perfect." He nuzzled his nose against hers.

"I have a virgin ass, by the way." She held a finger between them and closed one eye. "No ideas."

He tipped his head back and let loose a throaty laugh. "You." He flashed her a smile. "I could get used to having you in my arms like . . ." He let go of his words as if he couldn't bring himself to admit what she knew they were both feeling.

"What about your focus?" *Damn it.* She hadn't meant to bring that up right now. The last thing she wanted was for his conscience to steal him from her.

The man had way more layers than he let on; he wasn't some womanizing player. Not even close.

"Right now," he said while brushing the back of his free hand down the column of her throat, "you're all I'm focused on. All I want to be focused on."

"Good answer."

His other hand remained on her ass, and he squeezed again. "Can you turn around so I can properly admire you?"

She slowly whirled the other way, her eyes falling to the bed a foot from where she stood.

"Spread your feet apart and hold your arms above your head. Cross your wrists," he said like a command, and she followed orders and lifted her hands in the air.

She looked to the ceiling when he trailed a palm down her spine before both his palms went to her ass cheeks.

At the feel of his tongue at her center a moment later, and from that angle—her knees buckled, and she nearly lost her balance. "Geometry."

"What?" The word vibrated against her sensitive flesh.

"Snipers are good with angles. Geometry. I guess it comes in handy in more ways than—" A groan left her lips when he darted his tongue between her folds.

He replaced his mouth with his hand. "Only you would bring up math while I have my mouth on your pussy." She heard the smile in his voice.

"Liam," she cried out when his tongue returned between

her legs, and she did her best to remain standing with her arms above her head.

"I think you're warming up for me." He lightly bit at the flesh near her hip and kissed his way up her back as he rose, then he reached around for her stomach and spun her to face him. "Keep your arms up."

He smoothed his fingers from her wrists down to the soft interior part of her arm, tickling her, and he leaned in and sucked at her nipple.

She bucked, a desperate frenzied need for him to fill her etched a hard shot of desire through her body, and she clenched her teeth, clinging to the hope he'd ease the ache soon.

He stood and slung her arms around his neck. "Do you want me?"

"Yes, please," she cried, not even embarrassed by the plea in her tone.

He left her to retrieve a condom and rolled it over his length, and she positioned herself on the bed, her back flat.

He climbed on top of her and kissed her mouth before whispering, "I want you so much. I'll try to be gentle." He positioned his tip at the center. "You sure you're ready?"

"More than ever."

As he slowly entered her, stretching her, she clutched at the comforter on each side.

"You okay?" he asked, his voice tender. Caring.

"Please. I need you." Their eyes remained locked as he thrust inside of her in one fast movement.

He reached for her hands at the sides of her head and laced his fingers with hers. The muscles in his arms flexed as he held his weight above her, their palms clasped tightly.

She lifted her hips to try and take all of him, matching his pace with her own movements, arching her body, so her slit rubbed against him in the process, creating even more mind-numbing friction as they made love.

He was strong and gorgeous. There was no denying that. But his soul . . . it was so beautiful it was almost blinding.

"Emily, stay with me." He kissed her, pulling her back to the moment. She'd let her mind distract her, and he saw it. Knew it. No man had ever been so in touch with her thoughts and her needs before.

"I'm here," she said against his mouth.

She was on the cusp of letting go, of giving in to her orgasm, even though she didn't want to yet. She wanted him inside of her for as long as possible.

"I've got you," he whispered as they continued to move together as one. "I won't let you go."

* * *

HE'D MADE LOVE TO HER IN THE SHOWER NEXT. AND THEN UP against the wall. He'd said he wanted to remind her of their first time together in Vegas, and apparently—they'd been naughty that night.

"I've had so many orgasms I'm beginning to lose feeling south of the border." She bent her knees in the massive soaking tub and leaned against his chest as he wrapped his arms around her.

She dropped her head back to rest on his shoulder, her hair swept atop her head in a messy bun. "This is heaven."

His hands wandered to her breasts, which skirted the bubbly water line. "I agree."

"Can we just stay here? Pretend the world isn't so messed up?"

"I would love that."

"But—"

"No buts, let's just pretend for a few more hours that people in my profession aren't necessary in the world." The pad of his thumb caressed her nipple. "Are you tired?"

"Not really, but my body may need a break before you make me swear in three languages again."

"Yeah, I didn't know you spoke French, too," he said with a laugh.

He smoothed a hand over her abdomen beneath the water, but the little touch was a reminder of . . .

"I can't have kids," she quickly admitted, and his hand stilled. "Well, probably not. I, um, have endometriosis. It's pretty bad, and although I have the pain under control, for the most part, there's a chance of infertility." Her body tensed at the memory of being in a hospital gown after the doctor performed a laparoscopic surgery when she was twenty-five to confirm the diagnosis.

"I don't know much about that, but damn it, I hate the idea of you in any kind of pain." He hissed a breath that touched the back of her neck. "Are you sure it didn't hurt when we had sex?"

"No." She glimpsed him from over her shoulder, but his eyes were squeezed closed. "Whether I can have my own children or not, I still want to be a mom. I'll make it happen." She looked straight ahead. "I thought you should know, though."

"Is that why you split? When he found out?"

"I never kept it a secret from him. But when he told his mom I might have fertility issues she freaked out. He broke it off at her insistence."

He kept his hand on her stomach but his thumb moved in circular motions near her belly button. "You're better off without him." He pulled her tighter against him, wrapping his arms around her in an embrace, and the beats of his heart intensified against her back.

"After we split up, I've done my best to keep my heart safe from getting broken," she said, willing her voice not to crack. *I've been waiting for someone . . . maybe someone like you?*

CHAPTER TWENTY-ONE

"You get enough sleep?" Liam pulled a long-sleeved white shirt over his head to pair with his dark denim jeans.

He moved around the bed to where she was sitting upright, holding the comforter to her chest as if sunlight slipping through the cracks in the blinds would turn her to dust. Of course, daylight was never the friendliest to a naked body.

"I slept great. You?"

"I got a few hours, but I had to hop on a call with the team earlier."

"Oh?" she asked as he reached out for her hand.

She let go of the bedding and stood, slipping her hand into his, not caring he could see her naked in what felt like a spotlight.

He tipped his head to the side and eyed her slowly as if calculating geometry in his head again. Maybe he was contemplating a new move to try?

"They, uh, said . . ." He blinked and shifted his focus to her face. "Sorry. Distracted." He tightened his grasp of her hand and pulled her against him so her palms went to his chest.

"Thankfully I have no intention of leaving the room like this, so your focus can remain sharp once we're outside."

His free hand skated down the side of her body and to her ass cheek. "Yeah, this ass—it's mine. So that'd be a negative on the nudity outside of—"

"Yours?" A light laugh helped warm her exposed body.

He captured her bottom lip with his teeth and sucked at it, never letting go of his firm grasp of her. "You object?"

She allowed a tiny and purposeful moan to slip from her mouth while their bodies were pinned to one another. How was she already itching to have sex again when she was so sore? "So, um, what'd your team say again?"

He edged back a touch and brushed her hair behind her shoulder. "Harper's contact will be on overwatch keeping an eye on what goes down when the Spanish authorities arrive at Port Adra Tuesday night."

"That's something. Will it help take down Carballo somehow?"

He released his hold of her. "It depends on the cargo."

"Well, let's hope so. That guy doesn't deserve to be living and breathing. He's killed so many people." She sidestepped him to grab a tee from the chair by the window, feeling the need to be clothed when discussing a mass murderer.

"I promise we'll get him in one way or another," he said as she pulled on her shirt.

And she believed him, especially after he'd admitted last night he basically had a burning desire to rid the world of evil.

She glanced at her hand, remembering the blood she'd spilled the other night. There was no tremble. Not even a slight shake at the memory.

She reached for a pair of white PJ shorts that had never actually made it on last night. "Why don't I feel so bad about what I did to that Lamond guy anymore? How am I moving on so fast?"

He stood in front of her again, tossed the shorts aside, and gathered her hands inside his larger ones. "We all deal with death in our own way. I'll always remember my first kill, but I don't talk about it with anyone outside my team."

"Do you think you should've?"

He shrugged. "I don't know. Maybe."

"You can talk to me, you know."

"And I can be a good listener, too, if you decide you really haven't moved on from what happened like you think."

"Thank you." She went for the chain around her neck and grew frantic at its absence.

"It's on the dresser," he said. "Found it on the floor earlier. I'm sorry, I forgot to tell you."

"Thank you." She clasped her necklace. "What's our cover story today with Maria? We can't tell her we're Heidi and Decker."

"Reporters for the *Washington Post*. We'll tell her we're covering the story about Elaina's abduction."

"You think she'll talk to us?" She peered at him. The light pouring through the partially open blinds bathed him in a heavenly type of glow—he looked like an angel. Like a hero or savior. Of course, he already met that description in her book.

"Let's hope so. I've been known to be convincing when I have to be." He rolled his lips inward and wet them. "You sure you want to come with me?"

"Why, you okay leaving me alone and out of your sight?" Before he could respond, she added, "I'll be fine. I'll be with you."

His lips parted as if he were going to speak, but then his cell began ringing.

"More news?" she asked as he lifted his phone from his pocket and checked the screen.

"Hopefully. It's Jessica."

She moved past him and opened the blinds all the way to allow even more light into the room.

"Hey," Liam answered once he placed Jessica on speaker.

"The CIA managed to get our contract killing duo to talk with a little persuasion," Jessica said. "They provided a phone number for our mystery buyer."

Finally. Her hand landed on her chest, her heartbeat growing more intense as she waited for Jessica to continue.

"We tracked the number to one of those old-fashioned phone booths in London, which, as far as we know, is more of a piece of history than actually used."

"The buyer's in London?" Emily turned to look at Liam.

"Not necessarily. The line still works, but we were rerouted to another number . . . but it'd been disabled."

"Maybe the couple lied," he said.

"No, I don't think so. I checked the history of that phone booth, and there've been no incoming calls to it in three years —not until this past week, at least. It's been ringing off the hook."

"Like hitmen who want a chance at the bounty," Liam said. "But now the line's no longer working. You think they changed the number?"

"No," she replied. "The CIA picked up chatter the buyer placed the bounty on hold until further notice."

"Way to bury the lead," Liam grumbled.

"Why would the bounty be placed on hold? The buyer have a change of heart?" Emily asked.

"Unless someone offered the buyer compelling evidence they have Elaina already," Liam said.

"That's what I'm thinking," Jessica stated. "Lamond texted the video we sent him of Elaina before Jared shot him. It was to an untraceable burner phone, but if we assume Lamond texted the video to Patty, and she then forwarded the evidence to the buyer—"

"The buyer may not know Patty's in custody." Emily's brow pinched as she put the pieces together. "We need to get Patty to talk."

"She's not bending, but keep your fingers crossed," Jessica said. "And good luck with Maria. Call me after."

"Copy that." Liam ended the call and slid his phone back into his pocket.

"How do you handle all of this?" She sat on the bed, her legs painful and numb like the last time she'd attempted a spin class. "The cartel. Contract killers. And some mystery buyer. It's enough to make a juror's head spin if I were to ever bring all of this to the courtroom. But you guys talk like you're deciding what to have for dinner."

"I've been doing this for a long time." He sat next to her and reached for her hand. "And I think it's safe to assume this won't end in a courtroom."

* * *

"You can drop the Spanish." Maria didn't bother to glance Emily's way as she filled her computer bag with folders inside the lecture hall.

Emily shot a quick look at Liam, and he lifted his shoulders. "How'd you know?" She stood on the other side of the podium, waiting for Maria to look at her.

"Your accent. Your Spanish is good, but you're not a

native." Maria slung the strap of her work bag over her shoulder and circled the podium, her hazel eyes moving to Emily's outstretched hand.

"We work for the *Washington Post*." Emily shook her hand. "Could we have a minute of your time?"

"You must be here about Elaina," she replied, her voice so matter-of-fact she wondered if they were even talking to the right woman. "I saw on the news Americans took her."

"No, ma'am, that's a rumor," Liam began, "but we want to help find her." He'd traded in his accent for an American one. A touch Southern, too.

"How can two writers find a kidnapped girl?" She flicked a finger and pointed to the side exit. "If you want to talk, you must walk."

She matched Liam's puzzled look before they trailed after Maria out the exit and into the hall.

"We're hoping to ask you a few questions about what happened if that'd be okay." Emily walked fast, trying to keep up as Maria's heels clicked along the wood floors in the now-empty hallway.

"In my office then," she said with a sigh.

She couldn't wrap her head around the woman's attitude. Maria had no clue Elaina was safe, and so . . . was she somehow part of the kidnapping?

"I'm not coldhearted," she said once they were alone in her office. "I do care. I know what you're thinking." Maria motioned for them to sit in the blue velvet chairs before her desk. "But after losing my best friend, and now her daughter, I feel a bit numb." She sat at her desk. "Numbness is the only way I can handle what has happened to Elaina—at what I did to cause her kidnapping."

Emily straightened in the chair. "What?" She looked over at Liam, and the familiar angry tic in his jaw was there.

"What do you mean?" *Did you help Carballo abduct Elaina?*

Maria wrung her hands together and rested them atop the desk. Her hazel eyes flashed Emily's way before swinging toward Liam. "I didn't report what happened to the police, and I probably should have. Elaina might be okay."

"Report what?" Liam stood. His tall, muscular frame dominating the small office as he eyed Maria.

Maria leaned back in her chair, her hands going to her lap. Intimidation? Check.

"I received a call from some man almost three weeks ago, and he offered me a half a million dollars to take Elaina to the airport and put her on a plane."

"Who? Where?" Emily couldn't stop herself from asking.

"He didn't specify, but I said *no*. The man even upped his price to one million. Who offers a person a million dollars for a child?" She kept her eyes downcast. "They threatened to kill my son if I told anyone about this—so you see, it's my fault she's gone. They must've decided to just take her from me."

Liam's shoulders slouched a touch at her words, the anger toward Maria shriveling somewhat.

"It's not your fault." Emily found Maria's eyes. "Can you start from the beginning—from when Elaina came into your care up until her disappearance? Any detail might help."

"Do you need to take notes?" Maria asked.

"I'll remember." Liam sat back down, but he clutched the chair arms so hard they were probably on the verge of snapping off.

Emily returned her focus to Maria. "He has a great memory."

"Sounds like Elaina." She reached for a framed photo on her desk and stared at it. "I've known Elaina's mother, Talia, for years. We have similar research interests in biochemistry and neurology, but she's always been light-years ahead of me. I could never keep up with her mind. How fast she could think through a problem and then solve it." She sighed. "But Elaina," she said while tapping a finger at the picture and smiling, "she's even smarter. Her mind is exquisite. Like a work of art." She repositioned the photo back in its previous place.

Elaina was more than smart, though. Her heart and soul were out of this world. "I bet she's a special kid."

"She is, and Talia realized she might also be able to help with our work."

"Help how?" Liam asked, a bite to his voice.

"Talia and I were working on a project to try and find a way to repair brain activity in regard to memory loss. Talia began to study Elaina, to observe her brain while she engaged in challenging memory exercises, for instance. She believed somewhere inside Elaina was the answer to helping others restore lost memories," she explained, excitement now replacing the somberness of her tone.

"Were you successful?" Emily asked, but the idea of performing tests on Elaina also had her stomach on the verge of a revolt against the bagel she'd had for breakfast.

"The tests were too much for Elaina, so her mother stopped them. But we were on the cusp of something big, I could feel it. After Talia died in the accident, our lab—"

"Did you continue to use Elaina?" Liam was back on his feet, a roar to his voice.

Emily stood and gripped the back of his shirt, trying to get him to sit again, worried he was two seconds from going Hulk on the woman.

"I never supported Talia's decision to use Elaina, so no, I did not resume tests. But I did ask someone to have a look at the data collected with a fresh set of eyes." She looked toward the ceiling, and a flood of shame crossed her face.

"What'd you do?" Emily let go of Liam's shirt, a harsh and defensive anger zipping up her spine.

"I called Hans Zimmermann. He used to be a friend of Talia's. I asked if he could fly down and help. He said *no*, at first, angry at Talia for ending their friendship a while back. But I begged and pleaded, and when I explained more about the project and how we might be able to fulfill Talia's lifelong dream, well, he agreed to come for a weekend. He had a bodyguard with him, though. He said it was because of his job."

"And do you think Hans had something to do with Elaina's abduction?" Emily asked, emotion working in her throat as she imagined Carballo's people ripping her away from her home.

"Well, he's Elaina's father," she rushed out as if hoping to lessen the blow.

"What?" Liam rasped.

"Hans is considered one of the smartest people in the world just like Talia." She flipped open her laptop and powered it on. "They met at The Golden Minds Gala twelve years ago and became friends. The event is still held every year. A collection of the world's brightest minds gather, and it's funded by people with deep pockets. The money is raised to support a youth organization to sponsor gifted children from around the world to advance their studies."

Get to the damn point, she wanted to scream her thoughts. She was hanging on to the edge of control, waiting for Maria to explain how she may have jeopardized Elaina's safety.

"This is Hans." Maria spun her laptop around to show them his picture.

Tall, dark hair like Elaina, same eyes. The resemblance

was there, for sure. But what'd this man have to do with a bounty being placed on Elaina's head?

"The Golden Minds Gala has been held every year in a different city for the last two decades. And the night of the gala in Texas back in twenty ten, Talia got pregnant. She didn't tell Hans about the baby; she didn't think he could ever love a child the way he worshipped his work. And so, after Elaina was born, she moved to Santiago and took a position with the university and avoided Hans from that moment on. Never attended another Golden Minds Gala after that, either. Too worried Hans would discover the truth."

"Did you tell him Elaina was his daughter?" Liam asked, taking a step away from the desk, bumping into the chair behind him.

"No, but when he came to the lab, he met her." She combed her fingers through her jet-black hair as if buying herself some time. "He knew the second he saw her she was his, and I caught him poking her with a needle to draw blood the day after I'd lied about it to him."

"What happened?" The pain magnified as if her ribs were on the verge of cracking.

"He wanted her," she whispered. "And as much as I cared about Talia's wishes—shouldn't a child be with her father?" She lifted her shoulders. "Elaina was a lot for me to handle with all my work and classes. Plus, I'm a single mom."

"Did you even ask Elaina what she wanted?" Liam barked out, the vein throbbing at the side of his neck.

"No, I didn't know how to tell her." Her lashes fluttered. "Hans gave me what I wanted, and I was going to give him what he wanted."

"He was going to finish what Talia started?" she asked in surprise.

"He was smarter than Talia. Than me. It was why I called

him," she admitted. "His work has always revolved around attempting to give a computer the mind of a human but better, and well, his perspective helped." She released a breath. "We start test trials next week." Tears filled her eyes. "Hans didn't have to abduct Elaina, though, so it had to be someone else. Whoever called me asking for her, well, they called the day after Hans flew back to the U.S.," she explained. "It doesn't feel like a coincidence. Maybe my bringing him here somehow—"

"When were you planning on turning Elaina over to Hans?" Liam interrupted.

"He was planning on coming this Saturday for her. He has The Golden Minds Gala in London on Thursday, so he wanted to wait until after."

London? "What'd Hans say when you called to let him know Elaina was taken?"

"He never answered my calls, so I had to leave him a message. But Elaina's abduction made world headlines because of Talia, surely, he knows. Maybe he's trying to find her. I just hope if he does, he wants her because she's his daughter and not just because of her brain."

CHAPTER TWENTY-TWO

"You're back," Elaina whispered in a sleepy voice when Liam entered her room around two in the morning on Tuesday.

"I didn't mean to wake you." He squatted by the bed.

"I'm glad you came to see me. I missed you." Her lids were heavy, and her long lashes fluttered with the weight of exhaustion.

"Missed you, too."

She smiled. "How was Maria?"

His conversation with Maria crashed through his mind like a wrecking ball at Elaina's question.

He tried to force away the stir of emotions rising. "She's okay. Worried about you, though."

"Can I stay with you forever?" Her eyes dropped closed, and he nearly fell back onto his ass at her question.

"Elaina?" he whispered, but when she didn't answer he realized she'd fallen back asleep, saving him from having to disappoint her.

He left the room, quietly closed the door, and found Emily waiting for him out in the hall.

"She okay?" She leaned against the wall with eyes pinned to him.

"You could've come in."

"I wanted to, but—"

"You're becoming attached to her, and it'll be hard to walk away when this is over, right?" At least, that's how he felt. When Maria had divulged the truth about everything back in Chile, he'd been walking a tightrope of control, trying not to fall.

"Elaina must know she has a dad. No way does a kid like Elaina meet Hans at the lab and not put two and two together."

The idea had buzzed around his mind on the flight home, too. "She didn't want us to know."

"Because she doesn't want to live with him."

"Which means I already don't like the fucking guy, but let's focus on getting her out of harm's way right now."

Knox peeked his head outside the makeshift command center. "Hey, we finally have news. You're back just in time."

"Be right there." Once Knox disappeared behind the closed door, Liam reached for Emily's bicep. "I've mapped out the possibilities in my head of what could happen to her, and everything ends the way it should."

"Oh, you see the future?" Her lips twitched into a smile, her dimples popping. Goal achieved.

"I do." He returned her smile with an even broader one, then slid his hand down her forearm to take her hand. "Let's go." He guided her to the control room as if she could somehow get lost.

Jessica, Asher, and Knox were working at the table.

"Where's everyone else?" he asked.

"We've been taking turns sleeping," Knox replied, looking up from his screen.

"You find out if Maria's story checks out?" Liam eyed his teammates.

"Yeah, from what we can tell she told you the truth." Jessica removed her black-rimmed glasses and motioned for Liam and Emily to have a seat. "But I've got bad news," Jessica began, "and then some even shittier news."

"Which should I hear first?" He pulled the seat out for Emily, then sat next to her. He reached for her hand, which had become second nature lately, and focused on Jessica across the table.

"Hans is working on a top-secret project for NORAD out in Colorado," Jessica dropped the metaphorical bomb of the century into the room. "Looks like he landed the gig in January."

"NORAD?" Emily gasped. "As in the North American Aerospace Defense Command? They oversee and defend U.S. and Canadian air space and respond to unauthorized air activity—missiles, nuclear attacks, right?"

Knox nodded. "Hans is a computer engineer and mathematician. German-born but an American citizen now."

Liam had done his research on Hans when they were en route back to West Virginia. Of course, the NORAD part hadn't been disclosed online. It explained why the government sent a bodyguard with him.

"This conversation is going to get worse, isn't it?" Emily asked, and Liam gently squeezed her hand, hoping to reassure her.

Asher stood from his swivel chair and crossed his arms. "The president couldn't go into too much detail because of the classified nature of the project, but all we know is Hans's work involves the field of artificial intelligence."

Liam tried not to squeeze Emily's hand too tight. "Is he still planning on going to that upcoming event?"

"Yeah," Jessica said. "The Golden Minds Gala is being held at a convention center in London Thursday, and he's currently on a plane heading there now."

"Is his bodyguard with him, too?" Emily asked.

"He's less of a bodyguard and more there to ensure Hans doesn't leak intel," Jessica explained.

"Did he have the same detail with him on his trip to Chile?" Emily was in lawyer mode, and Liam couldn't help but smile.

"No. They rotate them." Jessica checked her computer. "The man with Hans for this trip is a former Marine. A stand-up guy."

"So, probably not a threat then," Emily said.

Liam knew what she was getting at. If someone had learned about Elaina as a possible weakness to use against Hans, it had to have happened right after his trip to Chile. "Is Hans's phone tapped?"

"Yeah, but not by the bad guys," Jessica responded. "NORAD has him under full surveillance because of the secrecy of the project. Emails, calls, his mail—everything is monitored."

"Let's just say he can't take a piss without Uncle Sam knowing," Asher added.

"Then who found out Hans has a daughter?" Liam voiced his thoughts. "He only just learned a few weeks ago himself. Regardless, it's the only thing that makes sense to me . . . use his daughter to get to Hans."

"Someone's been keeping tabs on our boy, Hans. Gotta be a friend or colleague he trusts that lives out in Colorado. I doubt NORAD's got a traitor on the inside." Knox braced the table with both palms.

"Not unless someone in NORAD is being blackmailed, the same way Don was, and they're being forced to keep tabs on him," Emily said, and Liam was damn impressed. "If Hans was under surveillance and received a threatening call or whatnot about Elaina, NORAD security would've intercepted that."

"Which means the information and threat were most likely delivered in person." Jessica sat. "Someone who knows the location of the surveillance cameras and how to avoid being seen talking to Hans. The person could've shown Hans a video of Elaina as proof they have her."

"If Maria hadn't brought Hans to Chile, Elaina would still be safe, and none of this would've happened," Emily said under her breath a moment later.

"We don't know that for certain," Jessica said. "And they probably would've found another way to get to Hans."

"And just like Talia, Hans has no other family," Knox noted.

"Family," Asher commented in a low voice, his eyes pinned to the woman he loved. "They're always the easiest target."

"What kind of father goes on a scheduled trip after his daughter goes missing?" Liam slipped his hand free of Emily's, an uncomfortable pain stretching through his chest.

Emily stood. "Hans must've told someone about his daughter when he got back from Chile, someone he trusted."

"But would Hans risk everything for a daughter he just discovered existed?" Knox asked, playing devil's advocate.

Liam thought back to what Maria had said about his work-focused life. "Maybe for her brain he would."

"Whatever these people are after has to be big. Thirteen mill to use Elaina to force Hans's hand isn't chump change." Knox shifted his swivel chair from left to right, clutching the chair arms. "And maybe whatever they need requires Hans to be on-site in Colorado because why not just take out his bodyguard and grab Hans on his field trip to Chile last month?"

"Clearly, someone wants Hans in London. Maybe threaten to kill Elaina if he doesn't go back to NORAD and complete whatever the hell it is they want." Liam's blood heated at the idea, even though his team had already spoiled the buyer's plans by rescuing her.

"They'll put a cap in his ass after. No way do they let Hans live when they're done with him," Knox said.

Liam turned away from the team, and when his eyes fell upon the whiteboard his arms dropped to his sides.

Elaina had drawn a picture of herself flanked by a man and woman holding her hands. And he was pretty sure the people were Emily and himself.

He pressed two fingers to the dull pain blossoming in his right temple.

"I'll do my best to get a list of employees at NORAD who Hans interacts with, but it may not be easy," Knox said, a grim tone to his voice. "We may have to turn that over to POTUS." He leaned back. "I don't want to end up in jail for hacking our nation's air missile defense center."

True. Liam shifted around toward Emily. Her brows were drawn inward. Concern, maybe fear, created bracketed lines along each side of her mouth.

"I'm sure this buyer will be at the event in London," Liam stated. "We need to let Hans know Elaina's safe."

"Does this mean we're going to London?" Emily asked.

We? Shit. How could he let Emily or Elaina out of his line of sight—but what if bringing them also put them in the crossfires of danger?

"Elaina should go with us," Jared announced, and Liam turned to find the spook creeping on them in the now open doorway.

"We might need to prove to Hans that Elaina is safe and with us if we're going to get him to talk," Jared said, edging farther into the room. "I don't like it, but I don't think we have an option. Another video of the kid might not work."

"We're telling Hans we have her then? We're going to approach him?" Emily folded her arms.

"We have to assume Hans is being watched, so we'll need to be careful how we go about it," Jessica replied. "They'll probably wait until the night of the gala to make their move. The place will be crowded. Lots of exits. They'll have him ditch the bodyguard."

"Plus, they're still waiting for Elaina to arrive in London," Knox pointed out. "What happens when they discover Patty can't deliver?"

"I don't know, and I don't want to find out." Liam stabbed at the air. "This needs to end Thursday night. I want the target off Elaina's head."

"I'll see about getting us tickets to the event," Jessica said. "Maybe we can catch a military flight out of Dover to the U.K."

"Not commercial?" Liam asked.

"I don't like flying commercial if Elaina's with us," she answered.

Knox leaned back into his chair and peered at Jessica. "If NORAD has been compromised, how do we know who we can trust over there to alert them to the mole?"

"Rydell will have to tell the general in charge what's going on so they can beef up security," Jessica began, "but until we find out who our suspect is and what they're after, the general will have to keep the information on the DL."

"Plus, whatever Hans is working on, Rydell doesn't want any other nations knowing about it, which means we can't alert the British about the mission," Asher pointed out.

"Unless we have absolutely no choice but to bring them in, it'll be Bravo and Echo Teams only."

"And one spook." Knox jerked a thumb Jared's way.

"You need me," Jared said with a shake of the head.

"Well, I think Owen should come with us, too," Liam added. "We may need a pilot."

"What about Sam?" Emily turned toward him.

"We'll have people from Scott and Scott protect her. We'll make sure she's safe," he told her. "We telling Luke yet?" he asked Jessica.

"I've got to call him. I can't keep him in the dark any longer. Honeymoon or not."

Honeymoons. Weddings.

Now he was focused on thoughts of Vegas and Emily and their night together.

But then Jessica looked straight at him with narrowed eyes as if trying to do some sort of Jedi mind trick on him.

And he was pretty sure he was receiving the message loud and clear: *don't break Emily's heart.*

CHAPTER TWENTY-THREE

"The boys have everything packed and ready to go," Liam said after spotting Jessica still at work on her computer in the command center later that Tuesday morning. "Can't you work while we drive?"

Jessica looked up at him. Dark circles beneath her eyes, two lines darting between her brows. The woman was a machine, but she was a tired one.

"He's right, babe. If we're going to catch the flight out of Dover, we should've hit the road ten minutes ago." Asher swirled a finger in the air, directing her to wrap it up and move out.

"Yeah, well, I think I found something interesting."

"What do you have?" Liam leaned into the doorframe and eyed her, but he was anxious to get back to the SUV where Elaina and Emily were waiting for him. Their Suburban had two built-in TV monitors, and he'd put one on for Elaina to watch during the trip.

After waiting and waiting for Jessica and Asher to leave the bunker, he'd won the short straw to go find them—Wyatt had worried they were "shagging" as he liked to call it.

"Can you give us the rundown while we walk?" He checked his wristwatch. "Those Air Force boys aren't going to wait on a bunch of supposed civilians."

He had no idea what the president told the commanding officer on the flight as to why a CIA officer, nine former Teamguys, one lawyer, and a kid, were catching a ride with them, but as long as they bought the story, that was all that mattered.

"Yeah, okay." Jessica pulled her hair into a messy bun and tucked her laptop under her arm once she was on her feet.

Asher's hand settled on the small of her back as they walked past Liam and into the hall.

"I've been going through the guest list. Looking at the main sponsors for the gala to try and see if our buyer might be connected to the event somehow," she said, a touch of excitement in her tone like she was onto something.

They climbed a set of stairs leading to the exit and Liam locked up before they returned to the land of oxygen and open spaces. He sucked in a breath of the fresh outside air, and the smell of honeysuckle hit him.

"What'd you find out?" He slid on his shades, the late morning sun beating down on his face.

"The main sponsor for this year's gala was Weston Tech. They design microprocessors, next-generation software and such for the U.S. and the U.K. All their products are geared toward intelligence and defense. Computer chips for drones and satellites." Jessica stopped walking to face Asher and Liam. "Early January they won a three-billion-dollar contract with NORAD in a bidding war."

"You said they *were* the main sponsor. What happened?" Liam squared his shoulders, his back muscles pinching together.

"Weston Tech pulled out in April after their factory in

Bristol, England, was burned to the ground." She grabbed her shades off the top of her head and put them on. "This wasn't the first fire, either. Their largest factory in Nottingham went up in flames in February."

"Arson?" Asher asked.

"The police couldn't find evidence of foul play, but the company took a major financial hit, and their stock plummeted. They could even lose their defense contract with England." Jessica tipped her face in the direction of the sunlight as if she were Supergirl drawing energy from the light to recharge. She was more often than not the team's personal hero, though.

"So, after the Bristol fire they bowed out?" Liam glimpsed Emily out of the corner of his eye.

Her back was turned, and she must've been talking to Elaina. She was so good with her. A natural. She'd make a great mom someday, and damn if he wished it could be him to . . .

He shook his head, realizing the danger of such thoughts, and he reset his focus to the mission. "Would anyone benefit from setting those fires?"

"Glad you asked." Jessica handed Liam her phone. "Blackburn Technologies. I need to do some research on them because they're a relatively new player in the defense arena, but not only did they fill in as the platinum sponsor when Weston bailed, they competed with them for the NORAD and British defense contracts."

"Competed but lost." Liam scrolled through the Blackburn company website. "Looks like they're an infant in terms of company years. No way would the U.S. hand over a bid like that to a newbie."

"How many other factories does Weston Tech have?" Asher asked.

"Only one left in Manchester," she said. "Five in the U.S."

Liam handed her phone back, glimpsing Wyatt sticking his arm out the window of his Chevy Tahoe, motioning them to get a move on.

But his mind was spinning with ideas now, and . . . "What if this Blackburn company plans on destroying the Manchester factory, too? And then gearing up to make a move against Weston Tech in the U.S. next?"

"The contract in England's worth seven hundred million," Jessica said. "Couple that with the three billion from NORAD, and yeah, I'd say that puts someone at Blackburn Technologies on a very short list of suspects."

"It'd be crazy," Liam muttered, "but it's the kind of crazy that would make sense as to why someone's after Elaina."

"But if they took over as the main sponsor in April, that's before Hans made his trip to Chile," Asher pointed out. "Before Hans even knew about Elaina."

"Maybe The Golden Minds Gala had been their target date all along since they knew Hans would be there," Liam suggested.

"That brings us back to the issue of why didn't they grab him in Chile while they had the chance," Jessica said with a sigh. "Unless our suspect wanted to be at the gala for another reason."

"Build up their rep and name brand?" Liam asked. "Street cred for the work they're doing?"

"Weston Tech falls short again, and Blackburn Technologies saves the day," Asher added. "That means they'd probably have a backup plan to try and force Hans to do what they want."

"Or maybe they had a different plan, but when they

learned of Elaina they opted to hit Hans where it'd hurt more," Liam grumbled.

Asher jerked his thumb toward the SUVs loaded with their equipment and crew. "But, um, we'll be flying economy if we don't get our asses on the road."

"Right. See you at the base."

"Liam, wait." Jessica wrapped her hand around his forearm. "What are we telling Elaina about her dad?"

"She deserves the truth." Whether Elaina wanted to hear it or not, he supposed.

She let go of him and gave a gentle nod.

He headed to the Suburban and hopped behind the wheel. "Sorry, Jessica was discussing a theory."

"Oh?" Emily turned around in her seat and strapped in.

"How are you doing back there?" he asked Elaina.

"Watching *Teen Titans*. I love it!" She giggled a few seconds later at something from the show, and his heart doubled in size.

"You buckled?" He checked his rearview mirror to make sure since she must've been too engrossed in the show to hear his question.

"So," Emily began, her voice low, "what'd Jessica have to say?"

"Working on the suspect list and motives," he said, not wanting to get too into the details with Elaina in the back seat.

"Do you think this mystery buyer will be at the gala?" Emily asked.

"It's looking that way."

"Revenge, money, or power." She untucked her necklace from her white tee and clutched the charm. "In my experience from the courtroom, those are the main three motivators."

"In my experience, too." He checked on Elaina again in

the mirror. She was squinting while watching the screen, so he dropped his and Emily's visors down to block some of the sunlight that infiltrated their windshield.

"Thank you," a tiny whisper came from the back seat.

"You're welcome, honey." He had to wrestle the words out as he thought about both Emily and Elaina.

Two people he never saw coming . . . and now they were two people he had no idea how he'd ever be able to watch walk away when the time came.

CHAPTER TWENTY-FOUR

Owen practically tackled Emily when he saw her outside the plane at the base in Dover, pulling her in for a bear-hug. "Sam and I have been so damn worried about you!"

"I'm fine, I promise," she said into his chest before he let her go.

"I can't believe I'm saying this, but I'm so relieved you got drunk and married one of my best friends." He gripped her shoulder and gently squeezed, his hazel eyes trained on her face as if in pursuit of an answer to a question he didn't ask. "If Liam hadn't been there that night with you—"

"I'm not going anywhere." She held up a palm. "I've already promised Sam I'll be a godparent whenever you guys have kids, so no way can I skip out on that duty."

Owen's attention skirted off to the side as Liam approached them. "Hey." He pulled him in for a quick one-arm hug. "I guess I owe you congratulations."

Liam toyed with the brim of his black ball cap, a silver trident stitched above the bill off to the side. "Not everyone knows yet."

224

"I assume you're planning on signing some papers when this mission is over?" Owen rocked back in his black boots.

"Uh, yeah," Liam said and his response had goose bumps fluttering across her skin.

"NORAD, huh? I've never been a big fan of too much artificial intelligence." Owen grabbed the aviator sunglasses hanging on his white tee and slipped them on. "I think we ought to stop where we're at with technology and call it a day. I'd prefer to drive my own car and make my meals, thank you very much."

"Yeah, I hear that, brother."

"The military guys we're flying with don't know who you really are, right?" Emily asked when a group of Air Force guys left the hangar and headed for the massive plane.

Liam and Owen exchanged a quick look. "Private contractors," Owen said.

"You think anyone suspects differently?" She couldn't help but worry about the risks they were taking being seen operating by so many outside their team.

"Nah, but the day too many people know the truth is the day I retire," Owen commented. "Anyway, see you on the bird." He patted her shoulder and headed for the plane.

"Same for you?" Would Liam ever give up the life?

"Yeah, but let's hope that's not anytime soon."

"Not ready to give up this world of danger and intrigue yet?"

"Not ready to stop helping people."

She glanced over at one of those people he was helping. Elaina sat atop some stacked boxes in front of Knox near the open cargo door to the plane. They were playing rock-paper-scissors.

She took a second to appreciate the fact Elaina had a chance to do something normal—something kid-like.

"I think I'll hang out with Elaina until we're ready to go." She reached into her pocket and procured a locket Maria had given to Emily before they parted ways in Chile. It'd been Elaina's, a picture of Talia and her inside the locket. Maria had found it on the kitchen floor the day Elaina had been taken.

She started to turn, but Liam caught her arm. "About the it-never-happened—"

"You don't have to explain," she said, ensuring she kept her eyes steady on his face, so she didn't give away the fact the idea of an annulment gutted her, which was insane. "We'll talk later."

She left before he could say more because, honestly, she couldn't handle hearing anymore right now.

"Emily!" Elaina hopped off the box and skipped her way over to Emily, then wrapped her arms around her waist.

"Can we have a minute?" Emily asked Knox.

"Of course."

She crouched in front of Elaina and opened her palm to showcase the necklace. "Maria said you lost this."

Elaina stared with wide eyes at the locket and then slowly reached for it. "The clasp is broken." She smoothed her fingers over the chain. "Can we get it fixed when we go home?"

Home. And where would that be for her when this all ended?

* * *

ASHER, JESSICA, AND A FEW OTHERS FROM THE TEAMS SLEPT in hammocks on the plane, which she'd learned normally did transport equipment like tanks or other vehicles. But today it was mostly Air Force guys, who were strapped into the seats lining the walls on the far end of the plane.

Liam was directly across from where Elaina and Emily sat, chatting with Knox. Knox had Liam cracking up almost every other minute, and Liam would attempt to stifle his laugh by covering his mouth so as not to wake anyone up.

It was a nice sight to see. Him in his element. And happy.

And wow, he was handsome. Plus funny. And smart. Caring. Basically, all of the things.

"Do you love him?" Elaina asked, her voice so small and innocent.

"Oh, um." *Shit.*

"He loves you, but I don't think he knows it yet."

Emily's stomach did a full-on free fall. Were there parachutes on board? Hell, she needed something to catch her. "What?"

"I see things." Elaina lightly shrugged as if it were no big deal. "And I see that."

Her words became trapped inside her mouth, just like at the wedding when the DJ had urged her to dance with Liam. Seeing him in his tux, and then having his eyes and hands on her while they danced had been her undoing long before the tequila.

"We're friends," she forced out.

"I read somewhere that the best relationships start out that way." She squeezed one eye closed. "*Cosmo,* maybe? Or *Vogue.*"

She chuckled. "Well, you're even more well-read than I realized." She waved a finger her way. "Just promise me you don't always follow the advice in those magazines, especially about how to win a guy over or something like that."

She grinned. "Well, like I said, Liam loves you." She

crinkled her nose this time. "He'll figure it out soon enough." She stood. "I'm going to go talk to him now."

And like that, she was off.

Emily leaned back in the uncomfortable seat, completely speechless.

Liam peered her way, and their eyes locked in one of those heart-stopping moments where the world fell away, and silence cocooned them as if they were alone together.

He rested his head against the wall—there were no luxuries in military transport—and he kept his focus on her until Elaina stole his attention.

"Hey," Knox said.

"Swapping places with Elaina?"

"That girl is one of a kind, isn't she?"

She glanced over to see Elaina chatting away, and she was beaming. How could she not? He'd won her over, too, but she was pretty sure Elaina was winning him over even more.

It was hard to believe Maria didn't want to take care of such an incredible child.

"Kids . . . they're stressful," he said. "Having a small life in your hands."

"You have lives in your hands all the time," she pointed out.

"Yeah, but kids, it's a whole other ball game."

True.

"You ever want some little ones?"

A warm whisper of hope touched her chest. "Yeah. You?"

"Oh, I don't know," he said. "I don't want to turn out like my old man."

"That bad, huh? Maybe I shouldn't vote for him," she teased and looked back his way. "He a strict guy?"

"He's a politician," he said in a glib tone. "Need I say more?"

She held an index finger between them and closed one eye. "Got it."

"But he has good intentions, just not when it comes to me."

"He didn't want you joining the teams, did he?" She'd met his dad a few times, and he seemed like a nice guy even though he was uber wealthy. But she'd also experienced how hard it was when her dad and brother were deployed. The worry and stress.

"He hoped I'd become a politician or doctor." His palms went to his thighs atop his khaki cargo pants, and he set his focus toward the plane ceiling as if wrestling with something —some sort of internal struggle, maybe.

"Sounds to me like he should be proud of you."

"He doesn't like how little money we make. Says we shouldn't be putting our lives on the line for pennies. His exact words." A hiss left his parted lips. "We don't do this for the money, though."

"Yeah, well, I can't say I don't agree with the fact our military should be better paid—and treated much better as veterans."

"Maybe he'll do something about it if he becomes president. Or maybe he's all talk." Knox shrugged and looked at her. "We'll see."

"Will he keep you guys around if he takes office?"

"He doesn't know about us, so if he becomes POTUS, I honestly have no idea what he'll do."

"He never served, did he?" she asked.

"Actually, he did. Served in the Iran-Iraq War in the eighties, and I guess his time made him worry—"

"You might get hurt?" she finished.

He scratched his clean-shaven chin and nodded. "Well, I

should let you get some rest, girl. Liam set a hammock up for you if you're interested."

She smiled. "I doubt I can sleep in one of those things."

"Ah, you get used to it. Sometimes they're more comfortable than an empty bed back home," he said, his voice dropping, making her think there was a bit more to his words than that. "Anyway. Goodnight." He left her side, and her attention wandered back to Liam and Elaina. She couldn't hear what they were talking about, but Elaina had his undivided attention, and he was grinning from ear to ear.

He'd make a great father.

Maybe he was busy saving the world, but she hoped he realized he could have it all. He deserved it all.

She thought back to what Elaina said. How could she possibly know what Liam felt for her?

Maybe she'd picked up on the lust. The flirting and charm.

But love? She wasn't sure if either of them were capable of that—were they?

CHAPTER TWENTY-FIVE

It'd been over a year since the team had ridden in a C-17. The familiar hum of the turbofan engines, the low chatter by some of the Air Force boys strapped in near the exit, would've normally lulled him to sleep. But he'd given up on catching any rack time hours ago, his nerves were jammed up with Emily and Elaina on board.

They were asleep in one of the hammocks ten meters away off to the right of where Asher and Jessica were sleeping. Elaina had tucked her little body against Emily's as if she belonged with her. He couldn't imagine what the kid was going through after losing her mother and now this. A damn nightmare. And he hoped they weren't about to walk her straight into a trap when they got to London.

"Hey, you're awake."

"Well, my eyes are open, and I'm sitting upright, so yeah." He looked over at Harper.

"Smart-ass," she said with a grin. "I was making a statement not asking a question." She flicked her wrist, motioning for him to get up. "I have news, and you're the only one not asleep."

He followed her through the maze of stacked cargo away from the military personnel, and she brought him to her temporary workstation. Her laptop was positioned atop three stacked boxes of MREs. "Should I get Jess and Asher?" She fiddled with the mouse on her screen and woke up the monitor.

"Let them get a little more sleep. Once the bird hits the ground they'll be going nonstop."

"Right."

He focused on Harper. "So, what do you have?"

"The Spanish authorities seized Carballo's cargo earlier at the port in Adra. Clearly, Carballo didn't know Elaina could give up the intel."

"What'd the police find on board?"

"Weapons and other explosive devices, but my friend on overwatch saw three suspicious men who'd been waiting at the port before the police raided the ship. They all made a run for it the second the police arrived."

"Tell me they were detained."

"Two guys were gunned down, and one got away. But my friend snagged a photo of the man who took off." She showcased three images on screen.

"The first two are known couriers for the Taliban." His team had known Carballo sold weapons to terrorist organizations in the Middle East, and so two more dead bad guys eliminated was a relief. Of course, it would've been nice to track the pricks back to their bosses, but fewer guns in the hands of terrorists was a win.

"The couriers were the two killed." She pointed to the third man next. "I've been running his image through our software, and I got a match."

He leaned in to view the image of a blond man. Late

twenties or early thirties. His hair shaggy and a bit long—not a military cut but that didn't rule out spec ops.

"Connor Grady's from London with no prior record. Hell, no job listed in the last two years." She tapped at the screen. "I looked through the last few months of the CCTV footage, and I got two more hits on him at that same dock unloading two containers. Once in February and another time this past April."

Liam crossed his arms at the news, hope beating like a drum in his chest.

"And guess what—those were the only two times a ship came from the San Lorenzo port out of Argentina this year, too."

"So, if this Connor guy is connected to our buyer, he would've known Elaina wouldn't be on that ship. But since he went there anyway, that means an arms deal was going down, too." He took a moment to process. "Did he leave a vehicle behind?"

"Yeah. The authorities seized it, but if this guy is a pro I doubt they'll find anything helpful." She held a finger between them. "But I did pick him up on camera buying a train ticket out of Barcelona to London."

"When does he get in? Instead of intercepting him at the station we should follow him and see where he goes. Whether he's working with our buyer or not, he works for someone we need to take down." He glanced at his wristwatch. They had an hour of flight time left.

It'd be three in the morning U.K. time when they arrived, and they'd have a two-hour drive from the Royal Airforce base in Suffolk to London once the bird landed.

Harper scrolled through the train schedule. "He has a layover in Paris before switching trains to London. He gets in at midnight. We'll have time to set something up."

"If we're lucky, he's connected to the buyer, and if not, we'll still take the fucker out." He patted her on the shoulder. "Nice work."

"Thanks." She smiled.

He started to turn but an idea caught in his mind. "You said February and last month?" He faced her again.

"Yeah."

He scratched his chin, already in need of another shave. "I assume Jessica mentioned to you the information about Blackburn Technologies before she fell asleep?"

"Yeah." It only took her a second to catch on to his line of thought, and with a determined nod, she refocused back on her screen and began typing. "February and April . . . you're right. The first Weston Tech fire in Nottingham was one week after Connor received a shipment at the port in Adra. And the second one in Bristol was a few days after Connor was at that port in April."

He tilted the screen up so he could get a better look. "Check every camera in Bristol and Nottingham around the time of the fires. I assume the security footage was destroyed since there were no signs of foul play found, but—"

"If he was in town I'll find out."

"Can you get a detailed list of the cargo seized in the raid earlier? I'd like to know exactly what kind of weapons were sold."

"Like something to burn down factories without evidence of arson being left behind?" She typed at the keys.

"If Blackburn Technologies is behind this, Manchester's probably the next target—a chance to secure the British defense contract," he said, thinking aloud. "Carballo's in South America. The cargo drop sites have been in Spain. If our theory is right, Blackburn's trying to maintain distance from what they're doing. It'd make sense why they wouldn't want to try and grab Elaina themselves. Too risky to have a kidnapping connected to a defense company."

"It's going to take me some time to go through everything, but I'll see what I can come up with." She glanced off to her left, and he followed her gaze to Emily and Elaina's makeshift hammock-bed. "How are you doing with all of this?"

He assumed she was referring to his growing attachment to Emily and Elaina. He wasn't normally so easy to read, but then again Harper wasn't just anyone. She'd been trained by the CIA, same as Jessica.

"Taking it a day at a time," he said, which had always been his motto.

"'The only easy day was yesterday,' right?" she asked, repeating a common SEAL phrase.

"Yeah," he whisper-said, thinking back to the wedding vows in Vegas that felt like light-years ago.

"She makes you happy, I can tell."

"What makes you say that?"

"You have that after-sex glow. Yes, men get it, too. But I don't think it's from sex. Well, not *just* from sex." She smiled. "I don't know you or Emily that well, but from where I'm standing, maybe it wouldn't hurt to fall so hard you hit the ground." She lifted one shoulder. "And you'll know she's the one if she's there to help you get back up."

An unsettling pain hit his chest at the impact of her words, and his gaze flicked to the tattoos on his arm. To the black band on his wrist.

"Yeah," he said under his breath, the throbbing pain worsening, "but what if I hurt her instead?"

CHAPTER TWENTY-SIX

"How many of these places do you have scattered all over the world?" Jared asked when Liam returned from putting Elaina to bed.

Jared did a three-sixty inside their black site location in Loughton, a town in the district of Essex about twenty kilometers northeast of the hotel and convention center in London where The Golden Minds Gala was being held tomorrow night.

It was an old twelve-bedroom bed-and-breakfast that closed down over a decade ago. The team had bought it, fixed it up, and converted the main living space into a command room with a safe off to the side to house their arsenal of weapons.

"Let's just say we've got our bases covered," Asher said.

"Sure you're *just* civilian contractors?" Jared grabbed his duffel bag.

"Well-paid ones," Wyatt answered with a wink.

Jared had asked the same question en route from the base to the B&B when Harper filled everyone in on what she'd discovered about the shipment from Carballo and their mystery man Connor Grady. Guess he wasn't done questioning them, yet.

Liam had a feeling working with Jared was going to end badly. Or worse, maybe the president would suggest Jared join their team. And that'd be a hard *no* from Liam.

"We use this place a lot," Asher said, "so the bedrooms should be good enough to sleep in. Pick any on the third floor," he directed his comment to Jared. "Everyone else, get some rack time. Sun is up in two, but I'm feeling generous—take four hours."

A couple of the guys rolled their eyes and muttered curses under their breaths.

"Oh, come on, you slept on the plane." Asher waved them off. "I'm about to drop the four hours back to two."

"Not all of us have the pleasure of getting shagged while on ops to cheer us up," Wyatt shot back.

"Screw you," Jessica said with a laugh.

"Pretty sure the big guy would murder me if I did." Wyatt kissed the air Asher's way.

"It's a bit early—or maybe late—for this, isn't it?" Emily flashed a smile at Jessica.

"These guys are nonstop. You'll get used to it." Jessica spoke as if Emily would always be around. And it killed him to know she wouldn't be. That she *couldn't* be.

"What's Luke's ETA?" he asked Jessica once the room cleared out save for a few of them.

"He'll be arriving tomorrow morning," she replied. "He just brought Eva back to New York."

Back to his daughter. Sometimes it was hard for Liam to believe Luke had a baby girl.

"You ready for bed?" he asked Emily. "You can sleep in the room connecting to Elaina's if you'd like to."

He grabbed her bag in one hand and his duffel in the other

and moved down the hall and to the back set of stairs, each old, creaky wooden step moaning.

"I'll stay in the room across the hall." He stepped inside her room and flicked on the light. "New sheets are in the closet. The ones on the bed have probably collected dust."

"Thanks for the heads-up." A brief smile crossed her face.

He dropped her bag on the chair off to the side of her bed and came up before her. "You can obviously sleep for more than four hours, you know."

"I rested on the plane."

"With Elaina," he added, going back to the visual in his head.

"True. I don't think either of us slept all that well given we were basically swaddled in a big net."

He chuckled, but when she didn't say more, he found himself simply staring at her full lips, envisioning what he wanted to do. What he wished he could do.

A soft brush of their lips.

A gentle flick of their tongues.

Then lose total control and claim her mouth completely.

"You okay?"

"Of course," he answered, but a hint of desire probably rattled loose in his tone when he'd spoken. "Are you?"

"I'm trying to be." She blinked a few times, her nerves showing.

"This life is—"

"Meaningful," she cut him off.

That word pinged around in his head, playing on repeat, masking the sound of Elaina padding into the room.

She'd changed into a long-sleeved unicorn top with matching pink pajama bottoms before they'd left the base. Her PJs served as a reminder of how young she was—even if she acted way beyond her years.

"I had a bad dream."

Emily crossed the bedroom to get to her and wrapped a hand over her wrist. "Sorry, sweetie. Can we get you something?"

"I'm kind of hungry."

Liam glanced at his bag. "I have something." He motioned for Elaina to have a seat on the bed, and Emily sat next to her, wrapping an arm around Elaina's shoulder like it was the most natural thing in the world to do.

He lowered to the floor, unzipped his bag, and grabbed Oreos. He stood and faced them. "I picked them up at the store when we filled up for gas on our way here." He peeled the top flap down to expose the rows of cookies and saw Elaina's face light up. "I don't have milk, though."

"That's okay." Elaina waved a dismissive hand. "The cookies are perfect."

He sat on the other side of Elaina on the queen-sized bed, the color of the bedspread matching her PJs. "If you twist the Oreo just right you have a fifty-fifty chance of guessing which side of the cookie the cream will end up on." He handed out the cookies.

"Actually, I'm ninety-two percent accurate in my guesses. Only eight out of every hundred times I've been incorrect." Elaina stared at the cookie. "Top side," she said and twisted the two halves.

Emily clapped her hands together. "You're right."

The kid was a genius. An adorable genius.

"Mm. Good." Elaina finished chewing then licked a crumb from her lip and focused on Liam's arms. Or more so on his inked right arm. "I like the artwork. Do you have more pictures I can't see?"

"Yup." He shoved up his pant leg to show a trident on the back of his calf muscle, then stood and shifted the material of his black tee to expose the skeleton frog tatt on his back shoulder. "I sketched this frog when I was about your age," he said when sitting back down.

"Navy SEAL, right?" Elaina asked.

He nodded. "I knew at a young age what I wanted to be when I grew up. What about you? Do you know?"

"Maybe an astronaut. But if I can I'd like to help people. Maybe be a world leader. We'll see." She shrugged.

Liam blinked a few times and caught Emily's eyes from over Elaina's head, seeing she shared the same surprised look. "I bet you'll do that someday. No doubt in my mind."

"Thanks." She grabbed another cookie from the package on his lap. "Are the pictures on your arm special?"

He skimmed a hand over the different images there. "I used to get a new tattoo every time I came home from being deployed."

"Because you survived?" she asked, her voice so full of innocence, and yet, she somehow understood the world. The problems with it.

For the people who didn't survive, but he didn't want to say that. "Sort of."

"I like the lion. It's bright and colorful. Very fierce." She put a hand in the air like a claw and growled, which had both Emily and Liam chuckling.

"I want to be strong like you and Emily when I grow up."

His heart nearly pressed against his breastbone as it pumped harder. "You already are, sweetie."

"And what do you do, Emily?"

"Lawyer." Emily crinkled her nose. "Not nearly as exciting."

"So, he catches the bad guys, and you make sure they stay behind bars." She looked left and right, back and forth between the two of them. "You make a great team."

"We don't normally work together," Emily admitted in a soft voice. "You brought us together actually."

"Oh. Well, will you two get married?"

How could he say that they already were, but it'd been an accident?

"That's okay. You don't need to answer. I know what you're thinking." Elaina stood. "I should go to sleep now. Can you take me? You sing better than Liam." She glanced at him. "No offense."

He held a palm in the air and grinned. "None taken."

Once the door was closed, he set the cookies on the nightstand, grabbed his bag, and went to his room and into the en suite to change and wash up.

After splashing water on his face and toweling his skin dry, he caught sight of Emily in the vanity mirror standing behind him.

"That was quick."

"She's burnt out." She leaned against the doorframe, her arms resting casually at her sides. "We have to talk to her about her dad, but I have no clue how to begin that conversation."

"I'm not looking forward to it." He tossed the towel and faced her. Her eyes moved over his inked arm like she was inventorying the designs.

"The tattoos," she whispered. "They represent people you lost, don't they?"

All he could do was nod. It wasn't something he talked about. Barely even with his brothers on the teams.

"That black rubber band you're wearing, I've seen Owen wear it before. Asher, too. But never at the same time."

He glanced at his wrist. "I'm not sure if you know, but we lost a guy from our team." He smoothed a finger over the inch-wide band. "Asher replaced Marcus on Bravo. Marcus always wore this, and when he died—well, his wife thought the bracelet should stay with the team. And now we rotate wearing it as a way to keep him with us on ops." His throat tightened. "He'd been the only guy on the team in a relationship before Luke began the domino effect of our brothers falling in love."

"I, uh, didn't know," she answered softly.

"The lion," he began, his own voice catching him by surprise, "I got that tatt after we lost him. Everyone always said he had the heart of a lion."

Her mouth tightened as if she were battling with what to say.

She crossed the space between them and reached for him. Her fingers gently wrapped around his wrist, her bottom lip quivered ever so slightly, and he knew she could feel the climb of his pulse as she held on to him.

Her eyes became the color of rich, glossy mahogany as liquid pooled. "I can't imagine what it must be like to lose someone you love." A tear escaped and slid down her cheek.

His shoulders sloped. His heart squeezed. An almost shaky breath followed. "I hope you never have to know." With his free hand, he brushed the pad of his thumb over a teardrop.

"Liam, I realized something," she said softly, sniffling back her tears. "I've been lying. I thought I was being honest with you, but I haven't been. And I've been lying to myself, too."

Liam went still, his shallow breaths mirroring Emily's, her obvious case of nerves showcased in the clench of her jaw. "What do you mean?"

"I told you I could do casual because in the two years since my ex I've never opened up to a guy. Never felt the need or desire to have anything more than casual."

And God, he didn't want to imagine her with any guy, not even the ones who came before him. But it didn't change the fact he felt like he was getting kicked in the nuts right now.

"I've always been attracted to you, and I hoped it'd go away. I think I subconsciously let Vegas happen—well, the sex part—because I thought it'd help me get you out of my head."

She let go of him, and he resisted the urge to tightly cross his arms to try and get through what she was saying.

"Instead of getting you out of my system, though, I want you with me now more than ever." She brought a hand beneath her nose and held it there as if somehow, she could prevent the tears that brimmed in her eyes. "Deep inside I knew that for me, it could never just be sex between us, and so I lied. I'm so sorry."

He had no idea what to say at this moment.

Admit that he'd fallen for her long before their accidental *I do*, only to break her heart when they'd have to split tomorrow? Or the day after?

He had to sever whatever this was between them sooner than he'd hoped, but God, it gutted him to think about it, let alone actually say or do it.

He covered his eyes with one palm, trying to summon the courage.

He could breach a compound with an unknown number of enemy combatants, take down terrorists, and jump from a plane, all in the same night—but a relationship with Emily and the chance of breaking her heart . . . no. He couldn't take the risk.

Fear. The fucking four letters that could be both the giver and taker of life.

Fear of failure kept his people moving forward. Pushing

to be the best. It motivated them on their darkest day and even on the brink of their brightest hour.

But his fear of hurting her was going to ultimately rob Emily from him—take away the only woman who'd ever made him want more in life than just the teams.

His lungs filled with air, an almost sharp stabbing pain hit his chest until he let the breath go. "I can't be with you," was all he could get out, all he could manage, but it was enough to have her stepping back.

"Is this about what I admitted to you back in Chile?" That slip of insecurity thanks to her ex touched her words, and it slayed him.

"What? God, no." The tension in the back of his neck and shoulders intensified. "You'd be more than enough for me," he said, in as steady a voice as possible.

"Then—"

"But it can't work for us." He roped a hand around the nape of his neck and squeezed, willing the pain to go away. Wishing it could truly fade with time. "I'm sorry," he said and brushed past her. "I'm so damn sorry."

CHAPTER TWENTY-SEVEN

TWO HOURS LATER, JESSICA HANDED LIAM A CUP OF COFFEE when he came into their command center. "You couldn't sleep?"

He sipped the jet-black liquid, just the way he liked it. "Looks like I'm not the only one."

Jessica tipped her chin toward Harper and Knox sitting at a table off to the side of the room near their safe, which was basically a wall with an access panel that opened up to their entire arsenal of weapons and other gadgets. "Harper and Knox have been working for an hour or so."

"We're making progress," Harper announced without looking up from her screen.

"And Owen took off twenty minutes ago to try and secure an off-the-books helo in case we need one on standby," Jessica said.

"Who do we know we can trust for that?" Using a helo in British airspace would be a first for them on an op like this without the backing of the U.S. government for an assist. And since POTUS didn't want the British government knowing about the op unless absolutely necessary—who the hell would they ask?

When Jessica's gaze darted Knox's way, as if she were uncomfortable with answering the question, well, enough said. "Emily's brother's tactical security company, right?"

"I know and trust them," Harper spoke up when Jessica remained silent. "When I was at the CIA we partnered with their agency on a couple off-the-books ops."

"Weren't all your ops off-the-books?" Knox smiled.

Harper leaned to the side and got him with a playful elbow to the ribs. "Anyway," she continued. "Most of the crew at the company in the U.K. is former MI6. They can get us access to helos."

"I trust them, but—" Liam began.

"They'll be our contingency plan. If we don't need to borrow a chopper or a drone for ISR, we won't," Jessica said.

"They can get us eyes in the sky, too?" He had to admit that'd be a hard offer to pass up.

Jessica nodded. "Owen's not mentioning Emily's involvement. This won't get back to her brother, either. They're on a need-to-know basis for now, and they're under the assumption we're private contractors—same as them."

The idea still made him nervous.

"We need British support in case things go south, too. And if the factory in Manchester is a potential target it'd be nice to have their help if we get into a jam," Harper added.

"Yeah, okay," Liam reluctantly gave in.

A.J. strode into the room a beat later wearing only his American flag boxers and cowboy boots, distracting everyone's focus. "Morning, ladies and gents."

"About time you got your ass up," Knox said with a laugh.

"You said if I got up there'd be two smoking hot women waiting for me in here." A.J.'s Alabama drawl was alive and awake that morning, more prominent than ever. "Clearly your idea of a good time is a little different than mine."

"There *are* two hot women in the room." Knox pointed to Harper and Jessica.

"Jessica's like a sister, and Harper, well, I don't want to scare her off just yet since she's new." A.J. plopped down on the sofa at the center of the room, which faced the drop-down screen on the far-left side wall.

Harper kept her eyes steady on the screen but replied, "Gee, thanks."

Jessica grabbed a pillow and tossed it to his lap. "I don't need to see your morning wood, thank you very much."

"Honey, this is—"

"Nothing I haven't seen before," Jessica said, "because you love to walk around practically naked." She waved a finger in the air. "And call me honey one more time, and I'll drop you on that Alabama ass of yours."

"Like you could."

Liam leaned against one of the white columns in the room and drained half his coffee. He was thankful for the distraction in front of him. It meant he could take a five-minute break from thoughts of Emily.

The look on her face before he left the bathroom . . . he hadn't been able to sleep after that.

"Well, I think better when I'm comfortable," A.J. said.

Wyatt came into the room just in time to join the conversation. "Okay, so next op you go in your skivvies." He spread his palms open. "And what, no hat this morning?"

"Jessica suggested I not wear it, or I won't blend in with you Brits."

Wyatt punched Liam in the shoulder—his morning greeting—then strode past him to get to the coffeepot on the desk near where Harper and Knox worked. "How come you call me a Yank when we're Stateside, but whenever we're across the pond I turn back into a Brit?"

A.J. propped both arms up on each side of him on the couch. "You're both, brother. But you tend to go full-on *Monty Python* whenever you're back home."

Liam almost choked on his coffee.

"I'm gonna go *Monty Python* on your arse in about—"

"It's too early for all of this testosterone." Jessica clapped her hands together.

"I see why you needed another woman on the team." Harper chuckled. "How have you handled this for so long?"

"They grow on you, I guess." Jessica touched her mouth, fighting a smile.

"You know you love us." Wyatt winked.

"Most days," she said. "But now that some of us are here, maybe we can focus and talk about the op?"

Wyatt turned around with his mug in hand. "Maybe we should wait until everyone else wakes up from their beauty sleep?"

"We'll catch them up," Asher said as he came into the room.

"Shouldn't you be kicking his ass or something for strutting around in boxers in front of me?" Jessica teased, elbowing Asher in the side after he planted a kiss on her cheek.

"You made me promise nothing would change on ops just because you and I are—"

"Making so much damn noise," Wyatt began while jerking a thumb over his shoulder in the direction of Asher and Jessica's bedroom, "that none of us could sleep if we'd even wanted to."

"Oh, so you weren't working, you were—"

"Don't finish," Jessica warned Knox. "Let's focus, boys." She grabbed a remote and cast a view of her laptop onto the drop-down screen on the wall. "Jeremiah Davis, Vanessa Blackburn, and Vanessa's ex-husband, Elliott, have won themselves a place at the top of the suspect list."

"I'm familiar with Vanessa from Blackburn Technologies, but are we talking about the same Jeremiah who is one of the ten geniuses invited to the gala tomorrow night?" Liam pushed away from the column at the news.

"He was a last-minute add when someone dropped out," Harper spoke up without looking up from her own screen.

"Why do I feel like this person who dropped out wasn't given much of a choice about it?" Liam asked.

"My thoughts, too," Jessica said. "And guess where Jeremiah works." She folded one arm under the other, propping a fist beneath her chin.

"Weston Tech?" Liam walked past the couch to get closer to the screen, committing every detail of the three suspects to his memory.

Jeremiah looked barely out of college, with long dark hair and brown eyes that were nearly black.

Vanessa was the polar opposite. Mid-forties, maybe. Pin-straight ice-blonde hair with eyes that bordered on paranormal looking—indigo-colored contacts, maybe.

"Jeremiah and Hans don't exactly like each other," Jessica said. "They're both geniuses in the AI space, but they competed for the project at NORAD and, as we know, Hans won, which pissed Jeremiah off. He went to work for Weston Tech shortly after that in January."

"Well, this is getting mighty interesting." A.J. stood and came up next to Liam.

"Keep the pillow with you, or I'll forget my promise to Jessica," Asher said, his brows rising, and Liam was pretty sure he wasn't bullshitting.

A.J. cursed under his breath and grabbed the pillow, holding it in front of his boxers, and Liam did his best not to laugh.

"Are you thinking there's a connection between Jeremiah and Blackburn Technologies?" Liam asked.

"I'm trying to see if I can ID anyone from Blackburn on camera with Jeremiah, but as for Vanessa, she's fairly reclusive. Well, she has been ever since her divorce from Elliott Nelson," she explained. "No one has actually seen her out in public in over a year."

"Elliott Nelson was her husband? As in Nelson Industries? Didn't the guy declare bankruptcy three years ago before going off the grid?" Liam set his empty mug on the coffee table off to his right and folded his arms.

"Yeah, but right before that, he and Vanessa got a divorce, and he basically handed her everything not nailed to the floor." Asher sat at the table on the other side of Harper and opened his laptop. "How often do rich assholes just offer their exes all their money and assets?"

"They do if they know they're about to lose it all," Wyatt pointed out.

"We're thinking the divorce was planned so Vanessa could protect the money for him." Jessica surveyed the team. "And then she used the nine hundred million from the settlement to start up Blackburn Technologies under her maiden name."

"Any idea where Elliott Nelson is now?" Liam looked to Jessica. "Will he be at the event tomorrow? I assume Vanessa will be there since she's the CEO, and her company is the main sponsor?" A.J. asked.

"Two seats have been reserved at Hans's table under the Blackburn Technologies name. That's all I know," she said.

"So, the divorce was basically a scam, and both Vanessa *and* Elliot are pulling the strings?" Liam suggested. "Guilty of the fires at Weston."

"I'm betting not only are they still together, but they're also in bed with Jeremiah," Asher said.

"Don't people know threesomes get you into trouble?" A.J. sat next to Wyatt on the couch again, resting the pillow on his lap.

"All I know is the more and more pieces we put together, the more it looks like Blackburn Technologies is not only gunning for Weston Tech's contracts, but they're hell-bent on doing it no matter the costs," Jessica said.

Asher shifted his focus to Jessica, a smile in his eyes. The man loved her and hard. Liam was happy for them. It was about damn time they got together.

"Any reason why they're targeting Weston Tech in particular?" Knox leaned back in his seat, palms on the table next to his laptop. "I get they're a major player in the defense space, and if Blackburn won the contracts, we're talking billions . . . but it feels almost personal in how they're going about it."

"Any chance Elliott Nelson blames Weston Tech for going bankrupt?" *Insider trading, maybe?*

"Nothing obvious, but that doesn't mean there's not a connection," Harper said.

Liam thought back to Emily's words when they were leaving the safe house yesterday. *Revenge, money, and power.* "It's the trifecta."

"What?" Asher's brows drew together.

"Sorry." Liam blinked and directed his attention Asher's way. "It's not just about money and power. I think Knox is onto something, and I bet revenge is also a motivating factor."

"Maybe for Jeremiah, too, since he lost the gig to Hans," A.J. noted. "They're all working together to take down their enemies for their own personal gains."

Jessica flicked her gaze to Harper. "I'm betting whatever Hans is working on for NORAD is somehow connected to the contract Weston Tech won." She held a palm in the air, her mind clearly working through an idea.

"Sabotage?" Harper followed her line of thought.

"They want the technology supplied by Weston to fail in a big-arse way," Wyatt suggested.

"And Jeremiah might get the job offer with NORAD if Hans is gone." Liam expelled a deep breath at the thought. "Did we find any connections between this guy Connor from the port and Blackburn?"

"Connor Grady doesn't appear to have any connections to them on paper, but I can place him in Nottingham shortly after he was at that port in Adra," Harper said.

"But not in Bristol?" Liam asked.

"No, but . . . just a second." Harper began working fast at the keys and Liam took the chance to refill his coffee, he was going to need it. "Got it."

Jessica went around behind Harper's chair to see her screen. "Jeremiah was at the lab in Bristol a day before the fire."

"I got a list of Carballo's cargo seized by the Spanish," Harper announced. "There's a special type of charge mechanism to set a fast-burning fire some of the Mexican and Colombian cartels have been notorious for using against their competitors. The charge self-destructs after the fire is started and all traces of arson are destroyed. The fires look accidental."

"So, Jeremiah could've placed that charge in Bristol and set it for the next day." Jessica stood tall, her eyes moving across the room to Liam. "If Manchester is their third target, we need to warn them."

"But the shipment was seized, and Connor is on his way back to England empty-handed," Harper reminded her.

"These people will have a backup plan," Asher said. "Knox and I can head to the train station tonight and follow Connor. With any luck, he'll lead us to Vanessa or Elliott before the gala, and we can end this early."

"I don't have either of them on the hotel guest list, but Jeremiah's staying there," Jessica added.

"I assume no residency for Vanessa or Elliott in or around London?" Liam asked.

"Wouldn't that be nice?" Harper's smile dissolved. "But maybe Connor can lead us to them."

"Right now, all of this is circumstantial," Liam said. "Aside from Connor being at the port, we have no hard evidence."

"Which means we need to wait until they grab Hans?"

Liam's body tensed at the sound of Emily's voice, and he turned to find her standing at the base of the stairwell open to the room.

"Maybe," Jessica answered. "We'll see what he knows when we try and talk to him before the event."

Liam still wasn't sure if talking to Hans was the best idea, but they needed to let him know Elaina was safe so he wouldn't attempt to do anything stupid.

"I guess I'm late to the party," she said with a little wave.

"Half the team is asleep," Jessica spoke up when Liam's throat muscles had decided to lock up on him. "No worries."

Emily's hair was damp, so she must've already showered. Dressed in her dark denim jeans, white Chucks, and a light pink V-neck, she strode farther into the room and sat on the other couch, off to Liam's side.

"Forgive A.J.'s attire." Wyatt elbowed A.J. "He was just going to get dressed, right, chap?"

"Damn Brit," A.J. responded with a chuckle then stood, pillow still fixed to the front of his boxers.

"You have twenty minutes to get ready." Jessica approached A.J. "I need you to do a perimeter sweep of the hotel convention center. I want to know every possible way in and out of the place."

"I'll go with him since I don't need to be at the station until close to midnight." Asher stood and stretched his arms above his head and ripped a moan loose from deep in his chest.

"Yeah, that's about how you sounded a few hours ago when you were shagging," Wyatt commented.

"Let's stay on track, guys." A soft blush touched Jessica's cheeks. "We should also get a room at the hotel across the street from the gala for observation."

"Overwatch during the event. Right." Liam finally got his voice to work.

"Yeah, I can have Luke there tomorrow night since I need you and Wyatt at the gala."

"Wait, what?" Wyatt was on his feet with palms in the air. "Don't tell me you're going to ask me to play dress up and put on a monkey suit. I just had to wear one of those things in Vegas."

"And you looked hot." Harper waggled her brows. Yup, she fit right in with them all.

Wyatt snickered and returned his focus to Jessica, a strain in his jaw visible beneath his trimmed beard.

"I think I found two couples on the guest list I can convince to relinquish their tickets, but we'll need legit guests taking their place," she explained.

Wyatt crossed his arms and dropped his head, and Liam had no clue what the hell he was missing right now.

"We can't raise any red flags." Jessica moved to stand in front of Wyatt, but he kept his gaze on the floor. Something sure as hell was wrong.

"We need real people, no time for creating aliases," Asher added when Wyatt still hadn't spoken. "If Blackburn Technologies is behind this, they'll be monitoring the guest list, especially any changes to it."

Now Liam was the one bowing his head. "You want me to buy a ticket under the Evans name, don't you?" His pulse intensified at what he knew Jessica was suggesting. "But I can't go as myself because—"

"Better not to have a known SEAL present at the gala," Jessica said, causing his throat to burn. "You look eerily similar to your older brother."

When Liam turned away from her, his eyes landed on Emily. Her lip went between her teeth as if she could feel the pain of what Jessica was asking of him.

Emily knew the truth about how his brother stabbed him in the back by marrying his ex, but no one else was privy to that particular detail.

Could he really pose as his brother?

"The guests are uber rich," Harper said from behind. "Your family has a lot of money, I'm guessing?"

He wasn't sure if Harper's question was directed at Wyatt or himself. But since Jessica was asking them both, it meant Wyatt had some well-kept secrets about his previous life, too.

"My family runs a company down in Sydney," Liam said without facing Harper because he couldn't take his eyes off Emily. "It's, uh, worth a lot. Not Bill Gates's kind of money, but yeah, my brother's presence there wouldn't set off any alarm bells."

Liam had hurt Emily, and yet, she still cared about him. She wanted to reach out for him, comfort him—he could see it in her eyes. And he wished he could let her.

"Will you do it?" Jessica asked, and at the touch of her hand on his back, he swiveled around to face her.

"Anything for the mission, you know that," he said in a low voice.

"Will he need a plus one?" Emily asked, her words like a discharged firearm in his ear. "We're married. It'd be legit," she added. "No need to—"

"Come again?" Wyatt jerked his head up and looked at Liam. He felt Harper's and Knox's eyes on him, too. "Married?"

He turned to the side, catching sight of Emily out of the corner of his eye, and he was certain she was having an oh-shit moment.

"Vegas. Lots of tequila," he offered a half-baked explanation that honestly made him feel like garbage after he'd said it.

"Well, uh, congrats," Wyatt said.

"But, I'm going as Brandon, and Emily doesn't look like his wife." Not even close. No, Emily was far sweeter. Kinder. More stunning in every possible way.

"I need Harper as Wyatt's date, and I need to stay on the cams and comms. It might look more realistic if you show up with a date," Jessica tried to rationalize, but he didn't like the idea of bringing Emily into a possibly dangerous situation, even though there'd be a ton of security at the event.

But his hesitation also had to do with the fact he'd now need to spend time alone with her when they could use distance instead.

"That's to say Wyatt agrees to go." Harper looked to Wyatt, a plea in her eyes. "I can't go solo."

"How can Wyatt go as himself?" Emily asked.

"I changed my name when I got U.S. citizenship before becoming a SEAL." Wyatt's announcement was probably news to everyone. Well, everyone except the team leaders. They'd surely know his background.

Jessica circled Wyatt and reached out to squeeze his bicep. "I'm sorry to ask you this, but—"

"NORAD." He huffed. "I'll do it, but if my family hears I'm in London I'm screwed. And it's bound to get back to them."

"Hopefully this all ends tomorrow night." Jessica offered him a weak, not-so-convincing smile.

"You want to tell us what's up with you?" Liam asked.

Wyatt sat back on the couch and rested his elbows on his thighs. "Wyatt Edward Frederickson the third."

"That's a mouthful of fancy names." Liam smiled, hoping to lighten the mood.

"*Lord* Frederickson the third," he said with a bitter bite to his voice.

"You're nobility?" Harper asked. "Is that still a thing?"

"You and your old man have a falling out?" Asher spoke up when Wyatt remained quiet.

"You could say that." He cracked his neck, irritation spreading across his face at record speed.

"Thank you for doing this," Jessica said when an uncomfortable silence filled the room. "I'll work on adding your names to the list and getting you guys checked into the hotel today." She turned toward Emily. "Can I have a word?"

Liam's stomach dropped, knowing exactly what Jessica planned on talking to her about, and he could only hope Emily would change her mind and stay back at the safe house and away from danger—away from him.

CHAPTER TWENTY-EIGHT

"ARE YOU ABSOLUTELY CERTAIN YOU'RE COMFORTABLE DOING this?" Jessica asked.

There was too much evil in the world, and she'd seen it in the courtroom when battling defendants on behalf of the government, but being on a mission to actually capture the bad guys . . . it took things to a whole new level.

"I want to help." She leaned against the wall by the door in the bedroom she'd slept in. Well, more like attempted to sleep in.

"We could always have Liam bring A.J. as his date," she said with a straight face.

"Uh, yeah, the cowboy and the Aussie? It might make for a great romance book, but it probably won't work for an undercover op."

"He could go alone and tell people his date got sick, I guess."

"But you need as many eyes in there as possible," Emily replied. "Liam needs someone at his side to help distract from the whole special operator look he always has going on, even when he tries to play it down with board shorts and flip-flops"—*thongs*, he'd instructed Alexa to call them, which felt like decades ago and not just last Friday—"he still looks like a SEAL."

Jessica smirked. "Yeah, the guys can't seem to drop that cocksure attitude and bravado, no matter what they wear. Even when Liam is in full charming-guy mode."

He was a charmer, sure, but he was a hell of a lot more than that.

"I can do this. I promise." She lowered her eyes to her toenails, the pink paint starting to chip. She'd need to polish up her look before heading to some swanky event for the rich and famous tomorrow.

"Okay. Thank you." Jessica crossed the room and braced a hand on her shoulder. "We'll keep you safe. Don't worry."

"Can you fill me in on what you know, or is it classified?" The idea of going into a situation without preparation was a bit more than she could handle.

"I'll tell you what I can," she said, then proceeded to give her a quick rundown of the new intel—including the fact her brother's security agency could get roped into all the craziness.

"You promise Jake won't find out?" she asked after processing the information. "My brother would leave his honeymoon if he knew I was here and involved."

"I know how brothers can be."

Yeah, she remembered when Jessica had been in danger —that couldn't have been easy for Luke.

"Jake won't know you're here. I promise."

"Thank you."

"Either Wyatt and Harper, or you and Liam, will talk to Hans tomorrow. You up for that?"

She drew up a clandestine mission checklist in her head, thinking back to shows or movies she'd watched over the years, mentally trying to prepare herself for every possible scenario. "Yeah." *Deep breaths.* "I can do this." She just needed another minute to process it all.

"See you down there when you're ready," Jessica said before heading out, giving her the time she somehow knew she needed.

After a few calming breaths, she finally got her feet to move and went back downstairs to the living room. She was surprised to see cartoons on the drop-down screen on the wall. Elaina sat next to Liam with his arm draped over her shoulder as they watched a show together.

The room had cleared out except for Liam, Elaina, and Jessica. Maybe now was the time to tell Elaina about her dad?

She sat on the other couch, catching Liam's eyes across the room.

His eyes narrowed as he studied her as if memorizing what she looked like so he wouldn't forget. With a memory about on point with Elaina's, she doubted he would.

"I didn't hear you leave your room," she said to Elaina.

"I heard you talking to Miss Jessica, and I didn't want to bother you." She pointed a finger at the screen. "Liam put *Teen Titans* on again. They're heroes like you guys! But they like to relax a bit more than you all probably do."

"We're not heroes." Jessica sat at a table where four laptops were scattered off to the side of the room. "Just normal people."

Yeah, okay.

"Sure," Elaina voiced Emily's thoughts, adding the perfect amount of sarcasm to her tone.

"Emily's going with you tomorrow." Jessica's quick announcement took all the air from the room. "She can go as your, um . . ." Jessica stumbled through her words, which didn't seem like the norm. "Your, uh, mistress," she forced out as if hoping Elaina wouldn't know the meaning of that last word, which was laughable given the kid's intelligence.

"Are you kidding me?" Liam's voice dropped so low you could freeze hell.

Emily's stomach knotted, and her hand fell hard to her lap.

"Emily doesn't look like your brother's wife," Jessica continued. "I checked Melissa's Facebook profile. She just posted a selfie with her baby bump. Congrats on almost becoming an uncle, by the way. You didn't tell me."

"So, you want to suggest I'm cheating on my pregnant wife, is that it?" he asked under his breath, his eyes on the floor.

"It wouldn't be the first time someone cheated on their wife," Jessica said flippantly. "And I checked, no one at the event tomorrow has any connection to your family's business or your brother. And I'll have Emily listed as a plus one only. No name."

He grimaced but muttered, "Fine," and she knew it'd taken a lot for him to give in, even to his boss.

"What about Brandon? What if he posts something online that proves he's not really in London?" Emily asked.

"My brother hasn't gone on Facebook since college. I doubt he'll start now."

"But she raises a good point." Jessica tipped her head in thanks. "I'll set up a program to flag Brandon's online presence from now until the end of the event in case I need to delete it from cyberspace." She grabbed her dark-rimmed frames from the table and slipped them on. "I worked some magic before you got up this morning, and I got your names on a flight manifest out of Sydney. The plane lands at Heathrow at two, so I've scheduled a limo to pick you up from there and take you to the hotel where the gala's being held."

"You were confident I'd say *yes* to this, huh?" Liam removed his arm from Elaina's shoulder and stood.

"Of course." Jessica flashed him a knowing smile.

"Can we have a *Teen Titans* marathon when we get back to the U.S.?" Elaina's out-of-nowhere question had Emily blinking.

"Sure, sweetie," Jessica answered but shot Liam a nervous look.

Emily wasn't so sure if lying to Elaina was the best option because, in truth, she had no idea if they'd all even go back to the U.S. together.

"I couldn't get you guys a seat with Hans, but I did get you a spot at Jeremiah's table." At the mention of Hans's name, Elaina's gaze dropped.

She knew. She had to.

"I'll put together a bag of everything you'll need since you won't be able to come back here before the event," Jessica continued, unaware of Elaina's sudden mood change.

"Will you have our outfits for the gala in there, too?" Emily asked with a small smile.

"It's a black-tie event, so you'll need a suit and a fancy dress. The color scheme is black and white. I'll make sure you have enough cash to go shopping," she replied. "I need Harper's help for a bit longer, and then I'll have her and Wyatt check into the hotel later this evening. We'll discuss strategy tomorrow when we have more to go on."

"Yeah, okay." Liam looked back at Elaina. "We have to go, but you're going to be safe with Jessica."

"I know. And I think Hans—my, uh, *dad*—will probably believe you when you talk to him because he won't want to help the bad people."

And a ton of *holy shits* batted through her mind at Elaina's words, at her admission.

Heat flooded Emily's cheeks as she peered at Liam, the same look of shock, or maybe concern, sweeping across his face.

When Elaina stood and threw her arms around Liam, hugging him tightly, Emily had to press a hand to her mouth to hide the quiver in her lip.

Liam was going to break two hearts, wasn't he?

* * *

LIAM HADN'T SPOKEN TO HER ON THE RIDE TO THE AIRPORT, or while they waited for their limo driver at Heathrow. And he'd chosen to sit in the front as if he needed as much space away from Emily as possible.

So, when he stopped walking and turned to look at her in the lobby of the hotel event center, she'd almost been surprised the man had remembered she was even there.

"Tell them the airline lost your bags," he rushed out. "My brother's mistress wouldn't travel empty-handed."

"Yeah, okay." She glanced at the concierge off to their right, but at the feel of his warm hand curving around her bicep, her eyes went to his extended arm, the muscle popping as he held her even though he barely squeezed.

"Are you sure you're okay with this? It's not too late to back out."

She forced her focus away from the arm porn and to his stunning eyes. The blue ring around the green darkening as he pinned her with his gaze.

She mustered out a quick lie, "I'm fine."

He leaned in and whispered in her ear, "What do you want your name to be?"

Her eyes fell shut at the proximity of his mouth to the shell of her ear, his warm breath there causing an abrupt and inappropriate arousal of her nipples.

"Better to stick with your first name and change only your last. Less confusing," he added, and she forced a nod, then he let go of her.

"Valenca. It's my great-grandfather's last name from my mom's side," she answered in a low voice before heading to the front desk.

"My friend and I would like to check in to our room, please." She pivoted to look Liam's way and held out her open palm. "You have the credit card, honey?" No way was she going to call him Brandon.

"It's already on file."

Right, Jessica wouldn't be able to create the copy of a credit card that fast, she supposed.

Liam looped his arm around her back, his palm going to her hip. "My friend and I," he began, speaking to the man behind the desk, "would prefer no disturbances while we're here. No calls. No room service." He slid a hundred pounds across the desk. "Are we clear?"

The man's dark brown eyes shifted to Emily before he took the money and tucked it discreetly into his pocket. "Understood."

"The airline lost my luggage. Armani." Emily pouted. "Could you be a doll and send a car in about thirty to take us somewhere so I can buy some new things? I can't exactly go to the gala tomorrow night in jeans, now can I?" She exaggerated her Southern accent, playing her role.

"Of course."

"Two beds or one?" she asked once inside the elevator, keeping her eyes steady on the floor and away from the mirrored doors as they ascended, not wanting to look at him right now. Role-playing would only get her so far—she wouldn't be able to pretend away her feelings for this man.

"A king," he answered. "It'd look kind of strange if I asked for two beds."

"Yeah, right," she said as the doors parted.

"I'll stay on the couch, don't worry," he said once they were in their room.

The suite was mostly gray, black, and white. Perfect for her current mood.

He dropped his bag by the door and went to the windows, the clouds hovered above the hotel across the street, threatening rain.

The back of his gray tee creased at the center as his shoulder blades pinched tight. Tension locked and loaded. The man was on the verge of exploding.

"You want to shower before we head out?"

"What?" she whispered, thoughts of their night in Santiago now clinging to her mind.

He drew the black floor-to-ceiling curtains together and faced her. "Shower? The car will be here soon, so you'd have to make it quick."

"I took one earlier."

"Right." He shook his head as if rattled a detail had slipped by him. "Here's what our suspects look like." He crossed the room and handed her his phone. She carefully swiped through the images of the people Jessica had told her about. "I doubt Vanessa or her husband will show up, but if you see anyone let me know. The boys will be positioned around the—"

"I'm sure you'll spot them before I do." Even though she'd learned years ago how to bury her frustration when talking in a courtroom—today wasn't one of those days, and this man wasn't a perjuring trial witness.

"Not if you're distracting me I won't." That sexy husky tone that most likely helped him earn his ladies-man nickname sent a shiver through her and touched her in places it was best not to think about. When he grimaced, she was certain he was kicking his ass for his slip-up.

"I'll do my best not to." Spying the two courtesy water bottles on the desk next to the mini-fridge, she sidestepped him, needing to cool off, but he wrapped a hand around her arm, halting her.

"You being here," he began in a gruff tone, "is all it takes to distract me."

"Sorry." She pivoted to face him again. "Is that why you're so angry with me?"

"You think I'm mad at you?" His brows snapped together as he quickly released her arm.

"Angry I'm a distraction, maybe. That I'm going to the gala tomorrow." She shrugged, trying to come off as casual. Not possible. "Angry you have to impersonate Brandon. I don't know. Just angry, period."

He turned away, his triceps flexing as he raked his hands over his head before cradling the back of his neck.

"I'm sorry you have to pretend to be your brother," she said when he remained quiet. "It can't be easy after how he hurt you."

A solid minute of silence dragged by before he looked at her, his arms falling to his sides.

"My shit mood doesn't have anything to do with him." His chest lifted and fell with a heavy breath. "Emily, I, uh."

When he said her name, the comforting sensation she usually felt was missing. Instead, that one word was delivered like a blow to the head. A hit of reality that could cause her to lose consciousness. Maybe forever.

"Spending more time with you is going to be hard for me, and—"

She held a palm in the air, hoping he'd stop talking, and she was grateful when he followed her silent plea. She couldn't handle excuses as to why he needed to break her heart.

"Finish the mission," she said, fighting to maintain her resolve. "Take down the bad guys. Keep Elaina safe." She bit the words out like a string of commands. "But when this is over, I'm not sure we can be friends."

CHAPTER TWENTY-NINE

HIS TYPICAL NEVER-ENDING STREAM OF THOUGHTS HAD BEEN replaced by a string of curses as they rode in the back of the limo to the next store. They'd hit three others so she could grab new clothes, and their final stop would be to find their outfits for the gala.

She hadn't said a word to him since they left the hotel, and hell, he deserved it. Maybe it was for the better. She was giving him the space he'd need to try and survive being so close to her for the next thirty-plus hours.

But the idea of losing Emily altogether after the op ended was intolerable.

He'd resigned himself to the fact that seeing her with a guy in the future would have him reaching for his pistol, or maybe he'd dust off his Winchester . . . but *never* seeing her again? No, he couldn't entertain the idea, even if he was to blame.

"Jessica told you about your brother's company, right?"

"Yeah," she said without looking his way. "You guys talked about working together just last Friday, and now maybe you will." She lifted one shoulder. "Guess he won't actually be here, but close enough."

"It's not ideal," he said in a low voice since the partition separating them from the driver was partially open. "But it may be a necessity."

"I get it." The emptiness in her tone was like a dagger to his heart.

"We're here," the driver announced, then came around to open the door for Emily, while Liam had to play the part of an ass and allow the guy to circle the limo and open his door next.

"Thanks, mate." He tipped the driver and joined Emily on the footpath. "You sure you don't want to eat first? You didn't eat lunch, and it's going on five."

"I'm good," she answered before they went inside the store. "I should help you pick out a suit. I have a feeling that's not your area of expertise."

"Um." He did a quick survey of the men's area off to the right. "Yeah, okay."

"Can I help you?" a woman asked after he'd spent a few minutes lost in the sea of tuxes and suits while Emily searched as well.

"No, I think I'm all set."

"I could measure you," she offered, her brown eyes traveling over the length of him.

"Nah, I'm okay." He tipped his chin toward Emily not too far away. "I think my wife"—*shit*—"girlfriend can help me." Based on the rise of color in the woman's cheeks, she probably assumed he was a cheating wanker.

"Of course. I'll have one of the girls bring some champagne over to you and your girlfriend as well."

"Got any beer?"

Her eyes widened as if he'd said something absolutely horrible. "No," she said, her voice flat, then she parted ways.

Emily appeared with only one suit in hand a minute later and pointed to the fitting room. "I think this is it. It's a classic."

Black trousers with a matching black blazer and tie, plus a crisp white dress shirt. God, he hated wearing a monkey suit.

He took the suit from her and eyed the size. "How'd you know my digits?"

"I'm good with details, too."

"You expect me to try this on for you?" He cocked a brow as she sat on a black leather bench in front of the single changing room.

"Of course." Her focus was on her clasped palms on her lap, and her downcast look may as well have been a shot to his groin. It hurt like hell seeing her upset, especially knowing he was to blame.

Inside the fitting room, he kicked off his shoes and removed his shirt, but then his attention fixed to the tattoos decorating his arm. The memories of every loss he'd endured raged through his mind.

But Emily's voice brought him back to the present. "It's been five minutes. You forget how to get dressed?"

Five minutes? Was she kidding? He finished dressing, sans blazer, and opened the door. The fit was spot on. The woman knew her stuff.

"Need help with the tie?" She pointed to the tie hanging loose around his neck.

"I'm a SEAL," he said since no one was around. "I know how to tie knots." He fiddled with the black fabric, but after a few frustrating attempts, she pushed his hands out of the way and took over.

His breath hitched when he looked at her standing before him, focused on the task at hand. And now the only knot was in his stomach.

"My dad took my brothers to a lot of black-tie events growing up," he found himself admitting, "but since he knew I didn't want anything to do with the company he never forced me to go."

"That's why you're not used to ties?" A smile touched her lips but only for a second as she stepped back and inspected her handiwork.

"Clip-on bow ties are my default whenever I have to dress like this," he said, unable to take his eyes off her, the music overhead fading into the background.

"Where's the jacket?" She twirled a finger in the air.

"Right." He grabbed it from the room, shrugged it on, and returned.

"Wow, I haven't seen a man wear a suit like that in—well, maybe never," one of the female sales associates commented. "You're one lucky woman."

Emily didn't blink. Hell, she didn't move. She remained staring at him, her eyes trained on his arm, or more specifically, the black band peeping out from beneath the cuff of the blazer as he fidgeted with the sleeves.

"Well, I assume you want it?" the woman asked.

Liam took off the jacket and set it on the chair where Emily had been sitting before. "Yeah, thanks." He undid the knot in his tie, never losing hold of Emily's eyes in the process. He allowed the suffocating device to hang loose while he popped the top two buttons of his shirt.

The woman said something to him, but he had no idea what. He'd been too focused on Emily and the change in how fast his heart pumped with Emily's eyes steady on him. Her lips parted like words hung on the tip of her tongue, but they were too dangerous to share.

"What are you thinking about?" He wanted to reach out and touch her cheek, but he resisted the impulse.

"You," she said, a look of sadness in her eyes.

Her response—more so how she'd said it—nearly knocked him off his feet.

"I'm going to look at dresses."

Diversion from the intensity of the moment. It was normally his specialty, and yet, she'd beat him to it.

"I'll, uh, meet you over there." He reached for the tie and removed it as she walked away.

It took him another solid minute to actually turn and force his feet to move from where they'd become stuck to the floor.

After changing, he handed the suit over to the woman at the front desk and crossed the store to find Emily in the women's section.

"I found a few options."

"Already?" he asked in surprise. "You're my kind of woman." His eyebrows furrowed. "Shopper," he corrected, and she forced on a tiny smile, probably more for his benefit because that was the kind of person she was—caring and compassionate.

"Speed shopping is sort of a super ninja skill of mine." The return of her humor, even if brief, had his pulse skipping back to sky-high.

"Explains how you picked out my suit so fast."

"It does make it easy when there are only three black gowns in the store that are my size."

"Well, you'll look beautiful in all of them." His eyes traveled back to her face, and she was once again wearing that for-his-benefit smile.

Maybe she was used to dealing with assholes in D.C. and

learned to smile her way through it, but he didn't want her to do that with him. "Emily." He reached out and wrapped a hand around her free forearm, but when she took a quick step back, his hand fell.

"I should try these on." She hurried to a fitting room. There were eight to the men's one.

He sat on one of the two white armchairs and placed his face in his palms, trying to get a grip.

I did this to her. It's my bloody fault.

After a few minutes passed, he figured she wouldn't be modeling the dresses for him. Not exactly fair, but then again, maybe he shouldn't see her walk toward him like a damn vision. He'd probably forget to breathe.

"Are you going to show me?" A guy's voice had Liam dropping his hands to his lap.

A man in a pinstripe suit sat in the chair next to him and began fidgeting with the knot of his tie.

"Do you want me flaunting my arse in lingerie to this stranger here?" the woman asked, and before Pinstripe Guy could answer, she kissed him on the cheek and disappeared behind a fitting room door.

"Champagne?" A different woman from earlier approached with two flutes.

"No, thank you," Liam answered, and the other guy shook his head.

"Champagne's only for weddings, right, chap?"

Liam glanced his way. "Uh, yeah." He wasn't in the mood for small talk with some guy who had a faint white mark wrapped around his ring finger.

"My girlfriend might want the champagne, though." He motioned for her to set a glass on the small circular table wedged between the two chairs.

The man retrieved his phone when it began screeching a

pop song for the ringtone. "I've got to step outside and take this, you mind letting her know I'll be right back if she comes out?"

"Yeah, sure." He'd wanted to say no, but he was playing the role of Brandon and not himself, and Brandon wouldn't have the urge to hit Pinstripe Guy just because he assumed the man was a cheater.

Brandon. And great, now he was thinking about another person he wanted to deck. Maybe he'd become so used to the anger it had become an extension of his body. Was it time to forgive and move on?

But when Emily exited her room, all of his thoughts fell away.

She was in a strapless, full-length black gown, embellished with crystals or something glitzy, and her full breasts swelled above the curved top. She'd pulled her hair into a bun, showcasing her long neck, and he wanted to trail his mouth down the line of her throat before gently biting her shoulder blade while he thrust inside of her.

He stood and jammed his hands in his pockets, trying to remember how to speak. "You look . . ." He was at a loss for words. An angel. A vision. *His.*

He let go of his thoughts when he realized her eyes weren't on him but off to his side.

The normally confident air she carried disappeared as a multitude of emotions floated across her face. Time seemed to move in slow motion while she grasped the material at the sides of her dress, lifted the hem slightly, and slowly padded closer to where he now stood.

Of all the times and all the damn places—so help him, if the asshole standing behind him was her ex-fiancé, he'd have to kill the son of a bitch, and that'd put a serious damper on the op.

"Emily? Is that really you?"

And . . . fuck. He hung his head for a brief moment, trying to get a handle on his sudden rage and the twitch in his trigger finger.

"Ryan," Emily said once in front of both of them, and the prick who now had a name was standing alongside Liam now. "It's been a long time."

Of course, they'd run in to her ex on a day like this. Fate had a fucked-up sense of humor.

"Emily." Liam spoke her name like he was dragging in a lungful of air. Begging for the privilege to breathe her oxygen.

He couldn't help himself, when this Ryan guy moved in front of him to get to Emily, he grabbed his arm.

"No." Emily sidestepped Ryan to view Liam. "It's not who you think."

Ryan looked back at Liam, his eyes wider than saucers. He might have also just shit himself.

"He's a friend," Emily explained.

Relieved, Liam let go of Ryan's arm, but the sour pit in his stomach remained. Something was still seriously wrong.

Ryan pulled Emily in for a quick, almost cautious hug. "Does Paul know you're in town?"

"No." Her fingers brushed over her collarbone and to her necklace. "I'd prefer to keep it that way."

Maybe Ryan wasn't her ex, but Paul probably was, and now Liam was back to hating this guy.

"I'm sorry things didn't work out, but he's a momma's boy and—"

"He told you why we split?"

Ryan rushed a hand through his wavy brown hair. "Just that his mom didn't approve, which is bollocks." His attention veered toward Liam, to Liam's clenched fists at his sides.

"How's he doing?" she asked, her voice soft. Still so caring, even though the guy had broken off their engagement and her heart along with it.

"He's married. Baby on the way." His tone was as somber as that of someone delivering bad news.

Liam watched Emily fight to keep her face from dropping, and his heart moved into his throat. Her cheeks flushed as her gaze lowered to the hardwoods.

"It was good seeing you and—" Ryan turned to Liam.

"Her husband," Liam interjected, unable to stop himself. Unable to keep his mouth shut.

"Oh, wow. Congratulations," he said to Emily. "I'm so happy for you."

"We're in a bit of a hurry, so . . ." Liam tipped his head in the direction of the exit. "And don't forget your girlfriend."

"Mindy's here?" Emily asked, but her eyes were glued to Liam as if still stuck on his mention of being her husband.

"No."

"Oh, I'm sorry. You split up?" Her focus went to Ryan, but when he didn't answer, she stepped back.

"We're separated." Based on the slight twitch of Ryan's eyes and how his lips had flattened after he'd spoken, the guy was lying. "I ought to go, though." He sidestepped her and rapped at the fitting room door. "Sure you don't want me to tell Paul you're in town?" he asked, looking over his shoulder at her.

"No." She pointed to the fitting room. "I'm going to change."

"Well, it was good to see you. Freakishly odd. But good," Ryan said before she hurried back to her fitting room.

Liam moved past him to get to Emily. He had to know if she was okay.

He knocked on her door and caught sight of Ryan leaving with the woman he'd come with out of the corner of his eye. "He's gone. Can I come in?"

"Just go away. Please." The angry grit to her voice faded at her last word.

"I can't do that." He shook the door handle. "You know I can breach this door, but if you don't let me in, I might just go after that guy, demand to know where I can find your ex, and proceed to do something really stupid."

And he meant that, too. The only lie was the part that he'd leave Emily alone.

When he tried the door again it was unlocked. He slipped inside, slid the lock, and faced her, willing his heart to slow down.

"Well, do you like it?" Her voice was so damn small. Almost lifeless.

"I more than like it." She was gorgeous, even in her sadness, but he didn't want to talk about the dress. He needed to focus on how she was feeling. No more deflection.

"I'll buy it then." She wouldn't offer her beautiful eyes to let him know if she was truly okay. "I guess seeing Ryan is better than running into Paul." Appearing to be lost in her thoughts, she reached for the side zipper and lowered it.

The strapless dress slipped, and so he quickly stepped closer and shifted her hand away to clutch at the material.

Her breasts peeked over the top of the fabric, free and exposed, and he did his best to focus on the problem at hand and pull her zipper back up.

When he edged back a step, he found her eyes on him, but it was as if she were looking right through him.

And as busy as his mind normally was, it was going

bloody blank at the moment with her standing before him smelling like roses from his parents' estate back in Sydney.

He wanted to breathe her in, to let her wash away the sins and memories of his past. *Mine.* Hell, he wanted her more than even the right to breathe.

She blinked out of her stupor. "I'm out of it. Sorry."

He turned and pressed his fists against the door.

Despite the gravity of the moment, seeing her partial nakedness had served as a reminder of their time in bed together—her moans as he'd sucked and licked her nipples, and he needed to calm his cock down.

"He's having a baby."

Her words worked to reverse the blood flow immediately, and he turned to face her.

"There's not an ounce of love for him left in me. You know that, right?" But before he could answer, she murmured, "It was just bad timing seeing Ryan. But maybe the universe is testing me, huh?" Her hand fell, and her brown eyes, colored with a touch of honey, sought his face.

He wrung his hands together in front of him, his forearms tightening in the process.

This woman was owning him piece by piece regardless of how much he'd tried not to let it happen.

"I need to change out of this dress."

And he needed to do something. To try and take away all of her pain. But he had no idea what to say or how to do it.

"Do you want to talk?"

She looked up at the ceiling. "Not in here, no."

"Right." *What am I thinking? We're in a women's changing room, and she just ran into a reminder of her ex-fiancé.*

"Liam?" She reached for his arm after he'd turned toward the door.

"Yeah?" He glimpsed her from over his shoulder.

"I'm glad you were here with me. I don't think I could've handled that moment alone."

"You're so much stronger than you realize," he said softly and opened the door. "It's me who's weak."

CHAPTER THIRTY

"It's starting to rain." She spread her palms at her sides and closed her eyes, tilting her face to the sky as the heavens opened up on them.

"Is it?" He couldn't rip his focus from her as they stood on the footpath outside the store, waiting for their limo to pull back around to pick them up.

The water glided over her, soaking her hair and shirt, and if he was getting drenched, too, he hadn't noticed. All he could see was her.

"Sir!" the driver hollered while taking the garment bags from him. "You're getting soaked."

He blinked away the drops of rain on his lashes and followed Emily. Once the limo was on the move, she reached for one of her bags from an earlier store they'd hit.

"Can you put the partition up?" she asked the driver, forgetting to maintain her deeper-than-normal Southern accent for her role. "I can't walk through the lobby looking like I was just in a wet T-shirt contest." She motioned for Liam to look out the side window so she could swap tops.

Yeah, he'd prefer her to change and keep her nipples out of everyone else's line of sight. Preferably forever.

When he realized he could see her in the reflection of the tinted window, he closed his eyes.

"Sorry," she said when catching him with an elbow while changing. "Done."

He shifted to face forward, and she nearly caught him with an elbow again, this time in the face, while combing her wet locks with her fingers. "Not much room back here for a limo." He peered at her and attempted a smile.

"Maybe this car is used for people who ride alone or with someone they care about." She grimaced. "I didn't mean it like that."

He took a moment to consider her words before admitting, "I do care about you."

But when she didn't say anything, his thoughts wandered to Australia. To his family. To Brandon.

Maybe it was time to visit home and forgive his brother.

Brandon had been willing to give up absolutely everything for love in a way Liam never could for Melissa.

"I think I should head home after the op is over." He hadn't meant to verbalize his thoughts, but it was too late now.

"Which home?" Her brows lifted. "I don't even know where you live." She crossed her arms as if chilly and gathered her focus to his face.

"I meant I was going to visit Sydney, but I don't actually have a permanent address in the U.S. I sort of bounce from place to place."

"Always on a mission?" she asked softly, even though the partition was up.

"Yeah."

Her eyes shifted down.

"I need to talk to my brother," he said. "My mum wants us to get along, and I think it's time I get over what happened."

He swallowed, hoping to hell he could ward off the emotion, to fix his attention onto something else. And thinking about Emily's ex was all it took to shake away the grip of sadness and redirect his energy toward anger.

"When's your brother's baby due?"

"I don't even know." And he didn't want her to feel the need to make small talk about babies, not after learning about her ex-fiancé's pregnant wife.

She held a palm in the air. "I'm okay. I promise." But when she looked back out the window, her spine bowed.

If she was feeling anything like him right now—then she wasn't even close to being okay.

* * *

He balled both hands, resting them on the vanity counter, trying to collect his thoughts, to get his head on straight before he had to face Emily again.

Steam from his hotter-than-hell shower still wafted around the room and covered the mirror, and he was grateful for the fact he wasn't able to see his reflection.

"Liam, you almost done?" she asked through the door. "I thought I took long showers."

"Sorry." He yanked a towel off the hook on the wall and wrapped it around his hips before opening the door.

She pressed a hand to her eyes and whirled away.

"Emily," he said with a chuckle, allowing every shit thought he'd been harboring to fade at her adorable shyness. "You've seen me naked." Memories of the precious few times he'd seen her naked—or even partially naked—hijacked his brain.

When he'd shown up at her door last Thursday, and she'd opened it clad only in a T-shirt and panties, his heart nearly exploded in his chest. The lazy buzz of alcohol flowing through his veins had been the only thing keeping it from breaking through his breastbone.

And since then, every time he saw her, it was like witnessing the sun setting on the horizon for the first time—a promise of a new day to wipe the slate clean.

"I know, but it's different now. We're supposed to only be friends and—"

"I thought you said we couldn't be friends."

She lowered her hand from her eyes then moved to the other side of the room and separated the curtains. The rain was still crashing hard and heavy.

Her shoulders sagged as if Lady Liberty's scales of justice were tethered to her arms, weighing her down.

"We can't be friends," he admitted. "You're right." They'd moved too far beyond friendship to ever try and step back in time and erase what had happened between them.

She slowly faced him. Her forehead creasing. Her pupils dilating.

He'd hoped he could push her away. Put distance between them to keep her safe, but it wasn't going to be possible, was it? He couldn't even last twenty-four hours.

"You need to understand who I am. Who I really am." *What I'm capable of.* "If that D.C. douche had survived last year, I would've beaten him to a pulp for what he did to you, and I'd only just met you then. So, you can imagine how I felt after we saw your friend back at the store."

She maintained eye contact, never backing down.

"A dozen ways of killing your ex-fiancé popped into my

mind when I thought he was Ryan." He kept his eyes on hers as he strode closer, his forearms tightening. "I even had time to think about how I'd destroy his body after."

"You wouldn't have done that," she said, certainty in her tone, but she gripped the justice charm on her necklace as if seeking protection from his threats of vengeance.

"That's not a wager you'd probably want to make."

His ability to kill was one reason he was afraid to be with her, and the reasons kept stacking like a pile of Jenga blocks, climbing higher and higher—and here he was pulling at a piece. Rocking the tower. Taking a chance. Risking the fall.

"You're not a killer," she whispered, and yet, she backed up against the window.

He crossed the short space between them and propped both palms over her shoulders. "That's my job, darling." The term of endearment was intended to lessen the blow, but maybe he should have just laid out the gruesome realities of his job. He needed her to truly grasp what he was capable of.

"I thought your job was to keep people safe." Her eyes flicked to his right arm, to the tattoos there.

He and his buddy, a former Teamguy, often hit the tattoo parlor together; it'd become sort of a painful ritual for them. A permanent reminder to be worn for the Teamguys they'd lost.

"I'm still a trained killer. The government spent a fortune making sure of it, too." His pulse increased as he stared at her, as he observed the woman who had the ability to flip his entire world if he let her. And God did he want to let her. So damn much.

She squeezed one eye closed and pointed a finger at the nightstand radio playing softly in the background.

He listened to the lyrics, trying to figure out the message she was sending. "Isn't this about a cheater?"

The edges of her lips briefly curved. "I didn't even pay attention to that part."

He continued to listen, trying to decipher her thoughts. "Time being able to heal the pain caused by your ex, then?" And then it hit him. "Or is it about moving on from whatever this thing is between us?"

She rolled her lips inward, her dimples deepening at the movement. Her palm went to his chest. "It's going to take a lot more than time for me to get over you. I guess that's my takeaway from the lyrics and the way the music is making me feel right now."

But he didn't want her to move on. Not anymore.

"Paul wasn't even half the man you are, though, so yeah, I'll need more than just time to get over you," she repeated. "I may not know your middle name, your ring size, or your—"

"I could come home in a box," he cut her off, desperate to stop her, knowing this was a battle he may not win if she kept talking.

She swerved her eyes to his, her stare glossy with unshed tears.

"Could you handle that kind of pain? Because time doesn't heal that," he said, his voice breaking, his own line of sight growing blurry.

He couldn't find the energy to deflect his emotions. Not now. And maybe he didn't want to. He was sick of hiding his feelings for the sake of the job. The missions.

"Time doesn't fucking dent the pain of a loss like that." He fingered the black band on his wrist.

"I know," she cried, her lip trembling. "And I'd never recover from that." Her head bobbed with a shaky nod, and she sniffled. "But it's because I wouldn't want to move on."

He pinched the bridge of his nose, trying to conceal the evidence of emotion in his eyes.

Her hand moved from his chest to his cheek, and he instinctively leaned into her touch. "I wouldn't want you to do that, though. Stay stuck like that." He lowered his arm. "If something ever happened to me, I'd want you to find another chance at love."

Her brows darted inward. "What are you saying?"

"Tell me, okay?" He brought her palm back to his chest and held it there as he struggled to fucking breathe without totally breaking down. "Tell me that you'd let me go. Promise me if we try to make this work and something happens to me —you'll let me go."

"Liam." Her eyes dropped closed, tears cascading down her cheeks. "Please."

"You have to promise me," he said, injecting a resoluteness to his voice he didn't quite feel. "It's the only way I can do this. It's the only way I can try."

She covered her mouth with the back of her free hand but nodded. "I promise," she whispered on a sob before he crushed her to his chest, needing her close.

"James," he said, his voice hoarse with emotion. "My middle name is James. And I don't have a bloody idea what my ring size is."

She half cried and half laughed.

He did his best to blink away his own tears. "And I'm not falling for you." He cupped her face with both palms, bringing his mouth near hers. "I fell a long time ago."

CHAPTER THIRTY-ONE

LIAM HELD HER. TOUCHED HER. KISSED HER SHOULDER.

He wanted to stay in the moment, to live in it for as long as possible, so he never had to worry about the *what-ifs* of tomorrow.

With her back to his chest, he smoothed a palm down Emily's sleek thigh and gave her knee a tap. She knew exactly what he wanted, and with an impatient whimper, bent her leg ninety degrees to allow him access to her center. He slid his tip through her silky wetness and joined their bodies, filling her slowly.

A groan tore from her lips. He hugged her tight, curving an arm around her waist to reach and rub at the sensitive folds between her legs as he thrust rhythmically, losing himself in her. His reward was another sputtering moan slash scream as she struggled to hang on.

He buried his face against her hair, still damp from the rain.

He wanted to bathe his cock in her wetness, wishing the rubber didn't separate them the moment he'd come and his worries would fade away into the black space of nothingness —leaving them completely alone and safe.

"I. Want. You," she said as she rotated her hips.

He shifted her hair and brought his mouth to the shell of her ear. "You have me, love."

"No." She twisted her neck to try and see him. "I want you to . . . to—"

"You want me to . . . what?" He smiled.

"Geometry," she cried out. "I want you from every angle imaginable."

He chuckled. God, this woman.

"How about you on top?" Without waiting for an answer, he flipped to his back and braced her hips, guiding her to sit on top of him. "Does that work for you?"

When she slid down onto his cock, taking all of him, she buried her fingers into his chest and cried out his name.

"I'll take that as a *yes*." He lifted his hips off the bed, giving her even more, burying himself deeper.

Tonight was more intense than their last time together in Chile. He hadn't thought *more* was even possible because it'd already been heaven.

He wallowed in the sensations—the bite of her short nails on his skin, her whimpering moans, the grip of her knees on his hips as she rode him, taking her pleasure. And with every slide down, she shifted around to hit that sweet, silky spot of hers against his skin, her perfect tits bouncing as she panted for breath.

He was on the verge of losing his fucking mind.

He kept one hand on her side while his other hand roamed up her abdomen to one of her nipples.

"Liam." She followed his name with a sigh as she rubbed against him harder and faster. He knew she was close, and when he pinched her nipple, he pushed her over the edge. "Yes. Yes. Yes!"

Her entire body trembled with her orgasm. And a sensation of complete relaxation washed over him as he came, too, then held her tighter now that they were both satiated.

. . . And then his phone rang like a kick in the balls.

"Must be Jessica." He cursed under his breath. "Sorry."

"No, I understand." She reached out for his phone and handed it to him. "**Boss Lady**?" she asked with a laugh, catching sight of the caller ID. "You have me programmed in there?"

He rolled flat on his back and clutched the phone as she stood. "Yeah. I have you listed as **Off-Limits**."

She chuckled. "You planning on changing it?"

"I was thinking about making it Mrs. Evans," he said without a second thought before pressing the speakerphone button. "What's up?"

"We have eyes on the HVT. I'd like you to make a soft approach tonight," Jessica said straightaway.

He shifted upright, placing his back to the headboard.

Emily grabbed his T-shirt from the floor and clutched it to her chest, and he shook his head.

She had absolutely nothing to be shy about. He loved her body. Her curves. So, he leaned forward and snatched away the shirt. She playfully rolled her eyes at him.

"Liam?" Jessica said. "You hear me?"

Shit. "Yeah, copy that. Where's he at?"

"Echo Two has him in his sights at the rooftop bar. His bodyguard is at a table off to his three o'clock. Tread lightly, but if you could get him to open up somewhat it'll make for an easier sell tomorrow," she said.

"HVT? Hans, you mean? But what if that makes him trust

us even less?" Emily spoke up. "Won't he wonder why we kept the truth from him?"

"It's a risk we'll have to take. See if you can get a read on him. His attitude. Mindset," Jessica said.

"Copy that." He ended the call and hopped off the bed and stood naked before Emily, then wrapped a hand around her waist, the condom still clinging to his shaft. Work was the last thing on his mind right about now, but it was his job to put the mission before desires.

A tiny hunger growl left Emily's stomach.

"You should eat."

"Does that mean I'm coming with you?" she asked.

"Yeah, I can't handle you out of my sight." He pressed his mouth to hers, stealing one last, quick kiss. It was time to get mission focused once again.

CHAPTER THIRTY-TWO

She resisted the impulse to reach for her forearm and pinch herself as she and Liam sat at the bar alongside Hans. Was she really on a covert op with Liam, and had he only two hours ago declared he'd fallen for her?

She did a mental pinch instead. Another two for good measure. *I'm awake.*

Liam ordered a beer for himself and a glass of wine for her.

She pushed her fingers through her still damp hair and tried to remember every detail of her conversation with Liam just before they'd headed to the bar. Liam had asked her to take the lead, and she didn't want to screw up.

They'd discussed the plan as she'd hurriedly put on one of her new outfits. A black fitted sleeveless dress that stopped shy of her knees, a dress Liam obviously found sexy. He couldn't seem to stop staring at her.

And as they were about to leave the suite, he'd pinned her to the door, and slid his hands up her thighs to grab her panties and lowered them to her ankles. Crouching before her, he'd tossed her panties over his shoulder, then buried his face under her dress and between her thighs.

"Stay just like this. I want you wet and ready for me when we get back," he'd said once standing tall after only a few seconds of teasing her. He'd then leaned in and taken her mouth in a searing kiss, giving her an erotic taste of herself. *"You make me crazy, you know that?"*

"Isn't there somewhere we're supposed to be?"

"I want to care, but—"

"You do care, and I love that about you." She'd grinned. *"We better go."*

"Yes, ma'am."

And when they were alone in the elevator shortly after, he'd pulled her against him and squeezed her ass cheeks to the point of a delicious kind of pain, all the while kissing her with his sinfully delectable mouth.

She crossed her legs at the memory, trying to tamp down the burn of desire.

But when her eyes fell upon a well-worn photo clutched in Hans's hand, his barely eaten steak forgotten, her ill-timed sexy thoughts came to an abrupt halt.

"She's stunning." Another furtive look revealed the picture was of Talia Alvarez, and she was the spitting image of Elaina. "She, uh, looks familiar."

Hans shifted her way, his eyes fraught with loss. "If you're here for the event tomorrow, you may have heard of her."

"The Golden Minds Gala? Is she one of the honorees?" she asked, playing her role even though a snag of guilt caught inside of her. She was worried she might totally unravel at the man's unmistakable melancholy.

He carefully slid the photo back into his wallet and

grabbed his fork, rolling it between his fingers. "I'm giving a speech tomorrow, in which I will talk about her. She had a brilliant mind."

"Did something happen to her?"

"She died in a car accident in Chile a few months back," he answered, his voice somber.

"I'm sorry. I'm sure she'd be touched you're honoring her in your speech. Were you close?"

He kept his eyes on his plate. "We were friends a long time ago, but we lost touch. Her death is a tragedy, and I can only hope she'll be replaced by . . ."

Elaina?

"I'm Hans Zimmermann." He set his fork on the plate and extended his palm.

She smiled and introduced herself, then leaned back slightly to introduce Liam on the bar stool next to her. "We had hoped for seats at your table tomorrow, but we got our tickets at the last minute. We're sitting with"—she snapped her fingers in the air as if trying to catch the name in her mind —"Jeremiah something."

"No idea who he is," Liam added and motioned for the bartender. "A refill of whatever he's having, please."

"Thank you." There was still a faint hint of German in his accent, even though he'd moved to the U.S. a long time ago.

"Where do you work now? Anything exciting?" she asked, keeping up with her role and her deeper-than-deep Southern accent.

Hans glanced over his shoulder in the direction of his bodyguard. "I can't talk about it." He took a sip of his newly delivered drink. "Do you have kids?" he asked, taking her by surprise with the sudden subject change.

Liam's hand went to her thigh at the question, and he gently squeezed.

"I want them someday," she softly admitted.

"Many people attending the event tomorrow believe our future is dependent upon today's children. It's up to this next generation to save our planet. It's why all the money raised tomorrow will go to funding scholarships to the world's brightest minds."

"And do you also hold that belief?" she asked, sensing doubt in his voice.

"People can't be trusted to do the right thing. Not even kids." He took another drink. "Selfish. Self-centered. Corrupt." He set his glass back down and pressed his palms to the counter as if preparing to push away and stand. "People are weak," he said in a low voice. "Even me."

"I don't under—"

"Have a good evening." He stood and tossed some bills on the counter.

"What do you think?" she asked Liam.

"He looks like a man who's very lost."

She reached for his hand atop her thigh and held it. "Why do you say that?"

He lowered his gaze to their clasped palms. "Because I was that man until I met you."

* * *

"About that dress." He peeled his shirt over his head, exposing the muscles that looked as if every line and curve had been carved into perfection by a master sculptor.

"Shouldn't we call Jessica? Tell her about the conversation?"

His eyes were on the hem of the dress as she lifted the material up. She was growing wet with his heated gaze on her.

"Give me five minutes to finish what I started before we call." With each step he took, she walked backward until she hit the wall.

"But the mission," she said under her breath.

"I've spent over fifteen years putting missions first." His pupils expanded. "I just want a few minutes to enjoy what's right in front of me."

"Okay," she said with a nod, her heart breaking as she thought about how much Liam had sacrificed over the years for his country. A man of valor and strength.

When he fell to his knees and fisted the dress—lifting the material to her hips, and darted his tongue along her wet center—every other thought in her mind was instantly obliterated.

Her focus narrowed down to his face, to the stunning man before her. A man she truly never wanted to imagine living without.

The base of her skull hit the wall as he licked and sucked. She grabbed hold of his head, not only to keep him in place as she rode out the orgasm but to keep herself from sliding down the wall.

"Liam," she cried as she shuddered and came.

He planted kisses from her thigh down to her ankle as if bowing before her. "Much better. Now we can call Jessica." He stood with a devious smile.

She shifted her dress back in place. "How are you going to focus like that?" She pointed to his tented jeans.

"I'm hoping by the time we're done with the call, you'll have had enough time to recover, and you'll be ready for me."

"Oh?" She smoothed her palm over his trimmed beard. "I think I'll always be ready for you."

"Always?" He cocked a brow as her hands slid down to the buckle of his jeans, and she unfastened it then popped the top button.

"Always," she whispered before kissing him.

CHAPTER THIRTY-THREE

LIAM HAD SCRUBBED EVERY INCH OF HER BODY WITH THE loofah and then proceeded to kiss every one of those inches as well, the shower water pouring over them.

"Do you know how many times I got myself off in the shower thinking about doing exactly this with you?" She rested her arms over his shoulders, and he brought his warm hands to her hips and pulled their wet bodies together.

"I think I can imagine." He nipped her lip. "There was a reason why I labeled you as **Off-Limits** in my phone."

"I didn't even know you had my digits before our wedding."

"Of course, I did. But every time I stared at your number, on the verge of calling, that label was my reminder why I shouldn't."

"You should've given in and called," she interrupted. "But then again, maybe it wouldn't have been the right time. I guess everything happens for a reason. Our drunken marriage saved my life from an assassin. The universe might not be so cruel after all."

"I'm just happy you decided to give me a chance despite

my fuckups." He brushed his lips over hers but then his cell beeped, alerting them to a text.

Once out of the shower, Emily shrugged on the white hotel robe and leaned against the vanity counter. She watched with appreciation as Liam rubbed a towel over the length of his body, then dropped it to the floor and remained commando as he read the text.

She peeked at his phone. "Why does Jessica want us to turn on the news?"

"She has a habit of leaving me in suspense." He flashed her a smile. "Lover of drama, if you can believe it."

"Well, you did wait a few minutes to call her after our conversation with Hans to—"

"You didn't enjoy having my mouth on you?"

Heat crawled into her cheeks at his words. The provocative tone had her prepping for him again—her body greedy and hungry for him.

"News," she sputtered before they became distracted again.

They left the bathroom, and she settled on the bed as he turned on the TV.

Vanessa Blackburn's face filled the screen as a reporter talked.

"Vanessa's dead?" Emily sat up onto her knees.

"Looks like it," he mumbled, eyes focused on the TV.

Elliott Nelson, Vanessa's ex, filled the screen a moment later. His jet-black hair smoothed back with gel, his skin flawless for the age of fifty, and his green eyes she remembered from photos, now pinned straight toward the crowd gathered around him.

A full-court press aggressively surrounded him, waving microphones and snapping photos. She recognized the backdrop to where Elliott stood—he was outside their hotel right now.

Liam moved to the window and parted the curtains.

"You see him?" she asked.

"Yeah, but my guys will have eyes on him." He let go of the curtains and returned to the TV when Elliott began talking.

"It's with a heavy heart I share the news today my ex-wife, Vanessa Blackburn, passed away at her estate in Seattle yesterday. I was with her when she took her last breath." Elliott pushed at the skin on his forehead as if trying to find the strength to talk. "She hasn't made a public appearance in quite some time because she didn't want anyone to know she'd been ill."

"What does this mean?" a reporter asked.

"How'd she die? What happened?" someone else spoke up. "Who's running the company now?"

More questions continued to hit the man.

"This is crazy," Emily whispered.

"My ex-wife and I had remained very close over the years. In fact, I stepped in to help run Blackburn Technologies during her illness. Vanessa officially turned the company over to me last week, knowing she was close to death." He kept his eyes on the sidewalk as if in unbearable pain.

Emily called bullshit, though.

"Before Vanessa passed she asked me to attend The Golden Minds Gala tomorrow night. The event is to raise money to help gifted children all around the world reach their full potential, and it was a charity Vanessa was very proud to sponsor." He cleared his throat and looked back into the crowd. "It's sad we have lost such a talented and intelligent woman, but I promise I will continue her groundbreaking work, and pursue her dream of making Blackburn the number one defense technology company in the world." He lightly nodded. "That's all I have to say at this time."

He turned from the cameras even though a dozen more questions snapped out from behind.

"He's entering the hotel. Is he staying here tonight?"

"Looks that way." Liam's phone began ringing. "Guess he's officially out of hiding."

"Yeah," she whispered, "but what the hell does all of this mean?"

* * *

EMILY EXTENDED A CUP OF COFFEE HIS WAY, BUT LIAM didn't seem to notice, his eyes fixed on his laptop screen. "You haven't slept, and it's four in the morning." Her mouth pinched with worry as she observed him.

He set the laptop off to his side on the couch and stood. He was in worn-out jeans, the top button unsnapped. No shirt. And as delicious as he looked, he also looked extremely tired.

"It's hard to get rack time when we're so close to figuring everything out." He accepted the caffeine and took a sip.

"You won't be any good to me at the gala tonight if you're sleeping at the table." She pointed to the bedroom, hoping he'd give in and at least sleep for a few hours, even though she'd just handed him a coffee to do the opposite.

He set his drink on the end table by the couch and braced her hips, pulling her a little closer to him. "I'm worried about Elaina."

They'd FaceTimed with Elaina before her bedtime last night, and she'd admitted she was scared.

"Something bad is going to happen," she'd whispered.

"Nothing bad will happen. I promise," Liam had responded in a calm, soothing voice. *"I'll protect you."*

"I'm not worried about me," was all she said before disappearing from the screen, leaving Emily's heart in her throat, tears in her eyes.

"She'll be okay," Emily assured him. "You and your people won't let anything happen to her. We're going to figure this out. We only have two suspects now, Jeremiah and Elliott, and they're both here at the hotel."

"Vanessa dying—I didn't see it coming."

"You couldn't have known. None of us could." She brought her hands to his biceps.

"There's something we're missing," he said, his voice so matter-of-fact.

"Your team will figure it out. I bet they always do, right?" When he didn't answer, she asked, "Still no movement on Connor?"

Emily had fallen asleep on the couch around midnight while he worked to find a lead and make sense of the turn of events last night. When she'd woken up to find him still glued to his computer—she'd felt guilty for having slept.

"No, Asher and A.J. are still parked outside Connor's flat in the city, waiting for him to make a move. It's better to let him lead us somewhere than for us to grab and interrogate him. We don't have days to get him to break."

"Maybe when he leaves his home, Asher can get inside his place and see if there's anything helpful?"

Of course, Liam's team surely already had a game plan, and so she was probably wasting her breath. She was a newbie to the world of covert ops, and they were pros. But that didn't mean she could just shut off her brain and stop the ideas spinning in her head.

"Yeah, maybe."

"Can I ask you a question?" Her hands slid down to his forearms.

"Anything," he said with a smile.

She let go of him and stepped out of his embrace. "I know the team has spent all night combing over every online image, every media clip, as well all the CCTV footage you guys could find of Vanessa over the last several years . . ." She took a breath and hugged her body as a chill chased over her skin. "And you came to the conclusion Elliott probably used Vanessa as a pawn to reclaim his fortune and his place in the tech world after he lost everything three years ago."

"Probably poisoned her to make it look like a gradual decline in health so her death wouldn't look suspicious or come as a surprise. And make it easier for him to take over the company," he noted.

"But what if Vanessa's not so innocent? What if Vanessa hurt Elliott in a way that had him out for blood and maybe not just hers?"

"Weston Tech," he said, and she nodded.

"What if she was in bed—literally or figuratively—with someone from Weston Tech while she and Elliott were still married? Maybe she supplied that person information about her husband's company, and it was her actions that led to the collapse of Elliott's business?"

"But why the divorce settlement?"

"Elliott's a genius, right? What if he discovered her betrayal but didn't let on he knew?" She'd seen similar scenarios in court. More times than she could count.

"So, he asks her for a divorce because he's going to lose everything, and it's his idea to start up Blackburn Technologies with the settlement money?"

"And she had no idea he was aware of her betrayal," she replied. "He could've been pulling the strings at Blackburn all of this time while slowly killing her off, choosing this moment to officially end things and take over the company."

"It's not just about taking the contracts from Weston Tech to advance the company," Liam said as if processing his thoughts out loud. "It's about totally destroying them as payback for whatever happened, which means it has to be the owner or someone high up at Weston if he's hitting this hard."

"But why would Vanessa secretly stay with Elliott after the divorce? Why not continue to betray him and take the money and run?" It'd been the only drawback to her theory.

"Because the guy she was sleeping with was probably married and had no intention of leaving his wife. Or maybe he used her for information."

"She was a smart woman—doubt she'd fall for . . ." She shook her head. "Then again, love can make people throw caution to the wind."

"Either way, I think you solved this. I don't know why I'm so surprised. You constantly impress me." He squeezed her arms and kissed her. "God, I love you," he rushed out then grabbed his phone, acting as if the most important combination of words didn't just fall from his mouth.

Maybe he didn't realize he'd said them. Or maybe she had imagined it?

She stood completely still as he rattled off the theory to Jessica over a secure line.

Her heart pounded and pounded like never before.

He'd said he'd fallen for her—but did the man just admit he loved her, too?

CHAPTER THIRTY-FOUR

"Are you okay? Is Emily?"

Liam barely heard Luke's questions over the phone line. He'd just admitted to his boss he and Emily had gotten married in Vegas. But right now, he couldn't stop thinking about how he'd slipped and casually dropped an *I love you* to Emily as if he'd done it a hundred times before calling Jessica three hours ago.

He hadn't realized what he'd said until he'd ended the call with Jessica. And then it didn't feel like the time to bring it up, especially since she didn't mention it, so he decided to save the conversation for after the mission.

But still, he couldn't get the words out of his head, even now. Even talking to Luke.

"Liam? You there?"

He faced the vanity mirror in the bathroom, finding his bloodshot eyes.

Maybe he did need to catch a few hours before the gala?

He'd slipped into the bathroom when Luke had called so he could talk to him alone, but damn if he wasn't doing all that much talking.

"Are you okay?" Luke asked again.

"Yeah," he breathed out. "I'm not going to fuck this up." He'd nearly done that, though.

Luke remained quiet as if not necessarily believing him, and could he blame him given his track record? Probably not.

"But, um, now that Jessica has caught you up, what are you thinking? You on board with the plan?"

Luke cleared his throat. "Yeah. Lay the news on Hans today and see what he says."

"Are Jeremiah and Elliott still in their rooms?" he asked.

"No movement on their end. Connor's still at his place in the city, too."

"Any evidence to prove the Vanessa-Weston affair angle?"

"We're pretty sure it's the owner of Weston Tech. He isn't married himself, but based on Jessica's research, he has a track record of sleeping with the enemy. Well, spouses of rival companies."

"So, this scumbag has built his success by stealing secrets between the sheets."

"For over a decade. We haven't placed him with Vanessa, yet, but we have enough evidence to assume this is his MO, and that Emily's theory is correct."

Liam left the bathroom in search of Emily to let her know what he'd learned, but she was asleep on the living room couch.

"We'll call you when we have eyes on Hans in the hotel. We have to assume his suite is bugged, so you can't talk to him there," Luke said. "Maybe get some sleep until you hear from me?"

Doubtful, but he'd try. "Any thoughts on how we're handling tonight?"

Now that Luke had been read in on the op, he assumed

Asher would pass the baton back to Luke as Bravo One to co-lead with Jessica.

"We considered a vehicle interdiction to grab Elliott after he leaves the gala—I assume with Hans—but then we're kidnapping on foreign soil. Besides, we may not be able to get him to talk."

"So, we need to follow and obtain hard evidence of what he's up to," Liam said.

"I'd prefer not to infil an unknown compound with God knows how many people and weapons there, but I think that's going to be the case tonight."

"Maybe we should consider getting help from our British counterparts, and then we won't have to deal with unknowns."

"I'm thinking about it." Luke paused for a beat. "It'd be nice to have eyes in the sky for an assist."

At least Jake was safely out of the country and wouldn't be involved. He sure as hell didn't want to make Emily any more nervous by risking her brother's life. "Let me know if you need me." He shifted to hold the phone against his ear with his shoulder as he looked down at Emily, sleeping peacefully on the couch.

"Just hang tight until we confirm Hans's position."

"Copy that." He scooped Emily into his arms to carry her to the bedroom.

"And, Liam?"

He set her atop the comforter, and she rolled to her side, slipping her hands beneath her cheek. "Yeah?"

"Break her heart, brother, and—"

"I'll let Asher hold me down while you break my legs."

There was no turning back now. He'd die before he let anything happen to her.

* * *

"You're sure this will work?" Emily took a Texas-sized breath as they stood by the window in their hotel suite living room.

Thankfully, they'd both had a chance to get a few hours of sleep, as well as freshen up.

"Having you flirt with Hans and lure him to our room is not my idea of a good time, I promise."

She chewed on her lip.

"You want to back out?" He wrapped a hand over her forearm. "Say the word."

"No, I want to help."

He stared at her for a few long seconds as if trying to navigate by way of the stars, without a compass or a good sense of direction. He was totally lost in her eyes. And for the first time in his life he was okay with that.

"Come to Sydney with me when this is over," he said before reason kicked in and talked him out of it. "I want to take you there."

Her eyes stretched wide with surprise, her lips forming that cute little "O."

"I mean, if you're not ready for that," he began while losing his hold of her, "I understand."

"It's not that." Her long lashes fluttered. "You're going there to talk to your brother, right? I don't want to get in the way."

"I want you with me. But if it's too much for you I'll go alone." He had to let go of the anger he'd held on to for too many years. Needed to make amends with his brother, if only so he and Emily would have a real chance at being together.

Her lips pursed together as if in thought. "I did tell Sam I wanted to plan a vacation to Australia after my case ended. At least now it wouldn't be a lie," she said with a small smile that quickly vanished. "Carballo," Emily whispered. "This isn't going to be over after tonight, though, is it? He's still out there."

"Not for long," Liam said as confidently as he could. "Knowing Jessica and the team as well as I do, she'll find him, and we'll lay him to rest." In one way or another, at least.

"Not an on-the-books team?" Her brows lifted in question.

"The boys at DEVGRU are trained for ops like this but whether or not the president can send them without Carballo catching wind first—doubtful. And I don't want our operators dying due to an ambush."

"Or you." There was an unmistakable hint of distress there. And he hoped like hell she meant what she promised him yesterday—that she'd truly move on if something ever happened to him. He couldn't bear to think of her spending a lifetime grieving his loss.

"Well, I guess we should go?" She left his side and started for the door.

A gut-wrenching pain hit him. "Are you sure you're okay?"

"I was just thinking about—"

"Elaina?" he asked because she'd been on his mind all day as well.

She nodded. "I'd bet she'd love to see Australia, too."

And he'd love nothing more, but . . . "Emily." His shoulders sagged. "You know we—"

"I know." She took another mammoth-sized breath. "So, um," she began, and he'd swear she was sniffling, "we need to have a public fight at the bar, then you'll take off?"

"And I'll come back to the room, but Harper will loop the feeds to hide I ever came back."

"So it'll look like I'm bringing Hans alone to my room to, uh, seduce him."

"Yeah," he said, even though he hated the plan.

It'd been her idea to flirt with Hans to hopefully get him to their room, but now that it was about to happen, it had his stomach tightening to the point of pain.

"Let's do this then."

He checked his watch. He'd traded in his G-shock for a high-end-looking silver one since his brother would wear something flashy and not so stealth-ops-like. "We only have four hours until we gear up."

"You think Connor will show up at the gala tonight?" she asked once they were inside the lift.

"He's not on the list, but he could be a plus one for Blackburn Technologies," he said as the doors parted, and he caught sight of Hans across the way, sitting in the same seat at the bar as he was last night. "You ready?" he whispered into her ear, and she nodded.

Once outside the lift, she turned and smacked him across the cheek with enough force it actually stung. He cupped his jaw. "What was that for?" he asked loudly, playing his part.

"You lied to me," Emily seethed. And damn if she wasn't falling into character. "You said you were in D.C. for work but you were with her, weren't you?" Her hands balled into fists at her sides.

"She's my wife, and she insisted on coming with me. What'd you want me to do?" He reached for her arm, but she swatted his hand away. "Nothing happened with her. I promise."

"I don't know if I can believe you." She held her hands in the air between them. "I need space. I need time to think."

"Fine." He turned back for the lift. "I'm going for a long walk. Get your head together before I'm back, or don't bother coming with me tonight."

Once inside, he rested his palms on the back-interior wall, doing his best to continue the act until the doors closed.

He grabbed his phone and called Harper as the lift began its descent. "It's time."

CHAPTER THIRTY-FIVE

"MEN," EMILY SPUTTERED AS SHE SETTLED ONTO THE STOOL next to Hans at the bar. "No offense."

"You looked happy last night," he said without looking her way, his gaze steady on the drink in his hand.

"He's married." She paused to let that sink in. "I get jealous when he cheats on me with his wife. Ridiculous, huh?" She released a flustered breath. "I just wish he understood how I felt. He never has to deal with jealousy since I'm faithful to him."

He finished his drink and ordered another one. "So, why are you?" A hint of casualness flowed through his words. Not as uptight as she'd expect from a father hoping to rescue his kidnapped daughter that night. Maybe he was coping with the reality of his situation by drinking, which would make her task of getting him to her room easier. Well, she hoped so, at least.

"Why am I faithful?" She traced a line from the column of her throat to the plunging neckline of her black silk blouse, hoping to draw his eye to her cleavage. She felt all kinds of gross doing it, but she'd take one for the team if it meant saving lives.

He was one of the smartest men on the planet, but he still had desires, and thankfully, he took the bait.

He zeroed in on her breasts when she lifted her chest as if taking a deep, cleansing breath.

"Yeah, if he's sleeping with someone else, why aren't you?" Hans brought his eyes back up to her face. His pupils had grown in size, desire eclipsing the color of his irises.

"Maybe I should." She raked her tongue over her bottom lip. "I find brainy guys very sexy."

Hans's attention dipped back to her breasts.

"This place feels a little stuffy," she said, exaggerating the Southern accent she'd almost forgotten to use thanks to nerves. "You feel like grabbing a drink in my room?"

"That's probably not a good idea. I have the—"

"Event tonight. Right." She allowed her shoulders to drop from their confident position. "I was looking forward to that, but I don't think I'll be going now."

"Maybe you'll make up before then." His eyes moved back to her face.

She wasn't going to be able to crack him. *Shit.* "I don't know." She thought through Plan B in her head. "I'm just sick of being alone. Even when he's around—he's not, you know, present in mind. Always working." She brought her palm to her face. "I'm sorry. You don't need to hear my problems."

He wrapped a hand over her wrist, gently lowering her palm and looked into her eyes. "I'm lonely, too. But I like my work. I don't know if I could give that up for anyone or anything."

What about Elaina? Her stomach squeezed. Would he be a good father to her? Did he really even want to be her dad?

313

"Maybe we can talk in your room." He let go of her wrist and stood. He extended his palm for her hand.

"Okay." She tucked her hair behind her ear, took his hand and hid a sigh of relief.

"I don't think this is a good idea," his bodyguard said after they left the elevator to head for her room.

"I won't be long," Hans replied, no room for argument in his tone, and relief hit her when the bodyguard didn't protest and stayed outside her door.

"Where's your bar?" Hans asked once inside her suite.

"The good stuff is in the bedroom." The plan was to get Hans out of earshot of the bodyguard, and so, she hoped he'd follow her.

When they entered the bedroom, she shut the door behind them, and Liam exited the bathroom.

"What's going on?" Hans sputtered at the sight of Liam and pivoted to find Emily's eyes.

"I'm sorry we had to do this," Liam said calmly. "We need to talk to you alone and out of the sight of the people threatening you."

Emily circled Hans and stood next to Liam. "We're not who you think," she got right to the point. "And *we* have Elaina," she rushed out before he made a beeline for the door. "We're with the U.S. government. Elaina's safe."

"No." He swiped the back of his hand across his forehead. "I don't believe you."

"After Elaina was kidnapped, we rescued her," Liam explained.

"No, you don't have her. I saw her on video." Emotion cut through. "I was told I wouldn't see her again until tonight."

"Elliott Nelson? Is that who threatened you?" Emily asked.

"I-I don't know who. My co-worker, he-he showed me a video and gave me a burner phone. He said I had to come to London, attend the gala, or she'd die. I couldn't tell—"

"Who at NORAD got to you?" Liam asked since it was still a part of the puzzle the team had yet to figure out, and so, they'd been forced to turn the search over to the president's people.

"No, I don't believe you," he whispered, sweat dotting his hairline.

"It's true." Emily carefully approached him. "We spoke with Maria. She told us what happened."

"I . . ." He covered his mouth with his palm, his eyes on the carpet.

"This is important. I need you to tell me who you talked to at NORAD about Elaina," Liam said.

"Prove to me you're not lying."

Liam produced his phone and dialed Jessica as planned.

"He's ready to talk to her," he said before placing the call on speakerphone, and a few seconds later Elaina came on to the line.

"Hello?" she answered, her voice soft. So innocent.

"Is that you?" Hans stepped closer to the phone. "Elaina Alvarez?"

"Is this my dad?" she asked. "I met you in Chile?"

"Maria told you I'm your father?" he asked in surprise.

"No, but I figured it out."

"Of course, you did," he said, a hint of pride in his words. "Are you okay? The people you're with, can I trust them?"

"They saved me, and now they're trying to stop you from helping the bad people."

"I-I . . . oh, thank God." He looked at Emily, a slight tremble in his hand. "I thought I was going to die tonight. Betray the country to save her. And then die."

"Elaina, we have to go. Talk to you soon, sweetheart," Liam said.

"Be safe," Elaina whispered before she hung up.

"Our being able to stop these people hinges on you telling us everything you know." He motioned for Hans to sit. "We don't have much time."

"Right." He blinked as if pulling himself out of a stupor and sat on the edge of the bed. "When I got back to Colorado, I met a good friend of mine for drinks at a bar. I told him about Elaina." He fiddled with the buttons of his shirt, his hands still trembling. "Then early last week he invited me to dinner and showed me a video of Elaina."

"Was it this one?" Liam showed him the video they'd made back in West Virginia to save Becky from the assassin.

"No."

Must've been from Carballo. "What'd your friend say to you?" she asked.

"That someone wanted me to do something, and that if I didn't, Elaina would die."

Blackmail. Elliott's MO.

"I was instructed to go to the gala as planned. Lose my bodyguard and head to the rooftop right after my speech. There'd be a helicopter waiting for me." He touched his chest. "I swear that's all I know. All my friend knew to tell me."

"What's your friend's name?" Liam texted Jessica the information once Hans had answered.

"I'm weak." His eyes welled. "How can I sacrifice my work—national security—for the life of one?"

"She's your daughter," Emily replied, her tone low and soft. "You're not weak."

"We're here to stop whatever they're planning, though," Liam added.

Hans touched the sweat on his brow. "And what will you do?"

"I don't want to risk placing a tracking device on you because they'll probably detect it, but I do want to clone your phone," he explained. "And then I'd like you to head to the helicopter pad as planned."

"But Elaina's okay. Why can't we go to the police? Why is it necessary for me to follow their instructions?"

"Our goal is to end this once and for all," Liam said. "It's imperative we infiltrate their location and collect as much evidence as we can to put these men away for good."

"I don't know if I can do this. I'm sorry." Hans stood and tried to move around Liam to get to the door, but Liam blocked his path.

"Hans, please. We need you." Emily took a deep breath and forced out, "*Elaina* needs you."

CHAPTER THIRTY-SIX

LIAM ACCEPTED A FLUTE OF CHAMPAGNE, OFFERED BY ONE OF the tuxedo-clad servers circulating the ballroom, and handed it to Emily.

There was a full orchestra performing atop the raised platform at the center of the room and a dance area off to the right, but no one was actually dancing. The entire event felt stiff. Boring. And he was way out of his element.

Most guests were crowded around the "top minds" of the world engaged in conversations about the latest tech or whatnot from what Liam could tell.

He glanced Wyatt and Harper's way as they talked to a couple at their table—the table where Hans was *supposed* to be. And then he did a quick survey of the rest of the room, ensuring all other targets were still present and accounted for.

He glimpsed Jeremiah out of the corner of his eye off to his nine o'clock talking to Elliott and Connor near the only door that led to the outside exit opposed to feeding back into the hotel lobby.

Connor had been Elliott's plus one, no surprise there.

Asher had breached Connor's flat as soon as it was clear

but hadn't found anything, so he returned to the hotel and was parked outside in a Range Rover waiting for the next steps.

Luke was on overwatch across the street, and Jessica monitored all the hotel camera feeds from outside in the back of a rental van they'd converted to their temporary command center.

"You look stunning in that dress," Liam said once his eyes landed back on her.

Her black gown showcased her curves, and her hair cascaded in soft waves over her shoulders, which had him remembering the hour they shared together before heading to the event.

Her hair had been up in a tight bun, but the moment she'd walked out of the bedroom in her dress—well, he couldn't resist her. He wound up destroying her hairdo as they made love like it'd be their last time.

"And shouldn't you be looking somewhere else?" she asked with a smile.

"Everyone is in position." *Except Hans.* "It wouldn't look realistic to be here with you and not have my eyes on someone so beautiful."

"Mm. Good point." She shifted to the side and eyed Hans's empty seat. "Will he show?"

"TOC, any movement on our HVT?" he asked into his mic, which was tucked beneath the sleeve of his blazer.

"We're thirty minutes in, and he hasn't left his hotel suite. I don't know if we can trust him to do the right thing," Jessica answered. "I'll keep you posted."

"Copy that." He shifted the sleeve of his blazer back in place.

"Anything?" she asked.

"Still in his suite."

She took a sip of her drink, trying to act casual, but he

could see her nerves in the way her lashes fluttered. "How do you think Elaina's doing?"

Elaina was still at their safe house with Jared, plus Knox for extra protection. The team had decided it'd be best to keep Knox away from the event with so many people who shared a connection to Knox's politician father.

"She's a tough kid. She'll be okay." And she would be. When this all ended, he'd make sure of it.

"What's going to happen when he discovers Patty won't be showing up with Elaina?" She glanced Elliott's way before returning her focus to Liam. "Patty hasn't even cracked, yet. Do you think she's innocent?"

"Hans is on the move with his bodyguard," Jessica said, her voice popping into his ear as he eyed Connor leaning in to whisper something to Elliott. "He has his luggage, and he and his bodyguard just exited the lobby. Looks like he's not coming to the gala as planned."

"And he's not the only one on the move," Liam said when Jeremiah and Connor left out the street exit. Elliott was on his way toward the lobby.

"Echo Two and Echo Four—pursue assigned targets," Jessica ordered.

Echo Four announced, "I have a visual on my target. He's hopped in a black Audi R8. Following."

"Copy that," Jessica said.

"Hans is leaving the hotel," he told Emily and reached for her free hand.

"Looks like they found out." She set down her champagne flute.

Liam connected eyes with Harper and Wyatt who were now excusing themselves from their table.

"Elliott has to be heading to the rooftop helo pad," Wyatt said when he neared Liam's location. "Luke should have eyes on him soon. Too bad Owen can't follow in his chopper."

"What do we do now since Hans is making a run for it?" Emily asked.

"Same plan. We follow the targets," Harper answered and left with Wyatt to get to their next required position.

"What about Hans?" She looked toward Liam, worry in her eyes. "Are we letting them grab him?"

"Hans shouldn't have run," he said. "But like Harper said —nothing changes. We follow and then take them all down once they get to their final destination."

"Okay," she murmured as if hesitant about the plan. "I just . . ."

Liam closed his eyes, his mind racing. That shit feeling in the pit of his stomach moved around to his back and hit the base of his spine before a chill zipped north.

Whatever doubt Emily was experiencing, it'd hit him, too.

"TOC," he said into his comm. "Can you get Bravo Five on the line?"

"I can't," Jessica said. "I just tried. Jared's not answering either."

"Keep trying." He grabbed Emily's arm. "We've gotta go."

"Where to?"

"The safe house. I think Elaina's gone."

* * *

"YOU DON'T HAVE CAMERAS AT YOUR SAFE HOUSE?" EMILY asked Jessica from inside the back of their mobile command center.

Thankfully, at 8 p.m. on a Thursday night, they didn't have to deal with too much traffic leaving the city for the safe house. Luke was driving, but he couldn't see or hear them from the front. They'd been updating him through comms the same as the rest of the team.

"We do have cameras. They've been disabled." Jessica clutched the sides of her computer to keep it from falling off her lap when Luke hit a bump on the back road as he drove the van.

Liam reached across and grabbed hold of Emily's hand, gripping tight. It was a toss-up as to who he was trying to reassure, her or himself.

"How would Elliott know Elaina was there? Or that we're in London?" Emily looked up at him, and he let go of her hand and scooted back onto the bench.

"They wouldn't," he responded, his voice grim. "Inside job. Right under our damn noses."

"Are you saying you don't trust everyone on your team?" she asked in surprise.

Jessica glimpsed at Liam from over her shoulder, guilt stretching across her face.

"Not my team." He tensed. "Jared."

"I gave Elaina butterfly earrings earlier just in case . . ." The earrings had a tracker, but the way Jessica spoke, that meant the tracker had been turned off.

"Jared knew about them," Liam hissed.

"He played us the whole time, and we helped the bastard deliver Elaina to London." Jessica's eyes narrowed, her pupils nearly obscuring the blue.

"But we don't even know if Elaina's gone, right? There could be another reason why they aren't answering the phones, or why the security cams went down." Emily was grasping at straws, and he didn't want to be the one to tell her because he wished more than anything Elaina was safe.

And then there was Knox to consider. Did Jared take him out? Kill him?

He pounded his fist onto the metal bench off to his left, needing to physically vent his frustration.

If anything happened to Elaina or Knox, he'd rip Jared apart. Limb from fucking limb.

"I never asked. I'll bet it was Jared who first approached POTUS about Carballo's ten mill payout to kidnap Elaina," Jessica suggested. "How could I have missed this?"

"It's my fault," Emily said, and when Liam peered at her, tears were developing in her eyes. "I vouched for him."

"No," he responded firmly. "This is on us."

"Jared's been after Carballo for years. It's hard to believe the double cross." Jessica grabbed her radio when it came to life with a pop of static, A.J.'s voice on the line.

"Connor ran Hans's town car off the road in Notting Hill. He shot the bodyguard and forced Hans into his Audi. They're heading west."

"Opposite direction as us," Liam muttered.

"I'll update you," he told them. "Harper and Wyatt are with the bodyguard waiting for the medics to arrive."

"We get a location on Jeremiah from Echo Four?" A.J. asked.

"Jeremiah's heading northwest," Jessica replied. "I'm assuming Connor will be shifting north soon. As soon as they reach their destination, I'll have our British counterparts get ISR over their position."

"Roger that."

Jessica set the radio on the other side of the bench off to her side. "So," she began, the wheels of her mind back to spinning, calculating possibilities of how shit went wrong. "I assume Jared hired the Lamond brothers to come after Emily and the AG to throw everyone off his scent since he had custody of Elaina at that time."

"He wanted us on the case, didn't he?" Liam asked. "He wanted us to make the connections. Discover Elliott was after her."

"He may not have counted on the fact Elaina would've been able to provide the coordinates to the ports," Jessica noted. "But the video we made of Elaina to get Don's wife back—"

"His sole purpose could've been a way to let Elliott know he had her and to call off the free-for-all bounty," he finished for her.

"It'd make sense as to why Jared wanted to make sure Lamond died. He didn't want the guy talking to us," Jessica pointed out.

"This is crazy," Emily said, nearly under her breath. "Do you think Elliott will really pay Jared the thirteen million bounty?"

"With his experience, Jared will have an exit strategy," Jessica answered. "Blackmail, or something to ensure he walks away alive after he hands over Elaina."

"Good." Liam stood once they stopped. "That way we can kill him ourselves." He grabbed a Glock from the weapons arsenal in the back of the van, as well as a flashlight, and opened the door. "Stay here with Jessica until Luke and I clear the house."

"Yeah," she replied. "Be safe."

He hopped out of the van and met up with Luke. The place was pitch-black, not a light on in the home.

Liam used the flashlight to guide their way, then found the closest switch to the door and flipped it on.

"Knox?" Luke called out.

"In the control room!" Knox answered.

Liam's chest nearly caved in with relief at the sound of his buddy's voice.

Knox's back was to one of the columns, his arms looped around it and tied at the wrists. Blood dripped down the side of his face.

"Elaina. The bastard fucking took her." Knox blinked a few times as blood hit his left eye. "He caught me by surprise and knocked me out." He hung his head as if in shame while Luke cut him free.

Liam grabbed a towel from the bathroom and wet it, then returned to the room and offered it to Knox to dab at the blood. "Did Jared say anything? Did you see anything?"

"I heard him talking like you were all in the room. It was weird. But I wasn't totally lucid yet." He patted the towel to his forehead and sat. "I'm sorry, brother," he said to Liam, somehow knowing Elaina going missing would hurt him the most.

He braced a hand to his shoulder. "This isn't on you," Liam said. "I'm just glad you're okay." He went outside to grab Jessica and Emily. "Knox is okay, but Elaina's gone." Jessica and Emily followed Liam into the house. "We'll find Elaina. Jared has to be taking her to wherever Hans is going." He had to stay strong even though he wanted to put his fist through a wall.

"Knox!" Jessica hurried to his side and hugged him.

Luke scanned the room with his usual thoroughness, holding his gaze toward the camera on the ceiling before looking across to Liam. "What if Jared *was* talking to us?"

"Like leaving us a message?" Liam gripped the back of his neck, the tension mounting.

"I'll turn surveillance back on. Maybe he did leave a message on camera before he disabled them," Jessica said, motioning for Luke to assist her with re-connecting the system.

Emily sat next to Knox and brought her forehead to her palm. As much as Liam wanted to comfort her, he couldn't think straight. He couldn't think beyond the details of getting Elaina back.

Jessica displayed the surveillance footage onto the drop-down screen on the wall, and Luke rewound the footage to before everything went black.

"There!" Jessica pointed to the screen. "Stop."

Elaina wasn't visible on screen, but Knox was on the floor behind where Jared stood. "I'm sorry," Jared began. "I don't want to do this, but I don't have a choice. I have to deliver Elaina to these people." He looked toward the floor. "Once I get the money, I'll slip the earrings into Elaina's pocket so you can track her."

"What's the time stamp on this?" Emily stood. "Can we intercept Jared's vehicle before he hands her over to Elliott?"

Luke paused the footage and zoomed in on the screen to showcase the time. "An hour ago. He may have already dropped Elaina off, but I'll alert the boys to be on the lookout." He pressed play, and the sight of Jared had Liam's stomach turning, yet again.

"I'll make the call." Knox left the room.

Jared stared up at the camera on the ceiling, standing almost where Liam stood now. "I don't want any harm to come to Elaina, or for our nation's security to be compromised." He lightly shook his head. "But I needed the money." His head bobbed with a few hard nods as if he were trying to convince himself his actions were justified. "Emily, if you're looking at this, the Lamond brothers were never sent to kill you, just to shake things up a bit."

Liam turned toward Emily at Jared's mention of her

name. Her eyes were shut. Her shoulders sloped with the weight of Jared's words. The son of a bitch had traumatized a kid for his own personal gain, and Liam was going to fucking end him.

"And Patty . . . well, by now, you've probably figured out she's innocent. You see, there's no CIA asset in Argentina."

Liam redirected his eyes to the screen. To the cowardly son of a bitch.

"Well, technically, there is an asset, but it's me. I've been working for Carballo long before the DEA tried taking him down in Mexico."

"And probably responsible for tipping off Carballo in Mexico and getting all of those agents killed," Emily whispered, the sound of her heart breaking evident in her tone.

"Once Carballo gets his grip on you, he never lets go. And I'm tired of it." Jared lowered his eyes again as if they were supposed to feel sorry for the murdering prick.

Liam took in a sharp breath, trying to fight the stabbing throb of pain in his chest.

Elaina was gone, and it was because of Jared.

"When I learned about Elaina, I thought I'd found my chance to get away from Carballo. Use the money to just disappear." He paused for a moment. "Once I'm safe, I'm going to email you all the intel I've collected over the years on Carballo so he can finally be taken down." He held a palm in the air. "I know what you're thinking, I could've handed the intel over and gotten free of Carballo—but you're well aware of how he operates. He'd know I was responsible and my parents and brothers would be killed. I couldn't take the risk." He looked at his watch. "I've got to go. Good luck." The cameras went dark.

"Can we trust him?" Emily stood to face Liam.

"We need to put together a new plan now that we know the truth," Luke answered.

Liam tossed his blazer and rolled the sleeves of his dress shirt to the elbows.

"What will you do?" Her eyes moved to the ink now exposed on Liam's right arm.

"What we always do," Luke replied when the words were stuck in Liam's throat. The familiar air of confidence in his tone. "We'll get her back."

CHAPTER THIRTY-SEVEN

"ISR JUST CONFIRMED SEVEN HEAT SIGNATURES GROUPED together on the second level of the mansion. Same location where we're picking up a transmission from Elaina's earrings," Jessica announced over her headset on the old British military helicopter they'd borrowed from Emily's brother's company.

Owen had picked up Liam, Luke, Jessica, Emily, and Knox, and they were en route to the final location where the rest of their crew remained on standby three klicks from Elliott's position—a home registered under a shell company owned by Connor Grady's brother-in-law.

According to the satellite images, the mansion had a wall of trees surrounding the property on one side, and a closed-down golf course on the other. Total privacy just northwest of the city center of London.

Liam repositioned his earmuffs with the built-in headset and asked, "How many in total are we talking?"

"Eight guards outside. Three at the back of the home, and three positioned at the front," she responded. "Heavily fortified walls, which include two overwatch towers on the east and west sides of the property."

Owen began his descent to their LZ—a field on the other side of the abandoned golf course, far enough away from notice of the mansion.

"We'll use the chopper to exfil the targets if they make it out alive. Owen can land on the eastern part of the golf course near the gate when we're ready for him," Jessica said. "And our British friends are on their way to serve as our QRF if needed."

Liam tensed as he eyed Emily sitting directly across from him. She was keeping her shit together pretty damn well. He hated she was so close to the action, but he didn't want to risk her staying at the safe house with Jared on the loose.

Liam grabbed hold of Emily's hand once the helicopter landed and they exited. He pulled her to his side, worried she'd forget about the blade at the back of the chopper as it died down, not wanting her to walk into it.

She'd changed out of her gown and into Jessica's clothes —jeans, a tee, and a lightweight jacket. Good call on Jessica's suggestion of the jacket given how Emily was now hugging her body as if cold. Probably nerves, too.

Harper and the rest of the team closed in on their position a few minutes later and parked near the chopper.

"What's the plan?" Harper asked once they were together. "They have a ton of arms and explosives. AKs. RPGs. You name it. Assume the last two shipments Connor picked up from the port had the same equipment recovered the other night."

"We'll need to do this fast," Jessica said.

"Is there any other way?" Knox asked.

Luke set a map of the property atop the hood of the Jeep Rubicon off to his side, and A.J. shone a light on it. "Wyatt and Liam will take out the guards in the east and west towers," he said while pointing. "Assume overwatch in the towers after."

"Similar setup to Argentina then?" Knox looked to Jessica since Luke hadn't been on the op to rescue Elaina.

"It might work," Jessica replied, but she didn't sound confident. "But if the guards manning the gate hear or see you shoot the tower guards, they'll alert Elliott and his men on the inside."

"I don't want someone holding a gun to Elaina's head." He couldn't take that risk.

"What if we wait?" Emily asked, and everyone, including Liam, looked her way. "I don't like the idea of leaving Elaina at that place for longer than we have to, but security might be laxer after—"

"We don't know for sure if Elliott plans on sending Hans back to NORAD, or if he'll have Hans help him at this site," Liam said. "We assumed Elliott didn't grab Hans before because he needed Hans on location at NORAD, but maybe he was waiting for this moment. Kill Vanessa. Announce to the world he was now owner and CEO of Blackburn. Make a flashy statement."

"Elliott was probably planning on grabbing Hans from the gala and putting a gun to his head tonight, but when they learned about Elaina through his friend they decided to add insurance to their plan," Harper pointed out.

"Elliott won't risk killing Hans or Elaina, even once they know we're on scene—as long as we get in there before Hans helps him," Luke said. "Well, *if* Hans chooses to help him, that is."

"So, what's it gonna be, boss?" A.J. stood off to Luke's left, flashlight stowed, waiting for orders.

"Remember that op in Dublin four years ago? The one

with the drunk woman asking for directions at the gate?" Asher asked. "Would that work?"

"Emily's not going in." Liam stepped closer to Asher, his pulse picking up.

"No, of course not." Asher held a gloved palm out.

"Harper was at the gala tonight. We can't send her in," Jessica said. "It'll have to be me."

Asher turned from the group and lowered his head as if the idea of sending the love of his life directly into danger was now an idea he regretted presenting. Of course, Jessica had been the "drunk woman" in Dublin, too, but the stakes were higher now.

"I've got this." Jessica pressed a hand to Asher's shoulder and glimpsed Luke off to her side. "Once they open the gates, I'll shoot the guard, then Liam and Wyatt take out the guards on overwatch. We ride in after that."

"You sure?" Luke asked.

"Harper can handle comms. If you guys need QRF—"

"I've got this," Harper interrupted her. "You can count on me."

"No one dies tonight. We all get out alive." Liam's eyes connected with Emily, and he motioned for her to follow him to the other side of the helo so they could have a moment alone.

She tightened the belt of her lightweight jacket. "I know you won't let anything happen to Elaina."

He removed one glove and brought his palm to her face before leaning in to kiss her.

"We'll get her out," he said when their lips broke. "I promise."

And it was a vow he'd die to protect.

CHAPTER THIRTY-EIGHT

SEEING LIAM WALK AWAY WITH HIS TEAM AND A RIFLE IN hand . . . it'd been pure hell.

"This is your second time working an op with the team?" Emily's nerves stretched to the point they'd snap at the slightest provocation.

Harper looked up from her computer screen on her lap from inside the Jeep Rubicon, parked about a half a mile away from the mansion on hole nine of the old golf course.

"I helped them out when I was still CIA—Liam saved me from near death—but yeah, this is my second official op."

CIA? Her assumptions had been right then.

Harper returned her focus to the screen, which showcased the aerial footage from the drone Jake's agency had provided. "I've worked with Jared five or six times, though. It's going to take a long time to wrap my head around his betrayal, and that his actions might've resulted in agents dying on that op in Mexico five years ago."

"You really think he has intel on Carballo he'll send us?"

"Maybe," she said softly, her voice distant. "But either way, we'll bring down both Carballo and Jared. I promise. I already have a program running to track down the transfer of funds made tonight between Elliott and Jared."

"That's good."

"Not all CIA officers are bad," Harper murmured. "The world just tends to only hear about the bad ones, so . . ."

"Sort of the way with everything, right? How often do you turn on the news and hear the good stuff?" She looked out her side window, wondering where Liam was right now.

She'd thought about asking Harper to explain the team's infiltration strategy, but part of her didn't want to know. It'd magnify her worry, and she was already scared shitless. Too many lives were on the line.

"We got lucky your brother's agency is here for the assist," Harper said after silence filled the Rubicon for a few minutes. "And with any luck, they can supply the British with the evidence about the Weston Tech fires."

"Maybe justice can prevail in a courtroom after all?" She reached for her necklace inside her jacket and pulled on the chain, needing to hold on to her charm. To draw strength from Lady Liberty. To know and believe the good guys would win and everyone would be okay.

Harper zoomed in on the screen and grabbed her radio a split second later. "We have movement," she announced, and Emily leaned to the side to observe her laptop. "Jessica's car is outside the gate now," she told Emily. "When the guard opens the gates to approach, she'll act drunk and ask for directions."

"And then shoot him, right?" She let go of her necklace at the news, that the operation was about to commence.

"She'll shoot the guard and drive in."

"I'm guessing some of the team is hidden in her car? Trunk?"

"A.J. and Asher." She pressed the side button on her radio. "Gate's opening," she said a moment later.

Goose bumps scattered across her skin beneath her lightweight jacket, and she wedged her thumb between her teeth as she averted her eyes to the side window, the rise of bile working into her throat.

"We're in," Jessica said after a moment.

"Echo One. Bravo Four. Take your shots," Harper commanded, and two pops punctured the silence in the Jeep.

"This is Four. Towers cleared. Moving to the next position," Liam said, and she gripped her chest at the sound of his voice.

"Copy that, Four," Harper answered.

"We have two heat signatures exiting the room on the second floor. Copy?" Harper informed the team. "The HVT has not moved."

"Is the HVT now Elaina?" she couldn't help but ask.

"Yeah."

Another painstaking silence filled the Jeep as they waited for the team. Asher's voice suddenly blasted over the line, "Bravo Four! Get the fuck out of the tower. There's a guy with an RPG tube prepping for launch."

Emily sat taller at the news, unable to truly accept what she'd heard.

"I have a shot, TOC," Wyatt said. "Taking him out now."

"Get your ass out of there, Four. That's a direct order," Luke came on to the line, his voice breathy as if he was running.

"Go," Emily said under her breath, her hands tightening on her lap. *Go. Go. Go!*

"Move, Four!" Wyatt yelled. "I took the shot, but . . ."

Emily clutched the door handle in a white-knuckle grip at the sound of an explosion over the line. "Oh, God." She turned to Harper, needing her to say everything was okay. "What happened?"

"Bravo Four, you good? Bravo Four, do you copy?" Harper asked, her voice shaky.

"I don't think he made it out, TOC," Wyatt said. "I'm on my way to him."

"Charlie Mike, Echo One," Luke ordered. "Bravo Five is on his way for Four."

Continue mission? No! She looked around the Jeep, frantic. She had to do something. If Liam was hurt . . .

"Give me a gun. I'm going with or without one." She held her palm open to Harper.

"Knox has medical training. He's on his way. Liam's radio probably just got messed up during the blast." Harper had managed to keep her voice calm, but the look in her eyes read anything but.

"I don't give a damn. I'm going!" She opened the door and stepped out. "Gun," she snapped out like an order.

Less than a half a mile. She could run that in four minutes. But would there be time?

"What will you do, Emily? The boys are in the middle of a rescue—you can't run into that compound. You could risk the entire op," Harper pleaded. "If something happens to you, Liam will kill me."

"I have to get to him." She found Harper's eyes. "I'm going, and you can't stop me."

"Wait," Harper yelled as Emily started to close the door. "Take this."

Emily leaned in and grabbed the pistol and a radio.

"Don't die," Harper hissed.

Emily nodded and slammed the door closed. She clipped the radio to her belt buckle and used the light attached to the gun to guide her way as she ran across the golf course and toward the mansion.

He's okay. She kept the words on repeat as she sprinted, her lungs burning as if a fire had been lit in her chest.

"We have a visual on the HVT," Asher said over the radio as she ran, and she tried not to slow her pace at his announcement.

The next rounds of gunfire she heard didn't come from the radio—she was closing in on the site. Close enough to hear the pops.

Flames engulfed the east side tower, stretching up, and everything inside of her went cold. Completely numb at the sight.

"TOC, come in," someone said over the radio. "The HVT and her father are secure."

Elaina's okay. She's okay. Oh, God.

She looked toward the sky in thanks. But Liam . . . she had to make sure *he* was okay, too.

"Emily's on her way to Bravo Four," Harper exclaimed. "I'm sorry. She—"

"There are still armed men in here," Asher interrupted.

"This is Echo One, I have eyes on her," Wyatt said, and the fact he could see her made her feel better. Safer.

She raced around the side of the tall cement wall, her arms pumping with the gun in hand.

"You have two tangos on the move," Harper said. "One appears to be making his way toward Emily."

"I got him." A gunshot followed Wyatt's words.

"Thank you," she said, even though Wyatt couldn't hear her. She kept on the move, closing in on the burning tower.

She slowed at the sight of Knox kneeling over Liam about twenty feet away from the tower at the base of a fallen tree.

She shook off the shock and picked up her pace, fear

pulsing through her body. "We need to medevac him now," he said into his radio. "He has a pulse, but it's too fucking faint. I don't know if he's going to make—"

"No!" Emily yelled out her anguish and dropped the gun.

She was disoriented from the explosion, even though she'd been nowhere close, and her ears still rang with the noise of gunfire. But it was the metallic scent of blood and the sight of Liam's lifeless body lying on the ground that forced her hand up to cover her mouth.

Blood everywhere.

His clothes torn.

Eyes closed.

Lips parted as if he'd already taken his last breath.

This can't be happening. No, God, please.

"You have to do something," she shrieked. "Do something!" she cried again, her lip trembling. Her entire body shaking as she fell to her knees.

"I gave him a shot of epi." Knox had already removed Liam's bulletproof vest and was performing chest compressions as he spoke calmly but urgently. "We have a defibrillator on the chopper. He might make it if we can—"

"He *has* to make it!" she cried, her chin wobbly.

She grabbed hold of Liam's limp hand and lifted his palm to her cheek, unable to stop the sob ripping from her chest.

"Liam!" a little voice yelled from behind.

"Stop her!" someone, maybe Wyatt, screamed. "Don't let her see him like that."

"No!" Elaina dropped down next to Emily. "You can't die. I need you!"

As much as Emily didn't want to let go of Liam's hand—she did it. She did it for Elaina. She did it so his team could get to him—to take him away. To hopefully save his life.

"He has to be okay." Elaina's words were strangled with

emotion as Emily pulled her into her arms and squeezed her tight. "We can't lose him, Emily."

"Tell me that you'd let me go. Promise me if we try to make this work and something happens to me—you'll let me go." Liam's words from yesterday ripped through her mind.

"No," she whispered under her breath as if Liam could hear her right now. "I can't let you go."

CHAPTER THIRTY-NINE

"HE'S BARELY HANGING ON."

"Blunt trauma to the head."

"Possible abdominal hemorrhaging."

Medical terms snapped from all around, and it was as if she were alone in the dark, walking through a tunnel being hit everywhere all at once.

Emily reached for the wall at her side as she followed the swarm of people surrounding the gurney—surrounding Liam.

"We're losing him!" another voice yelled as two wide double doors opened for the gurney.

"Miss?" A hand touched her shoulder, stopping her progress. A nurse, maybe? "You can't come back here. I'm sorry."

Emily held her arm in front of her face to block out the beam of light shining in her eyes.

"Are you okay?"

"I have to go with him," she said, feeling drunk and in a daze once the flashlight was gone.

"I'm sorry. We're taking him into the operating room now. Waiting room is down the hall and around the corner."

She stared at the woman. Not blinking. Not moving. Shock spiraling through her.

When the doors closed inches from her face, her hand went to her stomach as she fought away the rise of bile in the back of her throat.

She pivoted to the side and backed up against the wall and slid down to the cold linoleum floor. She wrapped a hand around her throat in a futile attempt to soothe the rawness inside.

She'd been thirteen when her dad's military helicopter crashed.

Jake had just thrown a game-winning touchdown. The running back had lifted him to his shoulders to parade Jake around the field, and Emily had cheered from the stands. Proud of her big brother.

But not even a minute later, Jake's gaze had zipped lightning-fast across the field, and she'd followed his eyes. Her hands had fallen to her lap at the sight of two of their dad's friends from the Army standing off to the sides of the bleachers talking to her mom.

Her mom's hand was over her mouth. Her head bowed.

Bad news had been delivered, and Emily's heart had slowed to a dull achy throb—life without her dad? How could her heart keep beating?

But her dad survived the helicopter crash. Somehow . . . he'd survived.

The waiting for news during his surgery had been brutal, though. All she'd been able to do back then was rock in place, an attempt to hang on, to keep it together.

Rock and rock and rock.

Jake had never wanted to follow in their dad's footsteps. He'd wanted to be a teacher. Coach high school football.

And she'd never believed she could be like her mom—the wife of a man who put his life on the line.

But Jake didn't play football or teach. He served in the Marines.

And now Emily *was* her mother.

In this very moment—she *was* the spouse hoping for good news—and it'd never occurred to her for a second when she began to fall for Liam she couldn't be with him because of his job. *That* hadn't been her fear, even though it'd been one for Liam.

But now . . .

"Emily. You okay?"

Everything was so white. The floors. The walls. So sterile and cold. But the place reeked not of surgical soap but of death.

Her stomach tightened. Little black dots appeared in her line of sight.

Stay strong, damn it. Be strong.

"Emily, you okay?"

The crushing pain in her chest advanced throughout her entire body. She dragged her eyes north to the sound of a familiar voice.

"Knox?" She tried to shake off her stupor—that loopy, semi-drowsy sensation, like the time she'd woken after her laparoscopic endometriosis surgery, hit her.

"He's still alive," Knox said. "You need to focus on that."

He was crouched before her. Blood on his tee. On his hands and forearms. *Liam's* blood.

"I need to be with him." She grabbed a tissue from the box Knox held out to her and wiped at her runny nose.

"Have faith. Believe in him. That man is way too stubborn to die on us. Besides, he just found you. He's not going anywhere."

"I can't lose him, Knox." She sniffled, sucking in air as she fought for a deep breath.

She'd been raised by a woman who'd remained stoic and brave all those years while her father had served, and maybe Emily hadn't planned on becoming her mom—but she hadn't planned on meeting Liam, either.

She couldn't lose him. Not now. Not like this. She hadn't had a chance to tell Liam she loved him.

"He made me promise I'd let him go if something ever happened, but this is . . . no, I can't."

"You won't have to say goodbye. You got it? We're not losing him," he said, his voice deep. Full of grit.

Knox moved to sit beside her and stretched his legs out, setting the tissue box on his lap. "Can you tell me what you know?" she asked once she'd gained better control of her breathing and slowed the tears somewhat. "And tell me the truth."

He turned his head to the left and looked into her eyes. "I'm hoping he was climbing down the steps to leave the tower when the missile hit, which would mean there was some space between him and impact before he got blown back." His eyes were now on his hands. On the blood. "No organs were punctured from what I can tell. No real external injuries aside from the gash on his head."

"And what about internal injuries?" The wounds they couldn't see were usually more dangerous, weren't they?

"When there's an explosion," Knox began, "the blast wave causes an intense over-pressurization impulse. Shockwaves travel through the body, resulting in rapid compression and expansion, pushing on the organs of the body."

"What-what are you saying?" She rubbed at the sharp throb beneath her breastbone, and her throat burned like she'd gulped a shot of whiskey and it'd gone down the wrong pipe.

"It's a severe trauma for air-filled organs. Lungs, ears, the GI." He was quiet for a moment and finally looked her way. "The fluid-filled cavities, too. Like the spinal cord and brain."

"There was a lot of blood coming from his head," she whispered.

"Don't think about that. Focus on the fact we were able to keep blood flow to the brain on the way here. He had a pulse when the helo landed, and so—"

"Thank you. If it weren't for you he might not have even made it here."

After a moment, he said, "I'd hold your hand, but the blood . . ."

She reached for his palm, anyway. "I'm sorry. I'm being selfish. You shouldn't be comforting me—he's your brother. Family."

"We all love him." Emotion threatened. He was trying to keep it together for her. But beneath that hard exterior she could see the pain. The worse-than-hell pain.

She eyed that damn stark white wall on the other side of the hall again. Her limbs heavy.

"I was wrong. I know that now," he spoke up after a few minutes passed.

"What?" She looked away from the wall.

He forced a tight-lipped smile, his eyes narrowing in the process. "At the reception in Vegas, I told Liam not to leave with you. I didn't want to see you get hurt." He cleared his throat, his eyes beginning to glaze as if he was on the brink of shedding a few tears himself. "I was wrong, and I'm so glad he didn't listen to me."

Emily gripped Knox's hand tighter, but before she could

answer, Harper approached them from the other side of the hall.

"He's in surgery." Knox let go of her hand and stood.

She stared at her palm, traces of blood there now.

Knox's back was to her as he talked to Harper, their voices hushed. And when he bowed his head and brought his hands to his hips, she knew whatever Harper was telling him couldn't be good.

"What is it?" She forced herself upright, using the wall as support, so her legs didn't give out.

Harper sidestepped Knox. "The president ordered Hans back to the base to catch a flight to Dover. Elaina, too."

Jessica and Luke had taken Elaina with them from Elliott's compound, but Emily thought they were going to bring her to the hospital.

Elaina couldn't leave right now.

"No!" She held her hands in front of her as if she could somehow make Harper's statement go away. Push it back.

"Hans refused to leave without Elaina. The president spoke with the PM and obtained clearance for them to go back to the U.S. immediately," Harper explained. "POTUS has to ensure there's been no breach of intel at NORAD." She gripped Emily's bicep. "I'm so sorry."

"This can't be happening." She turned out of Harper's reach, lifting her eyes to the ceiling. The color as blank as her thoughts.

"The president wants this situation wrapped up without media attention, or before the British authorities get wind of who we actually are." Harper removed her Yankees ball cap and clutched it between her palms. "We're not supposed to be on-scene during the aftermath of an op."

"But I didn't say goodbye to her." Emily whirled back around, her face pinching to the point of pain as she struggled not to break down again. "What if Liam . . . she needs to be able to say . . ."

"Everything will be okay. It has to be." Harper reached into her pocket and offered her a folded piece of paper. "Elaina said to give this to you."

She slid her palm over the side of her jeans, trying to remove the blood before she took the paper and unfolded it. Her eyes became glossy again at the words before her. "It's, um, a letter for Liam."

* * *

"Why does the weather always match my mood?" Emily stared at the River Thames out the waiting room window. No sight of the sun. A dark, angry sky. Rain pattering onto the river. "It's like someone else is writing our story. Setting the tone," she murmured. "They know how the story will end, and—"

"No." Knox strode next to her and peered out the window. "That would imply we have no control over what happens, and I don't believe that." He rested a hand on her shoulder.

She wanted it to be true, but lately, nothing seemed to be in her control. A frustrating helplessness, especially now, washed over her.

It'd been six hours and nine minutes since the doctors had taken Liam into emergency surgery. She'd noticed every tick of the clock. Every second that passed.

"Do surgeries always take this long?" She turned toward the room.

A.J. was next to Owen, and Harper sat opposite of them. Asher, on the other hand, paced in the hall outside the waiting room.

A man carrying an arrangement of lilies walked past the

open doorway, a reminder of the flowers Liam had snuck into her rental last week, and the sight had her burying her fingertips into her palms.

"Some surgeries take longer than others," Knox answered and motioned for her to sit next to Harper.

"When will the rest of the team get here?" They were wrapping up loose ends after the operation, and Jessica and Luke were on their way to the hospital after having dropped Elaina and Hans off at the base in Suffolk.

She wanted Elaina there with her. It wasn't right she was sent away, especially without the chance to say goodbye.

"The Brits think you work for Scott and Scott, right?" she asked no one in particular once sitting.

Owen gripped the arms of his chair. "POTUS told the police and PM we were operating on our own accord. Hired by Hans to rescue his daughter."

"Our story is that our team found Elaina, and we were fired upon by Elliott's men," Harper added. "Connor and the guards were killed during the rescue."

"And Hans is sticking to that?" Would Hans vouch for them? Would he do the right thing? He'd taken off from the hotel and nearly gotten his bodyguard killed.

"That's what Hans told the police," Harper said. "Same with Elaina."

"Elaina had to be questioned?" She should've been there for her.

"Yeah, and then POTUS issued the request to put her and Hans on a military flight," Owen said. "They should be in the air now."

"That's fast," Emily murmured.

"NORAD, so . . ." Owen lifted his shoulders. "Hans's friend from NORAD is already in D.C. being questioned.

Looks like he was blackmailed by Elliott to keep an eye on Hans."

Harper patted her phone atop her thigh, her leg lightly shaking. "Thankfully Elliott can't hurt anyone ever again."

"Gonna check with the nurse for an update." Knox left the room, his third time checking in the last hour.

"I don't even know what happened to Elliott or Jeremiah," Emily said at the realization. She'd been too worried about Liam and Elaina to think about anything else.

"We didn't know if you wanted to hear about it," A.J. responded, his eyes cutting to hers. "Jeremiah flipped on Elliott. He started squawking the second the police arrived."

"Not that we needed more evidence with the treasure trove of intel we collected at the mansion," Harper said, "but he's willing to testify that Elliott masterminded everything. Approached Jeremiah after Hans won the NORAD gig."

Asher strode into the room from the hall and joined their conversation. "The authorities have evidence Vanessa's death wasn't an accident. And they know about the Weston fires in Nottingham and Bristol, too. Elliott will be put away for a long time."

"Actually, the police discovered Elliott had plans to torch the site in Manchester this coming Monday—so, we saved some lives." Harper pressed a hand to Emily's shoulder, an attempt to comfort her, but honestly, nothing would help right now.

Even knowing the bad guys were behind bars couldn't ease the pain. She just needed to hear the words that Liam was okay.

Emily jumped to her feet at the sight of a doctor entering the room with Knox.

"I'm Doctor Lee." His light brown eyes surveyed everyone in the room. "Liam's stable now. A few fractures.

His right leg is pretty banged up, though. Plus the cut on his head required stitches. And we managed to contain the bleeding in his abdomen."

But. She could feel it coming from a mile away, and she clutched her stomach as she waited for the word.

"What is it, Doc?" Owen could feel it, too.

"There's some minor swelling in the brain." Doctor Lee held a palm in the air when her lips parted. "We've induced a coma just as a precaution to help the healing process and ensure he gets better, not worse."

"A coma," she said under her breath. "For how long? Is it safe? My brother was put into a coma two years ago." She hadn't known Jake had been hurt until he'd already recovered —giving her no time to panic. To rock. To cry. But . . . "When my brother woke up he had amnesia, and—"

"Each circumstance is different, but it was our best option to ensure he has a smoother recovery," he cut her off, sensing her obvious alarm. "When you injure an external body part it swells. Gets inflamed. But the brain is encased in your skull. Expansion can damage the—"

"Doc," Knox interrupted this time. "We understand."

"We'll be monitoring his electrical brain activity and keeping an eye on the swelling. It could be a matter of hours or days before we pull him out."

Owen looped his arm around Emily and kept her close to him for support.

"But he will wake up, right?" she asked.

"That's the plan," Doctor Lee answered with a so-called reassuring nod that did absolutely nothing for her.

"How's his breathing?" Knox had the medical experience, and thank God for that. "Tube through the mouth or a tracheostomy tube?"

"Mouth for now, but if he's under too long—"

"You'll switch." Knox turned away.

"Liam's in ICU," the doctor replied. "Who's family? I can take one of you back to see him."

"We're all family," Owen said, and the doctor rose a questioning brow.

Knox faced the room again and looked Emily's way. "She's Liam's wife. She should go."

"You're his brothers," she sputtered. They needed to see him, too, but the doctor flicked his wrist for Emily to follow him.

She couldn't stop the fresh tears from rolling down her cheeks. "I'm sorry. I'll tell him you're here." *He'll hear me. He'll hear me somehow.*

"You okay?" Doctor Lee asked when they entered the expansive intensive care unit, his tone soft. "Dumb question, I know. But are you sure you're up for this?"

"I have to see him," she whispered, and he pulled a curtain to the side to reveal Liam's bed.

Her heart thundered in her chest at the sight of him, so pale and lifeless. She knew it wasn't possible, but his strong, muscular body appeared smaller. A breathing tube in his mouth. A chest IV from the looks of it. Monitors everywhere.

She sat next to the bed and reached for his hand. The tears wouldn't stop. How could she ever stop them with him in this condition? "Why is he so cold?"

"Therapeutic hypothermia. We've found that by lowering the body temperature to thirty-five Celsius it's more effective in reducing intracranial pressure."

"Oh. That's good, then." She nodded without looking his way, unable to take her eyes off Liam, off the man she couldn't live without.

"Giving him a system reboot, so to speak." He circled the bed to stand opposite her and pointed to a device off to his side. "This is the EEG. It detects the brain's electrical activity."

Fat tears continued to hit her lips, and she used her free hand to wipe at her face. "Can he breathe on his own? If he didn't have this tube would he be able to survive without it right now?"

There was more he wasn't telling her. She could feel it.

He crossed his arms, a discomfort stretching across his weathered skin. "When he arrived he was in respiratory arrest. We had to do endotracheal intubation to open the airways, but he also had a collapsed lung." He paused for a moment as if to let her absorb the information. "There was air in his chest outside his right lung, causing his lung to collapse —a pneumothorax."

She did her best not to squeeze Liam's hand too tight. "But he's okay?"

"He's stable."

Was that a generic answer for *I don't know*? She touched her chest for the hundredth time. "His stuff," she sputtered. "Where is it?"

"I'll have a nurse find it for you."

She lowered her forehead to their clasped palms, allowing the sounds from the machines to fade away. "You can't leave me. I just found you," she whispered, hoping he could hear her. "We need more time." *Elaina needs you, too.*

"Miss?" A woman in scrubs held two white plastic bags in her hand and strode toward her. "All of his belongings should be here."

"Thank you." She reluctantly lowered Liam's hand to the bed so she could look through his things.

His coin was still in his cargo pants pocket, and the black band was at the bottom of the bag. *Thank God.*

She set the coin and band on the rolling table next to the

bed, then leaned closer and kissed his forehead, careful not to disturb the white gauze wrapped in layers around his skull where he'd had the gash.

"You're a survivor." She sat again and reached for his hand, gently massaging it. "I'm not ready to let you go, Liam James Evans. So . . . you have no choice but to pull through."

CHAPTER FORTY

"HERE. FINEST VENDING MACHINE COFFEE KNOWN TO MAN." Knox extended a cup her way in the waiting room.

"Thanks." She held the lukewarm coffee with both palms and eyed the dark liquid.

"When was the last time you ate or slept?" He crossed his arms, clearly gearing up to lecture her.

She couldn't believe it'd already been two days since surgery. "I slept."

"What? In the chair by his bed?"

"That counts." She forced the paper cup to her mouth, but her stomach protested. Maybe she needed to eat first before the caffeine burned a hole in her esophagus. "How much sleep has the team gotten?"

"We're rotating shifts. So, more than you."

"Liam's parents will be here soon, right?" She couldn't believe she was going to face his mom and dad, and Liam wouldn't be awake for the introductions. What in the world was she going to say to them?

He glanced at his wristwatch. "I'm picking them up at Heathrow in a few hours."

"Have you met them before?" She set the coffee down and chewed on her lip. Maybe she'd at least shower before they showed up.

"No, none of us have, not that I know of. Liam's never been much of a talker when it comes to his family. Well, aside from talking about his pops." He placed a hand over her shoulder and cocked his head. "Liam will wake up. And he's not going to lose his memory like your brother did."

"At least Jake's memories returned, but the idea that Liam could . . ." She shifted her focus to the white floors. No tiles to count for a distraction or a pattern to stare at. "Talia's research." She snapped her head back up. "Maria and Hans finished Elaina's mom's work—the memory loss test trials start soon," she rushed out. "Maybe we can—"

"It's not going to come to that. Liam's memory is off the charts. If anyone can bounce back from an accident like this it's him."

"Someone launched a missile at him," she whispered.

"And that someone got a bullet to the head," he said in a deep voice and lowered his hand from her shoulder. "He won't need any special drugs, okay? He'll remember you. Maybe not the moments leading up to the RPG, but everything else before that."

She found his warm brown eyes. "How can you be so confident?"

"Because he's my brother. And I have zero intention of losing another one."

She eyed the black band on his wrist, the reminder of the Teamguy they'd lost. Asher had decided the team should continue to wear the band and Knox had volunteered.

"I know he's going to wake up," she said as confidently as possible, "but what if he's not able to participate in team ops? Bravo's everything to him."

"Until he wakes up all we're doing is speculating and making ourselves crazy." His attention focused on the elevator doors.

"Emily!"

She whipped around to find her brother and his new wife on approach.

"Jake. Alexa. What are you doing here?" She closed the space between them, allowing Jake to pull her into his arms, while another sob rattled loose from deep in her chest.

"My team called," he said. "Alexa and I hopped on the first flight back."

"They weren't supposed to." She hugged Alexa next. "You were on your honeymoon."

"I'd bust their balls if they didn't." Alexa squeezed her tight.

"I can't believe you were here working an op with my guys, and you didn't tell me," Jake said when Emily stepped out of Alexa's embrace. "They said Liam got hurt. He's in a coma?"

All she could do was nod.

"What's his prognosis?" Jake blinked a few times, maybe recalling what had happened to him when his life had been in jeopardy two years ago.

She still couldn't get the words out, and Knox must've noticed because he stepped forward and introduced himself to Jake and Alexa before sharing Liam's condition.

"Mrs. Evans?"

Definitely not the way she wanted her brother to find out she and Liam were married.

Jake cocked his head, eying the nurse off to Emily's side, then leaned forward and whispered in her ear, "Did you lie to get visitation privileges?"

"No," was all she said before facing the nurse. "Any news?"

"We should probably talk alone." She angled her head toward the side hall as if there was some special room saved for delivering bad news.

Hell no.

"We can talk here." She folded her arms, trying to stand strong. Channel her mother's strength. Thank God Jake was there, though.

The nurse lifted a folder between them. "Do you know what Liam's wishes are in regard to life support and using extraordinary measures to sustain life?"

Her limbs grew cold in the space of a heartbeat. The blood drained from her face. *He wants me to let him go, so no, of course, he wouldn't want . . . but . . .*

"This is merely hospital policy and procedure," she added, her voice calm.

She relaxed and let go of a breath. "So, he's still okay?"

"His condition is the same as the last time you spoke with the doctor two hours ago."

"Any expectations about—"

"Are you also family?" the nurse cut Jake off.

"I, um." Jake lifted a shoulder and turned to Emily, a questioning look on his face. "I'm just the . . . brother-in-law," he said, his words slowly leaving his mouth as if he were coming to terms with what he was saying.

"My boss can have his DNR papers faxed over from our office in New York," Knox spoke up. "He doesn't want to be on life support."

His words weren't a surprise, but they still hurt. Knives plunging in the chest and twisting—yeah, that kind of hurt. Any version of Liam never waking up was . . . *damn it,* she was going to be sick.

"One minute, please." Knox motioned for Emily to follow him farther down the hall but everything was still spinning, and he must've sensed it because he reached for her elbow and offered her support as they walked. "We signed papers when we joined Bravo. Jessica had wanted to know our wishes if something were ever to happen."

"And his wish is to die?" She had to hear the confirmation, even though she already knew the answer.

"It's not going to come to that. But you know Liam, he wouldn't want to live hooked up to a machine. He'd want us to let him go."

"Let me go." Liam's words spun around in her mind, making her dizzy, yet again.

"I need a minute." She rushed to the nearest bathroom and dry-heaved into the toilet. There wasn't anything in her stomach to throw up, but her abdomen convulsed and shook.

"You okay?" Alexa appeared behind her and helped her over to the sink to wash her face.

"No," she whispered. "He made me promise I'd let him go if I ever had to, but how in the world can I keep that promise?"

"If you love him you will."

Her breath hitched, and she patted at the newly fallen tears with a paper towel and attempted to pull herself together. Probably an impossible feat.

"So, husband, huh?" Alexa asked a few minutes later when they left the bathroom. "Why didn't you tell us last week?"

"Because it was an accidental marriage."

"How do you accidentally marry someone?" she asked with a touch of *I-doubt-that* in her tone.

Emily stopped walking and faced her. "Accident would imply it shouldn't have happened, and I, uh, I'm happy it did.

So, maybe it wasn't an accident." She eyed the nurse standing next to Jake. "You do absolutely everything in your power to prevent us from ever needing those DNR papers, okay?"

The nurse nodded. "Understood." She patted her on the shoulder and left.

Jake folded his arms, and a smile tugged at his lips. "So, married, huh?"

* * *

"In other news, the owner and CEO of Weston Tech is under investigation for illegal business activities. Bribery, insider trading, and more. This comes as a surprise when it was only recently that Elliott Nelson of Blackburn Technologies was arrested for . . ." The reporter's voice faded into the background, and Emily glanced Jessica's way.

Jessica jerked a thumb toward Harper sitting off to her left. They'd all been taking turns in the waiting room—stealing moments alone with Liam. Luke was with him now.

Harper shrugged. "I may or may not have tipped the press off about that asshole," she said with a smile. "Sometimes the media can be our friends."

"Look at you fitting right in with us." Wyatt chuckled.

Emily stood at the sight of Luke returning from Liam's room. She wasn't sure how much time they'd all get once Knox brought Liam's family to the hospital.

"Mind if I go back there again?" she asked.

"I'll walk with you," Luke offered.

"Thanks."

They started down the hall when Luke blurted, "I threatened to break Liam's legs the day of the gala."

"What? Why?" She stopped outside the doors leading to the ICU.

"I told him that if he broke your heart, well, I said I'd . . . you know." He huffed as if angry at himself. "I shouldn't have said that. He's my brother, and I should've trusted he wouldn't hurt you. I'm a father of a girl now, and I get a little protective of—"

"You were looking out for me. I appreciate that. Liam understood exactly where you were coming from."

"You sure?" His brows snapped together. Real concern there.

"I am, but you can tell him when he wakes up." She squeezed his arm then entered the ICU.

She'd barely had two minutes alone with Liam before hearing the unmistakable sound of high heels outside the room.

"There's only one Mrs. Evans, and that's me!" a woman snapped.

Emily placed Liam's hand back on the bed. "That must be your mom," she softly told Liam as if he could hear her.

Closing her eyes, she quickly ran through various approaches, much like in the courtroom, on how best to handle confronting his parents without Liam being awake.

She stood and brought her sweaty palms to her sides, then swiveled around when the curtains parted.

His mom's tall, lithe body moved toward the bed, her black heels clicked across the floor with her gaze razor-sharp on Liam. "Liam!"

A man, obviously Liam's dad, hung back. His gaze moved from his son to Emily. A hard set to his bearded jaw. Same expressive eyes as Liam.

"I'm Emily." She approached him, giving Liam's mom a moment alone. "And I didn't lie to the doctors out there."

"You're married to my son?" His brows jetted together in surprise.

"Liam would never get married after what happened with . . . no, I don't believe you."

Emily turned at the sobering declaration from his mom.

She was American, but a touch of Aussie had moved through her tone. Her hair, the color of Chardonnay with streaks of caramel—just like her son's—was somewhat disheveled. Tears cut lines down her cheeks as she held Liam's hand between her palms, then leaned in to kiss his forehead.

A mother's grief.

She wasn't familiar from the perspective of a parent, but she knew what it was like to be the daughter. The sister. The friend.

And now she knew what it was like to worry as a wife.

"Well, it's true." Emily focused back on his father. "I'm sorry to tell you like this."

"When? Why?" There were probably a dozen more questions he wanted to ask, and she honestly had no idea if she had the strength to answer any of them right now.

"Maybe I should leave you alone with your son." She sidestepped him to leave, but his hand on the back of her arm stopped her.

"Are you really my son's wife?" he asked.

"Yes," she mouthed, her voice failing her. Without hesitation, she walked out of the ICU.

As she approached the waiting room, Emily saw Jessica, Luke, and Knox in the hall, talking to three men whose resemblance to Liam was unmistakable. She recognized Brandon immediately, and the way his eyes swept to her face, and his brows drew together, she realized he remembered her from D.C.

"Brandon." She moved closer to Liam's brothers as they stood like a wall of intimidation. "I've heard a lot about you."

Brandon's head lightly jerked back in surprise, and he eyed her as if she couldn't be trusted. "Bad things, I'm sure." He shook her hand.

"He cares about you." She looked at his other two brothers flanking Brandon's sides. "All of you."

"And now he's in a coma, and I didn't even get to . . ." Brandon bowed his head and slipped his hands into his pants pockets. "He can't die like this."

"That's not going to happen. He's strong." She needed to hear the words herself, too—a reminder not to give up hope. "There's something he wants to talk about with you when he wakes up, in fact."

"What is it? How do you know?" Brandon edged closer as if an eagerness snapped up his spine.

"I'm going to let him tell you because he *will* wake up."

"Who are you to Liam?" one of the brothers asked. The youngest, maybe.

Her lips pinched tight for a brief moment. They were bound to find out the truth as soon as they went back to see Liam and spoke to their parents.

"I'm the woman who fell in love with him."

CHAPTER FORTY-ONE

"WHAT HAPPENS NOW?" SHE STARED AT DOCTOR LEE, impatience burning through her.

It'd been eight days, seven hours, and nineteen minutes since he'd been placed into a medically induced coma. And she'd been on edge during every single second of that time.

"We wait for him to wake up." His smile was forced, which made her wonder if he was having doubts.

Liam was already healing. A week had reduced the cuts on his face and neck to faint marks. The bandage around his skull from the gash was gone, too. But it was the damage she couldn't see that scared her.

She'd spent too much time on Google. At this point, she basically felt qualified to operate.

"Listen," the doctor began while placing a hand on her shoulder, probably about to give her the same speech he'd delivered to Liam's mom earlier, "his brain activity looks great. And he's scored well on the Glasgow Coma Scale. It's time we see what he can do on his own."

No breathing tube.

No more meds to keep him in the coma.

And no more reduced temperature.

But *more* waiting.

"How long until he wakes up?"

"I wish I could answer that." He gently gripped her shoulder. "He's only been off the medicine for a few hours. But what I can tell you is I'm optimistic that when he wakes up, the road to recovery won't be all that bad."

She mentally went through the medical checklist of possible problems she'd read about. "Will he remember me? Be able to walk? Speak?" Tears started to once again build. "He's smart. Like really, really smart." *Like Elaina. God, she missed her, too.* "And I just—"

"We wait and see."

"Yeah," she murmured, understanding why Liam's mom left the room with such a somber face.

After almost a week of getting to know Liam's parents, they were starting to come around to her. His brothers, too.

Liam's grandfather had been the most comfortable with her. He reminded her of her grandfather. Same lively spirit.

Liam's brothers had been the toughest to crack, though.

Jesse, Grayson, and Brandon were a bit more suit-and-tie, no-nonsense guys, unlike Liam. She did manage to get them to put down their phones long enough to talk for a solid five minutes yesterday. She'd take that as a small victory.

Work for distraction—she didn't blame them. She'd phoned her boss a few times for updates in the last week. A lot had happened while Liam had been asleep.

"Can I have some time alone with him, please?"

"Of course." He left her side and pulled the curtain closed, and she positioned her phone by his bed and turned on the playlist she'd made for him.

"Remember this song?" She thought back to the rooftop

bar in Chile. "Sam Smith." She gathered his hand between her palms and settled in the chair by the bed.

She drew her eyes closed, allowing the memories of their time together to move through her. Comfort her.

She'd been playing the playlist every day since she'd discovered the possible benefits of music for patients in a coma.

An hour later, the playlist stopped, and she stood and leaned over the bed and brushed the back of her hand over his bearded cheek.

"I know you've heard this before, but all of the people connected to Elliott are behind bars, and to everyone's surprise—Jared came through. He sent the intel he promised."

No luck finding Jared, but they had to take the wins where they could.

"The president sent an on-the-books team to Carballo's home near the beach in Argentina—he resisted, and so Carballo didn't make it out alive."

And she wouldn't be shedding tears over his loss, either. She reached for her necklace with her free hand and smoothed the charm between her fingers. Years of waiting for the chase to ultimately end with Carballo behind bars, and now he was dead. Justice served. It was almost hard to believe.

"No American operator was hurt. I know you were worried about that." She let go of her necklace. "Jessica and Harper promise they'll find Jared, and I believe them."

She sat back down, trying to keep her voice steady. "And you'll never believe it, but you actually met my parents. They're still here. Our moms are friends. Kind of weird, right?"

She smiled even though tears started to hit her tee as they slipped from her cheeks.

"Your grandfather is awesome. But your brothers are a bit intense. Workaholics like you. I almost managed to pull a smile out of Jesse." She licked her salty tears from her lips. "I haven't been in here as much as I want because you've had a lot of friends visiting." She pressed a hand to her mouth, trying to stop the wobble in her lip so she could talk. "Lots and lots of people who love you. Pretty much everyone you know has shown up. The nurses said they've never seen anything like it."

Loved by so many. And me.

"I realized something while I was waiting to see you today. You don't know my middle name, and since you told me yours, you should know mine, right?" *Deep breaths.* "Emily Velma Summers. Velma was my dad's mom. She was the best grandmother. I used to shoot the hunting rifle with her, too. A strong woman. A role model." *Someone I wish my kids could've met.*

She retrieved Elaina's letter from her pocket at the reminder of kids and nervously patted the paper on her thigh.

"I have a note from Elaina." She lifted the letter between them as if he could see it. "She wishes she could be here. Hans has her with him in Colorado, but he's let me talk to her. She talked to you last night, too. I held my phone up so she could see you."

Yeah, her heart had shattered watching Elaina's tears spill at the sight of Liam in the bed.

She swallowed, trying to get rid of the cottony sensation in her mouth.

"To my Liam, I'm so sorry you got hurt." She struggled to get the words out while crying, but she had to do it for Elaina. "I haven't known you very long, but I like you. A lot. I'd really like you and Emily to stay in my life, too. I know my mom would want that. She'd like you both. I just know she would."

Tears streamed down Emily's cheeks, and her voice cracked as she spoke.

"And so, I was wondering, if maybe you'd think about being my parents when you wake up after you get better. I know you have a dangerous job—you save people—so you'd be worried about me being with you, but if you give me the chance to be yours . . . I'd be safe. I promise. And I wouldn't let you down. Love, Elaina."

She folded the letter, a few of her tears hitting the paper in the process.

"Hans is her dad, so I know it can't happen, but how can I tell her *no*?" She set the letter on the bed next to him. "I care about her, and I know you've come to care for her, too, even in such a short time. And I can't lose either of you." She clutched his hand and bowed her head, dropping her eyes closed. "I need you," she cried. "And I hope you remember me. I hope you remember her."

"You think . . ." She jerked her head up at the sound of Liam's voice. At the movement of his thumb atop her hand. "I'd ever . . ." His head rolled to the side a little, but his eyes didn't open. "Forget you." His chest rattled from a deep, raspy cough.

She was on her feet and standing over him, hand still locked with his, as she fought back a sob.

His lids lifted then closed. "This is-is . . . me . . . we're talking about," he whispered between coughs.

"Doctor!" She couldn't take her eyes off Liam, even though he went still again. Eyes closed and no more movement from him. "He talked," she shrieked. "He said he didn't forget me."

The doctor held a flashlight to Liam's eyes and separated his lids. "He's starting to come out of it." He looked back at her and smiled. "He's waking up."

Her shoulders trembled as she pressed her palms to her face and cried. Relief swelling in her chest.

Another hour passed until his eyelids fluttered open again. It'd been brief, but she'd take it. Any signs of life, of movement, she'd take in a heartbeat.

"Sweetheart." His mom stood on the other side of him now, gently smoothing a hand over his forehead.

"Emily." Liam's voice was low and raspy. He didn't open his eyes, but his fingers twitched like he was attempting to reach for her. "Emily."

His mom peered her way as Emily reached for his hand. "I'm here."

"What happened between you and Liam doesn't make much sense, but I can't question it," his mom said. "When I met his father, he swept me off my feet, and before I knew it, I was floating." A single tear slid down her cheek. "You love him," she said as if finally coming to terms with it, and Emily's body trembled. Hope climbing inside of her. "And he loves you, doesn't he?"

"I do," Liam answered, surprising them both. His eyes opened as if he found the fight inside of him to do it. "Emily . . ."

He winced, and his mom hurried from the room to grab the doctor at the sight.

"Emily Velma *Evans*," he corrected, his eyes falling shut again.

You heard me? She gently squeezed his hand, and a nurse hollered for security from outside the room a moment later.

"You can't all come up here! He needs space," one of the nurses cried out. "Way too many of you!"

"We're family." Jessica led the group into the room. There were too many friends and family members to fit in the confined space, but that didn't seem to stop them from trying.

"They're all here for you," she half cried and half laughed, and Liam slowly opened his eyes and blinked.

"We brought beer to celebrate." A.J. held up a case. "Good to have you back, brother."

"Now get your arse better and quick, mate," Wyatt said with a nod, and even though he was kidding—well, maybe partially joking—she could see the relief on his face as he closed in on the bed. "We expect you back soon."

"Five to six months." Doctor Lee shoved through the group of SEALs blocking access to Liam. "Don't rush him. He needs to recover. Injuries to the head can sneak back up on you down the road, and so you need to regularly monitor—"

"Four months tops, and he'll be back to himself." Knox winked at Emily and flashed her a smile. And she mouthed a *thank you* back to him.

Thank you for keeping Liam alive after the explosion. Thank you for his support and strength. For his faith everything would be okay.

"Now, can I get some space to do my job?" The doctor looked toward the crowd.

"Sorry, Doc," Knox said. "You're stuck with us." He kept his eyes on Emily when he added, "You are, too."

CHAPTER FORTY-TWO

Four Weeks Later

"I don't remember it ever being this hot in D.C. at the end of June," Emily said as they rounded the block in her new neighborhood of Adams Morgan, a vibrant area of the city wedged between Woodley Park and Dupont Circle. "Is the asphalt melting?" She eyed a wisp of steam rising from the road off to their right.

"There are a few benefits of this hot weather." Liam stopped walking, his gaze falling to her white ribbed tank top.

She peered down at the streaks of sweat dropping into her bra, her breasts practically swelling from the heat. "Funny," she said with a laugh. "No sexy thoughts yet. Doctor's orders." She tightened her arm around his to offer extra support as they began moving again.

"He didn't say anything about fantasizing, and you know I've been in bed for weeks, so how do you think I've kept my mind occupied?"

She slipped her sunglasses to the top of her head and

looked his way so he could witness her eye roll. A hearty laugh left his lips, and the sound was heaven.

They'd left London two weeks ago, and he'd already improved significantly in that time.

"When you're better I want to take you there," she said while pointing to a saloon. "Best whiskey in the area. Not that I drink the stuff, but you and the guys seem to love it. That and beer."

"Mm. You know me so well."

And she did, didn't she? She'd taken the last month off to be with him during recovery, and it'd given them a chance to learn all the other details about each other they hadn't yet discovered.

Like his love of dipping fries into vanilla ice cream—and then smearing the fry onto her nose before licking the cream off. He claimed it'd be her body next, but the idea of getting sticky was still up for discussion.

Liam's mom had stayed in London for ten days after he'd woken up, and Emily had promised to visit Sydney as soon as Liam got cleared by the doc.

"I think we should stop now."

"One more time around the block." He picked up his pace, and she tugged at his arm, trying to get him to slow down.

"You already pushed yourself hard at PT this morning."

"Knox took me, so how do you know I pushed myself?"

She'd hated missing the session, but she had to meet with her boss to ask for a few more weeks off. She wasn't ready to go back to work yet, and since they'd just moved into their new home a week ago, she needed more time to get situated.

"He called me. Says you're pushing too hard." She dropped her shades back in place, glimpsing the multicolored row homes off to their left.

"Nah, he's just worried about losing the bet."

"What bet?" She stopped walking again and faced him.

He pressed a hand to the top of a gate at his side for support. "As to when I'll be back on Bravo."

"Tell me you didn't partake in—"

"Three months, three weeks. Knox has me at four. So, he's worried I'm going to win."

"You're ready when you're ready," she exclaimed.

"But—"

"Don't even think about arguing with me, and just wait until I see the guys next. There's going to be hell to pay."

"So, I shouldn't tell you about the other bet, I guess." He smirked.

"Liam James Evans."

He chuckled. "You know when you use my name like that it only turns me on."

"Tell me," she said, struggling to maintain a serious look when she wanted to laugh.

"That I won't make it the six weeks until the doctor clears me for—"

"Sex?" she rasped. "Tell me you didn't join in on that bet."

"Maybe I went for longer." He lifted both palms in the air but then nearly lost his balance and grabbed the gate at his side again.

"Sure you did."

"Just talking about it has me horny as fuck." He tipped his head toward the sky as if he were in pain—well, in the groin area, at least.

"You're always horny."

"Like I said before, I've had a lot of time to contemplate all of the many positions we're going to try once I've got the OK."

Geometry. And now maybe she was getting horny, too.

Aside from a slight limp, no one would ever know an RPG had almost ended his life. In ash-gray board shorts and a white tee that showcased the muscles he was worried about losing—*not likely*—he looked relaxed and so damn sexy.

"Come on, let's get you back home. If you overdo it too much we might not get to make love in two weeks."

They began moving on the sidewalk again, and her eyes flitted from the bright electric cars passing on her right and over to him when he'd dropped a soft *thank you* into the air.

"For what? The sponge baths and massages?"

He gestured toward the wrought-iron bench off to the side of their new place as they neared their home. *Our home.* Liam's first permanent address in years.

She helped him sit, and he stretched his legs out, crossing one ankle over the other. One wide-strapped flip-flop nearly falling off in the process.

She interlocked their fingers together between them on the bench.

"Thank you for not giving up on me. Sticking with me through all of this." The deep timbre of his tone dropped a bit more as if someone applied pressure to his vocal cords. "Putting up with my parents and brothers. All the guys." He cleared his throat. "Knox told me about the DNR papers, too."

He hadn't brought this up before, and part of her hadn't been sure if Liam had been aware of what had been asked of her.

Her heartbeat picked up, and the heat from the sunrays continued to melt her, her sweat bleeding through the top of the tank. "I didn't want to agree to let you go, you know."

"But you would've." He fixed his eyes on hers. "And I know that couldn't have been easy and—"

"It would've been the hardest thing I've ever done," she whispered, fighting the tears in her eyes. "But I love you." She tried to shrug away the emotions and flicked her wrist. "But thankfully, I knew you were a stubborn ass and wouldn't leave me." She brought her finger beneath the frames. "And if the situation were ever reverse—"

"Oh, hell no! Extraordinary measures all the way for you."

"Liam!" She playfully swatted his arm, but when her gaze moved to a man walking by, a young girl atop his shoulders licking ice cream, her hand fell back to her lap.

"Knox told me something at PT today about Elaina." Liam's words ripped her focus back to him. "The boys found out that Hans's project at NORAD is complete, and he just took a gig in Paris. He starts in two weeks."

"Paris?" *No. No. No.* "Elaina won't want to go."

He unlocked their hands and looped his arm around her side, pulling her in close.

"Liam, you know what she wants."

"She has us. We Skype all the time." He paused. "She'll always have us, but she has a father who wants her, and I don't know how to compete with blood."

"Bravo. Echo. They're not blood. But they're family."

"We can be like the cool aunt and uncle, though."

"Is that what you really want?" she whispered, knowing damn well he felt the same about this as she did.

He lowered his head. "No," he said, his voice deep. "No, I want more."

CHAPTER FORTY-THREE

Two Weeks Later

"What time do we leave for your grandfather's house?" Emily called out from the bathroom, which was open to the master.

"We have two hours." He stared at the paper in his hand, his heart leaping from his chest.

Rubbing a towel against her wet hair, Emily strode before him in a fuzzy pink robe that stopped at her thighs, showcasing her shapely body and tan legs.

"You know what today is, right?" he asked.

She clutched the towel to her chest. "I thought your doctor appointment was tomorrow." Her eyes lowered to the paper.

He stood from the bed, his leg still hurting, but the pain was nothing like before.

He hated being away from his team and missing ops, but having six weeks alone with Emily, even though he'd been in recovery mode for most of the time had been some of the best weeks of his life.

"So, what is it?" She took the paper and scanned over it, then dropped the towel. "You want to go ahead with the annulment?" Her dark lashes lifted, her eyes stretching with surprise.

He reached into his pocket, his hand shaky—not the norm —but this moment hadn't been in his training, either.

"I was wondering"—he crouched to one knee to the best of his ability—"if we could finally rip it up?" He popped open a black velvet box. "Emily, would you *stay* married to me?"

She looked from the box to the paper. Her dimples popped as her lips rolled inward.

She lightly nodded and tore the paper in half before falling to her knees. "Yes." Her brown eyes grew glossy from unshed tears. And damn, he was pretty sure he was about to cry, too. "I would love to stay married to you, Liam James Evans."

He wrapped his arms around her, pulling her flush against him and kissed her.

"Did you wait to propose until we could have sex?" she asked with a laugh when he slid a white gold band with a solitaire diamond on her ring finger a moment later. "The doctor needs to clear—"

"I bumped the appointment. Already saw him." He winked. "There's no scenario where I ask you to marry me and then not make love to you after."

"Of course," she said with a laugh and narrowed one eye as if the sparkle from the diamond was blinding as she eyed it. "It's beautiful."

"It was my grandmother's ring." He brushed the pad of

his thumb over the fallen tears on her right cheek. "Pops wanted you to have it."

"I love it. I'm honored." She covered his hand with hers and smiled. "Are you sure we really can have sex?" she asked once they were both on their feet.

"Hell, yes," he gritted out.

"Then please, please, please . . . make love to me."

* * *

SHE'D KISSED HIS ENTIRE BODY. FROM THE TOPS OF HIS FEET and up his muscular legs to his ripped abdomen—then her mouth had landed on his lips, and her tongue had entwined with his.

He'd done his best to follow her orders and let her take the lead, but their second time around, well, he wouldn't be so obedient.

"Liam," she whispered as she slid down onto his shaft from her position sitting atop him. An honest-to-God cry-slash-moan followed. "These are happy tears," she promised, her body trembling against his.

He brushed his mouth over hers, kissing away the tears that chased over her lips. "I love you," he said as they remained connected.

"I love you, too." She panted, her beautiful breasts bouncing each time he lifted his hips off the bed so she could fully take all of him. "It doesn't hurt, does it?" She glimpsed her palms on his chest as if worried she'd break him, and he placed his hands at her sides and buried his fingertips into her flesh.

"No," he mouthed, unable to get his voice to work when she started to ride him harder, pushing more and more.

His chest tightened, and his entire body tensed with the burn of emotion shooting straight through him.

He slipped his thumb between her legs and touched her sweet spot, eager to hear the sexy whimpering sounds he knew she'd make.

Her back arched, and she tipped her head to the ceiling as her fingertips dug into his pecs, and she gave him exactly what he'd been fantasizing about—an earth-shattering groan.

She cried out his name over and over again as she rode out her orgasm, and he allowed himself to come, to fill her for the first time without the barrier of a condom between them.

Pure fucking bliss. No other way to describe it.

She collapsed on top of him, her heart pounding hard against his chest. "That was worth the wait."

"Wait until I get my stamina back." He brushed her damp hair away from her face. "You were incredible."

"Mm. We make a great team."

"That we do." He kissed her, not ready to pull out, but at the buzzing of her cell phone on the end table by the bed, she grumbled and rolled to the side.

She grabbed the phone. "It's Hans."

"What?"

She stood and clutched the phone to her ear, her breathing still labored. "Hello?" She paused while he spoke. "Yes, of course. One second."

He sat upright, trying to get a read on her.

"He's outside. He's here." She did a three-sixty in the room as if not sure what to do. "Clothes," she sputtered. "We need clothes."

"And a wet towel. You're a mess." He pointed to her naked body, his semen gliding down her thighs.

"Shit." Her hands flew to the top of her head, her eyes blinking rapidly. "Right."

"Honey." Liam shook his head and laughed.

"What?" She had the "deer caught in headlights" look going for her.

"You're pretty cute when you look all flustered."

"Liam," she said with a playful eye roll.

She hurried to the bathroom, and he took a moment to appreciate her heart-shaped ass in the process.

"Clothes," he reminded himself and grabbed a pair of shorts and a tee.

"What are you doing?" Her eyes widened when she came back into the room. "You can't go commando beneath your shorts with Hans here." She pointed to their dresser, which was still surrounded by a few unpacked boxes.

"I wasn't thinking." He smiled at the realization.

They hurriedly got dressed and dashed to the front door as if worried Hans would do a disappearing act before they made it.

The master suite was on the first level, which he was grateful for given he was still in recovery mode.

"It's been six weeks since we've seen her." She wrapped a hand over the doorknob but didn't open it, her eyes flashing to Liam. Her nerves showing.

"Which is why you should open the door." But hell, he was nervous, too.

She swung it open and immediately reached for Elaina without hesitation, pulling her into her arms. "We had no clue you were coming. I-I can't believe it!"

Hans's eyes were on the ground. His forehead creased, and his cheeks grew red and not from the summer heat. There was something wrong.

Liam's heartbeat hammered in his chest with worry, but he forced his attention back to Elaina.

"Liam!" Elaina exclaimed once Emily had let her go. She threw her arms around his legs.

He lifted her into the air and hugged her, not giving a shit about his injuries. "We missed you."

"Can we come in?" Hans asked when Liam lowered her to the ground.

Emily motioned for them to follow, ushering everyone into the living room off to their right. "Sorry about the boxes. We're still unpacking."

"This is a nice place you have." Hans sat on the couch and crossed his leg over his knee and held on to his ankle. "How many bedrooms?"

Emily sat on the opposite couch and Elaina dropped between her and Liam. "Four," Emily answered while glimpsing Liam out of the corner of her eye.

"I, um . . ." Hans started.

"He wants me to stay here!" Elaina burst out, and it was as if the world stopped rotating.

"Talia was right about me. I'm not cut out for fatherhood. I can't focus on my work if I'm taking care of her." The leg touching the ground began to shake. "I can't trust myself to put my work first if she's in my life, and it's critical my work takes priority."

"I don't understand." Liam had talked about this possibility with Emily, but they'd told themselves it'd never happen.

Hans cleared his throat. "I'm flying to Paris today. Elaina doesn't want to go, and the project will be for two years. I was thinking maybe I could stay in her life—calls and visits . . . but you could take her."

Take her?

"Like permanently?" Emily stood and crossed her arms.

"Is that something you'd consider?" Hans angled his head.

"What do you want?" She turned toward Elaina, but Elaina's eyes were on the ring on Emily's hand.

"You put a ring on it!" she squealed with a smile. "Like that song." She jumped to her feet and reached for Emily's hand.

"Just an hour ago, actually." Liam matched her smile with one of his own, but he was still a bit disoriented with everything happening.

Was Hans really offering them what they wanted?

"I knew the moment I met you guys we were all meant to be together." Elaina looked back and forth between them. "I just didn't know if you'd want me."

"Of course, we would." Emily crouched before her and braced her hands on both her shoulders. "I saved a room upstairs in the hopes you'd visit, but now . . ." She looked Hans's way. "You're serious?"

"She needs a family," Hans said. "I'm afraid I can't be the kind of father she needs. I'd like to start the paperwork if you're interested, but as I said, I want to keep in touch with her."

God, he was talking about Elaina as if she weren't in the room. If he wasn't Elaina's father—he might deck the guy.

"Adoption?" Emily murmured and stood upright.

"Please." Elaina tugged at Emily's hand, and it was Liam dropping to his knees this time, ignoring the pain in his leg.

"This is what you want?" He swallowed hard.

"Yes!" Elaina threw her arms around his neck. "I even brought my own Oreos with me in case you said *yes*."

Fuuu—he let go of the curse in his head, realizing he'd

probably need to work on his language with a child in the house.

And wow . . . there'd be a kid in the house.

Was this happening?

Elaina stepped back and placed a palm on his cheek. "You're crying." She angled her head.

"Am I?" He sucked in a deep breath and blinked a few times.

"You want to be my family, right?"

He looked up at Emily, tears streaming down her face as she nodded.

He stopped fighting the emotions, allowing the tears to steadily stream. "We'd love nothing more."

CHAPTER FORTY-FOUR

THREE MONTHS LATER – SYDNEY, AUSTRALIA

"WHAT DO YOU THINK?" LIAM SNAPPED A PHOTO OF ELAINA cradling her baby cousin in her arms.

"He's so cute." Elaina held David's little hand, and the baby's mouth stretched open with a yawn. "I like having a cousin." She looked at Emily off to Liam's left. "I think he smiled at me."

David was only four weeks old, so probably not, but he wasn't about to tell her. The baby looked more like Melissa than Brandon with his dark hair and eyes.

"Liam." Brandon motioned for Liam to follow him out of the living room of their parents' home, and Liam stowed his phone in his pocket. "Thanks for coming." He leaned against the wall in the hall with crossed arms.

He nodded. "How's Melissa?"

"She's still recovering from the C-section, but she's doing great." He wrapped a hand around the back of his neck and squeezed. They were more alike than Liam had remembered.

"She wanted to come over, but she didn't think you'd want to see her."

Liam looked him straight in the eyes, needing for him to believe him when he spoke. "I'm over what happened," he said without a doubt in his mind. "She can come."

"Your wife and Melissa at dinner tonight with mum and dad won't be weird?"

"Maybe a little, but Emily gave the green light, so as long as she's okay, I'm solid."

"I'd like that then." He lowered his arm to the side. "I'm so sorry again that I—"

"You don't need to apologize. I finally understand how you feel." He looked in the direction of the living room, catching sight of Emily holding baby David in her arms. "I have everything I want, bro. Absolutely everything, and I wouldn't change a damn thing."

"You mean that?"

He kept his eyes on his beautiful family.

God, he had a family.

He'd never grow tired of saying the word. Thinking it.

He'd been given a chance to have it all, and he finally realized he deserved it, too.

* * *

"WE SHOULD CONSIDER GETTING A PLACE HERE," EMILY SAID as they walked along the harbor, which overlooked the famous Opera House off to their left.

"Oh, yeah?" He wouldn't mind visiting his family more often, but he'd be going back to work soon so his schedule would get nuts.

He'd taken more time off than planned, but he hadn't

anticipated he'd become a father during his recovery, and he hadn't wanted to jet off so soon.

Emily stopped walking and tied her hair into a messy bun since the wind kept kicking it in her face. It was springtime in Sydney, one of his favorite times of the year there.

"Ice cream?" Liam pointed to a vendor and Elaina eagerly nodded.

"Good arvo," Emily said to the vendor.

Liam leaned in and whispered in her ear, "Look at you channeling your inner Aussie." He pressed a kiss to the side of her head. "So sexy."

"Oh, you'll see my inner Aussie when we're alone later," she whispered as he ordered three cones.

He slipped his shades up so she could see the look in his eyes—the I-want-to-pin-you-to-the-wall look.

Emily grinned and thanked the vendor for her ice cream. She stroked her tongue with purposeful licks over the vanilla, and damn if he knew exactly what he was going to be doing to her that night. Blindfold for sure to tease the living hell out of her when his tongue . . .

He blew out a breath and shook off his desire to the best of his ability and secured his sunglasses back in place. "So, um, up for the Taronga Zoo tomorrow?"

Elaina eagerly bobbed her head up and down. "Yes, please!"

"You'll love the—" His words were plundered by a boy walking past, the kid's eyes pinned to Elaina. "Did you see him check her out?" His lax stance converted to a tense one, his spine snapping upright. "He was probably twelve."

Emily pressed a hand to his shoulder and licked the ice cream attempting to escape down the side of the cone. "You have a daughter now. A smart and gorgeous daughter. This is going to happen."

"Well, I thought I had more time." He reached for his phone when Emily and Elaina began walking again, hand in hand, in front of him. He snapped their photo so he could have the moment accessible at all times, especially when he was gone on an op.

Two more weeks until he was back on Bravo.

He was looking forward to returning, but it'd be hard to leave them.

But now he had a family and home to come back to.

He had absolutely everything.

He started to put his phone away when it began vibrating in his palm. "It's Jessica," he called out, and Emily glimpsed him over her shoulder. "One second." He tossed his half-eaten cone and moved out of the way of pedestrian traffic. "What's up?"

"Enjoying your time Down Under?"

"Yeah, it was an awkward homecoming at first, but it's been great." They'd survived dinner with Melissa and Brandon, and it'd gone better than he'd expected. Emily was a champ, though, so there was that.

"Well, I should probably wait until you return home to tell you this, but . . ."

"Jessica," he said with a laugh. "You should've gone into acting, I swear. Or maybe writing. You just love to build up the sus—"

"We got Jared!"

He lowered the phone to his side for a few seconds and swiveled around to look at Emily and Elaina a couple of meters away. They had their backs to him, and Emily was pointing at the bridge off in the distance.

"Dead or alive?" he asked once he brought the phone back to his ear.

"A bullet in the leg since he resisted arrest, but he's alive.

The president wanted him that way in case he has other valuable intel. He's in a CIA black site getting a taste of his own medicine now."

"Where was he?" Not that it mattered, but damn, he wished he could've been part of the mission to take the prick down.

The bastard had orchestrated everything for money. Sacrificing lives. *Elaina's* life.

The son of a bitch had also been the reason why he now had a daughter, though.

"We tracked him to Amsterdam three days ago."

"Who led the op?"

"Harper and Echo took point. She wanted the chance to go after him," she explained. "Harper felt guilty for vouching for him, which is crazy, but I figured this was a good time for her to get a feel for handling things without me."

"Glad it went well." He followed his words with a sigh.

It was finally over. Justice had been delivered.

She was quiet for a moment, as if letting the news sink in. "We've missed you, but are you sure you're ready to come back?"

"Emily and Elaina support my job. I wouldn't do it if they didn't." They'd never ask him to make that choice, though. "Don't worry, I've made sure to hit the range while I've been away. My trigger finger is doing just fine."

"I'd expect nothing less. See you soon."

He ended the call and returned to his girls. *His. Damn.*

Emily slid her shades to her head. "Everything okay?"

He lifted his chin in the direction of the sun for a beat. "Jared's in custody." He smiled. "They got him."

Emily pressed a hand to her mouth, and her sunglasses dropped back in place, concealing the liquid he knew would be forming in her eyes.

"It's over." He pressed a hand to her shoulder and nodded.

Elaina tugged at the side of his shirt, and he crouched to find her eyes. "You okay?"

"Yes, but I was wondering . . ."

"Anything," he rushed out.

"You know how you asked me a few weeks ago if I'd want to visit Chile, and I said *no*?" She planted her lip between her teeth. "Well, seeing where you grew up, it makes me want to show you where I grew up, too. I thought it'd make me sad, but you're right—I shouldn't forget who I am."

"And I never want you to forget," he said, and Emily knelt next to him.

"But I'd also like to be Southern and Australian, too. Is that okay?"

He bowed his head, his chest squeezing with emotion. "More than okay," he announced when lifting his eyes to meet hers. "You'll always be your mom and dad's daughter, but now you're our daughter, too."

"We can head to Chile after here," Emily suggested once they'd all hugged. "Just no side trips to—eh hem—vendors while we're there."

Vendors? He closed one eye for a moment. *Ah, the arms dealer.* He'd still like to take that shithead off the face of the earth, but he'd promise to be good on this trip since it was about Elaina. "Right." He gave an obedient nod, which produced a smile from Emily.

"Sounds perfect. I can show you my mom's favorite places." Elaina stood between Emily and Liam and reached for their hands, and his mind skipped back to West Virginia.

Elaina had drawn a picture of this very moment, even the sail-like design of the Opera House had been on the whiteboard.

"Elaina?"

"Yeah?"

"Did you somehow know all of this was going to happen?" he asked.

She looked up at him and lifted her shoulders and winked. "Maybe."

EPILOGUE

Liam eyed all of the posters decorating Elaina's room. Two walls were a tribute to country singers and her new love of cowboys. And the other two were all about superheroes. "Ever since your brother bought her those boots and cowgirl hat last weekend—"

"You have a thing against cowboys?" Emily's lips pressed into a shaky line as if fighting a smile.

"Only when they're on the walls of my daughter's room." He held his palms open toward the pictures. He'd done his best to handle the superheroes because—well, she'd said the *Justice League* and *Avengers* characters reminded her of Bravo and Echo . . . but this?

How would he survive when she hit her teenage years?

Shotgun by the door felt too easy on her future dates. And he also didn't want a sixteen-year-old to piss himself at the sight of his long gun.

He had time to think about it, he supposed.

"This guy is Luke Bryan." Elaina pushed her chair in at her desk and pointed to a picture above it. "He's a really good singer." She strode past Liam and climbed atop her bed and pressed her tiny palm to the image. "This is Carrie Underwood's husband. Sort of reminds me of A.J."

Liam's stomach dropped. "Tell me she doesn't have a crush on A.J.," he whispered into Emily's ear. "I might have to kill him."

"Maybe get yourself some not-so-good-looking friends."

"Funny," he grumbled and pinched her ass.

But then reality settled in. They weren't in her room to discuss cowboys or men in tights. "There's something we need to talk about. You want to sit?"

Elaina's forehead creased as she sat atop her Wonder Woman bedspread. Thank God she was sleeping with Wonder Woman and not Superman. He'd take that as a win.

"Be right back," Emily said.

"I have to go on an op." He sat next to her. "The president needs me."

Emily came back into the room a moment later but kept her arm behind her back as she approached the bed. "This is his first operation since we've become a family, and so, we wanted to check in with you to see how you feel about it."

He'd been back with Bravo for two weeks, but he'd been able to stick around D.C. during that time. He had no clue where POTUS was sending him or what problem the president needed solved, but he'd anticipated this moment would be pretty damn hard for all of them.

The last operation nearly killed him, and although he'd gotten the all clear from pretty much every doctor on the eastern seaboard—being mentally ready to leave was more challenging than being physically prepared.

But being a Teamguy was part of him, a part Emily and Elaina loved.

It didn't make this moment any easier, though.

Elaina averted her gaze to Liam. "You'll be okay," she said with a nod. "You don't need to worry."

"Oh, really?" he asked.

"Yup."

Emily brought her arm around in front of her. "I want you to have this." She extended a glass jar to Elaina before sitting on the other side of her.

"An empty jar?" Elaina examined it before meeting Emily's eyes.

"It's not empty." Emily pointed at it. "It's filled with all the air kisses my dad sent to me whenever he was deployed." She paused as if struggling to get the words out. "And I thought you might like to have it for when Liam travels."

Elaina stared at the glass jar for a minute and brought it to her chest. "I love it. Thank you." She hugged Emily and then turned toward Liam and wrapped her arms around him. "Where should I keep it?"

Emily wiped at the single tear on her cheek and stood. "I kept mine in the nightstand by my bed."

Elaina pursed her lips in thought. "How about on top of my nightstand next to my pictures? I'd like to look at it whenever I start to miss you, which will probably be a lot."

Shit. Could he do this? Could he leave them both?

Elaina positioned the jar on the nightstand next to a collage of framed photos. "I know what you're thinking," she said when facing the bed, "but you're a hero. The world needs you. You keep us safe and give me the chance to be a kid."

He didn't know what to say, so he forced a nod. She was so special. And theirs to protect.

"Will you be able to have dinner with Grandpa tonight like we planned before you go? We were going to have pizza and play charades."

"I'll make time." He stood and pressed a hand to his chest.

Elaina smiled and grabbed a comic book and headphones before plopping back on her bed like a teenager and not an almost-nine-year-old.

"Are you okay?" Emily asked once they were in the master suite downstairs a few minutes later.

He turned toward her, cupped her face, and kissed her. "I'm more than okay," he said against her mouth.

"And you're sure you can stay for dinner?" Her palm smoothed down the center of his black tee. "I don't want you to get into trouble."

He stepped back and eyed his stunning wife before sweeping her into his arms. "I think the president can wait."

BONUS SCENES

Want more Liam & Emily? An all-new Stealth Ops Bonus Scene will be coming soon to newsletter subscribers. Subscribe at: brittneysahin.com

Check out the Stealth Ops Spoiler Room on Facebook to talk about the book or ask me questions! Also, join me in my reader group - Brittney's Book Babes.

Knox's book - *Finding the Way Back* - releases next.

PLAYLIST

Dancing With a Stranger by Sam Smith (with Normani) - ch 19 & 41

Be Alright by Dean Lewis - ch 30

Girls Like You by Maroon 5, Cardi B

Latch by Disclosure & Sam Smith

Tequila by Dan + Shay

Prayer in C - Robin Schulz Radio Edit - Lily Wood and The Prick

Don't Let Me Down - The Chainsmokers

Bailando - Enrique Iglesias, Sean Paul

ALSO BY BRITTNEY SAHIN

A Stealth Ops World Guide is now available on my website, which features more information about the team, character muses, and SEAL lingo.

Hidden Truths

The Safe Bet – Begin the series with the Man-of-Steel lookalike Michael Maddox.

Beyond the Chase - Fall for the sexy Irishman, Aiden O'Connor, in this romantic suspense.

The Hard Truth – Read Connor Matthews' story in this second-chance romantic suspense novel.

Surviving the Fall – Jake Summers loses the last 12 years of his life in this action-packed romantic thriller.

The Final Goodbye - Friends-to-lovers romantic mystery

Stealth Ops Series: Bravo Team

Finding His Mark - Luke & Eva

Finding Justice - Owen & Samantha

Finding the Fight - Asher & Jessica

Finding Her Chance - Liam & Emily

Finding the Way Back - Knox & Adriana

Becoming Us

Someone Like You - A former Navy SEAL. A father. And off-limits.
(Noah Dalton)

My Every Breath - A sizzling and suspenseful romance.
Businessman Cade King has fallen for the wrong woman. She's the
daughter of a hitman - and he's the target.

Dublin Nights

On the Edge - Travel to Dublin and get swept up in this romantic
suspense starring an Irish businessman by day…and fighter
by night.

On the Line - novella

Stand-alone (with a connection to *On the Edge*):

The Story of Us– Sports columnist Maggie Lane has 1 rule: never
fall for a player. One mistaken kiss with Italian soccer star Marco
Valenti changes everything…

WHERE TO FIND ME

Thank you for reading Liam and Emily's story. If you don't mind taking a minute to leave a short review, I would greatly appreciate it. Reviews help keep the series going!

www.brittneysahin.com
brittneysahin@emkomedia.net
FB Reader Group - Brittney's Book Babes
Stealth Ops Spoiler Room

Made in United States
North Haven, CT
24 August 2023

40704728R00243